Michael J. Hollows was born in London in 1986, and moved to Liverpool in 2010 to lecture in Audio Engineering. With a keen interest in history, music, and science, he has told stories since he was little. *Goodbye for Now*, published in Oct 2018, is his first novel, which he started as part of his MA in Writing from Liverpool John Moores University, graduating in 2015. *The German Nurse*, his second historical novel, was a top ten Globe & Mail bestseller. Michael's first short story 'Ashes of Grimnir' is available now. He is currently researching towards a PhD in Creative Writing, working on his next novel.

𝕏 @MikeHollows
www.michaelhollows.com

Also by M. J. Hollows

Goodbye For Now
The German Nurse
The German Messenger

The Violinist's Secret

M. J. HOLLOWS

ONE PLACE. MANY STORIES

HQ
An imprint of HarperCollins*Publishers* Ltd
1 London Bridge Street
London SE1 9GF

www.harpercollins.co.uk

HarperCollins*Publishers*
Macken House, 39/40 Mayor Street Upper,
Dublin 1, D01 C9W8, Ireland

1
First published in Great Britain by
HQ, an imprint of HarperCollins*Publishers* Ltd 2025
This edition published by HQ, an imprint of HarperCollins*Publishers* Ltd 2025

ISBN: 9780008530440

This book contains FSC™ certified paper and other controlled
sources to ensure responsible forest management.

For more information visit: www.harpercollins.co.uk/green

Printed and bound in the UK using 100%
Renewable Electricity at CPI Group (UK) Ltd

To all those who have fought fascism

Prologue

She packed the violin away in its case, observing how the lines of its wood shifted and shimmered in the dim light of her apartment. The windows were shuttered, as she liked them, keeping out the late autumn light, and the Hamburg wind. She was always careful to wipe down the violin's body to make sure that none of the oils in her skin damaged the wood. It was like a ritual when she finished playing.

The violin was precious to her and had been gifted by her late grandfather. It had blemishes and scars from when he had played it, but she treasured those. They told the story of him, his life and struggles. She felt that adding her own to it was somehow ruining the story and damaging the violin's reputation: her grandfather would have told her she was being too sentimental and to enjoy the violin as he had, but that thought of an argument with him brought a smile to her lips, and she cleaned it down out of familial spite. Her father had never understood her passion for music; it had skipped a generation, but her grandfather had fostered it in her and encouraged it even when her father told her she should concentrate on other things.

She knew her grandfather would have been proud of her, even if he never would have said it. She was studying, making a name for herself as a musician, and altogether being a valuable member of the Reich. She was finding her place in society. The only thing she was missing was a fine husband to sweep her off her feet, but that was rather complicated. He couldn't just be anyone, and he would have to be understanding about who she was.

She was good at keeping secrets. That was the reason she was about to embark on the next stage of her life. She loved her country and would do anything to protect it, no matter what happened. At least, that was what she had said during that interview. There was so much at stake. Her life at Hamburg University seemed small and insignificant in comparison. It was just a means to an end. She needed to find herself a position, otherwise she would be discarded.

She closed the lid of the violin case and placed it by the door. It was her way of reminding herself to take it with her when she left. She would bring it to the meeting. It would make a good cover, and then she would play it afterwards to calm her nerves. First of all she would need to get ready. She was expected to present in a certain way, and she didn't want to disappoint. She even had her hair down, after a trip to the hairdresser, to show off its length and sheen. And her wardrobe contained just the thing.

There was a sound from the hallway and she stopped. No one else was expected in the apartment and with recent events she had to be extra careful. While she paused there was no further sound. Perhaps it had been a stray animal, or something to do with the plumbing. Even still, she looked for something she could grab, something with which to defend herself. The violin case stood out, but she didn't dare damage it, and it would be too unwieldy. There was the blue-and-white floral vase on a side table by the chair. It would knock out an intruder if she could wield it effectively.

There was another sound. This time it was the creaking of a stair. She had meant to get them fixed, but now realised that it was an unexpected safety feature, warning her of danger. Someone uninvited was definitely climbing them.

She shot around on the spot to face the doorway as a shadowed figure appeared. Her heartbeat thumped in her ears.

'Oh, it's you,' she let out in a whisper. It was louder than she expected in the silence. 'You shouldn't sneak up on people like that.'

The figure in the doorway didn't say a word. He swayed as if he was drunk and she expected that he had come here for more than just a chat. She shouldn't have allowed him to just let himself in, but it had become a habit. The front door was downstairs and it was at times too much to go down and let someone in.

'Whatever you want, it's no good. I don't have time.' She decided to head him off. He'd had enough of her recently and she wasn't willing to give more. 'I'm due to meet someone in half an hour and if I don't make it then I'll miss out on an opportunity. You wouldn't want me to miss out.'

He was often quiet, but even this was unexpected. She moved closer to the doorway to get a better look, but he swayed and she stopped. There was something in his hand that glinted in the faint light from the shuttered windows.

'What's wrong?' she asked, already dreading the response. But there was no reply. He stepped into the room, reaching out for her as if wanting to embrace. She shook her head. Now wasn't the time. It would never be the time again; she had told him as much.

He stepped closer again and she got a better look at his features.

'No,' she breathed. It wasn't him. Their silhouettes were similar and the darkness had confused her, but it was not him.

She didn't have time to ask why he was here before he closed the distance and dragged her to him. Her instincts took over and she tried to push him away. But he was too strong for her. His arms slipped around her body and he pulled her around violently. The coarse leather of his gloves made her hairs stand on end.

The wire slipped around her neck and pulled up. She tried to grab hold of it, but her fingers would not find purchase.

'Please.' She tried to get the word out, but there was only pain. Her legs swung around and knocked the vase from the side table.

The china smashed across the wooden floor. Her vision blurred as her breath stopped. Her hands fell from the wire as darkness enveloped her, the blue and white shards of broken vase the last things she ever saw.

Chapter One

Hamburg, the red city. Of course, they had called it that even before the Nazis had taken over. It had been due to the red brick used in the building of the warehouses, but now the name wasn't so simple.

Charlotte Weber always felt like an outsider, even amongst crowds. It wasn't that Hamburg was lonely. She was always an onlooker, taking in the red and grey architecture, the Audi 920 that rumbled past her, a man at the wheel with his arm around a lovely blonde.

Her thoughts formed like she was observing from a distance, detached from her own life. This was just as true now as she left the university amongst a group of other students. None of them spoke to her as she walked along the street and crossed the road, with the wind buffeting her along. She saw faces she knew, like Greta's, in the year above her. But all she did was smile in Charlotte's direction and drift by. At home with her room-mate and friends it was like stepping into a different place, away from the outside world. At times it was because her mind drifted; at other times she was completely present and yet still she didn't

5

feel like one of them. Today was one of those days where her mind wandered. She pulled her coat around her, to stave off the autumn wind. Placing a cigarette in her mouth, she tried to light it, but the match guttered and went out.

She was a child of two nations: Germany and Sweden, and that only made things worse. Those who knew her background treated her as a foreigner, didn't understand why she was studying in Germany. Her friends were also students or worked at the university. In fact, her entire life seemed to revolve around the university. She was studying Philosophy because her father had always encouraged her to ask why people did the things they did and question the world. But she kept this feeling of being alone to herself. If she told anyone they would look at her in that way, somewhere between confusion and pity, or worse, have her committed. It was safer to pretend she didn't have these thoughts, to keep secrets.

Charlotte stepped from the street into the porch of her building. The chill air followed her wherever she went, and it was colder inside than out. Her key jammed in the lock, not for the first time, and she had to wrestle it to the sweet spot before it would open. She reminded herself to ask the landlord about it, but how many times had she forgotten to ask before? Add it to the list. But where was the list? Her mother had told her to find somewhere better to live, but this was the best Charlotte and Hilda could afford, and it had a comfortable charm.

During her first year, when her mother had returned to Sweden, she had moved into her flat with Hilda. Even though they had become good friends, the flat had never really become her home. It was supposed to be temporary, but she had a terrible feeling that it would become permanent.

Eventually the door opened and she walked into the kitchenette. Her heels clicked on the tiled floor, echoing around the apartment. The interior was unfinished red brick and she was reassured by the warmth of the aesthetic. At times, when she needed to focus her thoughts, she would run her hand along the bricks, feeling the pores and grit of each one. There was a wall above her dresser where she had worn a little groove. It wasn't a large apartment, not like the one she had lived in with her parents, but it would do while she was studying. After that she had no doubt that Kurt had big plans. His family would pay for it, but that wasn't what she wanted. She wanted them to make their own way.

She could hear her friends' voices before she saw them, then shuddered as the chill made her wrap her arms around herself. The apartment was unusually cold. Occasionally there would be a crack in the cloud cover and the sun would poke through, warming everything up. Then everything would go cold again. Charlotte wanted to sit by a warm fire and close her eyes. She wanted to let the heat warm her, but the news of war following her home reminded her rationing had been brought in last month.

She didn't want to ask for Kurt's help, even though she knew he would give it. His family would provide whatever money she needed: they treated her like their own child, but she didn't want to be more in their debt than she already was. They already had expectations of her she wasn't sure she could meet.

Inside, her friends were lounging around as if they hadn't a care in the world. Her room-mate Hilda took the armchair; Peter and Ilse were on the couch. Hilda waved at Charlotte as she walked over to them. Hilda's hair was a reddish brown that usually hung to her shoulders, but today she had tied up in a bun. She had a long, oval face, with sweeping eyelashes. Charlotte couldn't help but feel that Hilda would be a beautiful woman if only she took more care of herself, but she seemed determined to hide in the shadows. When Hilda had first moved in she had spent most of her time locked in her bedroom. At first Charlotte had thought that Hilda didn't like her, but they had since warmed to each other and become friends.

The others turned in their seats. '*Moin*,' they said almost in unison, which in Hamburg could mean anything from 'good morning' to 'goodbye', and then fell back into conversation. Peter was the epitome of a good German, strong and tall with short sandy hair. He dressed well. She didn't think she had ever seen him not wearing a formal shirt and trousers, even when lounging on the couch. Ilse, Charlotte knew less well. She was Peter's latest in a long line of girl-friends. Charlotte wouldn't waste too much time getting to know her until she was sure Ilse was going to stick around.

There was never enough room on the chairs for all of them, so Charlotte sat on the floor, leaning against Hilda's legs.

'Good day?' Hilda was the only one who ever asked, but she didn't expect an answer. Charlotte's nod was enough. They had fallen into an easy friendship now, where they almost seemed to know what the other was thinking without having to ask.

The apartment had become an impromptu meeting place for the group, but Charlotte was never really sure why. The friends had formed a sort of collective. Even if it was supposed to be Charlotte and Hilda's apartment, the others treated it like their home. At first it had frustrated her, but after a while she had got used to it and found the living area too quiet when they were not around. Like Hilda, she still needed to escape to her bedroom at times, to be alone, but today was not one of those days. At other times their friend Andreas would join them and occasionally Kurt would come by, but he kept his distance mostly. She wasn't sure whether he was intimidated by their intellectual conversation, or whether he simply didn't like her friends. He liked to read as much as the next man, so it was unlikely that he was intimidated. He had never said so, but she knew that he was often uncomfortable in her friends' presence. He would make his excuses and leave, or ask her to go out somewhere. She hated having to choose between him and her friends. Kurt's parents had wanted him to go to university, but he wanted a different life.

She faded back into the conversation as she heard the sound of the toilet flushing. Andreas entered the room. 'I cannot believe you would think that,' he said.

His cheeks were red and he shook his head as he perched on the arm of the couch. Peter laughed in response. Charlotte could tell Andreas wasn't joking. She didn't know what she had missed, but much of the conversations had been the same recently. She could guess what they were talking about.

'How can you think war would be good for Germany? For anyone?' Andreas was on his feet now. He had a way of raising his voice that wasn't quite shouting. It was like singing, enunciating and projecting at a higher pitch so that he could be heard. It always drew Charlotte in. 'I don't think you really believe that.'

In comparison Peter had a smug curve to his mouth. He knew that he could say whatever he wanted without consequence, and with a complete and unshakeable belief that he was correct. Charlotte had never found him an easy friend, but the others, including Andreas, seemed to like him.

'Of course it's good for Germany,' he said, the grin not leaving his face. 'Why wouldn't it be? We are back on the world stage after years of being forced into the shadows. Other countries are starting to take us seriously, will listen to us. And after Versailles—'

'But if the British declare war on us,' Hilda dived into the conversation, 'what then? I didn't think we wanted to repeat the mistakes of our parents' war.'

Charlotte reached for the last *Franzbrötchen* on the table, sure that the others had left it for her. There was a copy of the *Hamburger Anzeiger* half opened next to the plate, forgotten in conversation. Let them argue; she would listen and warm herself with the soft cinnamon pastry.

'That's just it,' Peter carried on, oblivious to the tone of the room. Charlotte wasn't sure he was even aware of anyone else's feelings. 'We're not going to repeat those mistakes. The Führer has a better plan, better generals. The Kaiser and the Jews won't betray us this time. They won't be able to.'

There was a cough from behind Charlotte as Hilda choked on her drink. None of the others stopped to check on her.

Charlotte could guess the reason for Hilda's response, but they had never formally talked about it. There was a reason Hilda kept herself to herself, and that was her business. If she wanted to talk about it, Charlotte would listen.

'But it is war, Peter.' Andreas was still incredulous. He shook his head as if talking to an ignorant child. 'War is never a good thing.'

'Never? Why never? Don't listen to the communists and the socialists. This is our way of reclaiming the land taken from us. More farming, more resources, more opportunities. It can only be good for the German people.'

'War means death. That's never good for the German people. Not for any of us.'

For once Andreas's words shut up Peter. He shook his head and pursed his lips, deep in thought. It was a rare thing when he didn't have a word to say, and Charlotte often found herself drowned out by his chatter.

'War is bad for all of us.' Andreas stood over them like a lecturer, imparting knowledge to his students. 'Do you think our studies will continue while our country is at war with the rest of Europe?'

'Why shouldn't they?' Peter asked. 'The university will still be there. You won't be needed for the fighting.'

'They don't let women fight.' Ilse shocked everyone by making a rare point.

'Exactly.'

'Well, then you're all right.' A wry smile crossed Andreas's face. The show of mirth was unusual for him, a man usually so quiet and distant. But this was how many of their conversations went. 'I feel I will not be so lucky.'

'Oh, I'm not sure about that, Andreas.' Hilda had stood and was appraising Andreas with a hand on her chin. 'You're far too skinny for the army. They want muscly young men for the great Wehrmacht. They'll leave the intellectuals to their books just in case you get in the way of those brave soldiers.'

It had been a joke, but the smile dropped from Andreas's face.

He wouldn't meet their eyes. Hilda shook her head and took another sip of coffee, then sat down.

'That thing in Czechoslovakia was supposed to be about reclaiming our lost land too,' Andreas continued, sensing his victory over Peter. 'How well has that gone?'

'Have you ever been there?' Ilse asked. 'Do you think it's nice?'

'No,' Andreas replied, frowning at the interruption. 'It is too far away. Why would I bother?'

'I wonder what the Czechs are like. I don't think I've ever met one.'

The conversation always went like this, without end. Eventually they would give up and leave.

'They'll sort it all out.' Hilda tried to regain some control. 'No one wants more war, least of all the British.'

Peter laughed. 'The British? Don't be ridiculous. They love war. They've been fighting for as long as they've been a country.'

For once the others feel silent. Peter didn't often speak sense. Most of the time he just repeated what others had told him.

'Don't you think . . . ?' Charlotte had to fill the silence. She couldn't handle them staring at each other. 'If the British attack, then they will come here. Won't they?'

'Possibly. But why would they attack us? They're only threatening war to get us to back down. It's Berlin they want.'

'But we have the industry, the copper, silver. What else?'

'Toothpaste?'

They laughed, but the silence quickly drew in again. She wondered how long they would stay, despite the lack of anything new to talk about. She was tired and wanted her bed. Instead, she went to the kitchen and boiled some water for coffee. The conversation began again, but she only caught snatches. Her mind was elsewhere, imagining the bombers gliding over the city.

As she took a step back towards the living room, there was a knock on the door. At first Charlotte thought she imagined it, but the room fell silent and there was another thump. The others

11

looked between her and Hilda. Andreas gripped one hand with the other and Charlotte could see that his knuckles were already turning white. Even Peter stared, his eyes slightly wider than usual, waiting for someone to make a decision. Even a few months ago this tension would not have happened, but now who knew who would be at their door? Charlotte wasn't sure how long it had been when there was another knock.

She was the first to turn towards the door. She was closest and she could feel their eyes on her back as she crossed the floor. She hesitated. Even yesterday she would have opened the door without thinking about it. Had the Wehrmacht come to enlist them all? Had the party decided that there was no longer a need for students and the police had come to round them up? It was ridiculous, but still these thoughts went round and round her head.

Chapter Two

Saturday, 2 September 1939

Kurt beamed at her as the opened door revealed his presence. She couldn't help but smile at his expression.

'For a while there, I thought you weren't in,' he said, his voice low.

Even though Kurt's family considered themselves to be fully 'Aryan', he didn't fit the mould of the perfect German. He was thinner than Charlotte, but about a head taller. In another life she could see him as a writer or academic, but it wasn't the path he had chosen. His sandy brown hair was combed back and stuck in place with pomade and his hair matched his eyes, at times making them seem dark and distant. He was anything but. When he spoke with passion, his eyes became the warmest things she had ever seen. She could get lost in them.

Due to his tall and thin stature, he had worked hard to be physically fit, to impress his parents and deter those who would mock him for his bookish looks. His biceps were muscled and despite herself she couldn't help but wish he would take her in those arms. She felt safe. She was that tired now that she could quite happily fall into them, but at the same time she didn't want to be touched. She realised she was still holding her coffee and put it on the side.

'Kurt, come in. Come, come.' She ushered him inside, saying his name so the others knew he was here, and placing a hand on his arm to help him feel welcome. 'You don't need to be so formal. Knocking is for strangers, and you're always welcome here.'

She flashed him the biggest smile she could manage and his lips parted in response. He moved in to kiss her, but she ducked away quickly.

'Come sit with us.' She held on to his arm partly so he wouldn't leave but also to make up for missing the kiss.

'I didn't know you had company. I will come back.'

'No, don't be ridiculous. You're always welcome.'

'I don't want to get in the way.'

'Nonsense,' Hilda called from the living room, before Charlotte could reply. 'Come join us, Kurt. We need a more interesting mind. This lot have run out of things to say.'

He blushed. Presumably he hadn't realised that they could be overheard from the doorway. He didn't respond well to compliments. He was just Kurt. She liked that about him, especially given his family. That he was completely unpretentious, never acted as if he was superior to her or anyone else.

'Good. Get all those immigrants out.' Peter had continued the conversation while she was gone. 'They shouldn't be here anyway. There weren't enough jobs for real Germans even before they came. Why don't they go somewhere else?'

Ilse nodded at Peter's words, but the others stared into the middle distance. Charlotte could empathise. Her father had often talked about how few regular jobs there were for people, even down at the docks. But that had all improved since the Nazis had taken over, or so she thought. But then her friends had struggled to find work while studying.

'The Nazis have brought in better controls, made the country safer. Look at the new rules for landlords. It means they can better vet their tenants and we don't have to live next to people who would cause us problems.'

14

'Like Jews?'

'Not just Jews, but other undesirables. It could be anyone.'

'What happens when they use it to refuse students? Don't you remember all the trouble we had with the landlord moving in? Have you forgotten how much we had to convince them that we were just students and not social democrat activists?'

'No, of course I haven't forgotten, but that's why the checks are in place.'

'We'd just have to prove that we are hardworking German citizens.' Peter was entirely serious and he almost puffed out his chest, but Charlotte couldn't help but laugh.

'What do you know about work?' Kurt glared at Peter. They must have met before, but she couldn't recall when that might have been.

She would have thought that Peter and Kurt would get on. If she had to pick one of her friends who would agree with Kurt the most it would have been Peter. They had similar backgrounds. Both came from wealthy families. Peter was a member of the party, like Kurt, and Peter was a student member of the university council. It made perfect sense. She could see them together in uniform marching off to the front, their rifles raised high. She just didn't know which of them would come back. Probably Peter. He had that knack for getting himself out of trouble. She recognised that in herself. She had always managed to talk or trick her way out of trouble, especially where her parents were concerned. But had they just let her get away with things? It was a question she'd never discover the answer to.

However, Kurt surprised her. The look he gave Peter was as if Kurt saw in Peter everything he hated about himself.

'There's going to be war.' Andreas was apparently oblivious to the tension in the room. 'There's no doubt about it. The only question is how long it will last.'

'And who will be drawn into it.' Peter wasn't ready to back down. 'If we're at war with Britain, we're at war with her colonies. And what about America?'

'Who knows about America? The newspapers are saying that after the Depression the Americans have no interest in war.'

They fell into silence. What the others were thinking Charlotte couldn't tell, but her own thoughts were occupied with questions of what would happen to them all.

'Listen.' Kurt leant over to whisper in her ear as the others were arguing. 'I came here because I think we should talk.'

Those words made her heart race. What did he want to talk about? He had turned up unexpectedly, when he was usually so reliable and predictable. Her imagination ran wild.

'I didn't quite want to do it like this. We're living in unprecedented times. But I think we should talk about getting married.'

There was a hush around the room as the others heard the words. It wasn't what Charlotte had been thinking, but she should have known better. It was all he had been thinking about for months, years even.

'Kurt, now's not the time. There are other things to think about. If we're going to war then what's going to happen? Marriage is the least of our worries.'

'But that's precisely why we should talk about it. With more war on the way, it's only a matter of time before they post me out to fight somewhere.'

The others shuffled in their seats, looking among themselves. They should have spoken about this in private.

'I don't want to think about that. We don't know what's going to happen.'

She knew she had disappointed him, but what was she supposed to do? She wasn't ready to be someone's wife. She loved Kurt, of course she did, but she was only a student: young, and she wanted more time to think about things. She needed more time. But the war would have other ideas. He was right about that, but even still she couldn't just marry him. It didn't feel right.

And he kept pushing and pushing, trying to get her to agree. He had asked her almost half a dozen times before in the middle of conversation. If she was going to marry him then that was not how she wanted to agree to it. She wanted it to be spontaneous, romantic. Not to be forced by a world that didn't really care about them.

'Charlotte, you need to marry me. If something happens to me I want you to be taken care of, and you will be better off as my wife. I can leave you a will. What about your dual citizenship? The party like the Swedes, but what if they decide you're not German enough?'

'Not the best proposal,' Peter muttered to Ilse. There was a sharp intake of breath from someone, but Charlotte didn't catch who. Her vision was blurred at the edges.

'Shut up, Peter,' Kurt growled.

'No, Kurt. Please. Not now.'

She stood up from the couch and retreated to the kitchen, to recover her half-made cup of coffee. In her grip the mug crashed down on the counter and a shard of china clattered off. She closed her eyes with a sigh. When she opened them again she realised Kurt had followed her. She knew he would. He didn't say sorry, but his eyes showed that he wanted to. From the hours she had spent staring into them she could always tell what he was thinking. That was one of the things that made them so good together. But she couldn't think about marrying him: she wasn't ready.

'Charlotte?' he ventured, reaching out to lay a hand on her arm. She winced at the contact and pulled further into the kitchen.

'I don't want to talk about this now. I think you should leave.'

He didn't say a word. He just nodded, looked back into the room then opened the door. With one long glance back at her, he left, his footsteps echoing down the hallway. He didn't close the door. She suspected it was because he wanted her to hear him leaving.

She shut the door behind him, feeling her friends' eyes on her back. She took a sip of water: it was brackish. The tap was another thing she needed to get fixed. If only there was a way to get to her room without passing her friends, but she would have to make her excuses. She hoped they would understand that she just wanted to be alone.

For the first time all evening the room was completely silent. All Charlotte could hear was the wind whistling around the window frames as it swept in from the sea.

As Charlotte stood there wondering what to do, Peter and Ilse left, shortly followed by Andreas. They each nodded their goodbye to her and left Hilda to retreat to her room. Charlotte was thankful for their consideration. She could already feel the tears pricking at the corners of her eyes. It wasn't the first time they had argued, but with the weight of the world crushing down on her, it had taken a different toll. She hated to leave things with him like that, to let him feel that she didn't care, but she knew he would be back.

The only thing that would prevent him from returning was if the war took him. She hoped that would be a long time coming.

Tuesday, 30 January 1933

The *stahlhelms* and brownshirts marched down Mönckebergstrasse, to the sound of a marching band. They weren't put off by the dripping rain and driving wind, and nor was Charlotte. Other children raced them, their parents grabbing at them to stay by their sides. The excitement was clear to see, from the waving flags to the movement of the crowd. Charlotte felt like she was being pulled along on its wave. The streets were so full it was difficult to see the parade, but this couldn't be the entire city here in one place. She knew there were elements of Hamburg's population who were keeping a low profile.

Hitler had been confirmed as chancellor of Germany and his supporters were celebrating. The dark evening was lit by the orange street lamps and the firebrands they carried, casting shifting shadows across the gathered onlookers and the walls behind them. Charlotte could only just make out the goose-stepping boots through the gaps in bodies around her. She jostled from side to side to get a better look.

Charlotte gripped Kurt's hand and led him around through the crowd. He resisted at first, but she knew that he liked to hold her hand, and that was enough to get him over his fear. She smiled at him in the gloom and she could sense him relax. Partners in crime, that was what they called themselves. They had been inseparable since they had run off together at one of her parents' parties. Now they were doing it again.

They couldn't see the parade from where they were, but she knew a place where they could get a better look. A place away from the adults. Charlotte and Kurt weren't the only teenagers out after dark. She caught glimpses of others, in some places standing with their parents. Unlike the others, the two of them raced through the crowd as if they were playing a game, hunting something amongst the ceremony.

The news of Adolf Hitler becoming chancellor had taken over the city like a festival. It was a great victory for Germany and everyone wanted to be a part of it. Except for the communists and the social democrats. They were keeping themselves to themselves, locked away in their homes, plotting as always. They had been a part of the problem, and now they would have to change their ideas. Charlotte didn't really blame them, although she would not admit that to anyone, and the argument was very compelling. They had let Germany down by being selfish and betraying German values.

There was something about the bright red flags, the hooked cross, the cheering and the singing. It was euphoric. Her parents thought Charlotte was too young to understand, but she was not as naive as they thought. She had read books, voraciously, taking in every detail she could. She had lived through what the Weimar Republic had done to Germany. They had all struggled, even those with money like her parents. Pappa always talked about how hard it was to make ends meet, how even a loaf of bread and butter could cost a fortune. But now things were going to get better. The National Socialists were going to help them all and cast off the restrictions of Versailles. They were going to make Germany great again.

'Here.' She hauled Kurt down a narrow alley. He pulled back at her, but didn't let go of her hand.

20

'Where are we going?' His voice had yet to take on the bass timbre of adolescence.

'You'll see.' Didn't he trust her? They'd known each other for years. Everything was going to be all right. It always was. Whenever they got into trouble, she always got them out of it. Yet Kurt was still scared. He preferred a life in the corners, left to read his books. If not for Charlotte he would probably be sat in his room now, reading some adventure story, lost in another world. She had helped him to come out of his shell, be a little more adventurous.

'What's wrong with here?' he murmured. 'Here is close enough. What if someone sees us sneaking around?'

'I can't see from here.' His lanky frame was already almost ten centimetres taller than her, and it was enough to give him a vantage point she didn't have. 'Come on, I want to get a better look.'

Charlotte pushed through the crowd again. Their movements were followed by frustrated glances and shouts as they bumped into people. It was like being chased on the school playground, enjoying the rush of her raised heartbeat. But unlike school, they never managed to catch up with her.

Pulling away from the crowd they ran down an alley. At first it led away from the parade, but she knew it would take them to a fire escape at the back of a building, which they could climb up to the roof. It was technically trespassing, but Charlotte didn't think anyone would notice them in all that was going on. Kurt kept pace with her now.

'The roof on the old Karstadt building,' he said, realisation dawning. They had climbed up there when it had first closed down, and it had been one thing she hadn't needed to convince Kurt to do. Uncharacteristically, he enjoyed climbing. It was why she knew he would follow her now.

As she turned a corner, she ran head first into a dark figure. The man elicited an oof sound as he doubled over, clutching his stomach. Charlotte fell back, landing in the dirt of the alley. As her

21

vision cleared she looked up into a face she recognised. Her hand shot to her mouth, before she scrambled around to stand again.

'Pappa!'

'Charlotte?' her father asked, after getting his breath back. 'What are you doing out here?'

'I think that's somewhat obvious.' She climbed to her feet and gave him a hug, but not before he gave her a look that said: *don't be flippant*. He winced again as her head came to rest against his chest.

'Who's that with you?' he asked, looking over her shoulder. 'Oh, Kurt. Hallo, *Junge*.'

'I . . . I have to go.' Kurt didn't even say goodbye as he disappeared into darkness back around the corner.

'Perhaps one day I won't terrify him.'

Charlotte could hear the amusement in her father's voice, even though she knew he was angry with her for being out.

'It's not you he's terrified of. It's the concept of you. He likes you, truly, but you're my father. He wants to impress you.'

'Hmm.' He placed a hand on her shoulder and gently turned her around to face the way she had come. 'You're incredibly perceptive sometimes. It can be quite scary. For now, you should focus on being young. It's the only time you can.'

She didn't know what to say as they walked along the alley. It wasn't the first time he had complimented her in such a way, but she wasn't perceptive enough to know what he really meant. Her father could be like that at times. He was an incredibly warm man, but he kept his secrets and sometimes spoke in riddles. At times he would close off, no matter how much she asked him a question, and wouldn't give her an answer. It was those times that truly scared her.

'Come on. Let's go home,' he said. 'It's getting late.'

'But the parade.'

'We'll be seeing more of the Nazis in good time, no doubt. I suspect this is far from their last party.'

He quickened his pace down the alley in the direction she had come, clearly expecting her to follow. She hesitated for a second, but in the end her obedience won. She ran to catch up with him and they walked side by side all the way home, in silence, the sounds of revelry fading behind them.

It was only once they had returned home after her father had clicked the front door shut and locked it that he turned to her. He was breathing deeply, but his brow was furrowed and there was a redness to his cheeks that suggested he was overheating. It was then that he became serious. His eyes lost their twinkle.

'We need to talk,' he said, fixing his eyes on hers to make sure he had her attention. 'You shouldn't have been running around the streets at night, Cha-cha. You're too young and it's dangerous.'

She had known this was coming, but still there was a flutter of anticipation in her stomach. She could always tell when her father was truly angry, and this wasn't one of those occasions. For a start he used her full name when he was telling her off, and his face always became a shade of beetroot. But it was when he was calm that it was worst. At those times she knew his anger had abated and he had become disappointed with her, unable to see any way to get her to do what she was told. What he thought was best for her. It was as if he had given up on her.

'Especially with boys,' he continued. 'I don't care how wealthy their parents are. It's all right for them. It's not safe for you.'

'I'm sorry, Pappa.' She looked at her shoes, noticing for the first time that they were covered in mud and dust from the city's streets. It was times like that she felt like a young girl. 'I just wanted to see the celebration.'

He sighed and hunched over to her height. He tucked a blonde curl back behind her ear.

'Don't be sorry, *meine Liebe*. Just be careful. I know those Nazis are promising everyone the world, and we had better play by their rules now, but don't forget to always question what others tell you. You promise?'

23

She nodded, unsure of the weight of his words. As far as she could remember he had never spoken about the Nazis before. Politics was a forbidden subject at the dining table, but Charlotte had heard her parents arguing when she was supposed to be in bed. Neither of them could agree what the Nazis were going to do to Hamburg, but they had never included Charlotte in those arguments. They thought she was too young to know. But she knew they were scared. That said, they had been scared for as long as she could remember.

Chapter Three

Monday, 4 September 1939

Charlotte got up early and left before seeing Hilda. There was still sleep in her eyes, even though she had washed. Normally she and Hilda would enjoy a breakfast of warm coffee and *Franzbrötchen* together, but she didn't want to talk about the argument with Kurt. She couldn't dump that on Hilda; it wasn't fair. And she too was wary of Kurt's links to the party. It was still too raw. So she was on her way to hide in the university, where no one would bother her.

Many in Hamburg cycled along the wide roads, but Charlotte preferred to walk. That way she could feel a part of the city, breathe it in. She used public transport where she could; the U-Bahn and S-Bahn made it easy to get around. She loved the city because of how open it was. She couldn't imagine living anywhere else.

The university felt like somewhere new. It was always fresh and exciting. Not just because of the learning and knowledge exchange that happened within its walls, but because of the students coming and going. It felt like the train stations, the city, everything was moving, shifting, and becoming something new all the time, with links to the world. Before the war, at least.

She got off the U-Bahn at Dammtor Bahnhof, noticing some other students getting off the train. Even though she was only a second-year, most of them looked a lot younger than her. They wore their clothes differently. Not exactly new fashions, but with a different sort of confidence she couldn't put her finger on. The hem of a trouser leg slightly wider, a blouse with a lower neck. They were fresh, inexperienced children. Were they nervous of their new surroundings as she had been? Even though she had been born in the city? In fact, she wasn't even sure that she had got over that feeling. While she enjoyed being within the university buildings, she often felt as though she wasn't supposed to be there. At any moment someone might come and throw her out as an imposter, an intruder.

Dammtor Bahnhof was the prettiest train station in Hamburg. The architecture a remnant of a time before the needs of modern Germany and the brutal concrete. Although it wasn't far from the central train station it served a vital part of the city, the Rotherbaum and the university. From there you could catch trains to Munich, Nuremberg, and Berlin. Its arch was smaller than the central station, but the stone towers either side of the building were both impressive and imposing. These days, of course, the red-and-white banner of the National Socialist party hung between the towers over the entrance, the swastika above them all.

She turned swiftly away from that sight to the park that lay on the other side of the road. Moorweide Park. Through it was one of her favourite walks in the city, not least because it led towards the university. It was almost as green as the Stadtpark to the north, where she had spent hours as a child playing in the Kinderpark with her mother and father. She could happily spend hours walking around those parks, but as she got older she found it more difficult to find the time. The weight of the war pressed down on her like a black cloud.

As she crossed the park the university came into view. The central hall was a domed building that could have been mistaken for a public library. Other stone and brick buildings were dotted around the campus for other departments. The entrance was through a pair of heavy wooden doors that hung at the top of a small flight of stone steps. She passed through on her way to the library.

Charlotte used the university as a place to be alone. The library allowed her to compose her thoughts and think about what she was going to do with her life, and it wasn't unusual for her to lose hours working there. It wasn't just how dense some of the philosophy textbooks could be, but once she got in that mind-set she could quite easily lose track of time. At other times she would find it hard to even get started, staring at the page of a book as the words flew around, not settling long enough to make any sense. Today was one of the former. She had lost herself in Baeumler's work on Nietzsche, a large book which she used to cover up a work by Thomas Mann underneath. The latter had been banned, but the university still had a copy. She was comparing the two, noting the differences in belief, when she was interrupted.

Two boys walked past, talking loudly. She glared at them, but they didn't notice. In truth she preferred noise to silence. Silence allowed her mind to wander, and she couldn't concentrate. Noise helped her to keep calm, to focus. But it was the irregularity of their conversation that distracted her. The disturbance made her heart rate rise. She couldn't be seen with the book.

She glanced at the wall clock before going back to her reading. It was two minutes past five, after the time she usually went home, but she didn't feel like being at home. Kurt would come to see her and she didn't want to argue. Let him think about it for a few days before she saw him again. It would do him good, help him understand she was only nineteen, too young to marry.

The words on the page no longer made sense. It wasn't that they were jumbled. She knew what each word meant, but as soon as she turned the page she forgot them. She picked up another book. It was Hans Fallada's novel *Kleiner Mann – was nun?* (*Little Man, What Now?*). She turned the first few pages, but it was no better.

She dropped the book onto the table with a thump and a boy at a nearby table glanced over at her. He shook his head as he went back to work and she wanted to stick her tongue out at him. What could be so important that it could not even be disturbed for a moment? The hypocrisy of her thoughts was not lost on her, but that was the mood she was in.

Charlotte put her head in her hands. It was no use, no matter how hard she tried to concentrate she couldn't. She couldn't stop thinking about her argument with Kurt. He could be so stubborn, so obstinate. If she could just let her eyes close for a moment, she could sleep here and not have to go home. She wondered whether anyone would notice.

She opened her eyes again. The only person in the library was the boy who had shaken his head. His head dropped to his books again as she made eye contact. If she had looked up a second later she wouldn't have noticed. Was he watching her? No, that was ridiculous. Yet every time she glanced away she could feel his gaze on her.

She hadn't seen him before. At first she had just disregarded him as a new student, but now that she looked at him, truly looked at him, she could see he was at the very least her age. He could even be a few years older. He had one of those faces that was hard to place and medium brown hair cut short. There was nothing remarkable about him. Now that she was keeping an eye on him he was making an effort not to look up. She was sure he was paying more attention to his books than he had been previously.

Had the Gestapo, the state secret police, sent someone to keep an eye on the university and she just happened to be in the wrong place at the wrong time? She couldn't think why, but there was no such thing as being too cautious. Not anymore. Could he have seen the Thomas Mann book?

Hastily she started cramming things into her bag and then stopped. She didn't want to give him any reason to think she was panicking. She wasn't even sure why she was. Instead of rushing, she did what she always did when she finished in the library; she collected up her books, put the ones she wanted to keep into her bag and placed the others back on the shelves. She had taken them; she could put them back.

She returned to the table and picked up her bag and violin case. She didn't go anywhere without her violin, and the best thing she could do now was to go and practise. She had not had enough time recently to play and, even when she was tired and distracted, it helped her keep calm.

The corridor was even more empty than the library. If anyone wanted to follow her they would have a difficult job. So she walked as slowly as she could, only picking up her pace as she turned a corner. The sense of a shadow at her heels led her in a different direction, towards the staff offices. This corridor was arranged with stained brown wooden doors along its walls, with name plates outside each one. Charlotte didn't know how many lecturers the university employed but it seemed like hundreds. She turned another corner, still conscious of something behind her.

Professor Bendorff was just coming out of his office. It was as if the fates had decreed it, the very man she was hoping to call on. He smiled as he saw her, tucked some paperwork under an arm, and shut the door behind him.

'Charlotte, what a pleasure,' he said. 'I didn't expect to see you out of term time.'

He was one of Charlotte's philosophy lecturers. She wasn't sure what he could do to help her, but his office felt like the safest location to be at the moment.

'Professor Bendorff.' She laid a hand on his arm. 'I can't explain out here, but I would like to speak to you in your office if you have the time.'

Professor Krüger came out of her office and locked the door behind her. She was another of Charlotte's lecturers, and she felt her cheeks redden as she realised her hand was on her professor's arm. What would Krüger think? She had to admit she admired

Stefan Bendorff, in a different way to anyone else. They always seemed to be on the same page. Then there was the way he smelt, so— She cut off that thought before it could blossom and focused on the scene in front of her, and kept her gaze on Professor Bendorff as Professor Krüger passed them down the corridor.

Bendorff's curly black hair was thinning at the temples, but it only served to accentuate his slightly oval face and fine nose. The moustache he wore flattened as his lips thinned and his deep-brown eyes widened in apparent concern. The stubble that covered his cheeks barely disguised the dimples she couldn't help but be drawn to.

'Please, Charlotte. Call me Stefan. I keep telling you I prefer first names.'

She nodded her assent and looked over her shoulder. The boy was walking behind a pair of academic staff who were coming her way. He made eye contact and his face was steel. Stefan continued.

'I was just on my way to a meeting across the university, but you're welcome to walk with me if that will—'

'Yes, yes. That will be fine. Let's go.'

She didn't wait to see if he followed as she dragged her gaze away from his frown and continued along the corridor. He caught her up after a few steps. The corridors were starting to fill up with staff now.

'I thought I was supposed to be the one in charge,' he said, raising his voice to be heard. There was a hint of humour in his tone. 'Where are we going?'

'I don't know,' she replied, honestly. 'I don't care as long as it's not here and you stay with me.'

'Wait a moment, Charlotte.' He grabbed her arm and pulled her around. Reluctantly she stopped. 'What's going on here? I'm flattered, honestly, but I think you should explain.'

His hand was still around her upper arm, the grip stronger than she had expected. It didn't hurt, but she wasn't sure she would get away if she tried. She didn't know what to say. Would he believe her? Something about those deep eyes made her want to confess everything. Her mouth worked silently, but she felt safer with him there.

'That boy back there.' She pointed vaguely in the direction they had come. 'I think he's following me.'

'What? Who?' Stefan looked back along the corridor. 'Who would be following you?'

'That boy there.' She resisted pointing. She didn't want him to know that she was talking about him. 'He was in the library watching me, and when I left he followed. Now he's here. We have to go.'

Stefan shook her arm. She thought it was supposed to be comforting, but it made her stumble.

'It's all right,' he said. 'The only people I see here are staff.'

He led her back to his office, opened the door again and ushered her inside.

'I can understand you're scared,' he said. 'But there's no reason to be. No one can hurt you here. Please, try to calm down. But we'll just wait a bit and make sure they're gone. Let's get you a drink.'

He took out a couple of glasses and a bottle from his desk drawer. It was Scotch, Lagavulin. She remembered he had spent some time in Britain before the war started. If the Gestapo found it then she was sure they would confiscate it as non-German contraband. But that didn't matter now; she needed a drink.

'Here.' He passed her a glass and she drank. The liquid burnt her throat as it went down, but she already felt warmer and more relaxed. 'We shouldn't really drink on campus, but I felt like the situation allowed it. Now, why would anyone be following you?'

She looked him up and down. Could this man with his soft voice and brown suit help her? Keep her safe? She had heard his lectures. While he was careful to never openly criticise the party, he did encourage his students to think. He was braver than she was. It was worth the risk.

'I was reading a banned book. I shouldn't have been, but I was comparing notes on Nietzsche.'

'In the library?'

She nodded.

'Show me.'

He held out a hand, indicating she should pass it to him. She took the Thomas Mann book out of her bag and handed it to him. His eyes widened only slightly, as if he had been expecting something worse. He cradled it in both hands.

'How did this avoid the book purge?' he asked, rhetorically. 'They're rare artefacts now; you should look after it.'

'I found it in the library.'

'That's no place for it. Take it home. Keep it safe and secret.'

She pulled the book out of his hands, without being invited to. She hadn't been sure what his reaction was going to be, but his almost reverence surprised her.

'I've been looking after it,' she said. 'But it was foolish to read it in the library.'

'Good. When the Nazis are through then we'll need the books again.' He gave her a look that suggested she shouldn't repeat his words to anyone else. 'But I've already said too much.'

His manner changed in an eye blink from the warm, comforting lecturer to being on his guard. She had seen it happen many times before, around the city. Whenever someone thought they had said the wrong thing, they shut up and withdrew. After she knocked back the dregs of her drink, he took the glass back from her and returned it to the drawer with the bottle.

'I'm sorry, I overstepped the mark,' he said, laying a hand on her arm as she had done in the corridor. 'But you're welcome to wait here for a while before you leave if it will make you feel safer.'

It wasn't unusual for a student to be in a professor's office, but something about the atmosphere had changed.

'I was on my way to a meeting.' He moved towards the door and opened it. 'So if you're all right here, I'll leave you be.'

'Thank you for taking me seriously,' she said, as she took a seat in the corner. He smiled and shut the door behind him. Now alone, she realised how fast her heart was beating. She would take a few minutes to compose herself and then she would make her way home. She hoped that she would have no need to call on help again in the future, but you couldn't be too sure in this world. If she did, she might have to go to someone other than Stefan Bendorff. Krüger might help her, but Charlotte didn't want to put her in any danger.

Chapter Four

Tuesday, 5 September 1939

Charlotte had woken from a dream about being chased, but finding that no matter how much she ran she couldn't escape the pursuing silhouette. At breakfast she had not wanted to speak of it. Hilda had been able to tell something was wrong, of course, but she knew better than to ask when Charlotte was trapped in her own thoughts.

She had packed her violin and headed to the university. It was freezing in the rehearsal room, as if a breeze was blowing in through the windows, but the one window in the room was painted shut. Charlotte pulled her coat tighter around her and was thankful she had brought it with her, even though it was early autumn.

The university had provided them with a space to practise. It had been a small office at the end of one corridor, around a corner. She thought at one time that it had belonged to an academic staff member: there were a few discarded books, a photograph frame and an empty filing cabinet. It wasn't ideal, but it was at least a space.

There was a musty smell of damp, and the windows were painted shut. Every now and then a strange knocking sound could be heard, which most put down to water moving through old plumbing, but which Charlotte couldn't help but feel was something more sinister. The times she waited to listen for it, she could hear nothing, but as soon as her attention was on something else it started up again. It was as if whatever was causing the sound was mocking her.

Her father had made sure that she practised every day. As long as she was studying and practising then he was happy. 'You can't have knowledge without art,' he would always say. One without the other was meaningless in his eyes. She missed his little sayings. Every so often she caught herself repeating one or another to someone else and it brought him back for a moment. She would fall into reflection, having heard it in his voice. On those occasions she would go and play her violin as if he was in the room watching her practise.

She sat on a piano stool, facing a corner. As soon as she had her violin against her chin, bow in her right hand, she found herself playing a tune. At first she couldn't place it, humming it to herself as she tried to find the correct notes. It took a few minutes of moving up and down the fingerboard before she felt confident enough in her memory to reproduce it properly, but after that it came back with ease.

Mendelssohn's 'Violin Concerto in E Minor'. That was the tune. She hadn't heard it in years. She hadn't played it in longer. It was amazing how much of it she could remember. She started again from the beginning. The bow almost slipped from her hand as she played a wrong note. Too sharp. She cursed then heard a chuckle from behind her. She turned, half standing and dropping the bow.

A woman she recognised was standing in the doorway.

'Greta? Were you watching me?' Greta stifled a laugh again in that way she always did. Charlotte didn't know her well, but on the few occasions they had met she had put the giggle down to nerves. But now she felt as if the other woman was mocking her. 'It's not nice to laugh at another's mistakes. I was practising.'

Her words were unusually defensive, but in truth she hoped that Greta was mocking her. The alternative was much worse. She shouldn't have been playing that piece. It was un-German, but for some reason the impulse had taken her. A half-forgotten melody from her childhood. Had her father played it to her when she was a child? She couldn't remember.

'Oh, I wasn't laughing.' The grin dropped from her face as she rushed to Charlotte's side. Greta's black hair hung curled over a sable stole draped over her shoulders in a way that showed her family's wealth. 'At least, I wasn't laughing at you. I'm sorry.'

She was always well dressed. No matter the weather, Greta never looked anything but impeccable. She could have been a model or actress. Charlotte was not only a little jealous, but also in awe of the other woman. Greta was in the university orchestra. She often seemed distant and aloof, but Charlotte considered the two of them friends. Greta was a year older than Charlotte, and they both played the violin. Some might even say they looked similar, if not for Greta's darker hair. For some reason they didn't spend much time together, but Charlotte wanted to learn more from Greta, especially about the orchestra.

'I was just thinking how much I loved Mendelssohn's music as a child,' Greta said. 'And well, your misplaced note made me realise how odd it was that I was hiding in the shadows listening to you play music that shouldn't be played. Music that should be in the shadows itself, if you like.'

'It was silly. I just remembered the melody and thought I would try and remember how to play it. I should have picked something else.'

Greta was in her final year of study, Charlotte going into her second, so they didn't have classes together. It struck her as odd that she knew more about the other woman than Greta knew about her, but none of it had come from Greta directly. There were rumours about Greta's family, but then there were always rumours these days. Everyone had a story about everyone else, and some were all too quick to report them to the Gestapo for some perceived slight or misdemeanour.

As far as Charlotte could recall, her own family was the only family that had escaped rumour. That was mainly because she didn't really have a family these days. At least, not in Germany. And before then, well, there hadn't been many rumours. They had only started when the Nazis had come to power. She and her family had been considered fully Aryan. Not just because of her blonde hair and blue eyes, but also because of her Prussian and Swedish heritage. Her father had never caused any trouble and he was not a member of any political party. As far as she knew he just went to work and did his bit for the community, as all good Germans should, before he had died.

She had once been annoyed that Greta had an almost automatic place in the university orchestra. So far Charlotte had failed to get in, despite multiple attempts, and if she kept playing the wrong note, she would have no hope at her next audition.

'What did you want?' One of the problems was that she never knew what to say to Greta. Her words caught in her throat whenever she was in the company of the other woman.

'I have seen you with your violin case, but I never thought to ask you about it. I never bring mine in to practise here; it feels too personal. But really it's a silly thought. Why shouldn't I practise here at the university like you? We should play together.'

Charlotte hesitated. Greta was trying to engage her in conversation, so why was she finding it difficult? It couldn't just be the fact she had been chased the other day and was still feeling wary of others. Could it be that music was too personal to her? That it reminded her of her father?

'I would like that,' she said after the pause. It was a genuine response. 'I haven't had the opportunity to play alongside someone in a long time. I'm a little rusty, but surely it would help.'

'Oh definitely. I could even see about you joining the university orchestra, but maybe we should just practise together first.' Greta sat on the other stool. 'We shouldn't even be talking about the forbidden music. But I won't tell anyone. I promise.'

There was a pleading in Greta's dark eyes. It was how Charlotte imagined the other woman would have got what she wanted as a child. It was hard not to fall into those eyes, to be mesmerised by them. She could see Greta wrapping a lover around her little finger. They would do whatever she asked. Charlotte thought that if she wasn't careful she would do whatever Greta asked as well.

Charlotte didn't reply immediately. She had learnt to bide her time and bite her tongue. Even a word spoken in haste could cause problems. She didn't want to have to explain herself to anyone, not even Greta.

'It's nice to hear someone else play,' Greta said. 'The halls here are so quiet now. I miss the music from my childhood. But we shouldn't talk about that. Where did you learn to play?'

It was the first time anyone had been interested in her music. Perhaps she had been wrong about Greta's aloofness after all.

'My father taught me. He said that no matter what happened, if I had music then I would never be poor.'

Greta stifled a laugh again, but Charlotte was beginning to realise that it was what she did when she didn't know what else to do. It would get her in trouble one day, Charlotte was sure, but she wasn't about to let it ruin their growing friendship.

'I don't think he meant poor financially, but rather that music makes us rich philosophically. He was fascinated by philosophy and anthropology. I guess that's why I'm here at the university too. Thanks to him.'

Of course, to get into university she'd had to do her service in the *Jungmädelbund*, the League of German Girls, but it had made sense at the time. All the other girls in her school were joining and it was logical to follow the crowd. For once, at least. It was the only way to make sure she could have the future she wanted. She remembered telling her father what she planned to do.

'Say, why don't we meet tomorrow?' Greta asked, but Charlotte was already lost in the memory.

It had been the first time she had seen her father angry.

Friday, 20 April 1934 – Adolf Hitler's Birthday

'I don't want her joining that organisation.'

It was the first time in Charlotte's life that her father had said no to anything she wanted to do. Normally he would listen and would compromise, explaining why he thought a different approach was best, but now he was flat-out refusing.

'Why not?' she asked, in the hope that he would at least explain his way of thinking.

'I don't have to explain it, Charlotte. I'm your father.'

'But, Pappa.'

He looked at her then in that way of his that suggested he knew better. His face was red, redder than she had seen it before. She couldn't understand why he was being like this and she only wanted to understand.

'I'm sorry, Cha-cha, but I just don't want you joining that organisation. It's not good for you.'

'But—'

'I don't think we have a choice, Max.' It was the first time her mother had got involved in the argument. Typically she would leave them to it, perhaps knowing that the bond between father and daughter was stronger, but on this occasion Charlotte welcomed her input. Her mother was making a pot of tea with her back to

Charlotte and her father. She would not be able to tell how angry her father was, but she must have been able to tell from his tone. As a result her voice was unusually soft and calm, like that of a teacher who wanted to take better control of her pupils.

'I know she's made up her mind, Linny. But please, you know what those organisations are like.' That was his pet name for her: Linny, for Linnea.

Charlotte's mother put the pot of tea down on the dining table and took a step towards her husband. She took his hands between hers and hushed him softly. Charlotte suddenly felt as if she was no longer in the room, as if they wanted to continue this conversation without her. She had grown used to them speaking about her as if she wasn't there when she was a child, their only child, but now that she was growing up she wanted to be a part of the conversation.

'This isn't just about Charlotte,' her mother said, still holding her father's hands in hers. 'The Nazis have decided that all children over thirteen are to be a part of their youth organisations.'

'Yes, but they won't enforce it. How can they?'

'They enforce everything. They're authoritarians and if they don't enforce it, someone else will do it for them. The danger—'

'It's worth the risk. They can't take her away from us.'

'They're not, darling. She's our only child, our precious daughter. If we cause any trouble it will be more dangerous for her in the long run. Think about it. There is no choice.'

There was a familiar look on her father's face, one that suggested he knew he had lost the argument. It was always the same when Charlotte and her mother agreed on something. There was no hope for him. He was outnumbered. It was time for Charlotte to say her piece; she had been left out of the conversation too long.

'Pappa, I want to be a part of the group, even if you disagree. I know you have my best interests at heart, but this time you're wrong.'

Her father pulled his hands out from between his wife's and stroked the hair at the side of Charlotte's head as he had done when she was a child. Instinctively she leant into it, but she knew it would diminish her argument.

'By why, child?' he asked. 'What do those people mean to you?'

'Opportunity, Pappa. If everyone else is a part of the organisation and I am not then how can I get ahead? I will be left behind while they get the important jobs, the best positions.'

'Such a mature head on such small shoulders. How did we create such a wise child, Linny?'

'I've no idea, husband of mine. But it pains me that she should have to be so mature at this age. What a world we have brought her into.'

She too stroked the other side of Charlotte's hair. It was the first time Charlotte had really heard her mother show such concern for her and she could feel tears pulling at the corners of her eyes. She willed them away. She had to show them how much she needed this, to be a part of something.

'If I don't join with the other children,' she said, 'I will also be an outcast, a pariah. They will treat me differently. I already have no friends and you always told me I should have friends.'

'You have friends, my dear. There's Kurt.'

'And who else?'

Her parents were silent. Once again her father had that resigned look on his face, but there was something else there. Did he have tears in his eyes too?

'You're right. Friends are important. I just worry about the type of friends. Do you really want to be friends with those people?'

'What choice do I have, Pappa? Everyone else will join the League of German Girls. I should be a part of it too. I'm sure I will find other good German girls to be friends with. Just you wait and see.'

'That's exactly what I am worried about.'

Charlotte didn't understand his comment, but she was determined to prove him wrong. Was it not her father who always encouraged her to make friends, to study and to make something of herself? This was the only way. This was the new Germany the Nazis were forging.

'If I want to go to university, or to be a musician, then I will have to join. They will not accept people who have not been a member of the organisations. I can't miss out.'

'All right, but I want to know everything that happens when you are at their meetings. Everything.'

'Pappa, I won't remember everything.'

'You must try. For me.'

Charlotte came back into the corridor to her waiting parents. She had donned the neat blue skirt and white blouse of the League of German Girls, complete with its embroidered swastika. Her mother put her hands on Charlotte's arms and gave her a kiss on the cheek.

'Look at you,' she said. 'You're growing up too quickly, my *barn*. You look like a young woman already.'

Charlotte looked to her father for his thoughts, but he said nothing. His lips formed a thin line and she was sure there was sorrow in his eyes. He could be expressing the same emotion as her mother, but Charlotte knew it was something else.

She just smiled at him. 'It will be all right, Pappa.'

Her words seemed to bring him to life. He ruffled her hair.

'I hope so, Cha-cha,' he said. 'I hope so.'

She made her own way to the park for the meeting, and when she got there a stern-faced matron took her name and filled in some paperwork. Then she led her over to a group of other girls, all dressed in the same uniform, their hair in pigtails.

'Weber. This is your section.'

The other girls turned to her, looking her up and down. They were holding dolls and one or two of them were pushing prams.

'What's this?' she asked them.

'It's a pram, silly. What do you think it is?' The other girl had a pinched face, which made her look as if she was always scowling.

'I know that,' Charlotte replied, as politely as she could. She didn't want to make enemies on day one. 'But why do you have it?'

'So that we can learn to be good German mothers . . .'

Chapter Five

Wednesday, 6 September 1939

Charlotte had planned to meet Greta in the rehearsal room at the university. For some reason she felt a little sick, as if she hadn't eaten. It wasn't just because she was an awe of her friend, her easy confidence and ability to do anything she put her mind to, but she still felt uneasy about being followed the other day. The university had become less of a safe space for her and that made her sad, but she didn't want to miss out on getting to know Greta better.

For once Charlotte was early, but Greta was already there waiting for her. She had her violin on her lap and was polishing the fingerboard and strings. She looked up as Charlotte arrived. When she saw Charlotte come through the door, a smile broke out on her face, showing perfect teeth.

'Charlotte,' she cried, but didn't stand. 'It's so good to see you.'

It felt a little like attending an appointment, perhaps due to the way Charlotte had made sure she was early, but Greta's smile helped Charlotte feel more at ease. Greta rested her violin back in its case and ushered Charlotte over to a seat near her.

'I thought we could make a morning of it,' Greta said, and

picked up a basket from beside her seat. 'It's not so often we get to enjoy ourselves these days.'

She had brought snacks, pastries, and a bottle of schnapps poked its neck out of the wicker basket. It was another show of Greta's wealth, but Charlotte took it at face value. Greta was happy to share, and Charlotte wouldn't complain about being included. Money had been tight since her mother had returned to Sweden.

Greta offered her a pastry and she gladly took it, mumbling a thank you through a mouthful. It melted in her mouth, leaving raisins and a cinnamon aftertaste. She took another bite, hungrier than she had realised.

Greta too was happily munching away, before she shot a glance at Charlotte.

'Say, let's play something we shouldn't.' There was a twinkle in Greta's eye that accompanied her grin. Charlotte wasn't sure whether it was a good idea. She wasn't sure whether Greta was trying to get her in trouble, but Charlotte was just as wary as everyone else at the moment.

'I'm not sure,' she said. 'It's not very private here.'

Greta looked over her shoulder at the door, seemingly suggesting how quiet it was in the corridor. The she looked back into the room and out again, before turning to Charlotte.

'Fuck, Charlotte. We don't get to just enjoy ourselves any more, do we?' She lit up a cigarette and took a drag. 'We're students; we should be painting the town red. What's wrong with a little banned music? It can't hurt anyone. Everyone is far too serious. It's fucking depressing.'

Charlotte hadn't expected to hear Greta swear. It seemed so out of character, but it also sounded so natural on her lips, as if it wasn't the first time she had uttered that word. Greta continued as if she hadn't even thought about it, in between drags of her cigarette.

'Play something for me, please,' she asked. The smoke drifted around her brown curls. 'I don't mind what it is; I just need to hear some music.'

Charlotte thought of what to play. Her mind went to all the songs the Nazis had banned, but she couldn't play them. Even though they were friends she knew better than to completely trust Greta. Then she settled on something that had come back to her from a distant memory. A second later her bow and violin were rising and she let the first note ring out from its wooden body. She let the melody come to her, by instinct. The rhythm was slow at first, but then she grew into it. The bow moved back and forth, and she swayed in time. Greta joined in, adding harmonies here and there, but before she realised what she was doing Charlotte was singing. The words slipped from her mouth as if the music itself had called them out.

'*Plaisir d'amour ne dure qu'un moment.*' *The pleasure of love lasts only a moment.*

Greta gasped and her bow fell to her lap, but Charlotte continued to sing.

'*Chagrin d'amour dure toute la vie.*' *The grief of love lasts a lifetime.*

She closed her eyes. The words came easily. She had heard them a hundred times. It was a song her father had sung to her when she was a child, and she could still remember every word. Her own bow fell from the violin as she sang. It was as if she was sharing a moment with her father again. Eventually she ran out of song, took a deep breath and then opened her eyes. Greta was staring at her with wide eyes.

'I had no idea you spoke French,' Greta said. 'Or that you could sing so beautifully. How many other languages do you know?'

'Well, I don't really know French. But I can sing a little.'

'Don't be so modest. Your pronunciation was perfect, like a Parisienne.'

'My father sang it to me when I was a little girl. I listened to him every night for years. Eventually we would sing together and

I learnt the pronunciation that way. I suppose he taught me a little French: he was fluent. But then I speak Swedish, my mother's tongue, a little Norwegian and Danish, and of course English.'

'That's incredible. I only speak German, French and English. Not nearly as smart as you.'

'Now who is being modest?'

'Who doesn't speak English? They spread their language and their empire everywhere.'

It was Charlotte's turn to gasp.

'Don't say such things,' she said. 'It's dangerous.'

Greta waved away her concern.

Charlotte wondered whether it was a good time to tell Greta about the boy who had been following her. Her friend seemed to think that the university was a sanctuary, but they couldn't be that complacent. However, she decided against it. Charlotte didn't want Greta to think she was being paranoid, and she didn't yet know whether she could completely trust her friend. She had once thought that Greta was a Nazi. Her words could have been a trap. Greta considered Charlotte for a moment, her brow furrowed.

'You're right, of course,' Greta said. 'Idle talk costs lives. Maybe we should only speak through our music.'

She picked up her bow and placed her violin in the crook of her neck. 'There's a little club I want to take you to sometime,' she said. 'The music there is simply divine. I think you will like it a lot. Why don't I play you something I heard there?'

Before Charlotte could respond, Greta was playing. With her bow in hand she plucked at the strings one after the other. The staccato notes beat against the walls and Charlotte felt her pulse race in response to the music. It was unlike anything she had heard before. Greta would bow a few notes then return to snapping a string with her finger, changing the beat. It was almost erratic, free-form, if not for the fact she returned to the same pattern every few seconds. Charlotte watched, entranced. She wanted to learn more about this music, but was wary of the questions. Surely it was un-German, banned.

'There. I thought you might like that,' Greta said, when she laid the bow back on her lap. She reached down to the basket and pulled out the bottle of schnapps. 'Here, have a drink with me.'

She unscrewed the cap, took a swig of the drink, and then handed the bottle to Charlotte.

'To music,' Greta said, taking the bottle back and raisingit.

A face appeared at the doorway. Charlotte thought she recognised it. She was up from her chair in a heartbeat. Somehow she managed to hold on to her violin, but the bow clattered to the floor as the chair fell over backwards.

'You can't be here; the university is closed for the evening,' a man she had never seen before said. He wore a smart suit that would have looked out of place amongst the academic staff, and a red-and-white party badge adorned his lapel.

The closure was news to Charlotte. As far as she knew the building was open twenty-four hours a day. Although few used it in the evenings. It could be that due to the blackout they had decided to close the university overnight. She was in shock at the surprise visitor and didn't know what to say, but Greta stood. She still held the bottle of schnapps in one hand.

The man looked down at her hand and his frown deepened. 'And you definitely shouldn't be drinking. This is a university, not some bar.'

Charlotte wasn't surprised that he was a party member. He had all the airs of a block warden. He may even have been employed by the Nazis to keep an eye on the university and make sure students were doing what they were supposed to be doing. They were taking over all aspects of life in Germany.

'You must come to my apartment sometime,' Greta said, turning to her and ignoring the man. 'There we can be truly free.'

'That would be nice.' Charlotte was still looking over Greta's shoulder. The man was tapping his wristwatch.

'You're always welcome if you want someone to practise with. It can be so boring on one's own.'

Once they had packed up, the man escorted them from the building. He held the bottle of schnapps in one hand, as if it was a dirty rag. His Reiter shoes clicked on the tiled floor.

Charlotte hadn't expected to deepen her friendship with Greta, with the new war, but she was glad for it. Everything felt more shut-in and claustrophobic, from the boy following her to the new restrictions. It was like everyone was watching her, waiting for her to make a mistake. She was going to need friends like Greta now more than ever.

Chapter Six

Friday, 8 September 1939

Charlotte was late, and it wasn't the first time. Her old friends were used to it, but Greta represented something else, a chance to play music with someone, a different connection.

She rushed around a corner and ran head first into another person. The violin case dropped from her hand and clattered across the floor. The blow took the wind out of her lungs and she had to stop and take a deep breath. The other person fell back against the wall. When her breath returned she realised it was Andreas. Charlotte was grateful it was someone she knew. He had shown her around the university when she had first arrived, and now he was one of her closest friends. She apologised and helped him regain his balance, before reaching for the violin case. The clasp had broken open and now wouldn't click shut. It wasn't as old as the violin, but it was frustrating that she would have to carry the case upright so that the violin didn't fall out.

'I can fix that for you,' Andreas said, getting his breath back, as he played the clasp back and forth. He was a short man and slight of frame. But then Charlotte was used to men like Kurt and her father who were taller than average, and she was taller than average height for a woman. It was Andreas's hair that was the most striking thing about him. It was cut so short that it almost resembled the shorn flank of a sheep. If he cut it any shorter he would be bald, but there was just enough hair to make it look like stubble. Charlotte had once caught him when it had grown slightly longer, and stray hairs stuck out above the cut. He had been so distraught at his reflection he had left the room in a hurry and Charlotte hadn't seen him for a couple of weeks afterwards. Usually when they were together, they fell into an easy friendship, able to endure any silence, or talk each other's ears off.

'Thank you.' She passed him the violin case. 'But be careful please. The violin is precious, a Hopf that belonged to my father and grandfather before him.'

He nodded, already too intent on the mechanical operation of the device to take in many of her words. That was the thing she loved about Andreas and why they had become friends. He could be grumpy and grow frustrated easily, but at times he grew so passionate about things and became so flamboyant in his defence that it was endearing. If he hadn't been a scientist then he would have made a perfect actor, walking the boards of theatres across Germany. She had once asked him why he hadn't gone into the arts. His reply was simple enough: 'No one respects the arts.' And that seemed to be the most important thing to him: respect.

'Where were you going in such a hurry?' he asked, passing the case back to her. The pitch of his voice wavered higher than usual. From his raised eyebrow she suspected he was amused. He didn't often laugh openly, but there were subtle hints in his body language that suggested when something had appealed to him. The eyebrow was one thing; his easy smile was another. Charlotte didn't see her friend smile often, but when she did it filled her with an unexpected warmth.

'I'm late meeting a friend.' She had almost forgotten. 'I'd better go. I'll bring the case to you later.'

'I am not surprised you're late. I'll walk with you.'

They continued together along the corridor in the way Charlotte had been heading. Andreas didn't say where he had been going, but it must not have been important. One of the other things she liked about Andreas was that they could lapse into silence and it would feel entirely natural. When he spoke it was careful and considered.

'So you're meeting a friend?' he asked, glancing at her as the crossed the hard floor. 'Do I know them?'

'She's a relatively new friend. I don't really know her too well yet if I'm honest.'

She had practised a couple of times with Greta since they had crossed paths, but Charlotte wasn't sure whether it was simply a musical relationship, or whether they were actually developing a close friendship like the one she had with Hilda. Charlotte preferred to call it a friendship for now and find out later.

'I'm joking, Charlotte. You're allowed to have other friends.'

Before she had a chance to reply, they reached the rehearsal room.

'Hmm, I haven't been in here before,' Andreas said as he entered the room. 'I think this used to be Professor Rosenbaum's office before he was asked to leave.'

It was empty. Charlotte had expected Greta to already be there, waiting impatiently for her. Perhaps Greta had already grown tired of waiting? Charlotte would have to apologise.

'Where's Greta? We were supposed to meet here.'

'Greta?' Andreas frowned. He was a kind man and a good friend, but was often forgetful.

'Yes, she's a violinist. Curly black hair. Approximately five centimetres shorter than me. We've never compared heights.'

She was rambling and she wasn't sure why, but there was something about this situation that had made her anxious. Greta could have decided that she had waited too long and left, but that didn't seem likely. Charlotte wasn't that late and they would have passed each other in the corridor. Her friend hadn't arrived, but why?

'I'm sorry. I don't know a Greta. Are you sure that's her name?'

'Definitely. You must know Greta. She's a student here.'

He shrugged and shook his head.

'Did you see anyone matching that description before I bumped into you?'

'No. You hit me pretty hard, but I don't think hard enough to affect my memory.'

Andreas's smile was entirely unwelcome in the situation, even if he was trying to calm her down. It wasn't working.

'I'm not playing a game. I'm serious. She should be here.'

'Sorry . . . I . . . Why don't you try her home? She might have forgotten she was due to meet you. I could go with you, but I really should get back to the lab.'

'That's all right.' She made to go back out of the room. 'Thank you, but I'll go on my own. I'm probably worrying over nothing.'

'We're all on edge at the moment.' He stopped short of saying why. None of them were sure, but they all had the feeling talking about the war could be considered dissent, so it was best to avoid the subject altogether. 'I'm sure it's nothing. She will be at home, completely unaware.'

'Thanks for your help. It's always appreciated.' She gave him a kiss on the cheek and ran out of the room.

She had a choice. Should she wait for Greta, or try to find her? Their meeting wasn't important, but she felt rude leaving. What if Greta too turned up late? But it seemed unlikely.

Charlotte remembered that Greta had invited her to visit her home. It wouldn't hurt to take a look and see if she was there. She could have forgotten entirely, and it would do Charlotte good to spend some time away from the university. Perhaps there was something at home that had slowed her down.

Greta had given her the address, but Charlotte had not yet visited. It wasn't far from the university, part of a more modern, nicer row of buildings. It was something else that made Charlotte think Greta came from money. As it wasn't far, she decided to go and see if she was there.

Only minutes later Charlotte stepped off the U-Bahn onto Greta's street. It was flanked by trees, but that wasn't unusual in Hamburg. One of the reasons Charlotte loved living in the city was because of how green it was. Even with such an industrial centre so nearby, it was one of the greenest cities Charlotte had been to, and it reminded her of Stockholm in a way. But the air was different. In Stockholm the air was always fresh, like a welcome breeze on your face in the middle of summer. In Hamburg there was a slight tint of salt from the brackish waters of the Elbe and the tang of industry.

Charlotte knocked on the front door and it swung back on its hinges. She entered and climbed the stairs. The second step creaked as Charlotte put her foot on it, and she almost tripped as she pulled her foot back. She felt like an intruder as she crept up the stairs, not wanting to alert anyone to her presence. The lack of noise from the building made her more cautious. Were the apartments empty? Did no one else live here but Greta? It was strange. Charlotte had assumed that Greta had money. Everything about her persona, the way she dressed and behaved suggested she did. But the state of this building suggested otherwise.

The stairway ended on a landing, from which only one door led off. Number four. Greta's front door was just as unremarkable as the others. Dark green paint flaked off in areas and there was rust around the door handle. Charlotte reached for it before thinking. She knocked again, this time calling Greta's name. She waited for a minute or two, but when there was no reply she reached for the handle. Just like the door onto the street, Greta's front door was unlocked and opened freely.

The door opened onto Greta's living room, and Charlotte felt like she was being permitted to some kind of hidden space that no one else had the privilege of seeing. There was something voyeuristic about the whole experience, as if this were a museum of Greta's

54

life and Charlotte was engaging in a private tour. If only Greta would come and help Charlotte feel less like she was intruding.

'Greta?' she called again, this time more tentatively. 'Greta, are you there?'

The only sound in the flat was the flapping of curtains as the wind poured in through an open window. The apartment was freezing, the breeze bringing the cool morning air with it. Charlotte made her way over to the window and closed it, shutting out the sounds of the city. Suddenly the apartment was warmer, but deathly silent.

Greta's violin case lay on the sofa. It was open and the violin itself wasn't properly placed inside. It was as if it had been abandoned. There was a plate on the coffee table, complete with crumbs and a sliver of discarded pastry. Charlotte moved to take a look at the violin and her foot crunched on something. Underneath the chair were broken pieces of a white-and-blue vase. She reached out to pick up a piece and her hand came back coated in some kind of sticky substance. She recoiled as she noticed the reddish-brown stain on her hand. Drops of the same liquid led away from the living room, and without fully being in control of her legs she followed.

The light in the bathroom was the only one switched on and it cast a yellow glow across the white tiles. As she stepped through that door, Charlotte's legs almost failed beneath her as she saw the scene before her. Instead she fell against the doorframe, holding on to it for support.

Greta was hanging from a rope attached to a light fitting. Her neck was at an unnatural angle, clearly broken. Charlotte gasped for air and reached for her friend, but there was nothing she could do. Thick globules of blood dripped from Greta's toe to the floor, pooling beneath her.

Her open eyes stared at Charlotte, imploring for help. Her eyes were pleading, desperate. But there was nothing Charlotte could do.

Nothing Charlotte was seeing made sense. If not for the blood then Charlotte would think her friend had taken her own life. But why would anyone hang her up like that if they were going to kill her? But why would Greta take her own life? As far as Charlotte knew her friend had everything to live for. She was first violin in the university orchestra, her studies were going well, she had money. It was true that Charlotte didn't know her as well as she would have liked. Perhaps Greta had secrets. Could something tragic have happened to cause her to take her own life? Charlotte had no way of knowing, but she had already lingered too long. If someone found her here then they would think the worst.

It didn't matter that she had no reason to kill Greta. Being found by her body would condemn Charlotte. The criminal police, the Kripo, would take her away.

She stepped backwards out of the bathroom, careful not to disturb anything. It felt like wading through snow, the weight of the situation pulling back against her. Had she left any evidence of her being there? She had to think. Something with her fingerprint, a foot mark, or even a hair could incriminate her.

There was the sound of footsteps on the landing. She pushed herself back against the living room wall and froze. From the doorway it would be impossible to see her, but if they came further into the flat, she would surely be caught. Her heart thumped in her chest and she willed it to be silent, but the more she did so, the more the sound filled her ears. She couldn't think. There was another creak of floorboards, then a voice.

'Someone's been in here,' it said, faint, but easy to make out in the silence of the apartment. It was a man's voice, approximately middle-aged, or at least used to authority. She didn't recognise it.

'You!' The voice was loud, like a cannon. 'What are you doing here?'

She perched on the balls of her feet, like a sprinter about to start a race. She looked one way and then the other. The man blocked the doorway, but if she was quick, she could make it before he had a chance to react. It all happened in the blink of an eye. He shouted, she reacted, and then she ran. She didn't know where she was going. If someone had killed Greta, then they could follow her too. Nowhere was safe now, but she would have to find somewhere. She would have to ford that river when she could. For now it was safer to run.

She had guessed, but a back door led onto a fire escape at the back of the building. It was unlocked and she was through it before the man even made it into the kitchen. She had to climb down, her dress snagging against the rusting iron. It tore the hem, then came free as she dropped a metre to the ground. Without looking back, she ran through the alley.

The streets of Hamburg had been her home for years, and she knew them well. She would have to find some way of losing them in the back streets. Her shoes were slowing her down, rubbing against her feet, but if she left them behind then they might be able to use them to find her. All of these thoughts raced through her head as she powered herself along the alleyway.

She turned a corner, hoping to put some distance between her and her pursuer. The streets of Hamburg were often wide and straight, but she thought if she could pass between the buildings then she might be able to throw him off her scent. A shadow loomed over her, and before she could react she was hit in the stomach by an unexpected force. The man tackled her, forcing her backwards. As they hit the ground he let go and she rolled. The attack had taken her breath.

She struggled to stand as the man righted himself and towered over her. He was thinner than the other man, and he stared at her with steely determination. She grabbed hold of a brick to try and pull herself up, but her legs failed. The brick crumbled in her grasp, flecks of red dust joining the red-brown stickiness already there. As she went down again, her head hit a hard surface. She just had enough time to notice the bile on her lips before her vision faded and she blacked out.

Chapter Seven

Saturday, 9 September 1939

At first her vision was like a dark theatre, then as more light came back to her, more shapes began to form and she realised she was awake. Charlotte was still sore and she had the taste of something bitter and rancid on her lips. She tried to swallow it away, but her throat was dry. She stretched her back and winced as the metal chair dug into her back. She was sitting in a cell of some description. It was bland concrete that looked like acned skin. The only item of note was the wooden door that sealed the cell. She had expected some kind of metal door that would be harder to escape, but this was clearly a room to hold people they weren't expecting to try and escape. A single, unshaded lightbulb lit the room, but her eyes struggled to adjust in the gloom. She reached to brush her hair out of her eyes, but her right hand was handcuffed to the chair.

She had heard the rumours about how the Gestapo got their answers; they all had. But even with the stark, unpainted concrete of her cell, this didn't feel like a Gestapo operation. They would have taken her to an abandoned warehouse down in the Speicherstadt. That was more their style.

Her mouth was dry and her tongue stuck in her throat. Her heart banged against her ribs so hard she could hear her blood pumping in her ears. She closed her eyes to still her heartbeat, but that only made things worse. She didn't want to be vulnerable in this strange place. At least not any more than she already was. She worked at the handcuff, but it stung. In the short time she had been in this cell it had already scratched her wrist and, as it moved up her arm, she could see red weals forming there. She placed her thumb onto her palm to make her hand smaller, but the cuff was too tight. There was no way she was getting out of it, and what then even if she did? As far as she knew, the door was locked, and she had no idea what lay outside. She could be left here forever.

Avoiding Kurt now seemed like a terrible idea. Kurt and her friends would realise she had disappeared, but they would have no idea where she was. She closed her eyes and counted to ten to calm her breathing. It was a technique her father had taught her when she had become anxious as a child. After a while she lost count and started again.

Eventually the door opened. Bright light spilled into the room and Charlotte had to cover her eyes with her free arm. It was another few seconds before anyone entered the cell, but it could have been a lifetime. She had expected to see the boy who had been watching her in the university library but it was the fat man from Greta's apartment who walked in.

'Miss Weber,' he said, grinning at her. 'You gave me quite some exercise back there. I did not expect you to run and you've got quite some legs on you.'

'How do you know my name?' There was no point in denying it or playing dumb, but even still he looked down at her with faint amusement on his face.

'Like all good German citizens. You carry papers.' He waved her identification in front of her as if he had found them on the floor and was admonishing her for forgetting them. 'I took the liberty of inspecting them.'

'You had no right. I've done nothing wrong.' She didn't know what she was angrier about, that he had taken her papers or that he knew her name. All of her frustration at being chased, locked, and tied up came out. She could barely hold it back. She didn't care if it made things worse.

He walked up close to her. Any closer and she would have her face in his groin. It was supposed to be intimidating, but thankfully his ample belly got in the way.

'Of course I have the right, Fräulein Weber. I can do whatever I want. I'm the police.' The look on his face as realisation dawned in her mind was one of triumph. 'Hah. Not what you were expecting, I think? That's right. I'm criminal inspector Richter with the Hamburg police, and running away from me was a very bad idea.'

'I had no idea. I ran because I was scared.'

'You should have known. You look like a smart girl. Why else do you think we were there? Sightseeing? Looking to engage with your friend in a spot of extracurricular activities?'

'What? Greta wouldn't.'

He gave that barking laugh again that made his stomach wobble. 'Don't worry, your friend wasn't a prostitute. At least not as far as we know. You'll let us know if she was, won't you?' He winked.

'How dare you?' Charlotte's voice echoed in the cell. 'If you're the police as you say you are, then let me go.'

'All in good time. I just want to ask you some questions first to discover why you were found in her apartment with her dead body.'

His words brought the flash of Greta's hanging corpse back to Charlotte's mind. She wanted to close her eyes to push away the image, but it would only make things worse. Her grimace seemed to answer one of his questions and he nodded then undid her handcuffs. He reached into a pocket and handed her her own handkerchief, which she used to dab at her eyes. He pulled another chair across the room and sat down in front of her.

'Yes. You did see her body, didn't you? Too bad. Perhaps you put it there and didn't have time to get away before we found you.' Any trace of his previous joviality had disappeared.

'No! I would never.'

'That's not much of a defence.' He took a step back, which had the effect of making the room feel even smaller. 'I've heard worse, but not by much.'

'Why would I kill her?' It was the only defence she had. Apart from the fact she didn't do it. She had Greta's blood on her hands. That had been a mistake, but it would be enough for them to suspect her.

'That's what I'm trying to find out.' He stared at her, perhaps hoping she would crack and admit to killing Greta. But Charlotte could only be honest.

'I can't believe it. I was supposed to meet her but she never came, so I went to look for her at her apartment. I can't believe she's dead.'

She pushed her handkerchief to her face, if only to give her the chance to close her eyes and think for a moment.

'That's life, Fräulein Weber. It's all misery and strife. But you're not making a convincing argument. What time did you arrive at the apartment?'

She didn't know why they were asking these questions, and it was no good asking her own. They wouldn't tell her anything. She couldn't be sure, she had been in such a rush, and she told him as much.

'Can you see why we might be suspicious of you? Your story doesn't hold up under interrogation. I'm just trying to think why you might want to kill her. Was it over a boy?'

'No. Of course not! I didn't hurt her.'

In her shock, she hadn't realised this was going to be an interrogation. She knew she would have to give a statement for their records, but what could they possibly want to talk to her about? She didn't really know Greta that well. They had played violin together a few times, but other than that Charlotte didn't know anything about her. Other than the rumours and whispers of other students.

'What then? Did she steal something from you? What could two young women come to blows over?'

'Nothing. You're being ridiculous. Greta is my friend. We practise violin together.'

She realised she was using the present tense. She hadn't really come to accept or understand that Greta was dead.

'Ridiculous am I?' He was almost laughing, the corners of his mouth turned up into a grin. That or he was enjoying her discomfort. She couldn't be sure.

'I found her. Why would I still be there if I killed her?'

The policeman nodded along with her words, then stood up.

'Well, that's precisely what I thought and what my colleagues said. But then I thought about it and it would make an excellent alibi. As you say, why stay on the scene if you had killed her? Why? Because you were too slow to cover your tracks and put yourself above suspicion.'

He slammed a fist on the table and she flinched. He looked incredibly proud of himself, a grin widening his features, but Charlotte thought he had read one too many detective novels. He wasn't the only one.

'Then what motive do I have for killing her? Why on earth would I want her dead?'

'You're a foreign national, of course. You have less respect for the German way of life.'

'I have dual nationality, and I was born here in Hamburg. I've lived here my entire life and consider myself German. Whatever you are suggesting is not true.'

'Perhaps.'

At that moment the door opened and another policeman entered. This one was slimmer than the inspector, but a sheen of sweat covered his features, which suggested he had been running. He looked harassed as he pushed a sheet of paper into the inspector's hands, then wiped his brow with the back of his jacket sleeve.

'What's this?' the inspector asked.

His subordinate looked over at Charlotte.

'Don't worry about her – get on with it.'

'Report from above. Asked me to give it straight to you, Richter. We need to redistribute our resources, stop wasting them on needless tasks.' He emphasised the latter part as if he was quoting someone else.

'What about this? This is what they're referring to. The doctor's report came back. It's been on your desk for a few hours while you were waiting for her to come to.'

He stopped talking abruptly as if he had said too much. He took a step back, but Charlotte couldn't imagine the inspector taking his anger out on his subordinate. But it wasn't his words he was worried about. He held out a brown file for the inspector, who snatched it from him a few seconds later. The inspector flicked it open while casting a sideways glance at his subordinate.

'I see,' he said, more to himself than anyone else in the room. 'Suicide. Such a tragedy.'

The inspector looked as confused as Charlotte felt, but then steel returned to his face.

'Suicide?' Charlotte asked, forgetting herself. 'You're saying it's suicide?'

'Yes, yes. That's what the doctor's report says. A tragedy. I can't imagine what reason a young woman like that would have to take her own life. Such a sad loss for the Reich.'

Charlotte looked up at the policeman. What did he mean a loss for the Reich? Was Greta's life only measured in what she could contribute to Germany?

'He's wrong.'

The inspector turned on her then. 'Careful, fräulein,' he said. 'The doctor is a well-respected member of the community, a member of the party, and suggesting that he is wrong would not be a very wise decision. Why would he be wrong?'

'But is he sure?'

'Well, would you like to have a look at the body? In your professional opinion? Hmm?'

There was no hint of humour on his face. She opened her mouth to utter a pithy reply, but he forestalled her. She had already interjected too much and she was only a civilian.

'Of course Herr Doctor is sure. It's his job to be sure.'

The other detective's eyeroll suggested that there was more to that than the detective was willing to say. Given how unprofessional they had been so far, Charlotte could well imagine the doctor giving only a cursory examination of Greta's body.

Why would she kill herself? But then, why would anyone want to kill her? What secrets had the woman been hiding? Of course she wouldn't have told Charlotte anything, but she liked to think that the two of them had at least bridged a gap. Charlotte had thought she could trust Greta, but now she wasn't so sure. She had so many questions, but none of them could be answered by the detective. They had already dismissed Greta. Just another victim of her own troubled mind. They didn't care.

The inspector half turned to her. 'Well, that's that then,' he said. 'You're free to go.'

'I didn't know I was being held.' One last act of rebellion. They couldn't keep her now, or charge her with anything. But even still, she was taking a risk.

'There's no need to take that tone with me.' He no longer seemed interested in her. He was staring at the report he had been handed as if it were a telegram from the front.

'What are you going to do now?'

'Well, the party might be interested in her death, but that's not my job. They can sort it themselves.'

That left Charlotte with even more questions. Why would the

party be interested in Greta's death? And why wouldn't the police investigate it if it was?

He pulled open the door and gestured towards it with the file.

'Something tells me we'll meet again, Fräulein Weber. Make sure you remain a law-abiding citizen.'

He held the door open for her and grinned. She was so desperate to leave, but she hesitated. Because of the way he was standing in the doorway, to get out she would have to brush past him. There was no good way to do it, so she walked as quickly as she could manage and all but barged him out of the way. He grunted and called after her. 'You really do want to find yourself in a cell, don't you?'

Thankfully, he walked in the opposite direction up the corridor, apparently no longer interested in intimidating her. He was exactly the kind of thug that the National Socialists were supposed to have removed. Completely un-German, and she hoped she never saw him again. But now he and the Kripo would be keeping tabs on her and she didn't trust him to keep himself to himself. She would have to keep an eye out. Yet another reason to look over her shoulder.

'Oh. There's just one more thing.'

She stopped in her tracks. She had suspected all along it had been a ruse and they were about to throw her back in the cell and lock the door. Or were they going to ask her to identify Greta's body?

'I'll need your address and telephone number . . . for our records.'

Charlotte gave her details to the inspector and only a few minutes later she was stood outside the police station, as if nothing had happened. She was on Neuer Wall outside the Stadthaus.

She clenched her teeth and leant back against the wall. It was the easiest way to stop herself from screaming. The slight pain was a welcome relief. Two policemen left the police station shortly after her. She saw them glance in her direction and mutter something between themselves. They thought she hadn't noticed, turned half away from them, but she had. In her state of mind she noticed everything, took in every detail, but they weren't to know what was going on in her head. After them came a number of other men in the uniforms of the Orpo, the ordinary police. But she had been lucky to be taken in by the Kripo, the criminal police. The Stadthaus housed the Gestapo and other departments of the Nazi government. If they had got hold of her, she didn't think she would be standing outside the building, apparently free.

She wanted to run and get as far away from the police station as possible, but it would do no good. Instead she took out her last cigarette from a pack, lit it, and placed it in her mouth, then decided she would go for a walk. If they followed her they would learn nothing useful from it. No doubt they already knew everything they needed to know about her.

She turned to her right and headed down the street, forcing herself not to look back over her shoulder. She walked at what she hoped appeared to be a regular speed. There was no doubt she was being watched, and she didn't want them to think that she was panicked.

Her stride took her past the Rathaus. It was the largest city hall in Germany. The seat of the Hanseatic city's government and parliament, before the Nazis had taken control. Its central tower loomed over Rathaus Square, now Adolf-Hitler-Platz, with its large clock face hanging above the arched entrance to the building. These days a Nazi flag hung between the two towers, but it didn't hang low enough to cover up the city's motto etched in gold-painted Latin. *Libertatem quam peperere maiores digne studeat servare posteritas. The freedom won by our elders, may posterity strive to preserve it in dignity.*

Those words had always stuck with her. She had never quite been able to catch what they meant or describe why they meant something to her, but there was something about the idea of freedom won that stayed with her.

66

She didn't know what she was going to do next, but she had a feeling she would be followed the entire time. There was no way the Kripo were going to let her walk away from a crime scene like the one she had found, with so few questions asked. They were playing a game with her, and she would need to work out what it was. Had it been the police following her all along, at the university? Why would they? None of this made any sense, but she owed it to Greta to find out what was going on. Even if it risked her own safety.

Chapter Eight

Sunday, 10 September 1939

Charlotte walked with her head down as if it was windy, but unusually the air was quite calm for Hamburg, which was more than could be said for her. She couldn't shake the feeling of the shadows behind her. She thought she had seen the face of the boy from the library on the U-Bahn. She moved down the carriage to mingle with the crowd of passengers, but when the man stepped off the train she realised she had been mistaken. She was becoming too paranoid, seeing faces everywhere.

The police could still be following her, keeping an eye on her, but she had nothing to worry about from going to see Kurt and his family. At least, that's what she kept telling herself. His family were well respected in the community and her connection to them could only be a good thing. It didn't stop her looking over her shoulder, but being with Kurt right now would be a relief.

Charlotte had been putting this off for days, but she needed to see Kurt now more than ever, to clear the air. Yesterday had been a strange day and the images still haunted her mind. It was worse when she closed her eyes. She wasn't sure she had slept at all.

She knocked on the heavy wooden door. Even from outside she could hear the echo in hallway. The Winmers's house was unlike Charlotte's apartment in almost every way. Located in the city's Altstadt area, it was an old house made of red brick, not like any of the new buildings the party had been manufacturing. There was no mistaking how wealthy the Winmers were from the façade of their house. It was as if they were announcing it to the street.

It took a few minutes for the door to open. As usual it was the housekeeper who opened the door. She smiled at Charlotte and admitted her with an upraised palm. Freida had always been kind to Charlotte. When she was a child the housekeeper would take her into the kitchen when she could tell she was feeling out of place and treat her to a piece of stollen or some other pastry. Freida was a woman of few words, but what she did say to Charlotte was often considered and warm.

Charlotte entered the house and asked after Freida's health. The other woman answered politely, but said little more. She knew Charlotte well enough not to ask in return. They always fell into a comfortable silence.

Charlotte passed down the hallway until she reached the expansive living room. Its door was always open, but there was a fire at one side of the room, casting flickering shadows across the plastered walls. The wall of heat that hit Charlotte as she rounded the corner made her sweat, and she passed her coat to Freida. To hang it herself would be unseemly. The Winmers behaved as if they were members of the British aristocracy, which wasn't completely surprising given Hamburg's historical links with Britain and the Winmers's trading background.

It was so far removed from her own childhood home that she always felt like an imposter. Her family had not exactly been poor, but her parents preferred to live in smaller accommodations. Their home had been one of the apartments so familiar in Hamburg life, and they had shared most of their space with one another. There were a number of times Charlotte had been thankful she had been an only child. She had free rein of their home. But here, with the Winmers, everything seemed far too large. In a weird way it made her claustrophobic.

Kurt's mother, Simone, was lounging on the couch when Charlotte entered. She had a white cigarette between her lips and blue smoke drifted around her ears as she turned to Charlotte. She put down the glass she had been holding in her right hand onto a nest of tables by the arm of the sofa.

'Charlotte,' she said, slurring slightly. 'Come in, my dear. Come, come.'

She waved her hands at Charlotte as if dragging her closer, but didn't rouse herself from the sofa as Charlotte took a seat opposite her. If anything she drifted further into the soft green cushions.

'It's good to see you,' Simone said, turning to face the fire.

Kurt's father would be at the factory, even on a Sunday, overseeing every little detail as he always did, leaving Simone to pass the hours at home. It was no wonder she liked to have a drink. What else was there to do? Kurt described his father as obsessive, but Charlotte wondered whether it wasn't something much more than that. It left Simone to languish in the house during the day with nothing to occupy her now that her children had grown up and had their own lives. In truth Charlotte didn't really know what Simone did with her time, but she had never seen the older woman do much at all. At times she would be listening to the radio, but now was not one of those occasions.

'Where is Kurt? I've been looking for him.'

Charlotte didn't want to get drawn into a conversation. Simone opened her mouth to reply, but before she could speak there was another voice.

'Too bad. He's not here.' The voice belonged to Kurt's younger brother Friedrich. He had entered the room behind Charlotte, a smug grin on his face. 'He's been out all day. Who knows where.'

Friedrich habitually wore the uniform of the Hitlerjugend,

the Hitler Youth, and he didn't miss an opportunity to tell you how proud he was to be a part of that organisation. His sandy hair was cut close, and at almost sixteen, patches of beard were starting to break out on his face.

'Well,' Charlotte replied, wanting to be anywhere else but in the same room as Friedrich. 'If you see him, let him know I came around and I'm looking for him, please.'

She always suspected that Friedrich was attracted to her. It made sense, given she had the natural blonde hair and blue eyes the party held up as truly Aryan, but even still it made her feel uncomfortable. Not just because she was in a relationship with his older brother, but because of the way he looked at her. She often caught him staring out of the corner of her eye, and often he didn't even look away when she turned to him.

'What's wrong?' he asked. 'Have you two had another argument?'

That smug grin still hadn't dropped from his face and she wondered whether he knew more than he should. He was always so annoyingly perceptive and it was another factor that made Charlotte's skin crawl whenever he was around. She didn't think Kurt really spoke to his younger brother, but she wouldn't put it past Friedrich to hide behind doors, listening and waiting. It was his responsibility to report anyone not following the German spirit, and she knew him well enough to believe that he took that responsibility seriously.

Yet, if she kept her silence it would only confirm his suspicions. The safest thing to do with Friedrich was to tell him something, but as little as possible.

'We had a disagreement, yes. But only that. I just wanted to see if he would like to have dinner together.'

'Why don't you join us for dinner?' Kurt's mother interjected.

'I wouldn't want to impose. You weren't planning on an extra person to feed.'

'Nonsense, it won't be a problem for the cook at all. I won't hear of you eating anywhere else. You're always a welcome guest.'

71

'Yes, we can celebrate the war and the impending invasion of Britain. After all it's only a matter of time until the Führer brings Britain into the Reich.'

A number of thoughts raced through Charlotte's mind, but she didn't dare voice any of them in front of Friedrich. He would run to the Gestapo as soon as she had opened her mouth.

'I have some things to do now.' She risked a glare at him, but his grin didn't falter. 'But I will come back for dinner. Thank you.'

Friedrich lingered by the door, holding it open for her as if he were some kind of butler, but she knew he thought of himself as anything but. He was far too self-important for that. He clicked his heels together and shouted, 'Heil Hitler!'

She looked him in the eye, smiled and returned the salute in the most deliberate way she could manage. She hoped he would believe she was exactly the kind of upstanding German citizen he wanted her to be.

She found Kurt outside her apartment door when she returned home. She needn't have gone looking for him, knowing he would come to her, and the smile on his face when he saw her showed that he was glad to do so. The smile quickly turned down as he saw how she looked. Without speaking she let him into the apartment, and dropped herself into the sofa. Hilda was nowhere to be seen, so Charlotte allowed herself to close her eyes for a second and take a deep breath as Kurt joined her.

'What's wrong?' he asked as she turned to him.

She stroked his arm as he tilted his head, concerned.

'It's been a long day.' She relaxed as he kissed her cheek.

'But something's happened. What was it?'

She warred with the idea of telling him about the police and Greta's death, but she didn't want to bring it all up again. The images still haunted her. He didn't know Greta and it would make no sense to him what she had been doing in the girl's flat.

72

He also wouldn't understand why she had been interrogated by the police. The last thing she wanted was for him to go down to the police station and cause more trouble, even if he thought he was helping.

'I don't want to talk about it,' she offered instead. It was weak, but she was feeling weak. She knew he would accept her words at face value. That was the good thing about Kurt. If she said she was not feeling well he would not press for a reason. He would just do his best to care for her. Sometimes it meant that he didn't realise when she needed comfort, but when she just wanted to be left alone it helped.

Charlotte leant further into his chest, filling her sense with his musky scent. His body was firm, but there was a softness there too, which was comforting. She wanted him to wrap himself around her, to feel a part of him. He kissed her forehead, then ran his hand through her hair from the nape of her neck. He had done the same thing hundreds of times before, but it still made her skin tingle. Sometimes they would stay like that; other times, like now, he would gently turn her head so that she was facing him, then he would kiss her cheek, messing up her makeup, until his lips landed on hers. They were always warm and, like his body, offered a faint resistance to her approaches. She liked it when he took charge; it was a far cry from the nervous boy she had grown up with. His clothing was coarse against her skin. The sensations were almost overwhelming and she closed her eyes so she could focus on them. As she so often did at times of stress, she wanted to be with him now. It felt good to be safe with him after the last few days, and she wanted to forget it all.

A few seconds later he was leading her by the hand to her bedroom. She hadn't realised she was doing it, but his shirt lay crumpled on the couch from when she had unbuttoned it. He kicked the door behind him and pushed her down onto the bed, reading her mind. He straddled her, kissing her neck and then her cheek, back and forth as she hurried to undo her blouse. He helped her pull down her skirt, his fingers deft and practised. Then they were both lost in the moment.

A while later Charlotte was lying with her head on his chest. The room moved up and down with his shallow breaths as she stared at the wall. Kurt was reading a newspaper, while he ran his other hand through her hair.

'They are bringing in rationing. It doesn't make sense.' She wanted to fill the silence, but regretted it instantly. She should have been happy lying there smelling the scent of his cologne. He threw the newspaper onto the side table and picked up a glass of water.

'It's just to make sure things don't get out of hand,' he said. 'While they sort out this mess with the British and the war. I don't suppose it will mean much. Look at this.'

He gestured at the newspaper, which slid onto the floor to land amongst their clothes.

'It says what I've been saying. This is just better for the German people and will only be temporary. You're always so gloomy about these things. If the newspapers are saying it then we should listen to them.'

'I'm sorry, but it just worries me.' She propped herself up on her elbows and his hand dropped from her head. 'All this talk of war. The last war was a disaster.'

'Yes, but this one won't be. They know how to right the mistakes of last time. That was all about the Kaiser. He let us down and betrayed us and we're done with him now. Once we have our *Lebensraum* then there will be more to go around and we will forget rationing was even a thing.'

Charlotte nodded, although she didn't feel like agreeing. Kurt was always optimistic and sometimes it frustrated her. She didn't want him to solve all her problems, only to listen and to understand. But he always had to try and convince her that everything was going to be all right, if only she could see things from his point of view. He stared at her while she was deep in thought and she could see that he was trying to form the words that would make everything better. As frustrating as he could be, she loved him for that.

'It's easy for you to say – you have your parents' money. It's not so easy for me.' She moved herself up the bed to rest against the headboard beside him.

'I'll always help you; you know that.' He laid a hand on her arm, but she pulled her arm away.

'Thank you, but that's not the point. I need to find my own way and be important in this life. Somehow, I need to find work, especially after university. My savings won't last forever. If I can play with the orchestra . . .'

He was quiet for a minute again, perhaps hurt by the removal of his hand. To make amends she laid her hand on his thigh and nestled her head into his neck.

'Marriage would solve a lot of our problems,' he said, a second later.

'How?' Her voice was muffled, but he heard her well enough.

'Well, for one, it would allow me to welcome you into the family. You would benefit from everything we have.'

'Do you think that's why I want to get married? For money? Surely you know me better than that after all these years.' He shook his head, but she continued. 'If we get married now, then I will lose everything.'

He sat more upright. 'How? We gain each other. A family.'

'We already have each other, don't we?'

'Yes but—'

'I will lose my autonomy. According to the state if I marry you then you get to make decisions for me. I'm supposed to become your housewife and mother of your children. I won't be able to be the woman I am now.'

'You don't trust me? You know I wouldn't do any of that to you.'

'That's not the point. You would be obliged to. The Reich marriage laws expect it of both of us. I'm sorry, Kurt. I know you mean well, but we'll just have to wait. We've got our whole lives ahead of us.'

She inwardly grimaced at the cliché. In wartime who knew just how much time they had? But she had wanted to reassure Kurt that it was nothing to do with him. She knew it was hard for him to understand. In his world they were effectively married and the certificate would only affirm things. He didn't look particularly reassured. His sandy fringe fell down over one eye as he sighed and looked at the floor. It was an affectation he'd had since he was a child, unable to face his parents' judging gaze. She didn't want him to think of her in that way, but so far she had failed to encourage him out of it.

'If you would rather separate—'

It was her turn to sigh. 'Kurt, please.' She shivered.

'If we were married you could move in with me and you wouldn't have to live in this draughty old apartment.' He pulled a blanket from the bottom of the bed up and around them, and tucked it in around her shoulders.

'I like it here. It's cosy. And it's mine, my own home.'

'You're always complaining about it. Have you even spoken to the landlord about the lock yet?'

'I've got used to being alone.' She ignored the question, but she stroked his cheek to show him that she wasn't dismissing him. 'Since my father died and my mother went home. But that doesn't mean I don't like your company.'

'Like? I was hoping it would be a bit more than that. I had thought that we would live together.'

'Kurt, I love you. But sometimes you expect too much. I don't need to live with you to love you. Besides, I like living in my apartment. I've made it my home. It's my sanctuary.'

'The party will support our marriage. A member of the Hitler Youth marrying his childhood sweetheart. You looking like the very image of an Aryan queen with your blonde hair and blue eyes.'

'I don't want to be some poster model for the party, Kurt. And I know you don't want that either. To be paraded around as some example of what it means to be a good German? That's not us.'

'That's not exactly what I meant.' He deflated and turned away to look at the wall. 'I was trying to pay you a compliment, but I misspoke. I'm sorry. You're stunningly beautiful and sometimes I just need to tell you.'

'I don't need you to tell me.'

She knew she was being unfair. It was his way of telling her he loved her when he couldn't find the words, but still she wanted to shout at him. She wanted to shout at something, anything and everything. Kurt was just unlucky that he was the nearest person to her. She should have been born a man. Then she would have had more control over her own fate.

'You don't understand,' she said. 'And you never can.'

He pursed his lips and frowned, hurt by her implication.

'That isn't a criticism. I know you try your best to understand. I need my degree first. It's not just about getting a piece of paper; it's not even about learning things and having a chance to expand my perspective. It's about having the right, as a woman, to do this. How many other women get the opportunity?'

He opened his mouth to answer, but she waved it away. It was her time to talk and she would not waste it.

'I have to do this. To prove I mean something.'

'You mean something to me.'

'That's sweet, but I don't just want to mean something as a wife. I am so much more than that.'

He frowned again.

'See, I said you wouldn't understand. I need to do this for my father. It's what he wanted for me, to have these opportunities and to take them. He doesn't get to see it, but I still have to do it.'

'Why can't you do both?'

'I wish I could. And I'm not saying I don't want to marry you, but my degree is important and I have to make sure that I don't waste it. After that, we'll have all the time in the world.'

'What about the war? We might not be so lucky.'

'It's a risk we'll have to take.'

She kissed him on the cheek, but he didn't lean in. He put an arm around her, but didn't pull her tight as he usually did. It was perfunctory. She knew how much he wanted to marry her, and it would take time and effort to help him understand why she couldn't, but she didn't have any choice. She couldn't give in to him, not now, not ever. That wasn't who she was. Some women were happy to be housewives, to look after children, and both of those things were admirable, but not what she wanted. Not yet at least.

She leant in to kiss him again, hoping he would relax against her. But as soon as she did the air-raid sirens blared into life around the city. Kurt sat bolt upright and she was only a second behind. Their worst nightmare had finally come.

Chapter Nine

Sunday, 10 September 1939

The sirens wailed from their positions down in the docks. They had all heard them tested before, but they had never quite expected them to be put into use. The newspapers were saying that they were just being overcautious and that the British were merely making idle threats. They would never commit to a full-scale war. It was impossible. Not after what had happened last time. No one wanted that again, did they?

Charlotte and Kurt pushed through the crowds, not really knowing where they were going. They had rushed to get dressed and leave the apartment, but now Charlotte felt lost. She didn't know what time it was exactly, but it must have been just after midnight. She wondered where Hilda was. Should she have searched the apartment for her friend? She knew Hilda could look after herself, but it didn't stop that pang of worry.

Searchlights flashed across the sky, trying to find the source of the bass drone. They wouldn't be protected by light alone, but maybe they would force the British bombers back. That or they would present an inviting target for their bombs. The guns the Wehrmacht had placed around the city barked into life, making

Charlotte jump. Their fire was sporadic and each time one opened up it caused a new shudder in her.

They came in low. Far lower than she would expect bombers to fly. It was as if the British wanted the aircraft to be seen, to say, *Here we are and there is nothing you can do about it*, but they were taking a terrible risk. Those around her ducked as if the bombers were aiming for them, but Charlotte stood tall. No amount of ducking would save them when it came down to it.

The guns kicked into life again, lines of fire racing into the air like fireworks. The British aircraft banked and lowered over the city. Charlotte braced. As another aircraft raced overhead, she pushed herself against the wall, willing it to provide some kind of shelter.

There were no shadows of bombs, no explosions. These aircraft came as a warning. As they soared overhead they released reams of paper, white sheets that in the gloom resembled feathers falling from a bird. Had the British decided that the fear of bombing was powerful enough? Or were they simply testing Hamburg's defences? It was not for someone as lowly as her to find out. Only time would ever give her the answer to those questions.

Thousands upon thousands of leaflets fell across the city. The people around her pulled back from the paper as if it were toxic or about to burst into flames. Kurt was the first of them to take one in his hands. This was more than a simple display of what they were capable of; they were sending a message that was more profound than *we are here and we can hurt you*.

It seemed like a waste of time. What were they thinking? That regular Germans would read their pamphlets and rise up against the Führer? The Nazis had been in power for six years. They would either win this war, or they would lose and everything would return to the years of poverty and strife before the Nazis had taken power. No leaflets were going to change that. She picked one up and looked at the words written there.

'*Warnung*,' it said. *Warning*. '*Mit fühl erwogenem . . .*' The Government of the Reich have with cold deliberation forced war upon Great Britain.

She didn't know why it surprised her that it was written in German, but it read like it could have been written by a native. The rest of it went on to say how the war would be worse than that of 1914. Kurt came up beside her having read his own pamphlet, distracting her from reading more.

'What the hell are these going to do?' He waved them in the air, like some kind of town crier. Charlotte had never seen him quite so angry. In a way it was refreshing, but she wondered why his anger was directed at the leaflets and not the people who were sending them.

'They're better than bombs. At least they won't kill people.'

'Are they? At least bombs would show they mean business. But these? It's nonsense.' Kurt pulled the leaflet out of her hand. 'The German public will either ignore them or laugh. They'll say they're just trying to scare us. The Imperialists wanted another war all along, and they're scared of the Reich.'

'Why? We were no threat to them, never made any statements about attacking Britain. Even Hitler didn't want that.'

'Because their empire is failing. It's jealousy. They can't see that the German way of life is the best way. They want to cling on to their old and dying empire and so they will not let us grow. But the Reich will defeat them.'

It was the first time Charlotte had seen him like this. His eyes were red-rimmed and he spoke like some kind of religious preacher, extolling the virtues of the Nazi way of life.

'It won't be like last time,' he continued, shouting over the drone of the bombers. 'Our generals have learnt the lessons of the past.'

She pulled him out of the street. The British might have only dropped leaflets so far, but there was nothing to stop them bombing them now.

'But won't theirs have as well?' she asked him, not really interested in his answer. 'None of us truly wanted war. We just wanted to be able to put food on the table again. To have a future. Now this war could take that from us, and we have no say in it.'

With Kurt following behind, she made her way back towards her apartment. They had only gone a few streets, but with the bombers disappearing over the horizon she didn't see much point in going to a shelter. The all-clear may take some time yet, but her home was warmer than the street or the shelter.

'You might not,' he said, from behind her, his voice quieter than it had been. 'But I do.'

She stopped in his path. They were outside her apartment building again, the cold air blowing at her coat, goosebumps rising across her body. 'What do you mean?'

'I will have to fight. At some point. I don't know when, but they will call on me sooner or later. Then it's up to me to make a difference.'

'You never know. Your job at the factory is important. The Kriegsmarine won't have shells for their guns without you.'

'For how long? It's only a matter of time until they call me up from reserve. And find someone else to do my work. Someone like you. Then I'll have no choice.'

'I won't let them take you from me.' She pulled him into an embrace. He wouldn't say what he was really feeling, but she knew him better than that. Just like the other party members it was all talk. Underneath it all was a scared boy trying to force himself to be brave. It was times like this that reminded her they were both young, growing up in a world they had little control over. The party expected them to be strong, patriotic Germans, but they were all scared of the war. They just weren't allowed to admit it.

She kissed him on the lips. Let them feel some comfort from each other. At first he resisted, but then he pressed back against her, looping his arms around her lower back. They pulled back for a second, catching their breath, then he put his hand at the nape of her neck and pulled her back in. They stayed like that for some time, pushing the outside world away and forgetting it existed at least for a brief time. All thanks to Kurt, the man she loved. They kept each other warm in spite of the encroaching cold.

Monday, 11 September 1939

The cold in Hamburg was only getting worse. Icy air blew along the streets and even down into the U-Bahn. Nowhere was safe from the cold. Charlotte had decided it would be better to go into the university than to stay in her freezing apartment, even though she had hardly got any sleep.

Charlotte didn't know what they were going to do when winter properly set in. It was bad enough in the autumn, and with the war escalating she suspected rationing would only get worse. They were at war with Britain properly now, and even though the bombs hadn't come yet, she was sure they soon would. She had seen the Luftwaffe going the other way, their grey fuselages resembling migrating birds in the dusk sky. Soon they wouldn't be able to find fuel to heat the apartment, let alone to be able to afford it. Hilda too spent most of her time in the university, but as the two of them studied different subjects, Hilda literature and Charlotte philosophy, they spent little time together outside the apartment.

Charlotte should feel thankful that she had access to the university. What did everyone else do? But she really didn't want to spend any more time there than was necessary. Not since that man had followed her down the corridor, nor since Greta had died.

Hamburg was a big city. People died all the time, and she was sure that a number of them were suicides. But Greta had given no indication of wanting to take her own life. The last time Charlotte had seen her, she had been full of life, jovial and even joking with Charlotte. No, it didn't make sense. Neither did the broken vase and the blood she had seen at the scene. The police had been too quick to call it a suicide, but Charlotte knew there was far more to it than that.

But how could she possibly find out what had really happened to Greta? If the Kripo couldn't do it and were happy to put it down as a suicide, then what made her think she could do any better? But even still, she had to try. She owed it to Greta. Greta had no one else to get justice for her.

It was time for her second lecture of the day. Charlotte entered the lecture theatre from the back, wincing as the door creaked. Professor Krüger was already mid-speech.

'You see, what is widely said about Nietzsche is not what we can infer from actually reading him. Newspapers may like to discredit the great philosopher, but I remind you to think who owns and edits the newspapers. Can we always trust that they do not have an agenda? Philosophers always tell us that we should question what we read, think critically, and that no text is entirely free from human bias.'

Some of the gathered students whispered to one another. One or two shook their heads. But that was exactly the response the professor was after. She had always pushed their understanding and knowledge.

'She needs to be careful,' another student whispered to Charlotte. 'Any one could report her to the Gestapo.'

Charlotte just nodded. It was entirely possible that Professor Krüger had already been reported, but then why was she still here? This was not the first time she had made these kinds of comments in one of her lectures, but she was careful not to directly criticise the Nazis.

'This is why we are here,' Krüger continued. 'To discuss and to learn. If we cannot question things, if we have no critical thinking, then we simply follow blindly and without progress.'

It was difficult for Charlotte to take in so much information, especially after arriving late, and she struggled to focus. As she went to leave at the end of the lecture, she made eye contact with the professor.

'Charlotte? Are you all right?' Professor Krüger asked as she was leaving. She must have noticed Charlotte's eyelids drooping. As the professor was one of the few female lecturers the university employed, Charlotte didn't want to set a bad impression. Truthfully she wanted the professor to take her under her wing and help her to become even half the woman she was, but Charlotte knew that was unlikely. The professor had little time to mentor students and if she couldn't even stay awake in her classes then Charlotte had no hope.

'I'm fine,' Charlotte replied, not wishing to get drawn into conversation. Krüger frowned, apparently thinking Charlotte was being rude. Before the war Professor Krüger had given talks internationally, but now that had become more difficult. Charlotte imagined those speeches were exhilarating, more so than these lectures she must have given a hundred times, but Charlotte had never had a chance to see one.

'Come on, Charlotte. Something is wrong – I can tell from your eyes. Have you even slept?'

Charlotte felt on the verge of tears and she pushed them back with the sleeve of her cardigan. Krüger reached out a hand to steady Charlotte but stopped before she could make contact. Charlotte smiled a thank you.

'I'm just struggling to keep up.' She thought it best to be honest. 'Everything that's going on just feels so overwhelming. I feel like I'm falling behind and I don't understand even the basics.'

Professor Krüger nodded and pursed her lips. 'I understand completely. It's a tough time. Why don't you go and see Professor

Bendorff? He can recommend some further reading. Give you a helping hand.'

Charlotte nodded her thanks again and turned to leave.

'Oh and Charlotte?' Krüger called after her. She turned to look back at her professor. 'Get some sleep.'

Stefan looked just as stressed as she felt. He was sorting through papers on his desk, moving them from one side to another. It seemed as if their lives were an endless stream of paperwork and books, and it wasn't reassuring to see that it didn't decrease in life as an academic.

At least she didn't have to decide what she was going to do afterwards yet. He took her reason for being there with the same knowing nod that Professor Krüger had done.

'I've got an idea of something that might give you back some spirit,' he said a moment later, forgetting the papers he had been shuffling. 'We're short on numbers in the orchestra, so I am pulling my hair out trying to sort that as well as a number of other things. It never ends.'

He flashed her a self-deprecating smile that made him look a few years younger. 'No rest for the wicked, I guess.' Then he nodded towards the violin case she was holding.

She had forgotten about Greta's role in the orchestra. While he hadn't mentioned her specifically Charlotte knew what he was getting at. 'You don't mean?' she asked, not really knowing what her questions was.

'Well, it all means we need someone to join the orchestra, and thinking about it, you're the natural choice. Actually I've been meaning to ask you for a while now.'

Why her? Why now? She had applied to join before and they had always rejected her. Of course she had performed before, here and there, but few people had heard her. She could still picture the polite 'no, thank you' she had received through the post. What had changed their minds, other than Greta's death? It didn't make sense.

'You'll need to audition, of course. But you shouldn't have any problem with that. Just come along and play and I'm sure it will all be fine. I'll put in a good word for you. I'm sure some good, uplifting German music will get you back on your feet. But you should probably get some sleep first.'

Why did everyone keep telling her that? It was as if they were treating her like a child. He went back to his papers, apparently forgetting she was there.

'Thank you,' she said as she slipped out of the door.

She only realised when she left the university that she had completely forgotten to ask him for book suggestions. Oh well, there would be other opportunities. For now, she was too excited that she had finally been given a chance to join the orchestra. It was a rare opportunity, particularly for a woman, even a female musician, and she would take it with both hands.

She almost skipped her way back to the U-Bahn station at Dammtor. Even in the gloom of the dusk blackout, things felt brighter. The orchestra might give her the chance she wanted to find out what had happened to Greta.

Chapter Ten

The music hall was not as big as she would have expected. It was a square wood-panelled room that looked more like a classroom. Charlotte pushed her way through wooden doors that squeaked on their hinges. The musicians gathered in the room stopped their conversations and looked in her direction. Some wanted to see who this newcomer was, curious. She knew a lot of them from around the university, but here in this room they all felt like strangers. She was a child, staring up at adults, not understanding their world, but desperately wanting to fit in.

The orchestra was composed of students and staff. By the looks of things Stefan hadn't arrived yet and it surprised her that she was apparently early. She couldn't help but smile at the whole thing. It felt like a rite of passage. Even with the enquiring faces turned towards her, she couldn't help herself.

She took them in one at a time, trying to find some warmth there. There were a few stony appearances, but many looked uninterested. If this was part of her audition then she was not going to be cowed by it. She knew that Greta had been popular, but Charlotte was here because she was a good musician and she would prove it to them. Everyone was getting their instruments ready, polishing the woodwork, or tuning up. Her eyes landed on Andreas. He was setting up his double bass and talking to another bass player. The instrument was larger than him, but he was very accomplished. He gave her a wave and a big smile, and immediately Charlotte's tense shoulders loosened. She could do this.

Andreas was about to come over to Charlotte, but one of the men from the group caught her eye and walked straight over to her.

'You must be Charlotte.' His hands enveloped hers, the following shake almost lifting her from her feet. He smiled the whole time and at no point did she feel he was trying to exert his power over her. Even still, she struggled to stay upright with the strength of his handshake.

She nodded, unable to find words. She could still feel the other eyes in the room on her, wondering how she could take Greta's place. The orchestra was a close-knit community. It wasn't the first time she would have to prove herself. She had come prepared.

'Come, come,' he said. He still hadn't introduced himself, but perhaps he thought that Charlotte should know who he was. It had passed the point in which she could ask without being rude. She would have to find out another way, ask Stefan or Andreas.

There was a heavy air in the room that Charlotte couldn't quite explain, and it wasn't just the cloying heat. She must have been imagining it. Could one of them be Greta's killer? But what reason would they have for killing her?

At that moment Stefan burst through the wooden doors, with his trumpet in hand. He was panting as if he had been running, and she could see his chest through the dampness of his shirt. He glanced in her direction and winked. She raised a hand to wave, but felt her cheeks redden and stopped. Stefan nodded at the orchestra leader who welcomed him then turned back to Charlotte.

'We might start with a little Wagner,' he said. 'Something we should all know by now, to get us properly warmed up. But while music is a serious matter in the Reich, we are here to practise. Mistakes are both encouraged and expected.'

His easy nature helped to relax her and she let loose a chuckle. Then she covered her mouth. Her laugh only served to encourage him more.

'There we are,' he said. 'You'll be one of us in no time.'

She couldn't help but laugh; his manner was infectious. She had gone from feeling completely out of place to feeling as if she was being welcomed into an exclusive community. It was as if she had made a new friend.

He led her over to the other violinist and pointed to a chair, before returning back to the front of the room. She scrambled to take her violin out of its case, which clattered to the floor. She just had time to kick it under her chair before the orchestra leader spoke.

'Listen up, everyone,' he said, his voice carrying easily over the groups of muttered conversation. He must have been another one of the professors at the university. His tone of voice suggested he was practised at projecting his words over a crowd or audience. He gestured towards her with a baton. 'I'd like to welcome Charlotte to our little orchestra. Let us hope her audition goes well.'

All of a sudden it was as if a spotlight had been placed on her. She hated being watched, but all eyes were on her. There were some smiles and applause and she returned an awkward smile.

'We will start with Beethoven's ninth symphony,' he continued. 'First movement. Remember it's in D minor and keep up!'

He lifted his baton as Charlotte's eyes widened. Had the mention of Wagner been a ruse? Had he said it to put her off balance and see how she would react? He gave her a wink as he counted them in.

The other musicians had sheet music, but she hadn't been that prepared. Nothing in the invitation had mentioned what they would be playing or what to bring with her. Some of the hairs of her bow stuck out in strands, flopping around her hand. The other musicians' bows were immaculate, but she could not afford to replace hers. She was out of her depth. She hadn't played the music in a while and the fingers of her left hand burnt as she struggled to keep up.

The conductor moved them on to another piece, then another. She was lost in the music and she could feel the corners of her mouth pulling into a smile. It was exhilarating, euphoric, and she couldn't help but be caught up in the moment. She had forgotten what it was like to hear the intertwined notes of an orchestra. It was like movement, pulling her one way and then another. She swayed with the notes, not even thinking what her fingers were doing. Her bow worked on its own; it knew what to do.

But like all good things it finished too soon and she was left waiting for them to start again. Her bow was raised and a bead of sweat trickled its way down her temple, but she would continue. She needed to continue. The others stared at her.

The conductor waved them to rest. Charlotte's chest rose and fell rapidly as her heart rate slowly lowered. She was too agitated to reach down and pick up her violin case so she just stood with her hands on her hips.

The other violinist looked at her. He was about a head taller than her and had short blond hair. His ovoid face was pockmarked, which made him look younger than his height and clothing suggested. He wore a simple brown suit that was a size too large for him.

'That was very good,' he said. 'I didn't think you would keep up. That was a nasty trick Muller played on you. He likes to throw something difficult in at the start for newcomers.'

'Thank you.' She wouldn't admit she had struggled.

'I'm Ernst.' He held out a hand and she shook it with pleasure.

She glanced over at Muller, the conductor, who gave her a shallow bow and a couple of emphasised claps, that smile still plastered over his face. He left the hall with a few of the other musicians, laughing and talking.

'I've heard about you.' Ernst broke into her thoughts. 'Listen, I was going to ask you something. It's hard to find musicians these days, what with the . . .' He looked around the room. Most of the orchestra had already made their departure, but a few were still around packing up and chatting amongst themselves. No one so much as glanced in their direction. 'What with all the Jews being pushed out of the university and the country. The orchestra used to have quite a few Jewish musicians, and they were very good. I shouldn't be saying this, of course.'

'It's fine,' she said. 'I understand what it's like. But it's to my benefit. I don't think I would have got in the orchestra otherwise.'

She tried a smile, but it was forced and dropped from her lips a second later. Thankfully he didn't seem to notice; he just nodded. It was true, many people like her had found an advantage in the absence of the Jews. After all, wasn't that what the Nazis had come into power to bring about? It didn't sit easy with her at all, but the orchestra was the opportunity she had been looking for and she wasn't about to turn it down. Doing so wouldn't help a Jew find a position within the orchestra.

'Listen, a few of us have a little side project and we think you might fit the bill.'

Despite herself she frowned. She just wanted to play music, but she had forgotten how there was a social element of performing as part of a group. He appeared to notice the look on her face and he laughed.

'It's nothing strange. It's just that the university orchestra doesn't always fulfil our musical needs. A few of us put together a smaller group to play some string concertos at various venues around the city. Sometimes the usual stuff, but other opportunities . . . arise.'

'That sounds great.' She knew the look on her face didn't match her words, but she often struggled to show the appropriate emotion. It had been an overwhelming day and too many thoughts were racing through her head.

He laughed again and shook his head. There was something about his laugh that appealed to her. It was warm, friendly, without a hint of ridicule in it.

'I understand,' he said. 'You're new here and you don't want to commit to anything before you really get to know the rest of us. I was the same when I started.' He turned to leave. 'Think about it?' he asked over his shoulder.

'I don't need to.' Was there a hint of disappointment in his eyes? 'It sounds like just the sort of thing I was looking for.'

'Excellent.' His pleasure made her smile. She had gone from being wary of the other musicians to being genuinely welcomed to join them and play more. That was all she had wanted. 'Here's a list of the music we regularly play.'

He gave her a handwritten note, almost as if he had been expecting this, and she glanced over it.

'I only know some of them, but I can learn the rest.'

'You'll need to find a copy of the music. It'll be easier. But the university library doesn't have any stock, and the usual suppliers are being funny with the Nazi's restrictions. They're only pushing the usual boring stuff.'

'I think I might know where I can find a copy.' She wasn't really sure, but a lie was better than admitting defeat. She would ask around, check in the library. Something would come up. Like her father always used to say: you had to make opportunities happen, and then you had to work for them. It was a risk, but Charlotte wasn't averse to risks and this was an opportunity that was too good to miss. She desperately wanted to be both accepted by this group of musicians and to have an opportunity to play more music. If she could make a living from music she wouldn't need to rely solely on her degree. Then she could build a career for a few years before marrying Kurt.

Ernst left her in the emptiness of the music hall. Even though the others had left she could still feel the music moving through the air. She closed her eyes and listened for a while, swaying with the tunes that filled the space.

94

Chapter Eleven

Saturday, 23 December 1939

The air pulled at her, cutting like a knife. The only defence she had was the grey woollen coat she pulled around herself, scrunching up her shoulders to make her body smaller, somehow convinced that was warmer. She longed to sit by a fire, close her eyes and breathe in the warming smoke, but she wasn't sure even that would help this chill. Had she experienced a winter like it before? She couldn't remember one as biting as this. The clouds threatened snow, but even they were too cold for this. Even when she visited Sweden it didn't feel as cold as this in the winter. It was a wonder she could think at all.

Charlotte had never set foot in the Hotel Vier Jahreszeiten before. It sat on the west of the Binnenalster on Neuer Jungfernstieg. It towered over the water like some kind of Bavarian castle, one of those buildings that was supposed to be stereotypically German, but which most Germans had never had the opportunity to see with their own eyes. Except, unlike a castle, the hotel had white walls and a copper roof.

It had always been intimidating, not just because of its size but also because of the amount of money one needed to spend a night there. On another occasion she would have hesitated in reception, waiting to be thrown back out onto the street at any moment. But now she wielded her violin case like an entry pass. The receptionist smiled at Charlotte, perfect white teeth matching the cleanly pressed white shirt under his navy waistcoat. Her heels clicked on the polished wooden floor as she walked straight past.

There was no question of excluding her; she was meant to be there. She even acted as if she knew where she was going, but that was far from the truth. It was amazing what one could get away with if one acted with confidence, but then she had seen men doing just that her entire life. They didn't have to worry if they were in the wrong place, or whether they were allowed to be there. They simply took over in the confidence that others would listen to them and agree with their point of view.

She mentally scolded herself. Her thoughts were getting carried away and her march had led her deeper into the hotel with no idea of where she was expected to be. The porter coughed from beside her and she turned to see the frown on his face. He was standing between her and a coffee house she had been about to enter in apparent mistake. He gestured at the violin case she was carrying with an extended index finger and then nodded his head to the left. She flashed him a smile, which wasn't returned, and walked in the direction he had indicated.

There were already patrons in the dining room. Each table was decorated with silver cutlery, which glimmered in the light. She longed to sit at one of those plush chairs, to sample the delicacies on offer. Her stomach rumbled and she pushed away the thought. It would only make things worse. She would be able to eat after the performance. Perhaps they would offer them whatever was left over in the kitchen.

The wide rectangular windows looked out over the Binnenalster, providing plenty of light. In the winter chill the water glittered like diamonds. As she walked, the room shimmered and shifted as the light caught different aspects of the decor.

She made her way to the bandstand they had erected at one end of the dining room. It was a simple raised stage, but it would allow them to be seen from each part of the room. There were a few musicians there already, whom she had met at previous rehearsals. As she had come to expect, they kept their distance from her. Did she remind them too much of Greta?

Two gentlemen in finely tailored suits were sitting at a window table nearby, discussing business, the details of which Charlotte could only just make out. She shouldn't eavesdrop, but it wasn't their conversation that drew her.

They ate lobster. Pulling the white meat out carelessly. It splattered on their suits. Charlotte could have guessed that in a hotel like this they would have access to the kind of food and drink that average Germans like her had no hope of acquiring, but seeing it first-hand made the bile rise in her throat. It wasn't just that she was hungry. She had been hungry before, so hungry she would eat anything. But it was that they ate with such little thought. They were devouring the food as if they had no care in the world, wasting bits that fell onto the tablecloth to be forgotten. There were Germans who would sweep up every morsel on that table and still be hungry, yet these men were unconcerned. Was that not what the Jews had been accused of? Their gross wealth and indifference had left thousands of Germans destitute and suffering. These men could not be party members. They were part of the problem, not the solution.

Ernst arrived a couple of minutes later. He saw Charlotte standing separate from the rest of the group and put an arm around her, before leading her closer to the others.

'Now, what's going on here? Why have none of you welcomed Fräulein Weber to the group in my absence?'

'Sorry, Ern,' one of the young men offered, but still wouldn't look at Charlotte. The others shuffled their feet and went back to tuning their instruments.

'Don't worry,' Ernst said to her. 'They're a friendly bunch when they open up. You just need to crack their tough exteriors first.'

Apparently Ernst had spotted the lobster too. He shrugged and set about opening his own violin case, propping it on a chair while he did so. She was too distracted by the diners to join in.

'This will be one of the boring performances, I'm afraid,' he said. He lowered his voice. 'No subversive music in a place like this.'

The two gentlemen were joined by another man wearing a leather coat with a Schutzstaffel badge on the lapel. He shouted 'Heil Hitler' and clicked his heels together. His voice echoed around the dining room, but as was so common these days, no one reacted except the two seated men who returned the salute.

Charlotte thought that she recognised him, but she couldn't be sure. He had the three silver pips and stripe attached to his collar that denoted he was an *Obersturmführer*, a senior storm leader in the SS. Charlotte would not have been familiar with the rank insignia except the SS seemed to be everywhere now. He could have been a member of the Gestapo, but as the name suggested the secret state police were hard to spot other than by their membership of the SS.

She put her violin case down and tried to drag her eyes away from their table. There was a member of the Gestapo sat only a few metres away from her. He hadn't yet looked in her direction, but despite that she felt trapped.

That couldn't be right. Charlotte wasn't sure what to think. She had not expected to be performing for party members, but that was where the money was. She should have known better, given the status of the hotel. Next time she would make sure that she invited Kurt. She would have liked him to be there, especially to form a buffer between her and the party members. Even though he was also a member of the party, he seemed less . . . fanatical about his beliefs. You never knew with other party members how dedicated they were and how much they would stick to the rules. She had never dared not to return the salute. It wasn't worth the risk. She hoped there was some money involved: she had used the last of hers to buy a new bow.

'Charlotte,' Ernst whispered at her elbow. 'Come on, we need to play.'

The three men settled in as Charlotte and the others began to play. They had agreed to perform the violin concertos that Charlotte knew, at least for now, and they started with Schubert's 'Trout Quintet'. Charlotte struggled to keep time as Leatherjacket turned his chair so that he was facing her. His cold blue eyes bored into her, as if she were being interrogated, and her mind flashed back to the police cell she had been held in. A faint smile turned the corners of his thin lips, but didn't reach those icy eyes. The bow slipped from her fingers, but she managed to catch it before it tumbled to the floor. She looked at the rest of the players, but they were lost in the moment. It was going to be a long evening.

Charlotte had been practising the music for weeks. At times she had missed Greta, but she would not have had this opportunity had her friend still been alive. She supposed that gave her as much motive as anyone. It was simple background music so that the diners could relax and talk, but even still she felt joy at playing for an audience. The adrenaline coursed through her, driving her through the music. When they were done, Charlotte felt elated, but the others only looked bored.

They were quick to pack up and leave the hotel, but Charlotte was in a daze. She didn't want to forget anything so she took her time to pack up her violin and other bits and pieces. It wasn't just the adrenaline of performing. That had been a truly wonderful experience and she couldn't wait to do it again. But she also felt that way because of the situation and surroundings. Thankfully the SS officer and the other men she assumed were party members had already left. As soon as the performance had ended, they had stood up from their chairs, shaken hands, given the salute, and then left the dining room without so much as a glance in Charlotte's direction. She supposed that the musicians were just like a part of the furniture to them. There for their pleasure only and discarded once they were done. Charlotte was grateful for that. She couldn't stand being under the glare of those cold eyes for much longer.

Ernst told her he'd see her next time and waved goodbye. There were a few diners left in the room, but it was oddly quiet now that everyone had left. She was just closing her violin case when she heard faint footsteps behind her. She froze.

'You didn't attend our arranged meeting,' the voice said.

Chapter Twelve

Saturday, 23 December 1939

Charlotte's mind raced, keeping pace with her heart. She didn't recognise the voice, but that made things even worse. The Gestapo man had left, but what if he had come back? Could it be the boy from the library? The voice didn't sound right; it was too deep. Whoever it was, she had to find a way out. To her right the windows didn't open and the doors were at the other end of the room. Her only way out was past the man who was now addressing her. She took a deep breath and turned.

'I'm afraid you have mistaken me for someone else.' She moved to walk past him, but he held out an arm. He had brown hair swept to the side of his narrow head. Going by the smell, she could tell he wore some kind of hair oil, and he moved a strand out of his eyes with a flick of his head. His top lip sported a thin moustache, which was the same colour as his eyes. His suit was almost as brown as the rest of him, except that it looked sun-faded.

'I think not,' he said. His voice was hoarse as if he had been shouting and she had to take a moment to process what he had said. 'However, your caution does you credit. We cannot afford to be lax in these difficult times.'

The man's manner was not cold, but matter-of-fact. Under other circumstances Charlotte might have made her apologies and walked away as quickly as possible. She was used to men approaching her and shrugging them off. But something about this man intrigued her. It wasn't his face, which was jaundiced and lined with age, nor the drab way in which he dressed. In fact, it was all of those things. Here was a man who had lived and had a story to tell.

'Who are you?' she asked. As far as she could recall she had never seen him before. It didn't add up.

He frowned at her as if she should know the answer to that question, then spoke again in that croaking voice of his. 'I think that's best explained over a drink, don't you? I know I could do with one. I think we may be able to help each other.'

'We can't talk here.' She touched him on the arm. She was taking a big risk, but his words intrigued her. Was he just some crazy man? Kurt would say she was being naive, but Kurt wasn't here. The adrenaline of the performance was rushing through her veins; she didn't want it to stop.

He looked down at her arm, in apparent surprise. She didn't think he was used to being touched. 'You're correct, of course.'

'Look. Follow me.' She led him out of the dining hall in the direction of a coffee room she had seen when she had first entered the hotel. It was just as quiet as the dining room and was perfect. At least here two people could be having a late evening conversation over cups of coffee and no one would think twice.

They took seats across from each other at a small round table and ordered drinks from a waitress. Once she was out of earshot, Charlotte dared to speak.

'Now, tell me exactly what it is that you want from me or I'm going.'

She wouldn't normally talk like that, but she was still riding the confidence of the evening's performance, how the music had buoyed her up. She wasn't prepared to hang around.

'They told me you were direct. That's good, but you will have to be careful. Not everyone we work with will respond too kindly to that approach.'

She shook her head. He was speaking in riddles, but perhaps he expected her to know more than she did. He had got the wrong person after all.

'Who exactly are "they" and what exactly did they tell you about me?'

'About you? Actually not a great deal. My superiors were quite vague about that, deliberately so. The less we know the less dangerous it is. Is that not so?'

'That's enough. I'm leaving.'

She made to stand up, but he grabbed her wrist and pinned it to the table. She wanted to reach out and rub away the pain, but thought better of it. 'Please, wait,' he said, letting go.

He could be from the Gestapo, but she didn't get that impression. He didn't give off that snake-like persona of the Geheime Staatspolizei, the state's secret police. His entire manner and dress sense spoke much more of a desk job in some forgotten government office. She didn't give him a response, instead she crossed her arms and gave what she hoped was a blank expression. After a silent minute or two he gave up and spoke again.

'They told me to meet with the female violinist. That you're to work for us.'

Charlotte stifled a gasp by passing it off as a yawn. The way he said 'female' made her squirm. Better to let this man think she was tired than surprised by his words. Why had they picked her? Then a thought came to mind. It wasn't Charlotte that he was supposed to meet with. She had replaced Greta. What had Greta been up to before she had died, and what dangerous game had she dragged Charlotte into? He thought Charlotte was Greta, and that opened up so many possibilities about how she had died. Why was Greta getting involved with shadowy men in expensive hotels? The inspector had been clear that she wasn't a prostitute, so what was she up to? The rest of the conversation was going to be even more dangerous than Charlotte had originally imagined, but there was only one way to find out what Greta had been up to. He couldn't have known Greta was dead, otherwise why would he be looking for her? That meant someone else must have killed her. Charlotte had so many questions.

'The Gestapo?' she asked, instinctively lowering her voice. He wasn't what she would have expected from a member of the Gestapo, but the secrecy seemed appropriate for the state's secret police.

He shook his head and scrunched up his face. 'I'm not from the Gestapo.'

'What then? The police? No.' She stopped herself. It was starting to make more sense, but there were still details missing. She took in a breath. 'The Abwehr?'

She hadn't expected that, he wasn't in uniform. The Abwehr were technically part of the Wehrmacht, the military intelligence, tasked with countering foreign espionage and gathering intelligence for the army. It was said if you ever encountered a member of the Abwehr then it would be the last encounter you ever had. Her cheeks flushed. What did they want with her?

He nodded shallowly. 'You're as perceptive as I was led to believe. The people I work for don't make themselves known to the public, but we serve the Reich just the same. We don't all wear uniforms. The Gestapo look inwards, we – that is to say the Abwehr – look outwards. It's our job to collect intelligence on the Reich's enemies and make sure they learn nothing about us.'

'So, what do you want with me?' Or Greta, she reminded herself.

'The same thing as you.'

She stayed silent. It was safer than admitting she had no idea what he was talking about. The entire conversation seemed predicated on the idea that she knew the meaning behind his words. Their drinks arrived a moment later. Two black coffees.

The man stared at her as if wondering what she was thinking. He made no attempt to reach for his drink. She had so many

104

questions about Greta, but she knew she couldn't ask them. This man thought she was Greta and in order to find out what had happened to her friend it would have to stay that way.

'All we want,' he said, when the waitress had retired, 'is to end the war as soon as possible. Then we can all return to our lives. Our studies, our jobs. If we can secure the right information then we can make sure that the British surrender as soon as possible, pursue the Reich's aims as expediently as possible. It's our jobs to save lives.'

'What if the British don't surrender?'

He lit a cigarette and took a drag from it, without offering her one. She could taste the tang of tobacco and closed her eyes.

'They must. It's our job to make sure that we win the intelligence war so that they have no choice. Anything else would be failure.'

If only things were that simple, but at least he was finally making sense. So this was what Greta had been up to before her death. Charlotte had had no idea. Greta didn't seem the type. She didn't seem the person to keep secrets, to pretend to be something that she wasn't. But then maybe that was the point. There was always something about Greta that Charlotte couldn't place, but she had thought it was her background, not this. At times she had seemed wealthy and uptight, like a Prussian aristocrat, but at other times she swore like a dock worker.

Had she taken her own life because she couldn't bear being a spy and keeping secrets? Charlotte didn't believe that for a second, and now she was getting wrapped up in it all. Charlotte would have to choose her next steps carefully. Whoever had killed Greta could come for her next if she didn't do what they wanted.

She took a sip of her drink. The coffee was warm and bitter, but reassuring. 'I don't know the first thing about intelligence operations. I'm a university student, a musician, not much more than that.'

'You're capable of learning. That's really all we ask for in a candidate. That and a willingness to serve the Fatherland. There will be training – don't you worry about that. We don't just send you into the field on your own and expect you to know what to do. We just need people to channel that information. To begin with it will be as simple as being a messenger of sorts. Coded letters, that sort of thing.'

He waved his cigarette around as if his words were of no importance, but Charlotte wanted to know more. How much was she going to risk for the Reich? She wasn't sure she could even answer that question.

'But what about my university studies?' She had to find some way to deflect, to find a way out of danger.

'We can fit in your training alongside those. You students don't do much anyway. After all the universities were infiltrated by Jews, you became lazy. This will do you good. And you will be doing good.'

She opened her mouth to speak, but he was determined to finish his sentence.

'You would be doing a great service for your country. You would be a hero.'

'I'm not sure that I want to be a hero. As you say, I wanted a quiet life.'

'Believe me, you are far more important to the Reich than that. Although you are not who I would choose for the role, but luckily for you it isn't my decision.'

She took a breath. Perhaps this was a way out of the conversation and the trap she was increasingly working her way into. But did she not want to see where this went?

'What do you mean by that?' she asked.

'You're a little . . . plump, but otherwise you look perfectly Aryan. In fact I don't think I've ever seen blonder hair or bluer eyes.'

She resisted the urge to comment. Her size was part of her nature. Her mother was a bigger build and her father had been a large man. No matter how much she tried, including starving herself as a teenager, it had never made any difference. It had absolutely nothing to do with diet or laziness, and everything to do with her background. She had come to terms with it. She was who she was. But that didn't stop others, particularly men like this, telling her that she should be thinner.

'If you lost a little weight you could be a model, or an actress. The Führer would be particularly interested in you, I'm sure.'

Again she bit her tongue. She had no desire to meet Hitler.

'But I guess we have a different path in mind for you now. Who knows? Work hard enough and excel in what we ask you to do, and you may still meet the Führer.'

She realised she had to say something. The noose was tightening around her neck. She kept falling into silence, incredulous at what was happening, but with each gap she was losing control of the conversation. 'That would be an unexpected and possibly undeserved privilege.' It was all she could bring herself to say, and she hoped that he didn't hear the dismissal in her voice.

'Perhaps. We will see. You should lose some weight anyway. It will help you perform your duties. We expect our agents to be fit and healthy, and well, you are . . .'

'I didn't ask for this—'

He cut her off. 'Everyone in the Reich must do their duty. Your particular skill set is useful to us and therefore you will be useful. There is no other choice. Especially by this point in the conversation. I have already told you too much.'

Her breath caught in her throat and she pretended she had choked on the coffee. He wouldn't see through her ruse, but she was becoming increasingly desperate. But this was her way to find out what Greta had been up to.

'I can do whatever you ask me to do,' she said, her voice louder than she had intended. 'But don't judge me by my appearance. That's exactly what Germany's enemies will do, and they would be just as wrong as you are.'

For the first time since their meeting his face broke out in a smile. It wasn't at all reassuring. 'You're confident. There's no doubt about that. Perhaps you're right. It's useful for an agent to blend in. We don't want too many eyes following you.'

'I know what I'm capable of. You have nothing to worry about. But why me?' It was a question she had been asking herself since the beginning of this conversation, but had not until now had a chance to voice. She took another sip of cold coffee to hide the wavering in her voice.

'Why? Because of who you are.' He grinned at her but it had the opposite of the desired effect.

'But you have absolutely no idea who I am. I'm not even sure I know who I am.' Her voice had risen an octave, despite her best efforts. It was something she had never admitted to anyone else, least of all a complete stranger. His grin turned to a frown before he shook his head and steepled his fingers.

'You're a musician,' he said, his tone suggesting he was talking to a child. 'It's as good a cover as any.'

'I am, but what use is a musician to matters of the state?' She leant back in her chair in a show of confidence she didn't feel. The cushioning was the softest she had ever felt and she wanted to close her eyes and let it wrap around her, all warmth and comfort.

'Not just because of what you can hide in that violin case.' He cut her off, gesturing towards the leather case and smiling at his own words. Apparently it was intended as a joke. 'But because musicians can go almost anywhere without drawing unwarranted attention to themselves. After all, here you are in one of the most expensive hotels in Hamburg, a hotel in which you can barely afford a drink, and yet no one has batted an eyelid at your presence.'

She nodded, remembering earlier. 'The violin does have its charm. And it works like a sort of passport, but it also gives people stories. They may want to know who I am performing for, what my background is.'

He waved a hand and took his own sip of coffee, before spitting it back into the cup with a grimace.

'People will always manufacture stories,' he said. 'That is not of our concern. If they are making up stories then they are too distracted from the truth and that is fine. We don't want them to get to the truth. For their own safety. But it's not just that you are a musician. You're also a student.'

'Me being a student doesn't mean anything. You cannot tell someone is a student just from looking at them, and it gives me no advantage over people. What do you mean?'

'It means you're young. People are more trusting of the young; they have fewer secrets. You're also a woman.'

She nodded. She had known that was coming but she didn't think he would be so obvious.

'You're perfect, don't you see?'

'I'm not sure if you're trying to flatter me or you just don't know how to talk to women.' She tried a smile, but it fell from her lips. 'There are many women just like me in the Reich. I'm not special.'

'I'm not playing games with you, fräulein. This is serious.'

'Now, hold on. A minute ago you were—'

'That's enough!' He banged a fist against the table and ash fell onto its wooden surface. No one else in the coffee room turned in their direction. 'We have spent far too long in discussion. There is nothing left to discuss. You are a woman. Women can get men to do whatever they want. You have a power over us.'

'I'm not sure that's entirely true.'

'Oh? What about if you were in a desperate situation? Men have less to offer other men.'

She didn't know what to say so she kept her mouth shut. Apparently seeing her unease, he waved it away with a hand.

'Besides,' he said, 'it's more that you can go many places unseen. Men get questioned. Women are part of everyday life. Many of you have roles that most take for granted, and even if you are seen where you shouldn't be, a woman like yourself would be admired rather than suspected. You're perfect.'

He took another sip of his drink, and straightened the cuffs of his shirt.

'For the role,' he finished.

What could she possibly say?

The Abwehr would give her another way of finding information. She could ask questions, see what they knew about Greta. But it would take some time to gain their confidence. To show that she was working for them and not for her own ends.

She knew it would be dangerous, but the mere fact they had approached her was dangerous. She didn't have a choice and she would use it to her advantage, for her friend. For the second time in a week life had thrown up unexpected opportunities. It wasn't going to be any easier but at least she had a way of getting ahead.

'The Führer has helped Germany. I might be young, but even I remember what it was like when I was a child. People giving up everything they had to buy a loaf of bread. We can't let them go through that again.'

He nodded at her words in agreement.

She had been left with an impossible choice. She wasn't naive enough to think that the war would pass her by and that she could carry on her life, her studies, unaffected. But she hadn't expected to be asked to take an active part in the war. She was no soldier and was thankful that the army didn't recruit women. That was a decision she would never have to take. But this decision was something completely unexpected and far beyond her experience. But then, there was a huge part of her that wasn't sure this was even a decision. What would happen to her if she said no? She couldn't just walk away and expect no consequences. That wasn't the world she lived in.

She wasn't fond of a number of the things happening in her country, but on the whole they didn't affect her, and she wanted to help. She wanted to make Germany a country that was prosperous, happy, and a place for the German people to be proud of. Progress always involved difficult decisions; that was the nature of the world. If her studies of philosophy had taught her anything, it was that life was never simple. There were always questions to be asked and sacrifices to be made. She took a deep breath and looked the man directly in the eyes.

'I'll do whatever needs to be done.'

Chapter Thirteen

Saturday, 24 December 1939

She spent a while walking around the city centre in the rain. Even though it had passed midnight, she couldn't go home; she was too pent up and full of something she could only describe as excitement. Kurt would be waiting for her and wondering where she was. They had agreed to spend the evening together, but she couldn't worry about that now. In her current mood she couldn't cope with him asking about marriage again. She couldn't explain to him that it didn't seem important when faced with the reality of what she had to do now. Life had changed dramatically in the last few months. It amazed her that Hamburg looked the same it had always done, when everything in her life seemed to be shifting and changing.

She wanted to walk around for a while to ground herself in the familiar. These streets had been her world for as long as she could remember. Her father had taken her for walks, talking of the city's history, its importance to the world through the Hanseatic league. Now, more than ever, that felt like a distant memory. She missed her father. She longed for his calm voice, the comfort he provided. But she wouldn't have been able to tell him what was going through her mind any more than she could tell Kurt.

She might not agree with everything the Nazis did, but she was going to be a spy for her country, for them. Some of her worries of the past few months had gone in the space of a conversation. She was going to be someone. She was going to be important and make a difference to the world. If only she could survive long enough.

There were candles everywhere, even in a few of the windows in the Rathaus. A large evergreen tree had been erected in the centre of Adolf-Hitler-Platz, but far from being the picturesque Christmas scene, the rain poured down covering its needles in drops of water. Charlotte was soaked through as she finally headed for home.

Kurt was in the living room as she let herself in. He wasn't just waiting for her, he had dragged in a fir tree and was attaching it to a stand in the corner by the window. The tree was bare, but he was covered in tinsel and resembled some kind of silver hedgehog. Rather than help him, Charlotte watched, a wry smile on her face.

After a second or two he turned, apparently sensing someone was watching him, and his face broke into a wide grin.

'You forgot the Christmas tree,' he said. 'You always forget the Christmas tree.'

'I know.' If she was honest, she hadn't forgotten. The last two years she had deliberately left it up to him. It had become a part of their tradition. She liked to see his joy at putting up the Christmas tree; it was the time when he was at his most pure, most innocent. 'You do it so much better than I do.'

He frowned. 'I don't think I can remember the last time you actually put up a tree. Come on, get dried off and then help me.'

The apartment was warmer than outside, but there was no fire and she was already beginning to feel the cold in her bones. He beckoned her over and she hesitated for a second, wanting to see what he was going to do with the tree. But she wanted to be close to him, feel the warmth of his body.

'Kurt, I've missed you.' She let herself fall into his arms, breathing in his aftershave. The events of the past few days whirled round and round in her head. She didn't hear his reply, but knew it was comforting. Even the indistinct vibrations of his voice calmed her, helped to block out her thoughts. If only for a moment.

'Ugh, you're soaked through.'

He stepped back and helped her pull her coat off, letting it drop to the floor before kissing her on the lips.

'You speak as if you've been away,' he said a moment later, as the kiss still lingered on her lips. 'It's not even been twenty-four hours since I last saw you.'

'I know, but a lot can happen in a day.'

His smile dropped. 'Has something happened? Is that why you were wandering around in the rain?'

She thought about telling him the real reason, but she couldn't bring him into her new world. She wasn't allowed. Even though he would think she was doing the right thing, she didn't know how safe it would be.

'No, nothing's happened. Nothing except the war and everything else that's going on. I'm just tired and I needed to think.'

He kissed her again and this time his lips pressed against hers for longer. She didn't want him to pull away again. She could have stayed there forever, feeling the soft warmth of his skin against her, the slight scent of mint. When she closed her eyes it was all she had ever wanted. But it was over too soon.

'Help me with the tree?' he asked again.

'Does the party have a list of approved Christmas presents?' she teased him. He frowned. He sensed the tension behind her words, and shook his head. It was one of the main reasons she was hesitant to marry him. While he didn't follow the party too closely, he was a member and that was enough to make her wary. She wanted to ask him what was wrong, but she knew he wouldn't tell her. She wasn't even sure he could recognise something was wrong himself. She laid the palm of her hand against his cheek. Despite the chill his face was warm, and she closed her eyes, cherishing the feeling.

'Don't say things like that. You never know who may be listening.' He stroked her hair and tilted his head to look in her eyes. 'I know you are joking but there are some party members who, let's just say, take things a little more seriously.'

'I know, but surely they would just ignore it and move on. There are bigger issues.'

'Some of them may not. It's not worth the risk.'

'The party aren't exactly friendly with the churches. What does it matter to them?'

'You know, that's the curious thing about them. They will always find something to pull you up on, if you're not following the rules as they decide them. It's best not to rock the boat. If you fall in the water, I won't be able to save you.'

It was the first time she had heard him be this honest about the party. She had thought that he was as sycophantic as the rest. She thought about the meeting she had just come from. If he knew how much she was risking by working with the Abwehr, then she wasn't sure he would be happy. Even if she was serving the Reich. Maybe she needed to reconsider her opinion of him, and have a deeper talk about their beliefs, but now was not the time.

'The party have circulated these for the tree.' He handed her a rectangular card box, a bit like a cigar box. She opened the lid and peered inside. It contained a carved wooden swastika with a conical base. She replaced the lid and looked back at him.

'I didn't think so either,' he said. Her sigh of relief was audible, but Kurt didn't seem fazed. 'It wouldn't disrespect the party to put a star on top of the tree. I'm sure we've got one around here somewhere.'

He started rooting through the boxes arrayed around the sofa. Charlotte dropped the swastika topper into one of them, hoping that Kurt would forget it. Then she picked up another box, looking for the decorations her father had left her. He had never wanted to decorate the tree either, but had always relented when Charlotte and her mother insisted they do it as a family. The other box contained some candles, but not what she was looking for.

115

There was a thump in the corridor and she tensed. She wasn't expecting anyone and the prospects of all the people she hoped it wasn't rushed through her head. The door opened and Peter came in. He was singing and it was clear from the way he swayed that he'd had a drink. It wasn't the first time he had shown up at her apartment unannounced.

'I wish you'd knock,' Charlotte said, pulling away from Kurt.

'It's Christmas!' Peter had rounded up Andreas and Ilse on his way. The former looked less pleased about it, but as usual he was immaculately dressed. Kurt wore a faint smile. It said, *What can you do?*

Ilse dropped herself into the sofa without so much as a hello. But before she could put her feet up on the coffee table, Peter pulled her up by the arm. 'Come on.' He handed her a bottle of schnapps. She tipped the bottle up to her lips then passed it to Andreas. He shrugged then took a swig and proffered it to Kurt. He shook his head. Charlotte had never known him to drink something without checking its origin first. Hilda came out of her room, yawning.

'Come on,' Peter said again. He took a few steps across the living room, almost hopping. 'Why are you all so glum? Let's have a sing.'

Hilda sighed and Ilse looked confused. They all knew that once Peter had an idea in his head he would see it through. He chucked his coat over the sofa then stood in front of them and started waving his hands like a conductor. Except, he had no idea what he was doing.

'Silent night,' he sang loudly. It wasn't bad. He could at least hold a tune.

'Oh God,' Hilda murmured, and Peter shot her a look. Charlotte started to sing. She didn't want her friends to argue again, least of all Peter and Hilda when she was in a bad mood and tired.

Peter started again, this time hoping they would all join in.

'Silent night. Holy night, all is calm, all is bright.'

Their hearts weren't in it. Even Charlotte, with her love of music, couldn't bring herself to do more than mumble.

'Only the chancellor stays on guard,' Peter continued as the others stumbled to keep up with the revised lyrics. 'Germany's future to watch and to ward, guiding our nation aright.'

'Why are we singing this version?' Charlotte whispered to Kurt. He nodded at Peter and then gripped her hand. He squeezed it tight twice and then intertwined his fingers in hers.

Peter's voice grew, trying to encourage them, but the louder he went the more his voice struggled. Still, he waved his hands in the air like he was leading a Nazi marching band.

Hilda pulled away from the group.

'I've had enough, Peter,' she said. 'I'm not in the mood.'

Charlotte glanced a warning at her friend. Hilda was taking a risk. Why couldn't she just play along? It would be better for them all. Peter stopped and his arms fell by his sides.

'I thought we were supposed to be friends,' he muttered, just loud enough for Hilda to hear. She turned to him, but he continued before she could speak. 'You all push against me. I thought we were supposed to be friends.'

'Peter, please,' Charlotte said. 'We are your friends. Of course we are, but do you really think this is appropriate now? The war . . .'

'The war. The war. It's all we ever hear about.' He was growing increasingly manic, waving his arms about again, but this time in frustration. 'Please. I think we need a distraction. Why don't you play us a Christmas song on the violin, Charlotte?'

She shook her head. 'I'm tired. I've already performed today. Please just let me go to bed.' She shot a look at Kurt.

'I have her violin at the university.' Andreas came to her rescue, stepping between them. 'To repair the case.'

She had forgotten that she had finally dropped it off there on her way home after waiting months to get him to repair it, such was her distraction. It had been quite a last twenty-four hours.

'But . . . it's Christmas.' He pouted like a young boy, and with his short blond hair he resembled one.

'I think that's enough, Peter.' Kurt cut him off before he could make any more demands. 'We're all tired. Why don't we just call it a night?'

Peter mumbled something that sounded like 'a silent night', but he picked up his coat from the back of the chair and pulled Ilse behind him. 'Happy Christmas,' he said as he approached the door. He didn't look behind him as he slammed the door, making its frame shudder.

The other friends looked at one another, but none of them said a word. They knew what Peter was like, how difficult it was for him to always have to impress his family. Their friendship was important to him, a second family, but he would come back and he would apologise. He always did after he had time to think. Hilda went to her room, and Andreas placed a gentle hand on Charlotte's arm and bid her and Kurt a good night.

When they were finally alone, Kurt did what Charlotte had wanted him to do all night. He took her by the hand and led her to her bedroom. There was something about the way they held hands. It was like they had always been one, one hand fitting perfectly in the other. There was no other way to explain it. He helped her undress and held her lower back as he kissed her again and again. After that they just lay in the bed, him behind her with one arm around her chest and the other under her head. She could feel his faint breath upon her hair as the candles burnt down to darkness and her thoughts eventually calmed enough for her to sleep.

Chapter Fourteen

Monday, 12 February 1940

Things in the new year slowed down compared to the last few months since war broke out, but they were no less frantic for Charlotte. No further British aircraft had been seen over the city since the leaflet drop. As Hamburg was the closest port to England it made sense that they would attack here, but so far the residents of Hamburg had avoided the RAF's attention.

Charlotte had spent her time reading her books, attending lectures, playing her violin, and when no one was looking she attended the Abwehr for her training. Once a week she headed towards the General Kommando building on Sophienterrasse. It wasn't far to walk from the university, and she enjoyed the stroll along the tree-lined avenues. She didn't go to the Kommando building's main entrance itself, used by the General Command of the army. The concrete structure, built in the typical Wehrmacht style, towered over her, with its brass eagles above the door. It was where Kurt would have to go if he was called up by the Wehrmacht, but she hoped that day would never come.

Instead she entered via a back entrance. To be seen by the imposing main entrance would invite far too many questions.

So, she had kept it secret, as she was supposed to. Thankfully no one had missed her yet as she strolled away from the university.

The first time she was there it was clear no one had been expecting her. She gave the handwritten note she had been left to a girl even younger than she was. Charlotte assumed she was the receptionist, based on her manner. The girl barely looked up or said a word to Charlotte. She could easily have been mistaken for Charlotte. The same blonde hair and blue eyes. She could imagine that the Abwehr and the Gestapo made a point of only hiring Aryan women. Something about that thought made Charlotte feel far less important.

Like Charlotte, the girl didn't appear to want to be there. She looked at the note Charlotte had handed her as if she had been given a piece of rubbish. Charlotte explained what it was but the girl's attitude didn't change. Instead she picked up a telephone receiver and, when it was clear the person on the other end had picked up, talked slowly into it. Charlotte could tell the enemy would never get anything out of her; she didn't know anything. Perhaps that was why they had been recruited. They were just useful bodies. Expendable.

That first time she had been told to wait and then had been admitted into an interview room by a short man in a poorly tailored suit. It reminded her of the police station, but also her first day of university. His bald head had bobbed as he had given her an aptitude test and made notes. Then he told her to come back at the same time the following week.

After that she had returned each week in much the same fashion. When she arrived the receptionist would pretend she didn't know Charlotte, then Charlotte would be shown into the room and asked to do a series of tests with the same man. He said very little at first and she worried that she had been caught up in National Socialist bureaucracy. She had been tempted to stop attending. What would they do? They didn't even seem to want her there. But even though she felt superfluous it was not worth the risk.

Besides, she wanted to see this out, see how far it could take her. That was until they started training her properly.

Then, he started to become more talkative, instructing her what she should do in particular situations. She could barely remember what he said, he directed her in such a monotonous voice, and they were unable to write anything down in case it fell into enemy hands. But thankfully he kept going over and over the same things, to the point she could almost repeat them by rote. If she had expected it to be easy, she had been mistaken.

She found it hard to pay attention to her trainer, until he had said something that truly shocked her. One day, completely out of the blue, he had turned to her and told her that her life meant less than the Reich, and if the information she had was ever likely to fall into enemy hands then she would be expected to destroy it and herself. The comment had left her speechless, and he had said nothing more of how she might accomplish it.

After that, he had continued training her as usual. She had expected to be called to represent them for the May Day celebrations, the day the Nazis celebrated national labour day, but instead everything had shut down and she had been given the day off from training to celebrate.

Then, her coding training had begun. Apparently they had picked up one or two things from the British. He placed a sheet in front of her, with a grid of letters that made no immediate pattern. At first she didn't understand what she was supposed to do. The letters were a jumble. She looked up into his rheumy eyes for an explanation, but he shouted at her.

It was the first time she had heard him raise his voice and she felt pushed back in her chair. She knew she was missing something, but couldn't think what it was. The letters on the sheet looked no more familiar than they had done a minute before.

'You have to be able to work under pressure,' he shouted again. 'The enemy will not give you time to think.'

That may be true, but he had given her no instruction and she had no idea what to do. She picked up a pencil lying in a groove on the desk. She played it through her fingers until the lead was facing the paper. She could still feel her trainer's gaze on the top of her head. It cut into her like a knife, and his rage had not abated. But what could she do?

She drew a line with the pencil separating the first four letters on the page from the next, then another and another, until the first line of forty-eight letters was divided into fours. She didn't know what she was doing, so she organised them like bars on a stave of music. There was something about the pattern that looked more familiar than it had done before, but she couldn't yet put her finger on it.

Her trainer stepped back and mumbled something that sounded like approval. He crossed his arms and watched. Like music there was mathematics behind the series of letters. She had never been good at calculations, but she was good at music. She added up the letters in each bar based on their place within the alphabet. Then wrote that number above each box.

'Good,' the trainer muttered. 'You surprise me at every turn.'

She surprised herself. If she assigned a new letter to each box given its number then she could form a new word. At first it didn't make sense, but if she decided that one of the codes must be a space, then she could start to form a new sequence.

Eventually it spelled out 'This is a code'. There was more to decipher, but she stopped and fixed her gaze on the trainer. He wore a loose smirk, and she guessed it was he who had come up with the task. He was pleased with himself.

'It's basic,' he said. 'But most of our operatives don't even know where to start when they come in here. What you did was very impressive.'

'You're right. It's simple.' She put the pencil down, a protest against continuing with the task. She didn't appreciate how surprised he sounded. 'If this is what you expect to beat the British with then it's not going to work.'

It was the first time she had been actively defiant towards the trainer and the Abwehr, but she was growing impatient.

'Oh, no,' he said, the smirk turning into a grin. 'This is only the beginning. We have a lot more complicated methods than this and you will need to be familiar with them in time. But I think you're almost ready to go into the field.'

He picked up the piece of paper and dropped it into a bin by the door. Charlotte didn't say a word, but it struck her how dangerous that was. Were they putting all their codes in bins? What if someone went through them? It didn't matter to her. She had other things to think about. He had said she was almost ready. She didn't think that would ever be true. She had been expecting to languish in training for years to come, and then the war would be over.

He held the door open for her. 'That will be enough for today.'

Her goal was to find out what had happened to Greta, but now Charlotte would have to keep an even more careful watch. Her life was going to be placed in greater danger. As she packed up her things and made for the exit, she wondered to herself what she had got herself into. Things were about to get a lot more difficult.

Chapter Fifteen

Friday, 17 May 1940

Charlotte pulled back the pin on the Luger and felt the satis-
fying click. She didn't want her weapons trainer to know she
had fired a weapon before. He was a big man, built like an
Olympian, and had a permanent frown stretched across his
brow. When he had first met Charlotte he had looked at her
like she was dirt, and he hadn't softened yet. Every time she
saw him he wore the grey Wehrmacht uniform, everything
pristine and polished.

He was supposed to be training her, and her ability with a
pistol would raise too many questions. Her father had taught her
to shoot. He had wanted her to be able to defend herself, but he
had never explained why. She handled the weapon firmly, so that
it didn't go off by accident, but she wanted to give an air of being
wary of it. She was scared of what it could do, but she also knew
how to use it. She wondered how many other women knew how
to fire a pistol properly. Probably not very many.

The instructor stood behind her and she could feel his breath
on the back of her neck. Clearly he wasn't used to training women
and his proximity was intimidating. He leant over her and took

hold of the pistol, and she got a whiff of his aftershave. It was musky and cloying.

'You need to hold it like this.' His voice was deep as he placed her left hand around her right, gripping them in his own. 'In both hands, otherwise the recoil will unbalance you.'

Her ruse had worked too well and she was desperate for him to take a step back.

'Thank you,' she said, without turning to face him. Her eyes were fixed on the target in front of her as she squeezed the trigger.

The Luger bucked in her grip and sent a wave of excitement through her arms. Its bark reverberated around the enclosed space, deafening. But she didn't fall over and it wasn't thanks to the presence of the instructor. There was a neat hole almost in the centre of the target.

He whistled. 'You're a natural.'

She fired off a few more shots, this time letting them fly wide of the mark. One missed the target completely, which was more than she intended.

'Hmmph,' he grunted and backed off. 'Must have been a fluke.'

But Charlotte was relieved for the distance. She took a deep breath of air and it helped the scent of his aftershave dissipate. It was already evening, her university studies taking up the day, and she longed to be anywhere else than training in the Kommando building with this man. Besides, she had a performance to get to.

She unclipped the magazine from the Luger and placed both of them on the workbench to her side. It was always best to make sure it was safe. It was the first thing she had been shown. But they didn't know that her father had shown her years before.

'What are you doing?' he asked. 'I say when you're done. Not you.'

'It's late,' she replied, turning to look at him.

He still wore the frown, but his uniform jacket was undone at the neck. He looked more relaxed than she had ever seen him, and as he reached forward she thought he was reaching for her.

125

She pulled back into the firing alcove, but he simply picked up the Luger to return it to the weapons cabinet.

As he turned, an air-raid siren screamed into life. It whirled through the building, even in these concrete depths. The trainer sighed and gestured to the door.

'Saved by the RAF,' he muttered to himself, while doing up his jacket with one hand.

Charlotte didn't hesitate. She grabbed her bag and made for the exit. She was supposed to be going to perform, but there was no way they would allow her during an air raid. But where else could she go? The sirens rang in her ears, following her as she ran out onto the street and into the blackout.

The drone was never-ending, like standing next to a row of taxis while they idled their engines, but spread across the night sky. Air-raid sirens cut through the din as they rose to a crescendo and the occasional anti-aircraft gun could be heard from a few streets away.

Charlotte ran. She hadn't run like that since she was a child, chasing Kurt through the streets. She didn't know where she was going, simply away from the sound of bombers. It washed over the city in a way that made it sound as if they were all around. She should have headed towards one of the bomb shelters. That was what they had been drilled to do and no doubt her building's warden would be directing the residents that way. But they had not accounted for her to be out in the city after dark.

A plume of orange flame erupted from the docks, the sound hitting her a second later. Involuntarily she ducked behind a wall and stopped to catch her breath. Whatever she had expected a bombing to be like, it had not prepared her for the reality of it. The noises were erratic. Loud in one part of the city, then another explosion taking over. It was like an orchestra tuning up, but an orchestra the size of a city.

She didn't know which way to run. A sound nearby made her start in one direction, away from the docks, then another crump from the other side forced her back into hiding. She was stuck against the wall, but she knew she couldn't stay there. If the building was hit, then she would be buried under piles of rubble. Would anyone be able to get her out? She didn't want to wait and find out. So she ran.

She ran in the direction she thought the nearest shelter was in. She saw a few other people, but they were difficult to make out in the blackout. Just blurred dark shapes running between the buildings as she was. Charlotte wondered where her friends were, but there was nothing she could do for them now. They would have made it to the shelters. They had to have done. But what about Kurt? Would he be in the factory helping them to put out any fires that may occur? It would be just like him to risk his life like that. She knew that running to him wouldn't help him, but she so dearly wanted to.

The crack of machine-gun fire joined the din of aircraft engines and the ack-ack of anti-aircraft fire. Noises blended into one another and washed over others. Charlotte was paralysed by the assault on her senses. She couldn't think straight, couldn't work out where she was or what she should be doing. It was like being shouted at. She turned into a child, losing her independence of thought and motion. She just stared at the sky, wishing it would stop.

'Charlotte. What are you doing? Come on!' Kurt called after her. She hadn't realised her legs had taken her out into the middle of the open. Kurt almost hopped from one foot to another, beckoning her to follow him. It was like when they had been children, but now Kurt was leading her. 'Why are you standing there? It's dangerous. Come on!'

Except, it wasn't Kurt. It was someone else. A man she didn't know. He hadn't said her name at all – that had been wishful thinking on her part. He must have been one of the air-raid wardens, as he led her to the nearest shelter, gently guiding her, and within a minute she was safely underground.

She had been in too much of a daze to realise where she was, but she thought it was under one of the department stores on Mönckebergstrasse. The basement was full of people and she had to push her way through them to find somewhere to sit. There was one spot free on a bench next to a family. A mother held her baby in a cloth blanket and shushed them to sleep while the father entertained a young boy on his lap. Charlotte hugged her violin case to her body and pushed herself into the corner.

From here the occasional rumble of a bomb landing was muffled, and seconds later she was drifting off, lost in exhaustion.

Chapter Sixteen

Saturday, 18 May 1940

'What are you doing here?' Kurt was wearing overalls over his shirt and there were smudges of grease on his cheeks and neck. She liked the way it made him look, somehow older. She couldn't tell him that she had needed to see him, to make sure he was still alive, still him. She would have to explain last night and that would be too difficult. She had to think of something else.

'I heard about the bombs landing here and I wanted to check that everything was all right. Is the factory heavily damaged?'

He put a toolbox down and took a step closer to her. He was about to hug her then looked at his hands. He wiped them on his overalls then shrugged. They were no cleaner.

'It's good of you to come,' he said. He walked over to check a machine, bending down and looking through some gears. 'Blohm and Voss got the worst of the damage. It's almost as if the British knew exactly where they were aiming, but that's impossible. Unless some idiot left a light on over there. But no, we remain unscathed. It's business as usual here.'

He ducked behind the machine. Charlotte would have liked to

have known what it did, but she felt foolish asking. In the Reich, it wasn't her place to know such things.

'I've always wanted to see the factory,' she said, shouting to be heard over the rumble. 'To see what your family does.'

Kurt's work at the factory was important to him, but she knew it wasn't his ambition. He wanted to be something else, but neither of them knew what. So he worked for his father, keeping a watch over the factory. It was good work, earning him around forty Reichsmarks a week, which she was sure his parents supplemented. She didn't hold that against him. If not for her own parents she would not be able to afford to live in her apartment, nor study at the university.

But most importantly Kurt's employment gave him a good argument against signing up for the Wehrmacht. Charlotte was sure that was why he continued to work here.

'I'll show you around.' His head appeared again around the corner of the machine and the broad smile on his face indicated he was glad to hear suggestion. It was the first time she had shown an interest in his work and she silently reprimanded herself. She should take more time for Kurt, but that would only get more difficult when the Abwehr progressed her from training to work.

He threw a dirty rag into a bin and took her hand. Even with the grease it was what she had wanted all morning, the reassurance of his fingers. He led her through the machinery, pointing out various components, but she didn't take any of it in. She was more focused on how at home he looked. It was as if he had built this factory with his own hands. Workers greeted him in each section, and those he spoke to he knew by name.

A second later Kurt stopped dead and her hand fell out of his. Kurt's father stood in a doorway between two warehouses. He was talking to another worker and hadn't spotted them yet, but it was clear Kurt had seen him. He tried to pull Charlotte to the side, but it was too late.

'Ah, Kurt. There you are.' Kurt's father took long strides towards them. 'And Fräulein Weber too. What a pleasure.'

His face didn't match his words. He didn't even look at Charlotte as he spoke. His scowl was reserved for Kurt. His face was similar to his son's, but where Kurt was lithe, Henning Winmer was rather more round. He looked exactly like the kind of man who was doing well out of factory ownership.

'Herr Winmer.' Charlotte held out her hand. Even though she had met them many times before, and they considered her almost a member of the family, Kurt's father was always overly formal with her. It was as if he didn't know how to act outside the traditions and strictures of what he had been taught.

He took Charlotte's hand in a quick grasp, barely wrapping his fingers around hers. She swept her hand back before there was any awkwardness. Their attention was drawn by a thump from across the floor.

A worker stumbled under the weight of the boxes he was carrying. A second later he fell, landing on his back with the boxes clattering around him. Charlotte made to aid him, but a look from Kurt stalled her. He shook his head shallowly and she stood back. Best not to get involved, he was telling her. Henning didn't even move and she thought she might have heard a slight tut. The worker struggled on the floor for a few more seconds, rubbing one hand against the back of his head. Then he managed to right himself. Standing, he stretched his back, much like an old man rising from a chair, but as soon as he saw the owner looking on he rushed to pick up the boxes. It was that kind of haste that Charlotte thought had caused the accident in the first place, but he managed to escape sight without dropping them again.

'There's a production section out of operation.' Henning's words were directed at Kurt. 'In the in-loading quarter. You need to get a team over there now.'

Kurt looked sideways at Charlotte. 'I'll see you later,' he said.

'Now, Kurt.' Henning's manner brooked no disagreement, and his son disappeared in the direction the worker had gone.

Henning shook his head and then turned his brown eyes on Charlotte. It was the first time he had acknowledged her presence, except for the handshake.

'You haven't come for dinner in some time,' he said.

She could try and think of an excuse but the simple reason was that she hadn't found time. With her studies, both at the university and the Abwehr, when she had got home she had done nothing but sleep. But she couldn't tell Henning about the Abwehr any more than she could tell his son.

'I'm sorry,' was all she could manage. He didn't even blink, and once again she felt she was failing in his presence.

'This evening,' he said. It wasn't a question.

Later that evening, after being escorted out of the factory, Charlotte was sitting at the Winmers's dining table, with the rest of the family. Even Kurt's brother Friedrich was there. They had eaten in silence, but once the plates were empty conversation had bloomed around the table. At first it had been idle chatter then talk drifted to the war.

Henning scowled across the table, past the candles and the silver platters of food. He had never been able to disguise his displeasure with his son. Charlotte wasn't sure whether it was the wine bringing out his anger, or whether he was in a constant state of frustration. Friedrich was definitely the favourite, despite being the younger. They made no secret of that fact. She hadn't caught what Kurt had said, but it had clearly upset his father.

'Do you not wish to serve the Fatherland?' Henning asked. Kurt's father had never been unkind to Charlotte, but she had never heard him say a kind word to Kurt. It wasn't just that he had known her since she was a child, but he was kind to everyone but his own family. Kurt seldom spoke about it, but she knew it affected him. He was always trying to work hard, to show that he was a good son, and to make peace whenever there was an argument. Not that there was ever an argument when Charlotte was around. They would never do that in front of her, it wasn't appropriate. But she wasn't naive – she knew what happened after she left.

'Of course, Father. But I will continue to work at the factory so long as I am needed and until the Wehrmacht call me up.'

'That may be sooner than you think, son.' Henning's scowl didn't relent. He gestured towards a newspaper on the side table. 'The Wehrmacht expansion into Denmark and Norway is going exactly as planned and they will soon be included in the Reich administration.'

In the rush of the day Charlotte had missed the most important news. She was too tired to process fully what that meant, but why didn't he call it what it was? An invasion.

'With Poland and these new territories the Reich is expanding quickly,' Henning continued. 'The Wehrmacht will need good young men to maintain order.'

There was an undercurrent to the words that it seemed only Charlotte recognised. Who would be next? Her mother's country? She could see no reason why they would invade Sweden, but she would have said the same about Norway before now.

'I am not a policeman, Father. There are men far better trained to do that than me.'

There was only silence in the room, not even the scraping of a knife upon a plate. Charlotte wasn't sure whether Henning's scowl was because of a perceived cowardice or through concern for his son, but she knew he would never say which it was. Fathers didn't do that sort of thing; they kept their emotions to themselves.

The conversation died at that moment, and she didn't feel like trying to revive it. Friedrich's smirk was enough to put anyone off their food, even the fresh apfelstrudel the cook had prepared. Charlotte knew that she would never eat like this at home, and it would be rude to refuse, but she was already full to bursting. She pushed the food around the plate and ate a little, a trick she had learnt in school to make it look like she had eaten more. If she thought eating it all up would allow her to go home sooner, then she would have done so.

Surprisingly Kurt and Charlotte were left alone after dinner. The candles had burnt down to their stands. His parents retired to their living room with one last glance at their son. Charlotte waited until they were out of earshot before speaking. She could feel Kurt's agitation beside her.

'You don't have to go and fight to impress your father,' she said. 'I don't think any less of you, in fact quite the opposite.'

'It's not about him. He will never be impressed, even if I become the Führer. It's about so much more than that.' He refused to look at her and she knew it was his way of not losing control. If he looked into her eyes then he was gone.

'What else? I don't understand.'

'It's about the Fatherland. Our home. This war is happening whether we like it or not. The only way to finish it is to fight it. That is my responsibility. I have to go and fight, otherwise who knows when it will end? What if the British win? What then? We all know how much they like to create an empire. They will just add us to it, and if we do not fit their way of life, then what?'

'It doesn't matter about the British. All that matters is you. Your life is precious. It's precious to me.'

'More precious than the thousands of other young men who have gone to fight? By staying at home I could be risking their lives.'

'You don't know that. You can't assume that you being there will make things any easier for them.'

He had no idea how hypocritical she was being. She wanted to tell him about the Abwehr, but now definitely wasn't the time. She knew that putting her life in danger wouldn't save his, but she wasn't doing it for the same reasons.

He stood up from the table and paced the room. 'You don't understand. You're not even really German. You're a foreigner.' His voice was raised, but not enough to be heard from the other room.

'How can you say that? You know very well that I was born here in Hamburg.'

'So?' He turned on her and she could see the trace of tears in his eyes. Either that or her own had become blurry. 'You're not completely German. Your mother—'

'Kurt!' It was her time to stand up. 'And you're being an absolute idiot. I know you don't think like that, so why say it?'

His shoulders dropped and he put his head in his hands. 'I'm sorry. I didn't mean it. You know I don't. Ignore me. The evening has played too much on my mind.' He reached out a hand and stroked her hair.

There was that familiar tingling again. At least, that was the only way she could describe it. It came on every time she was close to Kurt. It hadn't when they had first known each other, as children, but as they had both grown, as Kurt had grown into his shoulders and become a young man, she had seen something in him that hadn't been there before. It had been quite the surprise at first. Here was a boy she had always thought of as a friend, but now she was feeling something else for him, something that as a young woman she couldn't fully explain.

Thankfully he had felt the same. At least, once she had managed to get it out of him. If she was being fair they had both been shy at first, but Kurt was definitely the less confident of the two.

But she had not forgiven him yet. 'I should go home. It's late and I need to be alone.'

'I'll walk you.' He led her out into the corridor and retrieved their coats from the housekeeper. She should thank his parents, but she couldn't bring herself to talk to them now.

They didn't speak at all on the way home. She could see Kurt glance at her every now and then as if he wanted to say something, then look away, knowing better. Sooner or later he would find the words to apologise properly, but until then she could wait.

Once Kurt had seen her safely to her door, he gave her a kiss on the cheek and turned to leave. She knew it was his way of not showing he was upset with her, but she wished he could show it in another way. Any other way. They needed to talk, but that wouldn't happen yet.

Even still, she reached out and placed a hand on his arm. He stopped immediately and turned back. Despite knowing him for years there was a look on his face that she couldn't fathom.

'I know,' was all he said as he laid his palm on top of her hand and left the building. Tears filled her eyes and she fumbled at the lock of her apartment, wanting to get inside her flat as quickly as possible, before anyone saw her like this. She swore, but eventually the key turned and she rushed into her apartment. Thankfully it was empty. Hilda must have already gone to sleep. She would pick Hilda's brain about Kurt another day. It didn't matter to her in that moment. She wanted to be alone.

She awoke with a splitting headache. To say she awoke was an overstatement. She wasn't sure she had ever been asleep. The night passed in a fit of anger and frustration, her thoughts racing at an uncontrollable speed, and no matter how tight she forced her eyes closed they would not stop. Not a lot of it made sense. Her mind was that exhausted, and she knew that today would be even worse. Yet, somehow, she had to keep going. She only hoped that a shower and coffee would give her enough strength to get through the day. She threw some clothes on and went into the living room.

A white sheet of paper had been folded up and passed under her door. She reached for it, grimacing at the twinge in her head. There were only a few words written on the sheet, but it was enough to know what it meant. She looked over her shoulder. Hilda hadn't awoken yet. With hurried steps, she crossed to the cooker and lit the gas ring. The paper curled and browned before it turned to ash. If they were going to send her more notes she would have to warn them she didn't live alone. She turned the gas off. It wouldn't do to waste it, even if she was in their pay now. Headache or not, she would have to get dressed. She had work to do.

136

Chapter Seventeen

Friday, 24 May 1940

Charlotte walked along to the Café Brahms. For a long time it had been one of her favourite places to sit and while away her time, even when she wasn't studying. It wasn't just because of the musical heritage of the café, but because despite rationing, the coffee was still good and there was an excellent view where she could watch people go by across the street.

Rumour had it that the café had originally been opened by Jews, but now there was a sign in the window saying that Jews were forbidden. It wasn't the first business to cut all ties with Jewish ownership when the Nazis came to power. Even the department stores were not immune to their lack of favour. She hadn't seen the boycott herself in 1933. Her parents had kept her away from it with a trip to her mother's home in Sweden.

The door jingled as she entered now and she held the door open for a man in the uniform of a *Sturmführer* to leave. He tipped his cap and said, "Fräulein," to her as he pushed past her. Charlotte watched him go; she had never seen him in the café before. It wasn't unusual to see men in uniform in Hamburg, but the Café Brahms was typically free of soldiers. She hadn't yet managed to get Kurt to join her, even though he enjoyed drinking coffee.

The telephone call she had received as a follow-up to the note was still fresh in her memory, as if she could still hear the Abwehr agent's voice. It had been a brief phone call, passed on to her by the building's concierge. He had simply asked her for a place to meet and given her a time. The first place that had come to mind was the Café Brahms.

People she knew from the university seldom visited the café. It was often a place of quiet refuge for her, which was a good thing for what she had in mind. If she had been more practised in this sort of thing she might have chosen a café she didn't know. But then she would have been apprehensive for different reasons. Rather than finding an empty table by the window as she usually did, she worked her way to the back of the café and the rear room out of the way.

A couple were just leaving a table, and she smiled at them as they left, but they didn't return it. Too few people returned gestures these days, unless it was a salute. Then it was too risky not to reply. It was a shame that people didn't even give you a second glance, but Charlotte was often grateful. It gave her the opportunity to pass unnoticed, to not need to interact with other people.

She didn't know why she couldn't go to the office on Sophienterrasse, but it was probably better this way. The more she went to that building the more likely it became that someone would see her there. If anyone happened to see her enter the café, they wouldn't think anything of it. It was her safe space.

She took a table at the back, pulling out the wooden chair, which scraped along the tiled floor. No one looked her way. It was a typical sound for the café. She sat so that she could see the door and catch a glimpse of the street beyond.

One of the reasons she liked the café was because of how homely it was. Her apartment had never felt like home. It was supposed to be temporary, then she would get work and be able to afford her own place, but circumstances had got in the way and she felt as if she had been in temporary accommodation for years.

There was an old couple that were in the café almost every time she went in. They sat on a bench seat against the back wall, and stared into the middle distance unspeaking. Today they were holding hands and looking ahead, as if they had said everything that could possibly be said to each other, but still wanted, needed, to be close. She wondered whether she and Kurt would reach that point one day. In a way, with everything going on, she hoped so, but she also hoped they would have more in their life.

The couple's dark, leathery skin was today clothed in matching blue coats, which they kept on despite the humidity inside the café. The glass windows were often steamed up with the heat, but that was welcomed in the autumn and winter months. Sometimes, like today, they didn't even have a drink. They just sat there, thankful for the warmth. If Charlotte hadn't seen them leave from time to time, she would assume they were a permanent feature and the proprietors were too kind to remove them. For all Charlotte knew they could have been the proprietors themselves. It was never clear who owned the café and the staff was an endless turnover of students, like her, from the university.

At times she wanted to talk to the old couple, but she wasn't sure that they would respond. They seemed lost in their own world, and perhaps they were. The world was constantly changing around them. Charlotte herself had seen enough change in her own lifetime. Hitler becoming chancellor had only been one part of that.

A shadow fell over her. It was the man from the hotel who had recruited her to the Abwehr. She had been distracted by the old couple and hadn't spotted him coming in the door. He placed a newspaper at the side of the table. She couldn't see the masthead as it was face down, but she had a feeling it was a copy of the *Völkischer Beobachter*, the Nazi newspaper. He had no reason to hide where his loyalties lay. He pulled his chair in and folded his hands in front of him, but before he could say anything a waitress came to take their order.

'Peppermint tea for me.' She gave the waitress a faint smile, but received nothing in return apart from a shallow nod. He ordered a black coffee, the café being one of the places that had real coffee. It was one of the reasons it was popular and difficult to find a table.

Charlotte had made sure that they were sat at a table as far away from the other customers as possible, but even still he looked around to see whether anyone was listening to their conversation.

'Why did you pick this café?' he asked, turning back to face her. She hadn't been expecting small talk. In her mind her meeting would be a simple one. He would deliver her a mission and leave, with only scant detail and a reminder not to fail. But from his body language, leaning forward in the chair, it suggested that he was willing to take his time. On the other hand, she didn't want to talk any more than was strictly necessary.

'I like it here,' she said. The waitress put down a tray, placing the teapot and cup in front of her, then turning the spout towards the cup. She then placed a coffee cup in front of the agent. She lingered slightly longer than was appropriate and he glanced up at her.

'That much is obvious,' he said, when the waitress had gone. 'I suppose it suits the youth of today, but this is not the kind of café I would frequent when I was your age.'

She couldn't imagine him ever being her age. He talked as if he was old enough to be her father, but she couldn't gauge quite how old he was. His manner was that of an old man, formal and stilted. He had no lines or wrinkles that would suggest his age. He obviously took good care of himself. It gave him an ageless quality that unsettled Charlotte. But he was one of those men who had been born middle-aged.

She gave a short laugh, like some kind of film star, hoping that was what was expected of her. She could play the game as well as anyone.

'We can go somewhere else if you prefer?' She suspected he would have already made the suggestion had he wanted to leave. He was, after all, in charge.

He simply shook his head. 'Let's not waste time. I'm here to give you details of what we want you to do next. It's about time you started making yourself useful.'

She had no idea what he had in mind. Her training hadn't given her any indication in what way she might be an asset to them, but it brought back to mind their previous conversation. Was he going to have her infiltrate some orchestra?

'You're of course aware of the ongoing war and our operations in Denmark and Norway.'

She nodded. She couldn't voice her thoughts on those particular invasions. They were both countries she had expected to be free of German occupation. They were not as neutral as Sweden, but neither were they a threat to the Reich or, as far as she knew, had they been involved in the previous war. Had this man been involved in the last war? Was that why he was working from an office, rather than the field?

'We need someone to transport documents. Nothing too difficult at this stage, but it won't be easy. I will supply you with false identification, of a foreign national. That way you will be able to travel to other countries. It will not be infallible, but it should get you out of any tricky situations.'

She didn't like the 'should' in that sentence. 'There's really no need. I have a Swedish passport.'

'You do?' He looked into the middle distance as if he was thinking. 'But you are German?'

She nodded, unwilling to explain. If he hadn't done his research that was his problem, and she didn't want to explain about Greta.

'I wasn't informed of this. No matter. It will be useful. You are probably unaware, but here in Hamburg we are in charge of Scandinavian operations. You've just made yourself very useful indeed.'

She nodded. It wasn't something she had really considered before now, but the only thing she could think of was how she would get to see her family.

'Do you think you will be able to convince border guards you're supposed to be there? Are you a good liar?'

He took a sip of his coffee, waiting for her answer. It wasn't an easy question to answer. Yes, she was capable of keeping secrets. She had convinced him she was the violinist he was supposed to recruit, hadn't she? And no one else knew about her training with the Abwehr, but who knew what would happen should she be forced to prove herself?

'I can keep secrets, but I won't kill anyone or commit any action that will see someone killed. I'm not a killer. Leave that to the soldiers.'

'Quite, but that sounds like a luxury in war. The work you do for us may well see other operatives lose their lives. We hope that most of them will be our enemies, but that may not always be the case.'

'But I won't hold a weapon to their throat myself. I refuse. If that's what you're asking of me then I will leave now, quit.'

He considered her for a long time, playing his fingers around the handle of his coffee cup.

'Very well, then. But I cannot guarantee you will not end up in danger. We're at war. The Abwehr is part of the military intelligence. If I am being pedantic then as a member of the Abwehr, you are a soldier in the Wehrmacht.'

She didn't want to think about that. After telling Kurt not to be in a hurry to be a soldier, she was truly a hypocrite. 'What do you want me to do?' she asked, to move the conversation along.

'Of course,' he said. 'Nothing I say here goes any further than this table. If you reveal the details of our conversation to anyone else, there will be repercussions.'

Charlotte swallowed. She wasn't sure what the repercussions would be and how much he could really hurt her, but she wasn't willing to take the risk. He was behaving as if she hadn't had the training, but perhaps he was just unused to working with women. 'Go on.'

'Well, I'm sure you're well aware that Sweden is remaining a neutral country.'

She nodded. 'I'm aware. Famously so. But what does that have to do with me?'

He held up a hand in that insufferable manner of his. 'We're getting to that,' he said. 'If you are going to be this impatient then maybe I should reconsider your usefulness.'

'I'm sorry. I'm just . . . enthusiastic. Please go on.'

He couldn't sense the dishonesty in her words, which wasn't a good sign for his ability as an agent. But then she supposed that probably wasn't his purpose. He was there to give people like her the tasks. He was a pen pusher, sat behind a desk, or in this instance, a coffee shop table.

'The operations in Denmark and Norway have been incredibly successful, but given the topography of Norway, our forces in the north, in Narvik, are cut off from resupply.'

'You want me to carry weapons to them?' She smiled at him to show she was joking, but his frown suggested he either didn't understand or didn't care for her sense of humour. He carried on regardless.

'Don't be stupid. With the Swedish neutrality, it is making it difficult to get supplies to those troops. Without them then more young men will die.'

'Exactly. They need help, but the Swedish government are unlikely to sacrifice their neutral status. They're proud of how long they have avoided war.'

'I wouldn't suggest that our young men need help. They're well-trained, proud soldiers of the Reich.' Once again he reprimanded her with words. 'But Sweden's position is . . . a problem.

'Reichsmarschall Göring is deliberating with the Swedish government to come to some kind of agreement, but the Reichsführer wishes us to expedite things.'

143

Charlotte didn't miss that he dropped Göring and Himmler into conversation as if he knew them personally and they had sent him to issue her orders. It could be true, but it felt unlikely. The man sat opposite her was no senior member of the Wehrmacht, otherwise he wouldn't be drinking tea with her in a café.

'What we need you to do is to deliver letters to certain people in Stockholm. The contents aren't important, but you will need to express that our position is not to idly threaten. They must do as they are asked or pay the consequences.'

He pushed a sheet of handwritten names across the table to her. She looked at it for a second before placing it in her handbag. It was the same handwriting as the note pushed under her door. Next came a wad of envelopes tied together with brown string. They followed the note into her handbag.

'Each of these people has something to lose if they don't do what we ask. And coincidentally each of them is in a position to put pressure on the Swedish government to accept Göring's terms.'

'That's it? Extortion?'

He ignored her. 'Deliver the letters. Make sure they read them and understand them. Then leave. It's as simple as that.'

One day he would not treat her as a child, but for the time being she shrugged it off. He was a man clearly used to getting his way and he was dangerous. Of that Charlotte was absolutely sure. She wouldn't give him any reason to cause her or those she cared about harm.

'One other thing,' she said. 'What do I call you?'

He didn't hesitate for a second. 'You may call me Hermes.'

The symbolism wasn't lost on her; Hermes was the messenger of the Greek pantheon. She wasn't sure about the mission, but what choice did she have? Manipulating the Swedish government didn't sit well with her, as it was almost like her own government. But then what was going to happen would surely happen with or without her help. This way, at least, she was making herself useful

144

and in Germany being useful was important. Better to be useful as a spy than forced to be useful as a wife and mother.

'I want something in return.'

'I don't think you're in a position to make demands of me.' A faint smile played around his lips. It was the first time she had seen anything approaching what she would call humour from him. 'Besides that, what about serving the great German nation?'

She leant closer, wanting to mark the seriousness of her words.

'I will be risking my life for the German nation,' she said, her voice low. 'Should I not ask for something in return?'

'It's not quite as severe as all that. You're delivering some letters, not performing an assassination.'

'Even still. I want you to provide me with some information on a woman called Greta. She was a student at the university as well.'

She handed him a piece of paper with every bit of information she knew about Greta written on it.

'Don't you realise? This is a test of your suitability. If you fail in this task then you're done. And you're already setting a bad standard by asking me for something in return. Don't forget who you are and what you owe to the Reich. The Reich owes you nothing in return.' Then he saw the look on her face. She was trying her best to be stern. 'Very well, I will see what can be done.'

With that he was finished. He picked up his newspaper, tapping it once on the table, then left the café without a further word. It was almost as if the pleasantries from the early conversation were what he thought was expected of him and now their business was done he no longer needed to be polite.

She sat for a while longer yet. There was no reason for her to go home and she still had tea left in the pot. It was only just warm and going bitter, but even still she relished the taste. It was like a reminder of what she had and to treasure the opportunity.

A while later the waitress came by her table again to ask if Charlotte wanted anything else. Her cup was still half full of cold peppermint tea. She shook her head in reply and went back to her thoughts. What had her life become? Things were only going to get more complicated before they got better. If they were ever going to get better. She had no idea what was in store for her, but she would stand up and do what she had to do to survive. That was the only way in this world.

She picked up her violin case and made her way out of the café. She was due at a rehearsal. At least she had music to calm her soul.

Chapter Eighteen

Sunday, 2 June 1940

Sailing in through the archipelago to Stockholm was always beautiful – it didn't matter what the weather was like, whether rain or shine. The scattered islands with the red-painted huts, the way the greenery went down to the water's edge, which shimmered and shifted with the currents – it was a spectacular sight and Charlotte always made sure she was on deck to see it when the boat came into Stockholm. Even though it was still winter, there was a low, warm sun that gave the landscape an ethereal aspect. She could have taken her coat off and still felt warm enough, and the water below her almost glowed.

It was getting off the ship that was always the worst. She hated the change in movement as the moored ship shifted against the current and buffeted against the mooring. Her gloved hand clung onto the rail as she stepped down the gangway. She could feel how impatient the other passengers behind her were, but the Swedish were too polite to make her any more aware of it than that. They wouldn't even stand within a metre of her if they didn't have to.

As soon as her feet touched land she felt better, but it was as if she had come to a stop. The ground pushed back against her and she nearly stumbled. It would take her a day to get her land legs back, and she had lost count of how many times she had almost been sick at the sensation. From there she walked into the town, taking it all in with every footstep.

A dark green Volvo PV53 rattled past on the road. It had a trailer behind it with some kind of machinery that blew out noxious fumes. The smell was like an intense wood burner and Charlotte almost chocked on the smoke. There were a few other cars dotted around, some parked up by the pavement, but nowhere near as many as in Hamburg. One of the Nazis' crowning achievements was bringing the automobile to the greater German public, or at least that was what they said. In truth the Swedish preferred to use other means of transport in the city, such as the tram, and the ferries that took them from island to island.

She stopped and looked out over the water, leaning on the stone wall. The light reflected off the water, giving everything a blue hue. She could see Gamla Stan, the old town, and the Gothic spire of the red-brick Riddarholmen church beyond. She reminded herself she was here to do a job, not sightsee, but it was far too tempting to stare out at the beauty of the city and reflect. If the Germans came here then there was no doubt they would change it, add their stamp as they had done in Hamburg and other cities.

But there was something else she needed to do in Stockholm before she did the Nazis' work. She would deliver those damned letters when she had visited her mother. An extra hour or two would not change things. They could wait. What family she had left were more important than anything and she was doing it all for them.

Charlotte thought about knocking, but it felt so formal, and her key still worked in the lock. So she stepped right into her mother's home, the home she had inherited from her family. She supposed it was her home too. At least that's what her mother would have said. Charlotte found her in the living room dusting some bookshelves. She was always determined to do as much of her own housework as she could. She turned at the sound of Charlotte's footsteps and the duster fell from her hand.

'Mamma.' Charlotte pulled her mother into a hug, not allowing the shock to set in. She rested her chin on her mother's head. 'It's so good to see you.'

Only a few minutes later they were reclining in the armchairs drinking Löfbergs coffee with condensed milk. It was a tradition of theirs and as usual her mother didn't hesitate to get to the point.

'We worry about you,' she said, after a sip of coffee. 'Germany is becoming less safe.'

They had had this argument too many times for Charlotte to remember and she knew that she would never convince her mother. But she was an adult, she had to make her own decisions, and she couldn't just run away from her responsibilities. She wondered who the 'we' was, but didn't ask.

'It's my home, Mamma. My life is there. My friends are there.'

'You can have a life here. We have universities too. Some good ones, especially Uppsala, and music too.'

'Mamma, please. Let's not argue. I have to go back. I learnt my music from Pappa, but you always taught me to never quit. Leaving Hamburg would be quitting. I can't do it.'

Her mother closed her mouth in a thin line. She knew better than to disagree with her daughter when she had made up her mind. They were the same in that regard. Stubborn, unflinching. It was their strength and often their weakness. But this time, Charlotte hoped it wasn't a weakness. If she was wrong then the consequences would be fatal, not just for her, but for everyone she knew. The conversation fell silent as they drank their coffee.

'Your father would be very proud, you know? He loved his country just as much as you do. He would have stayed and fought for it too.'

A tear rolled down her cheek and she wiped it away with a handkerchief. Charlotte had no idea how her father would feel if he were alive to know the real reason she was visiting Stockholm. But she couldn't tell her mother that.

'I just wish it hadn't happened. I miss Pappa.'

Her mother crossed the room and took her into an embrace again, as she would have done when Charlotte was a child. It felt good to be comforted by her like that and it made her realise how much she had missed her mother. She wished she could confide in her more, but this would have to do.

'I miss you both so much. Even though my family is here, it hurts me that you are not.'

'It's not so far away,' Charlotte said, her voice muffled through clothing.

'Far enough.' Her mother stood up and took Charlotte's cup. 'More coffee?'

A clock tolled on the mantelpiece and Charlotte was suddenly aware of the time. 'I really must be going, Mamma. I'm sorry.'

'Aren't you staying? I thought you would be with us for a few days at least.'

'Overnight, yes. But there's something I must do before this evening.'

She stood too, towering over her mother. She wished her mum would take her in her arms again, but it would only slow things down.

'Please, won't you stay a while longer?'

'I'm sorry. I have to get back. My studies ... I have work to do.'

It hurt her to say it. She wanted more than anything to be able to stay with her mother. But she couldn't. Charlotte had responsibilities back in Hamburg. She thought about asking her mamma to go with her, but she couldn't do that to her. Her mamma was safer here, away from the war.

She thought of the brown paper bundle she had hidden in her rucksack. It needed to be delivered and the longer she waited the more difficult it would be to do. She didn't know why she had hidden it so well in her bag. It had been easy to get it over the

150

border – the border guards didn't care about that sort of thing – but she had still felt uneasy. And now, now she couldn't tell her mamma anything about it, but she had to make her excuses all the same. Find an excuse to leave the house.

Charlotte was in the hallway when the door opened again. She flinched, and she didn't know whether her mother noticed. She had become too used to living in fear, not knowing who was going to be arriving. A tall man with ear-length curly brown hair entered, shutting the door gently behind him. He had the build of a wrestler and his arms were twice the size of her thighs. She would have been terrified to see him had she not known exactly who he was.

'Åke, what are you doing here?'

'Cuz? I didn't know you were back. Your mum didn't tell me.' He wrapped her in a big embrace without waiting to see if she wanted to be hugged. He smelt of wood and cinnamon. A familiar smell that she breathed in, reminding her of her childhood. Åke was always friendly. The family always joked he should have been called Björn as he was like a big bear. He towered over them all and always had a grin for anyone he met. 'I came to see your mother. I've been doing some work for her.'

He had that singsong Swedish voice that she had missed so much.

'I was just leaving.'

'Oh no, cuz. You don't have to leave on my account. We've barely had a chance to catch up.'

'I need to go and see someone. I'll be back later.' Åke shared a look with her mother that suggested the two of them were going to talk about her secretive nature when she was gone, but there was nothing Charlotte could do to prevent that. She knew they talked about her anyway, but they didn't know the half of it.

'Come on, I'm sure your mamma has some cinnamon buns in the kitchen we can take with us. She's always baking something. Maybe biscuits.'

One thing she remembered about Åke was that he was always hungry. It was strange here where there was no war and everyone carried on with their lives as normal. Everyone looked at her as if she was in mourning. She could see the questions on their lips, but none of them dared ask what it was like. She wasn't sure she could answer if they did.

'You can't leave yet. You have to come to church with us.'

Her mother didn't even look at her to see whether she agreed. She put on her coat and headed to the door. It was as if she had just thought of it, but when her mother spoke like that there was no room for debate. It was just the way things were and if you didn't agree then you had better change your ideas quickly. Charlotte had to deliver the letters, but if she went to church with her family and then left immediately afterwards then she should still have time. But it would be pushing it.

'Mamma, please. You don't need me to go with you. You prefer to go on your own, see your friends. I'll just get in the way.'

'Nonsense.' Her mother continued stacking plates on one side of the kitchen as if she was making some kind of sculpture. She would return to them after church or have someone do it for her. But Charlotte knew her mother liked to have something to do around the house, to do things for herself. She had always rebelled against Pappa's insistence that they have staff for that sort of thing.

'My friends would love to see you. It's been too long. You're a grown woman now and some of them haven't seen you since you were a *barn*.'

'Come on, Cuz.' Åke beamed down at her. That was just what she needed, them teaming up on her. 'It would be nice to spend some more time with you. You've not been here long and already you want to go away?'

'It's just that . . . I don't really go to church anymore. I would love to spend more time with you all, and I promise I will come back soon. But I'm not sure church is the best place for it.'

She wasn't sure whether declaring she didn't want to go to church and be a parishioner would have the effect it would have on some families, but she held her breath waiting for their response.

'Don't you have churches in Germany anymore?' Åke's grin suggested he was teasing her, but her mother stayed suspiciously silent. Charlotte knew her mother went to church more for the social side than the religious side of things, but there was something else there she would have to investigate another time.

'Well, no. It's not really that,' she responded, meeting Åke's gaze. 'The government don't talk about the Old Testament obviously, and everyone around the university tends to be more secular. We're not atheist, but church isn't really something we do anymore. People are allowed their beliefs, but we tend to spend our time doing other things.'

She realised they were both staring at her. Neither had a university education and it occurred to her that she was speaking about a world that must seem so very different to theirs.

'Come for me?' her mother asked. 'I haven't spent quality time with you in years.'

How could she refuse? Charlotte should have known she would not win this situation, but still she had tried. Looking at her mother and noticing how age had changed her, she couldn't help but feel that it was a characteristic her mother had instilled in her daughter. She followed them out of the door. She should never have come. She should have done her job and got out, heading back to Hamburg before she could be drawn into family things.

She followed them all the way to the local church in silence. They led her down the aisle and to a row in the middle of the church. She had a vision of her father by her side, but she shook it away.

'See. We even have Germans here.' Åke nodded towards the back of the church and Charlotte followed his gaze. 'I told you it would be fine.'

She didn't dare remind him that she was technically German.

The German soldiers in uniform were working their way along the rearmost pew, one clutching a prayer pamphlet and the other with his cap in hand. They nodded and greeted those around them. They still had pistols clipped at their waists; not even church was safe from guns. Charlotte tensed and shot around to face the front again. She knew she should feel indifferent about their presence, even warmed by it, but something about them sitting behind her, watching her, made her uneasy. They could have no possible way of knowing why she was in the city, yet still she felt as if they were here for her, watching her and checking on her. They must have been stationed at the German Legation in the city, but she could not go to them for help, even if they were on the same side.

As they sat, Åke spoke again. 'Do you still have your father's gun I had repaired for you?'

She had asked him never to mention it again, but she should have known he wouldn't be able to help himself.

'Yes. I carry it everywhere.'

'Good. I've a feeling you may need it in Germany these days.'

'What the hell is this?' The man's face turned red and spittle flew from his mouth as he spoke. 'You dare bring *this* into my house?'

Charlotte tried to keep her face impassive. She was, after all, only the messenger. She had no idea what was contained within that envelope, but it had obviously had its desired effect. It was later in the evening than she had wanted once she had managed to get away from Åke and her mother, and she was getting tired. She would have to speed things along.

'I'm just the messenger,' she said. 'You know what to do.'

'I think you had better leave. And if you come by here again, I will call the police. Go on. Go!'

Charlotte didn't protest. She hadn't been prepared for such an extreme response and as far as she was concerned she had done what had been asked of her. It wasn't her job to deal with the result of the letters, only to deliver them, but yet she still didn't feel comfortable. Her heart fluttered in her chest and she had to sloe her eyes to control her breathing.

'*Vi ses*,' she said, as the door shut behind her. *See you.*

A car drove slowly along the road as she made her way to the next address on the note. She wasn't sure if they were watching her, but it was late and there was no reason to drive quickly in Stockholm.

The next man had stared at her chest from the moment he had opened the door. He hadn't even made any pretence of shifting his gaze to her face, not when he was talking to her, not even when he was leading her through the hallway to a room that he described as somewhere 'more comfortable'.

'How can I help you?' he asked after he had led her to sit down on one of the suite of sofas. There was a slight slur to his voice, but she wasn't sure whether it was the effect of alcohol or his age. She had pointedly avoided getting close enough to smell his breath.

She ignored his question. It wasn't his help she was here for, and there was no way she was giving him an opening for what he wanted. Instead, she opened her handbag, took out the letter with his name on and handed it to him. For the first time he took his eyes off her chest and glanced down at the letter. It was only for a moment before her looked up again.

'Now, now. If you're some kind of illegitimate daughter then I think some kind of warning would have been appropriate.' His smile was sickly and the fact he was still sizing her up despite wondering whether she was related to him made her sick. She longed to run away from that room as quickly as possible, but she had a job to do.

His eyes scanned the letter, then he jumped up from his seat, this time looking her directly in the eyes. 'Get out!' he said, waving the letter at her as if it would somehow fend her off.

He reacted in the same way as all the others, but she had got her wish to get out of there as soon as possible. She almost ran her way back to the front door, pursued by the staff. She wrenched the door open herself and once she had put a couple of street corners between them finally allowed the tears to flow. A car rolled past her again. Was it the same one? She couldn't be sure. She put her head in her hands and let the sobs come.

What did it matter if anyone saw her? Her father would not be proud of what she was doing. He always wanted her to be a musician and would not have liked her working for a government agency, even one who was supposed to be helping Germany end the war. He wasn't around to ask, but she knew he would have been frustrated just as when she had joined the League of German Girls. He never openly said he disliked the Nazis, but she knew he would not have been proud of her associating with them. She wasn't proud of what she was doing either, but it was too late now. This was who she had become and she would see it through to the end to protect her family and friends.

Wednesday, 9 November 1938

Glass smashed, cascading across the floor, and Charlotte ducked behind a shelf. Kurt wasn't far behind, rushing to her side to check she was unhurt. The sound of shouting followed after them.

Kurt had just kissed her, although she wasn't entirely sure he had meant to. He had leant across her to get a book from the bookshelf and when they both turned, his lips had brushed hers. They broke apart quickly, but it had still made her smile. She had teased him about it, then displaying rare confidence he had gone in for a proper kiss. Only, the second time, their teeth knocked against each other and she couldn't help but laugh.

She could still see how red his cheeks were and how forlorn he looked, thinking that he had done it all wrong. To make it up to him she ran her hand around the nape of his neck and pulled his head closer to hers. On the third attempt their lips pressed lightly together and she lingered for a few seconds, almost tingling with the electricity of the moment. But it had not lasted long enough for her liking, or for Kurt given the look on his face.

They had been disturbed by a commotion outside. Voices shouted over each other and it sounded as if they were coming closer. The bookshop was in a quiet street and it was unusual to hear much noise. Kurt frowned and then made for the door. That was when the glass window smashed inwards. Shards of glass crashed across the floor and a brick landed by their feet.

Her father had always told her to get home early and not stay out after dark, but she had been spending time with Kurt and was reluctant to cut it short. Pappa always worried about her when he had been alive, but she felt safe in the city, even when it was getting dark.

'What—?' Charlotte started, but the sound of the other window being broken drowned out the rest of her words. The men outside brandished weapons and shouted into the shop. Charlotte could only catch the word '*Juden*' through the destruction. She stared. She had never seen such anger manifest before. But it had been building for some time, even here far from Berlin and Munich.

'Charlotte.' Kurt pulled at the sleeve of her blouse. 'Charlotte, we need to go.'

The shopkeeper had disappeared through the back. There must have been another way out of the shop and Charlotte didn't hesitate to follow. Kurt ran with her as they passed the counter and through an apartment at the back of the shop. She was glad he hadn't left her, but she had put him in danger by lingering too long. The sound of crashing glass and the crunch of boot steps followed them.

A wooden door slammed back against its frame and Charlotte pushed it open again. The alley at the back of the shop was narrow and, more importantly, quieter. A shadow disappeared at one end. The shopkeeper. By Charlotte's reckoning he was running away from the direction she and Kurt needed to go, but did he know something they didn't? He had reacted far quicker than she and Kurt had. Perhaps he had been expecting the attack.

Kurt grabbed her sleeve again. This time he didn't stop to get her attention. 'Come on,' he shouted over his shoulder as he ran the other way down the alley.

That was it then – they were going that way, and as far as they knew they could be heading in the direction of trouble.

'I have to go. What if they're attacking my parents' business? Who knows what's caught up in this?' He visibly shook as he spoke and Charlotte wanted to pull him into a hug, but she knew better than that.

'Go. I'll be fine here. Go and see that your parents are all right.'

He hesitated and then kissed her on the lips. It was still unexpected, but she didn't think she ever wanted to get used to it. The tingling was a welcome sensation and she knew now that she would anticipate the next time.

'Go!' She all but pushed him out of the door.

Charlotte ran away from the shop. She should have followed Kurt, but it made more sense for her to return to her apartment. There, she could hide away from the chaos. The sound of glass breaking carried over the wind, but she wasn't sure if it was just her mind replaying what she had seen before. Still, she didn't slow her pace. She could also hear a rumble of voices of a crowd that reminded her of the victory parade in 1933.

When she turned the corner she could see why. The Bornplatz Synagogue was surrounded by people. Many of them were holding flaming brands and torches. They shouted their anger at the Jews and the volume of it carried easily over the flames, engulfing the stone building. Fire erupted from the round stained-glass window at the centre of the nearest tower, and Charlotte ducked. The intensity of the heat made her break out in a sweat, even though she was standing metres away.

No one was facing her, too intent on their destruction of the synagogue, but even still she couldn't help but cower. Her heart thumped like the beat of marching feet. If they turned and saw her not taking part then their anger may be directed at her. But she was saved by a Jew pushing through the crowd. He was shouting at them to stop, but they only laughed and jostled him away.

'The torah,' he cried, as he ran towards the now empty doorways. How Charlotte could hear him over the din, she had no idea. It was as if the crowd had quietened, hanging on his words. She reached out for him, knowing with grim certainty what he was about to do. But as soon as she moved, he was lost in the red glow of the flames. She gasped, unable to control herself. He had sacrificed himself to save their holy book. How could anyone endure that heat? She hadn't even seen the man's face. The crowd seemed undeterred, and Charlotte didn't have much time. She ran again, trying to put as much distance between herself and the flames as possible. The cries, the screaming, and the anger followed her all the way home to her own apartment.

'You think a block leader would be a Jew? Are you an idiot?' Kemper shouted.

The man pushed the door into Kemper's face, but the block leader stood firm.

'I'm a party member, you moron! Let me show you my membership.'

Charlotte had only just re-entered the apartment building and the concierge had ushered her in. Then it had happened, the brownshirts had knocked on the door. She wished that Kemper wouldn't keep calling the man an idiot. Surely it wasn't making things any better. Why wouldn't the men just go away?

As Kemper reached for his wallet, the door flung open and more men stormed in. The front window smashed in a shimmer of glass. She ducked away, but not before a sliver caught her on the arm. If not for her coat it would have cut deep. She had been lucky; there was only a tear through the cloth and her arm was unscathed. But it might not stay that way for long. The men were pushing their way into the building. They were wearing brownshirts, but each of their faces was red, like the armbands they wore. They might have been thugs, but they made no secret of where their allegiances lay. One of them kicked Kemper in the knee with the steel of his boot and the block leader went down. He crawled back up onto his other knee and swung a punch that caught one of the men in the leg. But it wasn't enough.

160

They kicked him again, until he was a ball on the floor, trying to protect his head with his arms.

All the time Charlotte watched on. She wanted to call out, to tell them to stop, but the sound caught in her throat. The brownshirts were angry, but it was better they were angry with someone else. She didn't think she could defend herself from them, even as Kemper was attempting to. She was not as well built as him, not as strong. She'd like to think they wouldn't attack a woman, but seeing their rage she wasn't so certain. It seemed as if everything in the city was a fair target.

She should run, but where would she go? Instead she cowered behind the stairwell, hoping the beating would stop soon. She willed the brownshirts to get bored and go away, but they kept kicking Kemper. There was no way he could fight back now. If she had not been frozen in place, she would have screamed.

Flecks of blood splattered across the beige floor tiles. One of the brownshirts noticed her as he straightened to deliver another kick. She sunk back further behind the stairwell, but he smiled at her.

'Come here, *Mädchen*. Take a better look at what happens to those who harbour dirty *Juden*.'

He beckoned to her and his grin widened, but she stayed where she was. What did he mean? Had Kemper been hiding Jews from the authorities? Why would he do such a thing when he was a party member? It didn't make any sense.

The men stopped their beating and looked at her. Their faces were red from the exertion. They resembled devils.

'Too bad,' he said as she stood still, before he returned to his mates.

She didn't know what quirk of fate meant they had left her alone, but she ran up the stairs to her own apartment without looking back. Someone else would have to help Kemper. There was nothing she could do.

For once the door opened easily and she pushed it closed behind her, checking the locks twice. The sounds of the chaos

161

on the streets followed her up the stairs, but she was safe behind the door. For now. She hoped the brownshirts were too busy to follow her to her flat.

Hilda was in the living room, putting items in a wooden box sitting on the sofa. She was working so fast that she dropped an item, which bounced off the edge of the sofa and landed on the floor. She retreated from the box like a trapped animal. Charlotte wouldn't have been surprised if Hilda had hissed at her, but instead she looked between Charlotte and the box.

Charlotte leant down and picked up the brown item. It was a leather-bound book. 'What's this?' she asked, opening the cover. It was a copy of the Old Testament. The Torah in German.

'You weren't supposed to see that.' Hilda was surprisingly calm, given the circumstances. It was as if she had given in already.

Charlotte didn't know what to do. She knew what she should do, what many others would do, but she couldn't turn her friend over to the authorities. Yet she had seen what the brownshirts had done to Kemper. Instinctively she looked at the door. She was sure it was locked, but what if they knew about Hilda? Charlotte hadn't known. But it didn't matter that she didn't really know her at all. Not now. Charlotte would hear Hilda out. There had to be an explanation. She handed the book back to Hilda who hesitated before taking it. A breeze blew through the apartment, bringing the sound of glass smashing somewhere nearby. Both of them flinched and Charlotte's heart thumped louder.

'Please, let me explain,' Hilda said.

This close to her room-mate, Charlotte could see the reds in her eyes. She had been crying.

Charlotte couldn't speak so she let Hilda continue. So many thoughts rushed through her head, mixed with the fear of what might happen to her and Hilda should anyone find them.

'My grandmother was Jewish. Although she converted to Christianity when she married my grandfather.' Hilda gestured to the suitcase. 'These are her belongings. I'm getting rid of them.'

'Why?' Charlotte asked. The first question she could form through the shock and the mental image of the brownshirts warring in her brain.

'Why? Because it's dangerous to keep them. I've held on to them too long and if anyone finds them then I'll be sent to the camps too.'

Charlotte shook her head and turned on Hilda. She couldn't bear to look at her. 'No. Why didn't you tell me?'

There was silence for a minute before Hilda replied. Charlotte could hear her rapid breathing. 'How could I tell you or anyone else? I couldn't trust anyone with this. And now you know, you'll be duty-bound to report me.' Her voice cracked at those last words and Charlotte felt a lump in her throat.

'You should have told me,' she said. 'You could have trusted me.'

'How could I trust anyone when you all hate us, blame us for everything that's wrong with Germany?'

'But you're not like the others. You're different.'

Hilda scoffed and shook her head.

'What does that even mean? Of course I'm different. For the last few years of my life I have been living in constant fear, hiding my background and who I am, because we're all different. Not even the Nazis are all the same, no matter how hard they try to fit into their Aryan ideal.'

Hilda's words conflicted with her thoughts. Everything she had been taught told her that this was dangerous. Her father had always told her to be kind to everyone, and to look out for those less fortunate. But then she had been told the Jews were liars, making everything about them and trying to trick you out of whatever you held dear. Hilda couldn't be like that; she couldn't. Hilda was her friend; she knew her. But still Charlotte couldn't shake the doubt.

'What happens now? What are you going to do?'

'That depends on you. I've been living like this for years now. I'm not sure I know how to live any other way, but if you don't feel like you can trust me . . .'

'Of course I trust you.' The words came a little too quick and a frown crossed Hilda's brow. Those deep green eyes gave Charlotte a look that was both questioning and as if Hilda was looking deep into Charlotte's soul to find the lie.

'I promise you, Hilda, I will never turn you in. And I will do what I can to protect you. You're safe with me.'

Charlotte helped her to store the last few items in the box. Hilda said nothing of it, but Charlotte could feel her friend's tension ease beside her as they worked, even in spite of the sounds from outside.

'Don't throw this away,' she said. 'Put it somewhere safe.'

Hilda nodded and disappeared into her room with the box. Charlotte entered her own room and moved a silver photo frame containing a picture of her and her parents and took down a wooden box. The lid lifted back to reveal a red velvet interior. On it lay her father's Luger from the war. She picked it up between tentative fingers, like a piece of fluff from the floor, and then she placed it in her handbag.

After that, Hilda and Charlotte did not talk of that night again. They carried on as if life in Germany was normal. Charlotte eventually fell asleep, when the sound died away to glowing embers and exhaustion took over. Ever since, she had carried that gun.

Chapter Nineteen

Thursday, 6 June 1940

Her shoulders were sore, as if there was some great weight on them. She lifted them up towards her ears, which gave some respite, but after a few seconds the ache returned. It was as if she had been carrying a large rucksack for days and her shoulders were protesting against the weight.

There was a knock at the door. From the sound she knew exactly who it was. She glanced at the letters on the worktop. She should never have taken them out of her bag in the first place, and while it wasn't the Abwehr at her door, she couldn't let anyone see them. There were questions that she didn't want to answer. She would have to find a way to dispose of the last couple of letters she had failed to deliver. She couldn't keep them on her for too long otherwise it would become even more dangerous. If Kurt or one of her friends found them then they would have questions she wasn't sure she could answer, and if the Abwehr found them then they would know she had only completed half of her mission.

'Just a minute,' she shouted, as she grabbed the letters. She crumpled them in her hands as she ran to the bathroom. She hoped it would be enough as she threw them into the toilet bowl. The water had to be processed and then drained into the sea. If not, she daren't think what might happen. She flushed the toilet and waited to make sure the crumpled mess of paper had disappeared before she went to the door.

When she opened it, Kurt walked straight in, excitement clear on his face. He put his hands on her arms and gave her a kiss on the cheek before he took his coat off and hung it up.

'Sorry, I needed the toilet,' she said, hoping the apology was enough. He didn't seem to notice.

'I'm just passing,' he said. 'But I've found the perfect house for us. It's a little out of our price range, but I think we can stretch with help.'

'Oh?' Charlotte had completely forgotten that they had discussed buying a house. Thoughts of settling down to a life together seemed so far away with everything that was going on. She looked to the bathroom, willing the letters to be completely gone.

Kurt saw her expression and his shoulders dropped.

'You forgot. What's wrong?' he asked. 'I thought you would be excited.'

'I'm sorry, I just have a lot on my mind. It sounds exciting, but you haven't told me anything yet.' She gestured to the sofa. 'Come. Join me, and tell me about the house.'

'It doesn't matter now. What's on your mind? Can I help?'

That was typical Kurt. He would drop whatever he was thinking about to check on her. But sometimes she wished he would stand up for himself and put himself first. She was worried he would one day put the party before himself and who knew what would happen then?

'It's nothing really.' She sat. 'I'm just a bit overwhelmed with everything. The thought of a house. It's a lot.'

'I know, and it's all right.' He reached for her hand. 'Do you have any idea how much I love you?'

'It's not just that. You keep saying you love me. But there's more to loving someone than saying it. You have to show it too.'

166

'What can I do to show you?'

She shook her head. 'I don't know. It's not that simple. You're not really listening to me.'

He dropped into the chair and let out a sigh. A coffee cup wobbled as he accidentally kicked the table.

'I'm trying to listen. We've known each other since we were children. Even our parents said we were inseparable. The next logical step in our relationship is marriage. Don't you think? I don't see where else we go from here.'

'That's not enough. I want to get my degree.'

He closed his eyes and rocked his head back. 'You mean I'm not enough.' His voice was a whisper. Resigned.

'No.' It sounded like she was shouting in the stillness of the flat. 'No, that's not what I mean at all. But just because we have been together for most of our lives, it doesn't mean we have to get married.'

His eyes were open again, scanning her face as if he was trying to analyse her words by her expression. 'But there is something holding you back. You say it's not true, but it feels like I'm not enough. If I was, perhaps if I was a wealthy man with greater prospects, you would not hesitate to marry me.'

It was her turn to close her eyes. She rubbed her brow to stop the tension building there. She didn't understand how he could say these things. Did he not know her better than that?

'You are a wealthy man, Kurt. You stand to inherent more money than I could ever wish for. And as for your prospects. Well, they're only held back by this damned war. Once it's over, you will be able to do whatever you want, study, work, whatever you put your mind to.'

'I suppose, but still that's not enough. I don't understand.'

'Because none of those things matter to me. I wouldn't care if you were poor. If you had no opportunities. Can't you see that? None of your background matters to me. It's not what drives me.'

'Then you simply don't love me.' He nodded as if it was the

most rational explanation in the world. As if she wasn't raging internally at how much he was wilfully misunderstanding her. 'That's why you won't join the party and marry me.'

'Ugh!' She jumped up from the chair, and he made to follow, but she shook her head. 'I'm going to the toilet. I can't hear any more of this.'

He followed her, but kept a respectful distance.

'If you must know, Kurt, you being an actual member of the party makes me want to marry you even less!' She knew there were plenty of people who agreed with the party, but not all of them were card-carrying members. To be a member meant that you truly believed and supported everything that the Nazis did. The party would want her to become a member too and Charlotte wasn't sure she could agree to that.

He pursed his lips. He knew that whatever he said would only make things worse, and yet she could see his need to say something, anything. She knew he was a good man at heart and she wasn't deliberately trying to hurt him, but he had been pushing the issue of marriage too much and she had heard enough. She loved him dearly, but now was not the time for such concerns.

'I'm just trying to keep you safe,' he said, eventually. 'Those who aren't members of the party come under greater scrutiny. Especially students and those with links to undesirables.'

'And that's the only reason you want to marry me?' The irony that she had flipped the conversation round on him was not lost on her.

'I want to marry you because I love you and can't imagine a life without you. I want to marry you because it's the only way I know how to give you everything I can in this world. That's all I want. To support you.'

'I don't need you to support me. I just need my own space.'

He nodded as if he was weighing up her words. 'I understand. I came in here talking about houses and everything else and it was too much. I'll give you some time.'

168

He stroked her arm gently as he passed, but said no more as he opened the door, then closed it again behind him.

She returned to the living room, then slammed the coffee cup down on the table and watched as it wobbled around. She almost picked it up again to make sure it didn't break. Then thought, let it fall, damn it. The shattering china would be a perfect metaphor for her mood.

Why did he have to be so annoying? It wasn't that he was being inconsiderate. She knew that he cared for her, but at times it seemed like all he cared about was making her his wife. At times she wanted to shake him. Shake him so hard that all the stupid thoughts, all the selfishness would drop out of him and he would return to the innocent, apprehensive boy she had once known and fallen in love with. He was no longer that Kurt and there was a part of her that sunk every time she was reminded of that fact.

He wasn't doing it on purpose, but even still she couldn't see his point of view. No matter how hard she tried.

She sunk back into the chair and closed her eyes. The groove accepted her like an old friend and it was like a warm embrace. She could sit there for hours feeling comforted, but still her mind raced. She wrenched open her eyes again, looking for some kind of distraction. She didn't want to think about Kurt. She knew that once she had a chance to sleep she would forgive him for not letting it drop. He didn't mean to emotionally manipulate her. Neither of them did. They would make up again and everything would be all right.

Her bow slipped off the string again, giving a screeching sound and she closed her eyes in frustration. She couldn't get her first mission for the Abwehr out of her head. It had felt like a failure. After she had seen a few of the Swedish politicians the others had refused to allow her entry. Word had travelled fast, but she hoped that it wouldn't get back to the Abwehr. What would they do if they discovered she had disposed of the letters? Would they think

169

she had failed, stop her training, and then she would lose her chance to find out what had happened to Greta? She couldn't get the faces of the gentlemen out of her mind's eye. Their disgust at her. She had returned to music to try and take her mind off it, before they asked her to do something equally distasteful, or worse. In truth, that was why she hadn't delivered the other letters or told the Abwehr; she couldn't do all the Nazis' work for them. She had to draw the line somewhere.

The piece of music Ernst had shown her was tricky, but she was sure with enough practice she would get it right. It would help if she could find the sheet music for it, but for now she would keep going through the patterns he had shown her at their last rehearsal. When she opened her eyes again an old man was sweeping the floor by the door. His silhouette almost made her jump.

His silver hair was thinning and cut close in a way that was similar to a military cut. He was old enough to have fought in the last war, and there was a lost look in his eyes every time he glanced towards her. He didn't ask her why she was still there so late, but his manner suggested he was thinking it. He kept brushing closer and closer to where she was sitting, with a glance at her each time he filled a pan with dust. She couldn't help but feel in the way and she wasn't even sure there was any more dust on the floor.

'Sometimes you can practise too much.'

At first she wasn't sure he had spoken, but then his quiet, gruff words filtered through her perception. When he realised she had heard him, his lips cracked open in a faint smile to reveal yellowed teeth.

'Take this floor, for example. No matter how much I sweep it, it's not going to get any cleaner.'

She couldn't suppress her laugh, and even though his lips formed a line she could see the amusement in his eyes. They were brighter than before and the faraway look had gone.

170

'You're right. I just can't seem to get this section right. And the more I play the more mistakes I make.'

'That happens,' he said, setting his broom against the wall and regarding her violin. 'You also need to change those strings. The dullness will only contribute to your feeling of not getting it right.'

She plucked at one string with a finger and heard the clang it made. She hadn't realised how old they were.

'How could you possibly kn—?'

'I was once the premier violinist in München.' There was a glint in his eye as he spoke and she had no idea whether he was telling the truth or making a joke. He was an enigma. 'I performed with all the greats. But life moves on. You might say I practised too much. Forgot to practise what was truly important, and came to the attention of people who wanted me to fail.'

'What happened?' she breathed.

'I said "you might say that", but who really knows what the truth is? Many things get forgotten in the sands of time. Songs we have performed, the people we love.'

'I don't understand.'

'No? Perhaps that's the problem. Why are you here?' When she made to open her mouth he interrupted her. 'You don't know why you are here. You're hiding from something. I know that look all too well. I've seen it on thousands of faces across this country and others, on battlefields and in trenches. Playing the violin may soothe your soul temporarily, but it will not solve your problems. Neither will hiding in a university storage room. I should be enough deterrent for that.'

She sighed and placed the violin back into its open case.

'If you wanted me to leave, you might just have said.'

He laughed then, for the first time. It was like the bark of a single rifle shot. 'And miss the opportunity to give my very own lecture? I don't think so. This was much more fun.'

She shook her head and couldn't help but feel the smile come across her face. She laid the bow across her lap and regarded him.

171

'How have I never met you before?'

'I'm not sure that's a question I can answer. I have been here for years. It's not my fault you have never noticed me before.'

'I'm sorry, I—'

'That's too bad,' he interrupted her. 'You've had your mind on other things ever since you came here. There's no reason why you should notice an ageing, scruffy caretaker. Why would you? I am so far beneath you students you don't even recognise me.'

'It's not that, I assure you.' She didn't know why she was defending herself. He was right, and by the faint smile that had returned to his lips she could tell that he wasn't insulted by it. But for some reason she wanted this old man she had only just met to think better of her.

'I can count on my fingers the number of students I've had conversations with in the years that I've worked here.'

He held up his hands and for the first time she noticed he was missing his little finger and half of the next finger on his left hand.

'But you should know, I was a student once too. And I ended up here, back at a university, sweeping up after you all. There's a lot you could learn from me.'

'I'm sure. We all lead strange lives, and now the war makes things more complicated.'

'Soon it will just be me and you female students. I'll have to teach all the classes as all the men will be at the front. And I'm far too old for that. They don't want me, and I saw enough of that in the last war so I'm thankful. They can keep their uniforms and their guns. There's more to life than that.

'And if the party have anything to say about it you young women shouldn't even be here. You should be at home making good German babies.'

He was being incredibly open for someone she had just met. How did he know that she wouldn't go straight to the Gestapo and report him? She decided to repay his trust.

'I don't want to do that.'

172

'No. I'm sure you don't. But I do agree with them that you shouldn't be here. It's far too late.'

'I like the evenings here. There's a charm to the building. It's cosy.'

He frowned at her, all trace of the smile gone. Looking at him now she couldn't imagine him ever smiling. He reminded her of her grandfather, but he had died when she was little. All she remembered of him was his face, pulled into a frown of disappointment. According to her father, his father was perpetually grumpy.

'You're a terrible liar.'

She really hoped that wasn't true, but somehow this old man could see right through her. It must have been his years of experience around the university, but there was something uncanny about him that she couldn't quite put her finger on.

'I'm not—'

'Come on now. You've got a life to lead, before this war gets in the way of that.'

She stood, collected her belongings, and reached out to shake his hand. 'Thank you,' she said.

'That's the wrong salute,' he replied. 'You don't need to thank an old man for having an opinion. There's far too many of us for that, although not as many as there should have been.

'Say, what happened to the other violinist who used to practise in here? I haven't seen her in months.'

'She . . . died.' Charlotte didn't want to go into the grizzly details, but she felt she owed him some kind of explanation.

He simply nodded. They had got used to people dying, whether it was the bombing, being sent to the front, or through some other means. Death wasn't unfamiliar to the people of Germany. He didn't need to say it; she could tell he was thinking the same thing.

'Too bad. You look a lot like her, you know? Except for the colour of your hair. You could have been sisters.'

'Thank you.' Greta had been a beautiful woman, who in another life could quite easily have been a film star. 'I'd never considered it.'

Greta had been playing on her mind since Charlotte had found her and the guilt was strong, but it had not truly occurred to her how similar they were before now. They had shared a lot more than friendship. She had made a decision; she wouldn't let Greta just be another statistic in this war. She had asked for information, but she hadn't got it yet. Greta deserved justice and somehow, someway, Charlotte would get it for her.

Chapter Twenty

Sunday, 4 August 1940

Charlotte hadn't been in Greta's apartment since that terrible day she had found her friend's body. It had been almost a year, and she was unlikely to find anything new, but she hadn't had any time at all last time to get a look at what had happened. As soon as she had found Greta's body she had been discovered by the Kripo and she'd run. She still didn't know why she had run, it had only made things worse, and she had been looking over her shoulder ever since.

The street was dark, but then she was used to that. There was only a faint light from a cracked window on the ground floor and Charlotte was amazed that no one had reported the owner. But then it was unlikely anyone else was out during the blackout. It was not sensible for her to be here, but she couldn't resist the impulse.

The door to the apartment building was open and as far as Charlotte could tell there was no concierge. Even still, she took light steps through the hallway and to the stairs. She didn't want to explain what she was doing here, especially after last time. Thankfully, Greta's apartment was on the first floor and the stairs made no sound as she crept up them.

She looked back out onto the landing to make sure that she was alone. The apartment building was eerily quiet. Had the tenants moved on after Greta's death, or had they been thrown out by the Gestapo? She had heard a number of buildings were left derelict after their tenants were removed, but she couldn't imagine Greta living alongside those kinds of people. This was a respectable neighbourhood.

Charlotte tried the door. At first the handle only moved a couple of millimetres, accompanied by a scraping sound. But it was enough to suggest that it could be opened. Perhaps she could force it. She pulled her sleeve down and used it to provide friction against the brass handle. With a jerk the door clicked open and swung back a few centimetres on its hinges. She was surprised it was unlocked, but she suppressed any reaction. If it was unlocked that could mean someone else was in the apartment. As far as she knew, Greta had lived alone. Like Charlotte her family was not in Hamburg. Charlotte had no wish to be caught there again. She wasn't sure she could explain it away this time. Looking for some sheet music was not a good enough reason, but would the killer return to the scene of the crime? It was far too risky and they had no reason.

The police had finished their investigation before it had even started. Had the killer returned because they had been looking for something and had come to find it? The apartment had been too tidy to suggest that they were hunting for something amongst her belongings. There was only the shattered vase and the blood.

No, if there was anyone in the apartment they were from the police or the Gestapo, and she didn't want a run-in with either. But what choice did she have? She had been too busy and scared to visit Greta's apartment in the last few months, but she wanted to find the music. She also wanted to see if she could find any clues to why her friend had been killed.

She realised she had been lingering outside the door too long. If anyone was inside they might have heard the door open and the only thing for her to do now was to plunge in and take the consequences.

Reaching out, she pushed the door further open so she could fit through the gap. It squeaked as the hinges turned and she flinched at the unexpected sound. There was nothing for it now. Anyone inside would know she was there. She strode in like a model on a catwalk, hoping that a show of confidence would help her explain her presence. It was better than skulking around, and she wanted the door wide open in case she had to make a quick escape.

The living room was empty. There was no sound from the rest of the apartment, only the faint rustle of the breeze coming up the stairs and through the hallway. Surprisingly, Charlotte was alone. The apartment had been left, but it was not exactly as she remembered it. She took a further few steps into the apartment, wondering what it must have been like when Greta was living here. She could imagine it full of sound and laughter.

Charlotte knelt down. Someone had taken care to clean up the mess, scrubbing the blood from the floorboards and collecting the pieces of shattered vase. She ran a gloved hand along the floorboards. There was still a faint red tinge to the wood, but the rest of the apartment lay much as it had done then. It was as if it was a monument to her memory, preserved as it had been in her life. Except, there were a few subtle differences. Charlotte couldn't put her finger on them at first, but a sense at the nape of her neck told her that she wasn't the only one who had visited recently.

She would have liked Kurt to have come with her, but he wouldn't have understood. So far she hadn't told him anything about Greta's death, or her own run-in with the police. She would have to explain why she was here, and she wasn't one hundred per cent sure herself. If the police found her here she would be in trouble again, but she had to come and look. Didn't she? But what was it she was looking for? And who had been here before her? Had a member of Greta's family been looking for some personal belonging? If that was the case, why would they leave everything else as it was?

She found Greta's violin case, but it was empty. That was strange. Who would have taken the violin, but not the case? If someone had taken advantage of the empty flat they would have stolen a lot more. The violin was worth a few Reichsmarks, but the other contents of the flat would be worth something too. She reached around inside the violin case, and there was a slight bump at the bottom under the felt. She found a knife in the kitchen and ran it around the side of the case. It took a minute, but eventually the bottom lifted out. It was old and almost disintegrated in her hands. Inside were sheets of music score and some other documents that looked like birth certificates and other official papers. She grabbed them all and put them into her handbag. The case would draw too much attention, even if it was only sheet music. It felt more like theft than borrowing a few sheets of music.

She put everything else back where it was and made her way out onto the street. When she left the building there was an Opel car parked across the road. It hadn't been there before – she was sure of it. It was too dark to see if there was anyone inside, but she had the feeling she was being watched. Had the police put a guard on the building to see if the killer returned? Why would they when they thought it was suicide? She knew she was being paranoid, but she wanted to cross the road and peer inside.

It would be far too dangerous. Even if the car was empty she had spent too long near Greta's home. She would already have been spotted, but she hoped that no one who had seen her had any reason to question who she was and what she was doing there.

After only a brief pause, she turned right along the street in the direction of the U-Bahn station. The pavement was empty except for a couple on the other side of the road walking in her direction. She kept her head down and pulled her hat lower, but they were too intent on each other to notice her. They giggled and the man pulled his partner closer, planting a kiss on her lips.

Charlotte could see it all from the other side of the road. Oh how nice it would have been to be so carefree. Charlotte hadn't felt that free to walk the streets since that day in the university library, and it had only been compounded by Greta's death. Charlotte longed for the confined space of the U-Bahn and, for once, her apartment.

The car rolled along the road behind her. It was driving unusually slowly even for a built-up area. She turned a corner down a back alley to see if it would follow. The alley would take her farther away from the U-Bahn station, but she had to try something.

Thankfully the car trundled past. She fell back against a wall, closed her eyes, and took a deep breath.

'Hey!' someone shouted from above and she started. There was a man standing on a balcony above her, smoking a cigarette.

'What are you doing down there?' he asked as she made her way down the alley, keeping to the shadow of the walls.

She ran from the alley and out the other side, onto the main street at the back of the apartment building. The Opel rolled past again and she caught a shadowy view of the driver. It was the boy from the university library. She was sure. It may have been dark, but she would recognise that face anywhere. His features had stayed in her mind's eye since she had first laid eyes on him. She saw him everywhere, but this time she was sure it was him. He frowned at her in that same way, pretending he hadn't seen her and was concentrating on something else. But why then was he following her?

She kept moving, increasing her pace to put as much distance between them as possible. The U-Bahn station was only another street away, and she could reach it via a shortcut, which the car would be foolish to follow. She could see the steps leading down to the station and she made a break for it.

Another motorcar, a Volkswagen, rattled past, but she didn't wait for its fumes to dissipate as she rushed across the road. She thought she could hear footsteps behind her, but she didn't stop to look. Faces turned to her, surprised to see a woman running in the street, but they quickly looked away. They didn't want to risk themselves for her, and she could understand that. She would have ignored it in their situation. There was no point in asking them for help. They would hold up their hands, say '*Entschuldigung*', and move away. Instead, she took the steps to the U-Bahn station two at a time. A man was coming the other way and she barrelled into him. He fell to the concrete steps and she wobbled, but managed to regain her footing. She apologised, but he only glared after her. Glancing back, she could tell the shadow was still there, ever following.

The stairwell led onto the eastbound platform of the U3. She let out a breath as the train rounded the corner, screeching on the iron tracks. Its silver finish reflected the sunlight and would have blinded her if she hadn't shielded her eyes with an arm. She was on the train as soon as the doors opened, not letting any other passenger off and receiving grunts of anger in response. She pushed past them into the carriage hoping to get lost in the crowd.

She would take the train to the next station, get off and then cross the platform and get a train going back the other way. Her follower would assume she had carried on, or had got off and gone into the city. Even if he thought that she would travel back in the direction she had come, he would have little chance of catching up with her. She only hoped he had no idea where she lived.

She lurched as the train started its journey again, almost falling into the lap of a male passenger seated beside her. He grinned up at her, but she moved on. Her path took her nearer to a door and a presence behind her blocked out the light for a moment.

'Hey.' It was the same voice she had heard in the alleyway. She was caught with nowhere to go. How could the boy have followed her onto the train so quickly? Her only hope was that he wouldn't do anything drastic while there were witnesses, but even of that she was not sure. If he was from the Gestapo then he could do whatever he wanted and no one would be able to stop him. She turned.

'Why are you running away from me?' a man in a clean beige mackintosh asked her, as he moved along the carriage towards her, swinging from handgrip to handgrip with the movement of the train.

It wasn't the boy from the library. She had been mistaken. This man had a similar face, but he was at least ten years older. His eyes were slightly wider and his hair was a different colour.

'I'm not.' She made to move away from him again, but was restricted by the press of people. It seemed that every word out of her mouth had become a lie.

'Stop it. You are running from me. You kept looking over your shoulder and speeding up. I want to know why.'

'Why were you following me then? Why shouldn't I run away from someone following me?'

'You dropped this.' He handed her a sheet of music. 'I was only trying to return it and now I'm two stops from my home. You're welcome.'

He shook his head and moved back down the carriage. His coat got caught between two passengers and he yanked it free with an apology.

So he had been following her, but only to return the sheet music she had stolen from Greta. She wanted to be angry with him for not making it clearer, but she couldn't bring herself to. Her heartbeat was still thumping against her chest, and she knew she had been right to be scared. This time it was an innocuous misunderstanding, but next time it would not be so simple.

Chapter Twenty-One

Tuesday, 17 September 1940

Charlotte had just left the library when she dropped a book. It hit the floor with a slap and slid along the highly polished surface before she had a chance to grab it. It was her fault for not putting it straight in her rucksack, and she couldn't explain why she hadn't. She should have known better. Usually she would have packed up everything while in the library, but she had been in a hurry and in desperate need of a drink. Her mouth was dry and her thoughts foggy. Only a coffee would make a difference. She had been on her way to the regular, monotonous, Abwehr training session. It was as if they suspected that she wasn't up to the task. They hadn't given her another mission since Stockholm and she was desperate for another opportunity: it might lead to the truth about Greta.

She reached down for the book and a shadow loomed across the wall. The shine of a polished black shoe was visible just behind her.

A voice followed the shoes. 'Heil Hitler!' it said.

Charlotte bolted upright. She almost fell against the wall in her haste to turn. Having a party member behind her was not a welcome experience. She could smell his greased hair. It was slicked back and was almost the same shade as the wood-panelled walls. The man wore a neatly cut, black pinstripe suit, which framed his long, oval face. If she had seen him in the street she would have thought him a lawyer or someone involved in business, but she knew better. He had an SS badge on his lapel. He had a pinched face as if from the cold and a slightly hooked nose bisected two ice blue eyes. She thought he may have been the man she had seen in the hotel dining room all those months ago when she had first performed with the violin group, but she couldn't be sure. She hadn't been as close to him before. His smile turned to a frown as she forgot to return the salute while in her daydream. He must have assumed she didn't want to return the gesture. Throwing her arm up, she almost hit him in the face, and dropped the papers she had been carrying. She cursed, which only made matters worse. But to her surprise the man laughed.

'I didn't mean to startle you. It appears you have a habit of dropping things. Let me help.'

He knelt down on one knee and gathered up the papers with gloved hands. He shuffled them into order before returning the neat pile back to her. He gave her a faint smile that didn't do enough to turn up his hollow cheeks. She had seen him before, but where? The way he looked at her and glanced down at her arm suggested he was still expecting her to return the salute.

She threw her arm in the air and barked those words as quickly as she could. He nodded and a faint smile spread his lips.

'It's my fault,' she said before he could lecture her. 'I was deep in thought. I wasn't paying attention to where I was going.'

His hand briefly touched hers as he put a piece of paper back on top of the pile she was tidying. The hairs on the back of her neck rose and she suppressed a shudder.

'I can see that now,' he said, his hand lingering. 'I should have been more aware.'

'No harm done.' She searched for something to say to remove herself from the conversation. Some instinct told her to be anywhere else but here.

'I was wondering, fräulein,' he said, breaking her train of thought. 'Would you be able to show me where the lecturers' offices are?'

She glanced over her shoulder, giving away the direction. But he probably knew where they were anyway; he was just trying to be polite. She didn't want any part of what he had come here to do, but disobeying the Gestapo had consequences. She decided to risk it anyway. Surely a Gestapo man would agree with protocol and correct procedure.

'Visitors should check in at reception,' she said. As he frowned again she cut in before he could complain. 'I can show you the way.'

She led him back down the corridor from the direction he had come, wondering how he had got past reception in the first place. Perhaps they had been too busy, or too afraid, to stop him, or maybe he had come in through one of the other doors. Once again she reminded herself that if he was here to arrest her then he would have done so by now, but that didn't stop the feeling in her chest.

She pointed at the reception desk and he gave her a shallow bow before marching over to speak to them. His heels clicked on the tiled flooring and Charlotte watched, waiting to see what happened next. He took off his gloves one at a time and folded them on the desktop, before speaking to the receptionist.

'Good afternoon,' he said. 'I'm from the Geheime Staatspolizei.'

There was an intake of breath from the people around the reception area. Like Charlotte they had stopped to observe, the spectacle far more interesting than whatever they were supposed to be doing. That or they were frozen in fear. Wherever the Gestapo went they had the same effect on people. It was part of their power. Charlotte wanted to run away, but she couldn't move. She was holding her breath like everyone else, waiting to see what happened.

Charlotte couldn't believe the arrogance of the man, that he would so openly declare that he was with the secret state police. But then they didn't fear anyone. They were a law unto themselves.

'How can we help you?' The receptionist's voice cracked as she spoke, like a boy going through puberty.

'I'm here to arrest Professor Krüger.' There was a silence again, this time even more pronounced than the last time. 'If you could have her brought to me I would appreciate it.'

He turned to look around the hallway at those who were watching him. His lips were a faint line and it was unclear whether he was impressed by the audience. He did nothing to dissuade them, but people started to drift off, pretending to be busier than they had been before.

A professor she didn't know appeared at her shoulder. He was older than most of the others she knew, with curly white hair. 'One of Göring's dogs,' he said. 'I missed the beginning. What the hell does he want with us?'

Charlotte had only caught snatches of the continued conversation between the Gestapo man and the receptionist, who to her credit was asking questions and appeared uneasy following orders.

'They are saying Professor Krüger is a Jew,' Charlotte said, without turning to the professor.

'That's absurd. There aren't any Jews left in society, not since the SA arrested them all last year. They're clutching at straws.'

Charlotte shrugged. What else could she say? Krüger was one of her idols, a respected professor and the kind of woman she wanted to be. But had everything been a lie? The professor continued as Krüger appeared along the corridor, summoned by one of the aides.

'She doesn't look like any Jew I've ever seen. At least not as far as any of the racial science says.'

Professor Krüger walked calmly, as if she was simply going to another lecture, but Charlotte knew that inside she must have been panicking.

'That's the problem with Juden.' The Gestapo man had apparently overheard the professor's words. He cast his dark eyes over them. 'They subvert everything. Hide in plain sight.'

'No. I can't believe she is a Jew. It doesn't feel right. Someone would have complained by now. They wouldn't want to be lectured by a Jew. Can you imagine?'

The Gestapo man walked over to the pair of them. His mouth was set in a grimace. 'She's been masquerading as an Aryan. Covering up her Jewish roots to sow dissent and disorder in this university. She cannot be allowed to teach such un-German things.'

Krüger had finished her long walk to punishment. 'What's all this about, Herr . . . ?'

'Schulz. I am Obergruppenführer Schulz of the Geheime Staatspolizei.' It was as if he was addressing the whole room, so that they would remember his name. Charlotte wasn't sure she would ever forget. 'You're to come with me. I'm arresting you for illegally holding employment as a Jew.'

Charlotte made a spur-of-the-moment decision and stood between them and the door. 'No you can't,' she said, raising her voice.

'Please stand back, fräulein. I can and I will. This is my job and if you have a problem with that then take it up with my superiors.'

The grin he flashed her was inhuman and something bestial. He was enjoying this. Charlotte had thought that he was a man just doing his job in a difficult world, but seeing that he was relishing destroying this woman's life, the truth hit her harder.

'Professor Krüger is a respected—'

Krüger gave Charlotte a slight shake of the head and cast her eyes downward. Charlotte knew she had admitted defeat, but couldn't allow the woman to go without a fight.

'It doesn't matter. She is a Jew. A Jew who lied to all of you, pretending she wasn't a Jew and now here we are. Do you not want her punished for her crimes? For lying to you?'

'Yes, but—'

'Then please stand out of my way. Otherwise I will have no choice but to arrest you as well.'

Charlotte looked around the hall. Everyone else refused to meet her gaze as she turned to them one by one. She would get no help there. And yet they still looked on, marvelling at the spectacle. Not one of them had stood up for their fellow academic and Charlotte wanted to call them all out and their shame. Then she saw Stefan. He had come out of an office behind the reception desk.

She could never quite place Stefan's age. His closely barbered hair was turning silver at the temples, but the softness of his skin around his eyes gave him the look of a young man, and he was energetic and too often on edge, as if he would rather be climbing in the Alps that be stuck in this university.

Stefan put his hand around her upper arm.

'Officer, let me deal with this. I will remind the student of her duty to the Reich and about the actions of this Jew—' He almost spat the word. '—of her crimes. There's no need to waste any more of your precious time on this issue.'

With a tug he pulled Charlotte out of the way. The Gestapo officer grinned again and nodded at Stefan, before manhandling Professor Krüger out of the front door. Before the door closed behind him he turned back to the gathered crowd.

'We will be back to make sure that you are teaching what you're supposed to be teaching,' he said, before clicking his heels together and throwing his free hand in the air. 'Heil Hitler!'

Chapter Twenty-Two

Tuesday, 17 September 1940

Stefan pushed her into his office, still clasping her arm, and spun her around in front of the desk. She almost stumbled over a pile of papers, which had slid down to cover the floor. She righted herself as he closed the door and looked down at her, his brow furrowed.

'What the hell were you thinking?' he asked. There was sweat on his brow that she hadn't noticed before. What had he been doing before he found her? It didn't matter now. She pushed back against him, to reach the door, but he stood firm. Her hand lay on his chest, pushing, but he wouldn't budge. Under normal circumstances she would be embarrassed at the familiarity, but these were not normal circumstances.

'Charlotte,' he said. 'Charlotte. Look at me. This needs to stop. Now.'

He stopped short of shaking her, but she could feel his hands gripped firmly around her upper arms. She refused to meet his gaze, but she could feel the inhale and exhale of his breath through her hair. She didn't dare look him in the eye, not just because they were too close, but because of what she might see there. He had let the Gestapo take Professor Krüger, the woman she respected. Of course, Charlotte hadn't known that she was a Jew. But even now she couldn't believe it. The Gestapo officer had to be lying. She was a respected professor.

'We should have done something,' Charlotte said. 'We should have helped her.'

'I know, but against the Gestapo? Would good would it do? They would as quickly lock you up as the professor.'

'But someone had to do something.' Her heart was still thumping in her chest and it was taking up all of her willpower not to chase after the professor. If Stefan hadn't been standing between her and the door she might have done.

'Perhaps. But not where the Gestapo are concerned. They will lock us all up if they can. They only care for party members and neither you nor I are worthy of their mercy.'

'You could have stood up to them more than me. You're a professor.'

'I can't just stand there and tell a Gestapo officer to go away. I'm a civil servant; the government, the Nazis pay my wages. They would still have taken Professor Krüger away, and then they would have arrested me too. I would have lost my job, my livelihood, and my means to live.'

'Stefan? What are we going to do?' She looked up and realised how close she was standing to him. In her distress she had almost fallen into him, and the cut of his waistcoat filled her vision. He didn't move, and she could feel his breath blow through the strands of her hair. She still hadn't got used to addressing him by his first name, and this felt even more informal.

'For Krüger? There's nothing we can do for her now. But maybe we can protect others from the same fate.'

She realised she had been standing staring at his chest and she wanted to lay a hand on it, feel his heartbeat, to check if he was more human that the Gestapo officer. She hadn't noticed it before but the heat in his office was suffocating. She wanted to undo her collar, but that would only make things worse.

'We should have seen the war coming.'

'I think we did. We just refused to acknowledge it. Those who tried to warn us were shut up before we had a chance to listen. But you are more perceptive than most, Charlotte. It's what I admire about you.'

'Why didn't you do anything? Why did no one do anything?'

She sat down in the chair facing his desk, but only lasted a few seconds before she was back on her feet. Stefan still stood between her and the door. She didn't think she was going to run anymore, but he had no way of knowing that.

'What did you expect me to do?' he asked simply, with a slight shrug.

'Stand up for her. Protect her. Something.' Stefan winced at every word and she realised that her voice was raised. Anyone in the corridor would be able to hear her. At least he didn't attempt to hush her.

He shook his head. 'If only it was that easy. In a way I'm glad that you feel this way, but we have to be more careful. We couldn't have done anything. That *Obergruppenführer* was close to taking you with him.'

'He wouldn't dare. He had no grounds to arrest me.'

'Obstructing an arrest? Even if he was a regular police officer he would have grounds, but when it comes to the Gestapo it doesn't matter. They make their own rules. There is no law in Germany anymore – surely you can see that. It's run by thugs and gangs, and even they turn on their own when they no longer suit their purposes.'

'So what do we do? She wasn't just some immigrant that was draining the economy, she is . . . was a leading professor.'

'Don't tell me you believe that? No immigrant has drained the economy. They come here and work, and most of the Jews who have been labelled immigrants were born here.' He sighed. 'It doesn't matter. We can't do anything for them. All we can do is keep up the fight against the Nazis, but subtly.'

She stood in front of him with her hands on her hips. 'You sound like you've been thinking about this for a long time.'

'I have, believe me. Maybe it's too late. Maybe the Nazis have too much control. They have too much influence over the younger generations, but maybe in time we can make a difference.'

She looked over at the window. If she couldn't escape through the door because he was preventing her, could she make it out of the window? She had wanted to stand up for Krüger, but she wasn't sure she was ready for what Stefan was suggesting. This very conversation was sedition and could easily see them follow the professor to wherever she was being sent if anyone cared to report them. And someone must have reported Krüger for her to be revealed as she was.

'They can't fight this war forever.' Stefan wasn't done. 'Sooner or later they will run out of young German boys. Just like last time, even with the Jews fighting for us too. Yes, they fought alongside your father and the others. And then the Nazis blamed them for surrendering.'

'You know nothing about my father,' she replied. For some reason his words had riled her. She didn't want her father brought into this. He was at least spared from what Germany had become.

Stefan frowned at her words then shook his head. 'I'm not just a university lecturer. I have friends around the city. They all feel as I do, as you are starting to. They know that this isn't right. And they want to do something about it, but listen. We've been in here too long talking. People will start to ask questions. You should go, but we'll talk about this more another time.'

He took a step closer to her, allowing her a path to the door, but she had lost the will to run. She had more questions, and she knew she wouldn't like the answers.

'If Schulz can just turn up here and arrest someone, a leading professor no less, and no one does anything, what's to stop them from turning up here and arresting anyone they dislike?'

Stefan didn't answer, he just pursed his lips and stared at her, but there was something in his gaze that said, *Exactly*. That or she had become too used to him saying it. She could hear it in his voice.

'You will need to lie low for a while. If he comes back looking for you he might decide to make trouble.'

'But I didn't do anything. Not really.'

'You don't understand. That doesn't seem to matter to the Gestapo or the party. Professor Krüger didn't do anything either, except for being Jewish. And even then I think she was a half Jew, a Mischling. That was enough for the Gestapo to drag her away. And we will never see her again, you can be sure of that. I don't want to lose you in the same way, Charlotte. We have to be careful. Any talk against the party and the Gestapo could come for us. They can decide at any time that something is not German or Aryan enough. A philosophy professor they don't like, or a half-Swedish woman who tried to defy the Gestapo . . .'

She stifled a gasp. Before today she hadn't truly thought she could be taken away like that. Of course, she had panicked about them following her and not knowing what they wanted, but after having a run-in with an actual Gestapo officer she was even more scared. If they decided she was a threat to Germany then they could do whatever they wanted with her. Now it all seemed real, but she couldn't admit that to Stefan, nor anyone else. She had to stay strong.

'I won't let them take me,' she said. 'I won't give them the chance.'

'Good. You deserve better than this world. Me? I'm just a sad, pathetic, and lonely man. Everything good in the world and everything I loved have gone. All I've got left is to try and do something good, try to make the world a better place. But I have to pick my battles and so do you. And I will protect you with my life.'

She hadn't been expecting those words and she didn't know whether it was the heat in the room, the height of the moment, or whether she had been wanting it all along. She had longed for Kurt to say something as romantic to her for years, but he wasn't here now. She let herself fall against Stefan's chest as he wrapped his arms around her and made soft shushing sounds against her hair. She wasn't sure whether the sound of her heart thumping in her ears was caused by her guilt at betraying Kurt, or because being in Stefan's arms awoke something in her she hadn't been expecting. She closed her eyes and dreamed of better times.

Chapter Twenty-Three

Charlotte hadn't seen much of her friends recently. The orchestra had taken up much of her time, as well as the university. She wondered whether they were avoiding her. Had her attitude changed since she had been recruited by the Abwehr? Did they suspect that she was keeping secrets from them? How could they? She longed to speak to Hilda, but she was simply being paranoid. They were all busy, trying to survive through the war.

The blackout across the city was almost complete. Only faint light shone from a reflective surface here and there. She could see the various church steeples poking into the sky above apartment blocks and office buildings. It was a clear sky and so Charlotte had brought Kurt to the roof of the apartment building. There were stars as far as the eye could see, the various constellations her father had taught her as a child. She was sure that he had made some of the names up, but she was too embarrassed to ask anyone else what their true names were.

She had never seen the sky above Hamburg like this. It was like being in the countryside, away from the taint of light. There was one good thing to be had from the blackout after all. She could see more stars than she even thought possible and she couldn't drag her eyes from them. She had the almost uncontrollable urge to sing '*In Hamburg Sind Die Nächte Lang*': 'In Hamburg the Nights Are Long', but she didn't want to ruin the moment.

She wondered what life was like in those distant reaches of the galaxy, away from the war and the struggles of being human. If she ever finished her philosophy degree, that was where she would like to take her studies: considering the role of humanity on earth. But now, in the middle of another war, that dream seemed too far away.

She couldn't be sure, but if she looked long enough she felt she could see a faint green glow across the northern sky, but as soon as she blinked it was gone again. Kurt lay at her side, propped up on one elbow on the blanket she had brought up with her. Even the docks had frozen over in the winter chill and they didn't want to freeze to death.

'We shouldn't be up here.' He looked at her rather than the stars and she wondered how he could pay attention to anything other than the wonder of the universe. He was always the cautious one, and more than once she had been scolded for getting him into trouble with his parents. But he had become more confident as a result over the years.

'There's no one to stop us. The concierge never comes up here, especially not at night.' She rolled over to look at him, but by then he too stared up at the sky as if mesmerised. 'Have you ever seen anything like it?'

'No. No I haven't. But it's not just that there's no one stopping us. It's not safe. What if the British decide to attack tonight?'

And yet he couldn't draw his eyes away from the stars.

'I've never known you to be afraid before.' She pulled his gaze down to her with a hand on his cheek so that he could see she was joking, but a frown lay on his brow. She knew that look well. It meant he was serious, but instead of insisting he sighed and leant back.

'You know,' he said a few seconds later. 'It really is an incredible view.'

They fell into silence. It was a good few minutes before either of them spoke again. The breeze swept across them and she huddled closer to Kurt to feel his warmth.

'I often think about what it would be like to run away and live in another country,' he said. 'But then I'm not sure that I could do it.'

'Why not?' She took hold of his hand. 'Why don't we run away to another country?'

'Everything is here. My family. You. I couldn't do it.'

'You could, I know you could. We could go away together. Away from all of this.'

She pulled his chin towards her and kissed him. He kissed her back and then pulled away. Her heartbeat rose at the thought of running away with him.

'And miss out on these sights? Besides, I thought you always said this was your home.'

'It is.' She hesitated. 'I just thought that, well. Maybe I could make a new home somewhere else with you. Where we didn't have to worry about this war.'

'That would be nice. But you know we can't leave. Not now. If we all got up and left, then what would happen to Germany then?'

'I don't know.'

'It would never again become the great country it was. We would be turning our back on the Fatherland and everything we believe in.' He got to his knees and stood up, then crossed to lean on the wall at the edge of the roof. 'No. I couldn't do it.'

She closed her eyes and sighed. Kurt was too far away now to hear her disappointment, and she was glad. She didn't want to let him down. Even still, the mood of the evening was shattered. She started to roll up the blanket as the air-raid sirens burst into life. She closed her eyes again. Was it too much to ask for one peaceful night?

Kurt rushed over to her and took her arm. 'Let's get off this roof. Come on.'

He led her down the staircase in the darkness, each step careful, but hurried. The creak of the wood the only thing that reassured her at the strange sense of descending disorientation. The concrete steps jarred her knees as they ran down and down, and then out through the main entrance and onto the street.

The sirens continued their incessant wailing. They made her want to cover her ears and retreat into a corner where she could close her eyes and shut it all out. The drone of the aircraft as they approached only added to the overwhelming atmosphere. It wasn't just a leaflet drop warning this time. She could feel it in the air, and after a few moments she could see a change in the horizon.

The bombers were so far away, they looked like toys. As the lights played across the clouds, occasionally landing on the wing of an aircraft, she felt she could almost keep away from them if she kept an eye on where they were going and kept out of their shadows. But she knew that wouldn't be the case.

'They're really coming this time,' Kurt said, wheeling her around and in the direction of the nearest shelter.

Charlotte didn't quite believe it either. They had worried about it for so long that they had started to believe it was all posturing between the two nations. But the drone of the bombers' engines was unmistakable. It almost drowned the city.

'I have to go and check on the factory.' Kurt raised his voice to be heard. 'Will you be all right?'

It was clear that he didn't want to leave her. He hadn't let go of her hand. Charlotte knew she should have been in one of the shelters, but she couldn't cope with sitting there and waiting. If the Reichsluftschutzbund, the air-protection wardens, saw her, then they would probably escort her to the nearest shelter. But from what she knew of the air-protection wardens, they didn't want to do the compulsory volunteering any more than she would have wanted to. She nodded, pulling her hand out of Kurt's.

'Go,' she said. 'Don't worry about me.'

She knew she couldn't ask that of Kurt, but he had a responsibility as foreman of his parents' factory. He hesitated for a moment, lifting an arm as if to reach out for her again, and then ran in the opposite direction. She watched him go and once he had disappeared around the corner of a building she walked calmly away from her building. Her walk took her in the direction of the docks, but along a different route to Kurt's. She wanted to see what was going on. Explosions and gunfire punctuated her every step.

From the hill she could see fires down on Landungsbrücke near to the harbour. Even now firefighters would be tackling the flames. If the fire got anywhere near the oil refineries then there would be no harbour left. She was torn between going to look and running in the opposite direction.

She didn't think that her observations would be useful to the Abwehr, instead she had a kind of morbid curiosity. She walked down the hill, wary that she was heading towards danger rather than from it. Everyone else would be running, but she knew she couldn't run from the bombs. It wouldn't help. Surely the bombing raid would end soon? But the aircraft were relentless. Their drone was like a swarm of bees, constant and threatening. A bomb whistled nearby, then silence, before it hit a warehouse and erupted in a cloud of orange.

The bombs didn't stop. She should have been in the shelter, but when she had last gone in there she had felt trapped. Better to be out above the ground where she could see the danger than underground where she couldn't even see her death coming. The waiting was the worst feeling of all. At least up here she could move, pace, see the damage that was being done to the city. Even if she was getting closer and closer to the fires.

She could feel the heat of the fire pricking at her skin. It made her want to retch, but she couldn't retch. She doubled over and coughed. Her lungs were filling with smoke and she needed to get away. The warehouse toppled like a drunk leaving a pub. Red bricks were scattered across the corner of the road.

There was a huge crash. The shockwave rocked the ground and Charlotte fell forwards. She managed to keep to her feet, but she hit another wall and bounced off. A second later a shadow loomed over her. She kept running, but something took her leg out from behind her. Sprawling, she hit the ground, putting her elbows out in front of her. The breath was pushed from her lungs.

She fell onto her face, and the red sky was replaced by blackness.

Chapter Twenty-Four

Thursday, 21 November 1940

She had been knocked out. She didn't know how but it must have been during the bombing. The side of her head was sore as she touched it, and there was a pressure at the back of her forehead. It fell over her eyes, making it difficult to focus. It was worse than when she had come to in the police cell. At least this time she was on a comfortable bed. It appeared as if she was in a private room, but it had seen better days. The white paint peeled from the walls and window frame, and the window itself was covered with thick iron bars.

Charlotte hated hospitals. She had done ever since her father had died in one, and she'd been unable to do anything. There was a copy of the *Hamburg Echo* on the desk in front of her next to some stale slop. Her stomach rumbled but she wouldn't eat it. There was no way of knowing what it was. She checked the date and her heart dropped. It was the twenty-first, and she was due to meet Hermes. Her stay in the hospital had only been one night, but she had no idea of the time. She may have already missed the meeting, and if she did she had no idea what would happen to her. Would Hermes assume she was trying to get out

of her responsibilities? What would the Abwehr do to her and her friends if they thought that?

Raising herself up on her elbows she looked for her escape. Her body ached and there were bruises down the right side of her stomach, but that didn't matter now. She had to make the meeting. If she didn't then who knew what the Abwehr would do to her. They might not know she had ended up in hospital. They had made mistakes before.

She pulled her bedclothes off and winced as they caught on her dressings. She didn't have time to worry about that now. When the meeting was over she would have time to inspect and clean them properly. She grabbed the clothes she had been wearing when they found her and headed out into the main corridor.

'Hey. Where are you going?' a nurse called after her, but she didn't stop. She ran past other nurses and hospital workers who stopped in confusion at the running figure. She bumped into a woman who fell back against a wall. Charlotte apologised before running out of the front doors followed by more calls. It was freezing outside, and there were already signs of Christmas decorations around the city. She was outside the Marienkrankenhaus on Alfredstrasse. It would take almost forty minutes to walk to her meeting place, so she made her way to the nearest U-Bahn station, hoping she still had time.

He was already waiting for her. She didn't like being late, and she had hoped that she would arrive before him. That it would give her a chance to think. But Hermes had other ideas. He looked as if he had been there all day, calmly sitting on that bench, waiting for the tidal change that would never come. He didn't acknowledge her presence, but she guessed that was deliberate. They weren't officially meeting – it was supposed to be a secret. She hadn't seen him in months, relegated to training rather than being a full operative.

She took a seat next to him on the bench, but far enough away for another person to sit between them. To an outside observer it would just look as if they were sharing the same bench. Taking a deep breath, she leant back observing her surroundings and waited for him to speak. He was reading a newspaper, and she wondered whether she would ever see him without one.

She wasn't entirely sure whether she had sat on this bench before, or one of the others along the Binnenalster. She must have done, but she had never really thought about it before. Now it had taken on a different significance. She had come here when her father had died. At least, she thought she had. At that time her thoughts had been a jumble, she had felt numb, and she had wandered all over the city. Walking for kilometres, she had been lost in her own thoughts, but she had the vague recollection of passing the great reservoir at the centre of the city.

'The Reich truly is beautiful. Don't you think?'

It was so faint that at first she wasn't sure he had spoken. She didn't respond. The Binnenalster was beautiful of course, as were other parts of her home city, but she didn't think that was what he was referring to. It was best to remain in silent reflection where the Abwehr were concerned. It was easier to say the wrong thing than to get it right. Often a shallow nod would suffice. She gave him one now, hoping he would move on. Unlike the Elbe, the Alster was not tidal, and the water came right up to the sides. On days like this it almost looked as if one could walk right across it, if not for the faint rippling of the water. Charlotte didn't know how deep it was, and she had no intention of finding out. Hers wouldn't be the first body to be fished out of the artificial lake.

'It's much nicer down here than in that café of yours, don't you think?'

Once again she kept quiet. It wasn't that she disagreed, but the café served a different purpose and as beautiful as it was down by the lake it was cold in the open air. He laid the newspaper on his lap, took a cigarette out of a packet and lit it. She didn't mind that he didn't offer her one. Smoking would only cause her bruised ribs to hurt more.

'You lied to me.' He took a drag of his cigarette. It was such a matter-of-fact statement it threw her.

'No,' was all she said. It was the truth.

'You're not the woman I believed you to be.'

At no point had she pretended to be Greta, to lie to him or give him the impression she was anything other than Charlotte Weber, the German-Swedish Philosophy student and musician.

'You never asked to confirm my identity. Nothing I told you was a lie.'

'Yes, that may be true. I don't remember the entire conversation. The woman I was supposed to meet in that hotel was killed. The police didn't bother to report it, so it didn't filter through to my department until recently.'

'You believe she was killed?'

'Killed . . . killed herself. It doesn't really matter to us. She is no longer an asset. And it seems you have taken her place. Whether that is a good thing or not I have yet to decide.'

'I did what you asked of me in Stockholm. Not that it appears to have done any good or made any difference.' He couldn't know that she had not delivered all of the letters.

'That much is true. It seems the Swedish relented in the end.'

'Once the Norwegians had surrendered.'

'Quite.' He looked at her for the first time. His dark eyes appraising her. 'It is because of this astuteness that I am going to keep you as an asset.'

She broke his gaze, unable to stare into those eyes. The way he looked at her made her skin crawl. 'What if I decide I've had enough?' she asked.

'Your mistake, fräulein, is acting like you have the luxury of choice.' He took a drag of his cigarette and let the smoke play around his nostrils. 'Your role is not up for debate.'

She sat back in the chair, partly to give herself distance from that acrid smoke but also to give herself time to think. She wanted him to think she was unfazed by his words.

'What would happen if I simply said "no"?'

He stubbed out his cigarette on the metal arm of the bench and then lit another. The smell was tantalising and she couldn't help but breathe it in.

'I don't wish to threaten you, but it seems you are having second thoughts. I thought we wanted the same thing. To see the end of this war.'

'I do. But I'm not the person you want for this job. You didn't answer my question.'

'If you decline our invitation, then maybe you will no longer be useful to us. And people who are no longer useful have a strange habit of becoming our enemies. Only enemies let down the Reich.'

Her heart was racing and her face was beginning to flush from the heat of the room, but she had to plunge on. There was no other choice.

'What could you possibly do to me if I refuse? I'm a nobody. I have no family in Germany.' She knew she wouldn't refuse. If she did she would never be able to use them to find out what happened to Greta.

'You have family outside of Germany, as you so freely told me when we first met. But there are other ways in which you cease to be useful to us. You are a student. Do you think you will get to keep that luxury in a country at war? It's not as if we are in desperate need of young women who have studied at university. The Reich demands that all women should find themselves a good home to maintain and produce children for the future of Germany.'

She failed to stifle a gasp, but stopped short of covering her mouth. She gave him a look that she wished could kill. 'You wouldn't dare. You need me. I earned my place at the university. I did my service in the BDM as a girl.'

'The university doesn't matter. They will do what we ask, or risk further recriminations. The Führer himself believes that universities should only be teaching useful subjects. Do you think they will support you when they risk losing any credibility they have? They do not need you as much as you claim we do.'

She closed her eyes, feeling the temperature rise in the room again. When she wrenched them open again he was smirking at her.

'So you see, finally. There is no choice. We all work towards the great German Reich. Some do it freely, others need a little encouragement, but the end result is always the same.'

Finally he offered her a cigarette and she took it gladly, even if it signalled her admitting defeat. Her lungs felt as if they were being compressed as she smoked and she had to sit upright to prevent the ache in her side.

'You will go to Stockholm in the new year and once there you will meet with a man named Miller. Of course that is not his real name, but it is irrelevant. From him you will procure documents and return them to the Reich.'

'Why can't he do that himself?'

He turned to her again. She had expected him to stare forward the entire time, pretending that they did not know each other, but he kept looking at her as a disappointed teacher.

'You're letting yourself down,' he said, facing out toward the lake again. 'But if you must know it is dangerous for him to enter the Reich. He is for appearances a Brit, working in Stockholm on official business for the country's steel industry. If he were to be seen entering the Reich then his identity would come into question and he would no longer be able to return to England. We would lose a vital information link. If you get the information from him, then he can return without question.'

'If I go to Stockholm, I put my family in danger anyway.'

'You really do not have a choice. Even if you were a party member. No, especially if you were a party member, you would have no choice but to do your duty to the Fatherland. We've given you your training; now we expect you to use it. If you need more motivation, I'm sure we can find it. Those friends of yours. I bet that have some secrets of their own. Maybe your boyfriend. Are his family hiding something in their factory?'

Charlotte knew she had nothing to be afraid of. Hermes was posturing, trying to assert his control over her. But could she say the same of her friends? Hilda was vulnerable and Charlotte couldn't let Hermes get anywhere near her. And even though Kurt's family were all party members, that didn't mean they were completely innocent. The conditions at their factory were poor, but could they be hiding something else? Kurt had often told her the best way to avoid the attention of the Gestapo was to join the party. Why would they investigate upstanding National Socialists? It was the Jews and the Bolsheviks they were after.

It didn't matter. Hermes had that power over her and she would do as she was told. The consequences of refusing him could be too dire. She didn't want to end up in a camp, nor did she wish that for her friend. She stared at the lake.

'If I do this for you then I want you to give me the details I requested about Greta. I need to know what happened to my friend.'

Out of the corner of her eye she saw him give a shallow nod. 'I will provide details of the meeting to you in due course. Heil Hitler.'

He didn't wait for a response as he folded up his newspaper and walked away, leaving Charlotte to look out over the lake towards the Alsterhaus department store with its stone and glass façade. Did the shoppers in there have as many worries and responsibilities as her? Even with the war she doubted it. What would it be like to lead a simple life?

Chapter Twenty-Five

Thursday, 21 November 1940

Charlotte fell into her own armchair, and winced as it put pressure on her bruises. She was glad to finally be alone with some peace and quiet. She hadn't seen Hilda in weeks. It seemed as if their lives had drifted apart, but no matter what was going on in Charlotte's life, she was determined not to lose her friends. She was coming to realise that friends were one of the most important things in life. She wanted to tell Hilda everything, admit to her secret life, but she knew that wasn't possible. However, just spending time with her friend was relief enough. It was as if Hilda knew her soul, could see the real her anyway. She would take Hilda out for coffee when they next had time, and try and find some of the real stuff. Not the ersatz stuff that was allegedly made from acorns and tasted like bitter hot water.

The front door opened with a creak and Andreas stomped into the room then collapsed into a couch. He rubbed his eyes for a few seconds before he noticed Charlotte on the other chair. Their eyes locked and he stared at her, before letting out a sigh.

'I didn't realise anyone was at home. Apologies. I came in here for some peace and quiet. My own apartment felt stifling.'

He closed his eyes again and leant back into the couch, letting the cushioning envelop him. His lithe body was almost lost between the folds. Charlotte could empathise.

'You've had a bad day?' Charlotte hadn't really been in the mood for conversation, but something about her friend's manner suggested he needed to talk.

'That's an understatement.' He groaned again and sat up. 'I'm sorry. I shouldn't direct my anger at you, it's just that damned university. How am I supposed to work like this?'

'Why don't you tell me what the problem is?' She too sat up, matching his posture, but every movement hurt and she struggled to stifle a wince. 'Maybe there is a way I can help. We're all struggling at the moment.'

'I don't know where to begin.' He got up and walked with heavy steps over to the kitchen, where he opened a cupboard door then another before turning back to Charlotte. 'Coffee?'

'Afraid not. Unless someone goes to the shop. Someone with more money than me.' She made a show of turning her purse upside down. The only thing that fell out was fluff.

He shut the last cupboard with more force than was necessary and stood there eyes downcast. 'As if this day couldn't get any worse.'

'There might be some tea in there.'

'Tea. Tea? Ach, what good is tea when I need a boost. I'm not British. Tea!'

Charlotte had never seen Andreas act like this before. She wondered what must have happened at the university to make him so completely out of sorts and she wanted to ask more questions, but she knew if she let him be he would talk eventually.

'I can't do my work. Or rather they won't let me. It's utterly ridiculous.'

'There must be a good reason.'

'There is absolutely no reason. A university exists to expand knowledge and understanding. All we are doing is standing still.

In fact, it's worse than that.' He glanced at her then rubbed his hand on his chin as if in thought. The sunlight through the window threw the creases under his eyes into shadow. Charlotte wondered when he had last slept. 'I really shouldn't say any more.'

'Listen, Andreas. You can say what you want in this apartment. We all know that. None of us, except maybe Peter, are going to run to the Gestapo. We have to be able to trust each other.'

'It's those damned Nazis.' He raised his voice again and despite her words she hoped no one could hear them in the hallway. 'They have their fingers in everything. They forced out all of the good scientists because they disagree with them and those of us that are left have to work on tiny budgets because they don't care.'

'They have to make the numbers work just like other businesses.'

He gave her a look that said she had not understood what he was saying. 'They said the same thing, but it's not just that. Don't make me say it.'

'Say what? You've lost me, and I'm trying to help.'

'I can't do my research on genetics, because the university directors say that I'm wrong. What do they know about biology? Nothing! They are just businessmen and pfennig counters.'

'But isn't it up to you to show them that they're wrong?' In truth Andreas's work at the university was so different to hers that she really didn't understand. Where she was a student being brought up to speed on current thinking in her field, he was a researcher pushing that thinking further. She might get there one day, but she wasn't sure if it was what she wanted.

'You might think so, but they won't listen to me. None of my sources are on the list approved by the Nazis. They are actively controlling knowledge. Not only by controlling what we read, but by controlling the literature and writing. They've destroyed books that they considered dangerous.'

There was something refreshing about being able to talk to Andreas without holding back. Since the Gestapo had come to the

209

university she had many questions, and Andreas was one of the few people who would give her reasonable answers.

'How can a book that details how human beings actually work be wrong?' he asked before she could form a question. 'A book that has been peer reviewed by biologists across the field and helps to progress our understanding of human physiology.'

'I don't know.' It was the same in philosophy. In music. The Nazis decided what was and wasn't appropriate and Charlotte couldn't help but feel they were missing out.

'Ach. It gives me a headache!' He landed on the couch again, causing one of the cushions to fall on the floor. He didn't pick it up. 'My work is useless. No longer relevant in a world that doesn't understand it. I can't go on.'

She moved to the couch to sit next to him, taking the fallen cushion with her. She placed a hand on the back of his.

'That can't be true,' she said. 'Don't give up. Every researcher has had hurdles to jump, obstacles to get around. If you give up now, you won't change the world and I've no doubt that the work you are doing is important.'

He pulled his hand back and scratched his chin again.

'Did you know they destroyed an entire biological research institute in Berlin? You won't hear of it, they burnt any reference to it. But it has set us back years and years. The work they were doing. Well, it was important.'

'I remember the book burnings. My parents stopped me from seeing them, but I remember seeing the piles of ash afterwards. I don't know how anyone could burn a book.'

'It wasn't just novels and stories. The Nazis called it deviance. But biology is incredibly diverse, even Darwin proved that. That research centre was important to understanding our sexuality and the diversity of human gender, but the Nazis decided man and woman was far more important, and without that they were worried that there would no longer be families, no more young Nazis to prop up the party.'

Charlotte didn't have a response. She had never heard Andreas talk about his subject area in this much detail, and he was right. If the Gestapo heard about what he had said then he would be in trouble.

'I understand,' she said. She placed her hand on his again and this time he didn't pull back. 'What are you going to do?'

'I will go back in tomorrow and do what I always do. Work. If I cannot work then I am nobody. But I thank you. Without your words, I might have given up. You're a special person, Charlotte. Don't ever let them force that out of you.'

He let has head land softly against hers and they shared a moment. It seemed they had both needed to get their pent-up anxiety out somehow and she could now hear Andreas breathing softly next to her. She was grateful for the peaceful sound. There had been enough talking for one day.

'I've been thinking,' Andreas said softly, a few minutes later.

'Oh?' Charlotte had almost nodded off, but the pain in her side had kept her conscious.

'Did you ever find your friend? You know, that time when you were in the university and you were trying to find a woman called . . . Greta, was it?'

Charlotte's stomach dropped and she squirmed in her seat. Andreas lifted his head away, apparently noticing her discomfort.

'I did,' she said. It was the simplest answer she could give, in the hope Andreas would accept and drop the subject.

'That's good,' he said. 'I was thinking about it and I did know a Greta, but I had been confused at the time and didn't think of her. We knew her as Garbo and I'd all but forgotten her real name.'

Suddenly Charlotte was more intrigued than wary. At the time she had expected everyone at the university to know Greta, but since that day she had come to realise that Greta had drifted in and out of the university, barely coming into contact with anyone else but her. It was as if she didn't really exist, and that explained why the police were so eager to dismiss her death as a suicide. They didn't care.

'So you did know her?'

'Yes. It slipped my mind at the time because I didn't think she was the sort of person you would want to spend time with.'

'What makes you say that?'

'Well, I was led to believe she was an out-and-out party-card-carrying Nazi.'

Kurt was slightly out of breath. A faint sheen of sweat was visible at his temples, and a fringe of his hair was out of place, but he was still impeccably dressed. He wore a perfectly fitted black pinstriped suit, which served to accentuate his height and make his shoulders appear broader. He palmed the hair back in line with the rest as he stood in front of her, then he checked his watch and shrugged.

'Just in time,' he said, with a smile.

She was still heady from the performance. Beethoven's music had lifted her at all the right moments.

'We've already played,' she said. 'You missed us.'

She knew it wasn't really his fault, but she couldn't help but feel grumpy with him. He should have been there. She wanted him to be there.

'But the note you left me said seven o'clock.' He checked his wristwatch again. 'It's only just gone six forty-five. If anything I'm early.'

'They changed the timing. It's not my fault.'

'I know, I know it's not your fault, I wasn't blami—'

'I wish you'd come sooner.' She cut him off. 'It would have been nice to see your face in the audience.'

He left his open mouth hanging, apparently unsure whether if he spoke again she would interrupt him. She was being unfair. She knew it, but she couldn't help herself. It had been a strange evening and she wanted Kurt there to support her. She couldn't do what she was doing without him to support her, but she couldn't tell him that. She didn't want to admit any weakness. She had worked hard, had needed to be strong to get where she was, and he would only revisit their argument about marriage again. She didn't want to have that argument again, especially now. But he looked so sad, standing there not knowing what to say to make things better. At least he'd tried.

'Look, I'm sorry,' she said. 'I'm not feeling well. Maybe we should go.'

It was the best apology she could manage, even if it was a slight lie. She had started lying to him a lot and it didn't sit easy with her, but what choice did she have? She could only put him in danger.

'What's wrong?' He reached out to console her, but she waved him off. 'What can I do to help? I should have come with you in the first place. It's my fault.'

Why could he never get angry with her? It was frustrating. He deserved to be angry with her; she was being unreasonable. Saying she was ill had been a mistake.

'I'm just tired. It's nothing, but I would like to go home.' She wiped the perspiration from her face, not caring if it marred her makeup.

'All right, let's do that.' He reached for her violin case and then stopped. 'I'll get your coat.'

A minute or so later, Kurt came back with her coat. As was typical of him, he draped it around her shoulders and held it out so she could put her arms in the sleeves. He was always a gentleman. She could shout at him and he would still treat her with respect. In many ways she didn't deserve him, but then a voice at the back of her mind said she deserved everything she had coming to her.

Chapter Twenty-Six

Monday, 13 January 1941

Charlotte felt more comfortable amongst the crowds in the Hauptbahnhof. Her instinct had been to go to Dammtor, but she had wanted to blend in and to make sure that she got on the train before anyone else. The best way to do that was at the central station.

Smoke drifted just above their heads, rising to linger in the corners of the glass roof. It was as if there were clouds inside the building. Charlotte's father had once told her that the station had been modelled after the Galerie des machines at the Paris expo, but as she had never been to Paris she only had his word for it. He was always in awe of architecture, and tried to tell Charlotte about everything they passed. When she was younger she had been interested, if only for the quality time spent with her father. But as he started to repeat the same old stories and she grew up, that interest had waned. Now he was no longer here, she felt as if she should pay more attention to what she was seeing. Was there more there that he was trying to tell her than she had originally realised?

The station's architecture was open and impressive, and she always marvelled that the ceiling managed to hold up despite having no internal pillars amongst the platforms. It resembled a larger version of the warehouses down in the Speicherstadt district, but made of iron and glass. She had no idea how many thousands of people came and went through the station, but she knew it was one of the busiest in Germany. It was the best place in the city to get lost in a crowd and that was exactly what she wanted at that moment.

The blue-painted train was already waiting on the platform. She hauled up her case and stepped onto the train as a guard blew a whistle. The short, sharp tone warned passengers it was time to leave, so she made her way along the carriage and found an empty seat. She would try and sleep on the long journey north.

This time she had decided to take the train to Stockholm. She was used to taking a ship, but she had wanted to see the countryside, and to see Denmark from a different perspective. Since the country had been occupied it should be easier to get across the border for a German citizen, but she wanted to put it to the test. She needed the time to think.

These trips weren't exactly what she had been planning to do with her life, but in a way she was glad she was being useful. It was a position that gave her work as long as the war lasted, and even once it had finished she was sure that the intelligence services didn't just stop. It was probably more than she could hope for from her university degree. Who knew what jobs that would provide her with in Nazi-run Germany? But she wouldn't give up. It had been important to her father that she get a degree, and she would honour that.

Later that day her train pulled into Copenhagen station. It lurched to a stop and suitcases rattled in the racks. Charlotte was shaken from her light sleep in time to see a pair of Wehrmacht soldiers join the train. She sat up straight at the sight of them, but had to remind herself she had nothing to worry about. They weren't there for her.

One of them headed her way down the carriage and stopped when he got to Charlotte. A young, clean-shaven face smiled down at her. He couldn't have been more than eighteen, but his eyes looked much older.

'Papers,' he said, reaching out a hand, used to being obeyed. It was as if every Nazi she had met was absolutely in control of their own lives. She wondered what that was like as she handed him her passport.

'Good,' he said, flicking through its pages. 'You're not a Jew, or Mischling. Not that you look like one. Far too pretty for that.'

She wondered what this situation would have been like if she had been. The wink he gave her was bad enough, but at least she didn't feel like he was about to lock her up because he was attracted to her.

'I could have been a gypsy,' she said, surprising herself at her own words. It was one way to get rid of him, but it wasn't worth the consequences if he believed her.

He laughed and pushed her papers back into her hand. 'Good thing you're not. You're free to carry on.' He moved along, but something about his leering glance suggested he was disappointed to do so.

Within minutes the soldiers were off the train and Charlotte sank back into her chair. It was not over yet, but soon she would be out of occupied territory. Charlotte was amongst only a handful of people left on the train after Copenhagen.

The train continued into Sweden, joining the ferry at Helsingør to Helsingborg. From there it continued its long journey to Stockholm.

She hadn't been expecting to see the swastika here in Stockholm, as she stood on The Strand looking over the city, but she shouldn't really be surprised. You couldn't mistake which of the buildings along The Strand was the German consulate. If not for the giant red flag hanging from the upper balcony, the men in field grey uniforms coming and going were as good a reminder as any.

Here in Stockholm she didn't expect any of the soldiers to recognise her from back home, but she couldn't be too sure. They may be from Hamburg, have studied at the university, or be a friend of a friend. She edged her way away from the building, hoping that her behaviour looked as normal as possible. She also hoped that she wouldn't ever need to enter that building and ask for help, but the way her life was going it was looking more and more likely. Would there be someone from the Abwehr in there? Almost definitely. But someone she could rely on? Very unlikely.

She didn't doubt the Gestapo also had a presence here, even if their role was to look after the home territories. She turned away from The Strand. She had a meeting to attend and she couldn't linger any longer. She walked along the street and then crossed the Djurgårdsbron from the city buildings arranged in blocks to the almost unsullied green island the other side of the bridge. She passed the statues of Heimdall, Odin, Freyja, and Frigg, wondering what they must have thought of the war.

When she had been to Stockholm previously she had no reason to go to Djurgården. Her family's ancestral home was in the Solna region of the city, farther away from the islands that made up the historical core. The island once belonged to the royal family, but it had not been private for some time. Walking through the lush green landscape, she wondered why her parents had not brought her on one of their visits when she was a child, but they must have been too busy catching up with family members.

Anyone in the city was free to walk across the green parkland that took up most of the island from the Djurgårdsbron to the north, down to the shipyards in the south-west of the island. But that wasn't where Charlotte was going. She hadn't come here for a stroll. The handwritten note she had received had simple instructions on it. "Miller. Nordic Museum. Noon."

The Nordiska Museet was a national monument, but Charlotte had never stepped foot inside. It resembled a huge cathedral, crafted from red brick and granite, with bronze towers that were now tarnished green. It dominated the island, and could be seen from miles around. Stone steps led up to the main entrance, and she took them one at a time so as not to appear too eager, even though she could feel the butterflies of anxiety flitting around in her stomach.

The central hall was also like a cathedral. Once Charlotte had walked up the stone stairs into the hall proper, she was exposed. There was nowhere to hide in this expansive building, and she couldn't understand why it had been chosen as a meeting place. Even the actual cathedral, Storkyrkan, was smaller than this and would have provided more cover. But maybe Charlotte was too used to being in Germany, with the prying eyes of the Gestapo. No one here in Sweden would notice a woman waiting by herself. There was no war here. It felt . . . safe. She couldn't remember the last time she had felt safe. But then, she couldn't really shake the feeling of being watched.

'You must be the person I'm looking for.'

Charlotte flinched and turned at the voice behind her. A man was smirking at her and leaning against one of the stone pillars. He spoke in English and there was a slight American twinge to the accent.

'Miller?' she asked, whispering in case her voice echoed around the cavernous interior. In response, he touched the brim of his trilby and took three strides towards her.

Anyone could see them here. There were museum visitors walking around idly amongst the exhibits. Some looked in their direction while others didn't notice them at all. Even the ones who saw the two of them stood together gave them a wide berth as was usual amongst Swedes. None of them liked to be too close to one another, lest they take up personal space. It played to their advantage, but it didn't stop them being observed from a distance.

'What exactly are you looking for?' It felt good to speak Swedish again. The language had a melody to it, a melody that German was lacking.

'Well,' he replied in Swedish. The American twang was gone. 'To look at you I would think you were just a normal Swedish

218

citizen taking in the wonders of the national museum, perhaps on a break from work. But no, there's more to you than that.'

'And why do you think that?'

'Because you look so damn nervous.' He barked a laugh, which was far too loud in the hall. The man obviously didn't care about being overheard as she did. Was he less paranoid than her, or were they safer here than she thought? She stood to her full height and flicked her hair behind an ear.

'I took a brisk stroll along The Strand. It's unusually warm.'

He chuckled again. 'And of course they sent me a woman. But I suppose you have your charms, and they're a powerful tool in our line of work.'

'What are you implying?'

'Oh, you know. Don't be naive – it's most unappealing.'

'I'm not trying to be appealing.'

He took a step closer to her and the single footstep clicked around the hall. She could smell his aftershave, like oil mixed with sandalwood.

'That's more like it,' he said. 'I prefer it when there's a fire in your eyes.'

She wanted to hit him. It was an almost-overwhelming urge, but she knew that way lay danger. Her best option was to get his messages and then get away from there as soon as possible. Then she could blend back into the world and take a deep breath. 'Let's get this over with.'

He winked, but thankfully said nothing further. He pulled a box wrapped in brown paper out of a satchel and handed it to her. It was tied with white string and as heavy as a hardbound book.

'How am I supposed to get this back into Germany? They will search my bags.'

'You'll find a way. You're doing the Reich's work. Just bat those sweet eyelids of yours and you'll have the officials eating out of your hands. Say it's a present from your sweetheart. They'll be too disappointed to check.'

He folded the flap of his satchel back and begun to buckle it up. As he did so she caught a glimpse of a badge with a red background and a white hammer in the top left corner. Not quite a swastika, but close.

'That means you're a member of the Swedish Socialist Party.'

'And? What exactly were you expecting?'

She shook her head. It had been stupid to mention that party so openly. They had aligned themselves with the Nazis, but they weren't popular in Sweden. There had been a number of disagreements and brawls between the parties that rejected the Nazis and those that agreed with them.

'You think you're better than us because your party has conquered most of Western Europe?' His manner had changed from the easy ladies' man of a minute or so ago. Now a vein bulged on his forehead and he no longer slouched. 'And North Africa too? Well, our time will come. You'll see.'

'I'm sorry, I didn't mean anything by it.'

'Your Swedish is good, but you're not one of us. You wouldn't understand. Germany and Sweden are similar, but too long have we been passive, too cowardly to take back what belongs to us. Norway, Denmark, Finland. They all belong to Sweden.'

'So that's what you want? To take over those countries again? And you think the Nazis will help you? You're more naive than you think I am.'

'How dare you?'

She didn't know why she was saying the things she was saying. They were on the same side. They were both here to help each other, but something about his manner put her off. Those other nations had suffered for their independence from Sweden. It was all in the past. Why did they want to drag it all up again? Hadn't they had enough of war? That was all she wanted: an end to this. For all those young soldiers to come home and stop killing each other. She would do whatever it took to bring that about.

'I'm sorry. You're right. This is getting out of hand. You've given me the package; we should leave before anyone spots us and reports us to the police.'

'That won't happen here. You're free here. The police can't stop us meeting in a public place or passing each other "gifts". You're not doing anything illegal.'

'What joy. But really, I must be going.'

He pursed his lips and frowned. 'We'll be seeing each other again.'

He wasn't the first man to say that to her. She could only hope that next time they would send someone else. She left, expecting him to leave after her. Even still, as she stepped out through the arch of the national museum she couldn't help but feel as if there was a dark shape behind her. She took a few steps then, despite her head telling her she should carry on, stopped and turned. There was no one behind her, not even a museum curator, but her instincts told her otherwise. She was not as free here as the man had claimed.

She had become too casual since returning to Stockholm. She had thought as he did that this was a different country, that there were different rules here, different perspectives, and while that was true she was no safer here than she was in Germany. The Reich's agents were everywhere. She was one of them, for God's sake! But they would not trust each other; none of them even knew the other existed. It was enough to make anyone paranoid and she would have to watch her back. But she was determined not to let it change how she behaved.

She tried to convince herself that the best way to stay safe was to not let them know she knew they were following her. She started again, walking away from the national museum as calmly as she could. Every instinct told her to run, but she had nowhere to run to. They would always find her. Besides, she had to do what she had really been sent to Stockholm for otherwise Hermes wouldn't give her the information she had requested about Greta.

* * *

'No one pays attention to the staff, even if they're pretty blondes. Just make sure you play something that blends into the background and you will be fine.'

That was what Hermes had said to Charlotte when he had told her of her latest mission. She played the words over and over again in her head as she sat in one corner of the private dining room and watched the assembled men talk amongst themselves. All she had been told was that they were a group of senior Swedish officials and they would be meeting with some Nazis to discuss Swedish involvement in the war.

She swept her bow up towards the violin at her neck. For the violinist it was like taking a deep breath, preparing oneself for the performance ahead. No number of deep breaths would still the beating of her heart. She had wanted to be a performer to play her music for people, but she hadn't expected to use her music as a means of getting into places she wasn't supposed to be. It wasn't just the music that made her nervous, even though she had practised it for hours at home, it was playing on her own in front of these people. She longed for an orchestra by her side. If these people asked her questions she wasn't sure how long her prepared answers would appease them before they became suspicious.

The notes of Sibelius's violin concerto rang out across the small room, but none of the men looked up as her bow glided across the strings, back and forth, gently singing. The music meant nothing to them; they simply carried on talking amongst themselves and smoking cigars. The room soon filled with blue smoke.

She didn't think she would have been able to play for senior politicians in Sweden. Surely they would be suspicious, but she had blended into the furniture as usual and they had not even taken a second glance at her. They must have felt safe, so far away from the war. But what she was doing could bring them into the war. She was at war with herself, but she had to do what she was told, otherwise her life would be forfeit.

Eventually they drifted off on a tour of the facilities, as she had been told they would. She stopped the music, now that she was finally alone. She put the violin back in its case and put the bow down. She didn't have a lot of time. They would be back any minute. Her heart thumped but it only served to spur her on. She rushed across to where they had been sitting.

The briefcase she had been told to look for was leaning against a leg of the chair. It was bound in a blue leather, and the dignitaries were so confident in their safety that they hadn't thought to hide it better.

She entered the code she had been given into the briefcase lock. When the note had been handed to her at the central station she had memorised it and then burnt the piece of paper. Any evidence like that could be incriminating.

She slid the Leica camera out of the hidden pocket sewn into her dress and took a couple of photographs of the documents inside. They meant nothing to her, but that wasn't the point. They were not for her eyes. She flicked through each piece of paper, taking two photographs each time, just to be sure. She didn't want to return home and find that they were out of focus. She would be punished. But she was wasting time. She had to be quick.

There was a sound of footsteps in the hallway. Heels clicking against the tiled floor. First one then another, and another. She placed the pieces of paper back in the briefcase as she had found them and closed the lid.

There was a click, but as soon as the door opened she was back in her seat. Apparently she had been there all the time. But she'd had just enough time to lock the briefcase again before she had sat back down. It was not placed exactly as it had been before, and she stared at it while she played. Her heartbeat thumped along to the music like a drum, but thankfully no one noticed. When the evening was over she would return to Hamburg as soon as possible, and never show her face here again.

Thursday, 14 November 1935

'Pappa?' Charlotte's voice broke. 'What happened?'

His face was covered in red patches and dried blood. She thought he attempted to look at her, but his eyes were cloudy and rolled into the back of his head. The two men who were carrying him didn't stop for her; they took him through to the living room and lowered him onto the sofa. A faint sound escaped his lips, but they were broken and swollen.

Charlotte knelt by the sofa, taking her father's hand in hers. He groaned with the movement. She didn't ask him again. Whatever had happened to him he needed to rest, but she was desperate to discover what had happened to him. Her father wasn't a fighter, and she had never seen him with a single bruise, let alone covered in them.

The two men left her to it and one went to find her mother. Pappa was trying to say something, but Charlotte couldn't make out the words. A few seconds later her mother came into the room. Charlotte expected her to show as much emotion as she had done, but she should have known better. Her mother took one look at her father then turned to Charlotte.

'Get her out of here,' she said, indicating her daughter.

One of the men put his hands under her armpits and lifted her up. 'Come on, dear,' he said, not unkindly.

'No!' She tried to resist, but he was far stronger than her and she only managed to slow him down. 'I want to stay with Pappa. What if something happens?'

'Not now, Charlotte. Your pappa needs you to give him space.' She didn't even look at her daughter; she was busy preparing some water and cloth to clean his wounds. 'Go with Fredrik now, please.'

Charlotte didn't have a choice. She was led away by the large man. But rather than kicking and screaming she stayed silent. Father would have wanted her to be calm, to show resilience. That was what he was always telling her. "Never overreact. Let your enemies do that and they will play into your hands." She wondered whether her father's enemies had overreacted and that was why he was now lying almost unconscious on the living room sofa.

Fredrik eventually let her down in the kitchen. Mother had been cooking something and the smell of warm pastry lifted from the oven. It would have been a comforting smell if not for the dread that filled Charlotte's stomach.

Fredrik looked at her with his head cocked, but didn't say anything. She had so many questions, but she didn't know this man, nor did she trust him. As he stood there she took in the quality of his clothes. His grey cotton jacket was frayed at the ends and there were small holes that could have been from moths, but on closer inspection were burn marks. His trousers were a size too short for him and showed thick woollen socks that were in almost as sorry a state as his jacket. He had a faint line of stubble on his chin that suggested he hadn't showered for a few days. He looked every bit the docker, and not the kind of man her father typically associated with. She backed off a step.

'You'll stay here?' he asked. In the heat of the moment, she hadn't noticed how deep his voice was. It was like a foghorn. She only nodded in response, words failing her.

He turned to go back to the living room and then hesitated.

'Here,' he said. Then reached for the violin bow that was lying on the kitchen table and held it towards her. 'Why don't you play for us? Your father us told us how brilliant you are. I would like to hear it.'

This strange man was not a stranger then. Her mother had known him by name without being introduced and he had clearly had conversations with her father. But why then had she never seen him before? She took the proffered bow. Who was Frederik? She didn't think she could concentrate to play, but she would try. For her father.

Why was no one calling for a doctor? Was it already too late for her father? She wanted to run back in there and demand they tell her, instead she gripped the bow until her knuckles turned white.

Her mother came into the kitchen. She looked at Charlotte in the same way that Frederik had done, but her mother looked tired. Her eyelids drooped and her eyes were bloodshot. Had she been crying? Charlotte didn't think it was that, just weariness. Her mother reached out and laid a hand against Charlotte's cheek.

'What happened, Mamma? What happened to Pappa?'

'Shhh, darling. He's all right. He will be sore for a while, but he will recover.' She pulled Charlotte into an embrace, putting one hand on her head and stroking her hair. Charlotte almost came up to her mother's chin, and she would be taller yet.

'But what happened to him? Please, I don't like secrets,' she asked from the safety of her mother's chest. Her voice was muffled, but years of experience lent her mother a helping hand.

'Your father got himself into a fight. I don't know all the details yet, but Frederik has told me some. We'll find out more when your father has had a chance to recover. Some men who disagreed with your father's politics. It is happening more and more these days. We all want Germany to be better, but we have to be patient, and most importantly, we have to be careful.'

Charlotte could sense that there was something her mother wasn't telling her, but she would ask her father when he roused. In his state he'd have no choice but to be honest with her.

'As I keep telling your father. We can't do it all on our own. Not even with good men like Frederik on our side.'

'What are we supposed to do, Mamma?'

Her mother thought for a moment as she always did when Charlotte asked a difficult question.

'We rely on our friends. They're the most important thing, and without them none of this . . .' She gestured around herself. 'None of this is worth it.'

Her mother reached out and stroked her cheek again.

'But we must also fight for our friends. Remember that. We never leave them without a voice and we never let them face trouble alone. We would expect the same from them.'

'But I have no friends.'

Chapter Twenty-Seven

Friday, 27 June 1941

'All these trips to Sweden are getting in the way of your studies, and your music. You need to concentrate. What are you even doing there?' Stefan was forever shuffling papers in a way that suggested his heart wasn't really in the question. It was as if he was just going through the motions, that it was expected of him. It felt as if he had the entirety of the world's knowledge in his office. She had wondered whether he was simply forgetful, but after a while she had come to realise that he did in fact need all of these notes. His lectures took a lot. They were so detailed. Impressive . . .

'You don't understand. I need to go. My family . . .'

'But I also don't need to remind you how lucky you are to have a place here. You don't want to jeopardise that. The Nazis will find any excuse to kick you out of university.'

'I know, I know, but I have to go. I'll catch up. I promise.'

He made a face that suggested he had heard the same words from a hundred other students, but then he smiled.

'I have an idea,' he said. 'I will help you study. There's also a little club I want to show you. They play some great music there. I think you'll like it.'

'That sounds excellent. Thank you.'

'Don't thank me, just get those assignments in, otherwise I will have to come to your apartment and get them myself.' He flashed her a grin. It wasn't the first time he had asked to go through her paperwork when they had been together. 'I don't want to have to hold you back any more. You're too good to be an eternal student.'

She thought about his words. Did he say something similar to all students in a bid to inspire them? There was something about them that felt more personal, as if he was looking out for her. She picked her bag up and made for the door.

'Charlotte,' he called after her. 'You'll come?'

'Of course.'

Charlotte didn't often come to St Pauli. It was close to the docks in Hamburg and because of that many of the sailors and ship crews stayed here. With them came all the other associated parts of that culture. Charlotte knew of the brothels and other dens in the area, but she had never seen them herself.

Stefan had promised her that this wasn't that sort of place, but she only had his word to go on. It was so far outside her experience that there was a queasy feeling in her stomach that she couldn't get rid of. She desperately wanted a glass of water, or a tea. Did they even serve those kinds of drinks here? Or was it only alcohol? She wished she'd asked Stefan more questions before agreeing to come with him, but he would only have laughed at her and tried to reassure her it would be all right.

Stefan met her outside and led her down the stone steps at the back of the building and through a steel door. There were two men waiting inside like guards. They looked up from whatever they were reading with frowns that softened as soon as the saw Stefan. 'Come, come,' one of them said, taking hold of Stefan's arm and leading them towards another door.

The whole thing reminded her of the American speakeasies

from the 1920s she had read about, and she hesitated. She wanted to trust Stefan, but he should not have been taking her to places like this.

'What's the matter?' He noticed her pull back against him.

'What if people see us together? In a place like this?' Her voice was a whisper. For some reason she didn't want the two men to hear, whether it was because she thought they would be offended or laugh at her, she wasn't sure. Stefan smiled, which wasn't the reaction she had expected. His teeth glinted even in the dim light, and emphasised the dimple in his right cheek.

'And who do you think they will tell? Anyone in that room has just as much reason to keep it quiet as we do. If they tell anyone then they risk their own safety. We'll be fine.'

He tried to take hold of her arm, but she wouldn't let him.

'That may be, but it's still risky.'

What she had read about the speakeasies told not just of their decadence, but of the debauchery and criminality involved. The American underground was exactly why American culture was so corrupt, why they would never embrace National Socialism. Stefan was supposed to be taking her out for a nice evening, but it seemed he had other designs for her.

'If you don't like it, we can leave. I promise.'

That smile played around his lips again and Charlotte wondered what was going through his mind. He was clearly enjoying himself. But she still wasn't sure. She was risking a lot even being with him, but that smile was infectious.

The doorman opened the inside door and beckoned to Stefan and Charlotte. Music spilled out of the room, utterly unlike the sound of the orchestra. There was a murmur of chatter underneath and the clink of bottles and glasses.

A band played at the opposite end of the room. Their stage was only raised about twenty centimetres from the ground and it was as if they were part of the audience. They had brass instruments and a drum kit, which was almost deafening in the close confines.

Dancers moved and shifted in front of the band, dresses swirling around and sequins catching the light. Charlotte felt underdressed, but Stefan led her further into the crowd. He let go of her hand and disappeared. For a second she panicked, but then she saw a face she recognised amongst the crowd.

'Ilse? What are you doing here?'

She moved closer so that she could hear better over the sound of the band. Ilse wore a sparkling silver dress that Charlotte could only describe as American. With her curls she looked like a film star. Charlotte didn't know her well, and if truth be told hadn't really liked her at first, but now she had to admit how impressively attractive the other woman was.

'I could ask you the same,' Ilse replied, but there was a smile on her lips that suggested she was being friendly. 'What is a respectable woman like you doing in a club like this?'

Charlotte panicked again. What if Ilse had seen her with Stefan? How could she explain that away? But then Ilse wasn't really a friend. She had only met her through Peter.

She was about to make up some excuse when she noticed there were tears in the other woman's eyes. They were bloodshot and sore.

'Forget all that. What's happened?' Charlotte asked, putting an arm around Ilse and moving her away from the dance floor.

At first Ilse said nothing and just shook her head. Then fresh tears pricked the corners of her eyes.

'Oh, Charlotte,' she said, over a sob. 'I didn't want to think about it. That's why I came here to escape.'

Charlotte couldn't help but ask again. 'What's happened?'

Despite herself Ilse laid a hand on Charlotte's arm.

'It's Peter,' she said. 'He's dead. They killed him. They killed him.'

A wave of shock hit Charlotte. She hadn't been expecting this news, not in this strange club of all places. A part of her wanted to run away, pretend it wasn't true, but she was trapped. In truth

Charlotte didn't even know they had still been together. She hadn't seen Ilse since Peter left to join the fighting last summer. It must have been more serious than she had initially given credit to.

'What?' she asked. 'Who killed him?'

Ilse had managed to gain control of her tears. Her face had turned to anger.

'The Nazis. The Nazis killed him. They sent him to war and he died, and it's all their fault. When will it end?'

'I don't know.' Charlotte tried to console the other woman by stroking her arm, but it felt weak in the face of the news that her friend had died at war. She couldn't believe that she hadn't heard Peter had died. Why did she have to find out like this?

'That's why I came here,' Ilse continued. 'I just wanted to be surrounded by the music, the people, to escape. To pretend there's no war outside these walls and forget myself.'

She finished off her drink with one gulp and then took a step away from Charlotte.

'Now, if you don't mind,' she said, 'I will get back to the dance. It's all too much, and you remind me of him.'

With that, Ilse was lost in the crowd and Charlotte was left with her thoughts. Was it true? Could Peter truly be dead? She had always expected him to come back, cocky and assured, but now he was gone like so many others. She couldn't believe it.

She too was caught up in the sound and despite herself she moved closer. She wanted to forget too, pretend what she heard wasn't true. But she would never forget Peter. She also wanted to see what the band were playing, how they were playing it, feel it. She moved past the dancers, this way and then that, as if they were an ocean she was wading through. A man caught her by the waist and twirled her around. The room rotated around her and she closed her eyes to take in the sensation, then she was gently propelled in the direction she had been walking.

Stefan appeared again and handed her a glass of some clear liquid. 'I thought you wanted to leave?' He laughed then pulled her around to the dance floor. He hadn't noticed the look on her face, the tears in her eyes. But why would he?

She didn't know any of the moves, but it didn't matter. The music took over and they both just moved with it. Occasionally she would glance at one of the other pairs around the room, but it put her off and she almost stumbled. They danced for what seemed like hours, but she never wanted it to stop. Unfortunately, as she rounded the room again, the band announced they were going to take a break. She wheeled into Stefan's arms who gripped her as if she was about to fall.

He held her at arm's length then look at her from head to toe.

'See? Not so bad,' he said with a grin. 'I need to go and talk to someone. You'll be all right here?'

She needed to catch her breath, so simply nodded in reply. It didn't occur to her to ask who he was meeting. At that point the only thing that mattered was the music.

The band were relaxing in the corner by the bar. Usually she would leave performers to their break, but something drove her towards them, as it had done when they had been playing. She crossed the floor in a few strides, no longer restrained by her anxiety. The trumpeter looked up as she approached and fixed her with a smile. His skin was almost as dark as the room.

'Hullo,' he said, tipping the corner of his hat. It didn't surprise her that he didn't give the standard national address. Nothing about this place surprised her anymore, and despite herself she was relieved about not having to raise her arm and shout in the club. It was as if they had walked through that door and left Germany for another world altogether.

'That was fantastic.' She went straight into conversation. 'I had no idea anyone could play like that.'

'Thank you.' He offered her a cigarette and she took it without hesitation. Finding good cigarettes these days was almost impossible, especially as she was a woman and under twenty-five. They didn't give women like her cigarette rations and if he was going to offer her one then who was she to refuse. It seemed that the only way to get what she wanted sometimes was to get it from men. As much as that angered her, sometimes she had to relent.

The smoke tickled her throat in that pleasing way and she closed her eyes. She let it drift around her nostrils before taking another pull. There was something so calming about the sensation that she really couldn't replace. Even if the rationing laws had tried to prevent women from having cigarettes at all. They all still found a way. The Nazis couldn't control everything.

'I play the violin,' she said. 'But I could never make music like that.'

She felt like a child meeting a famous film star and she wished she had something more interesting to say.

'Sure you could,' he replied. 'It's easier than a violin. Let me show you how it works.'

He started taking apart his trumpet, removing the mouthpiece and then adjusting the valves. He explained each piece as he went along, but it was hard to hear over the din of conversation. She leant in closer, hanging on his words.

'It's the mouthpiece that's the trickiest part. Here.' He handed it to her. 'Why don't you have a go. Try and blow through it, but don't spit.'

She placed the cold brass to her lips and with a glance at him she tried to force air through it. Her cheeks puffed out and she made a *pfft* sound, but nothing more. He laughed, and she couldn't help but laugh with him.

'Thank you,' she said. 'But I think I'll stick to the violin.'

A second later Stefan appeared again from a door in the corner that she hadn't noticed before. He was talking to a man who was shorter than him, but dressed in a black pinstripe suit. His bald head reflected the lamp on the wall and he laughed at something Stefan said before retreating back through the door.

'Ah there you are,' Stefan said as he walked over to her. 'Sorry I was gone so long.'

'It was only a few minutes.'

'Sam.' Stefan nodded at the trumpeter and shook his hand.

'Prof. Glad to see you're looking well. Excuse me, I'd better take that break.'

Charlotte shouldn't have been surprised that the two of them knew each other, but she didn't think Stefan would be the kind of man to get to know everyone's names. She expected him to stick to the shadows, to watch and take it all in. She liked this new side of him.

'Can we get some fresh air?' She had become aware of the smoke lingering around everyone in the club and the evening was making her dizzy. Stefan led her up a different set of stairs at the back of the club. This time they came out into a square between buildings. An alley led from each side. The cold hit her immediately and she wrapped her arms around herself.

'Here.' Stefan took off his jacket and put it around her shoulders.

She thanked him and took a step out of the shadow of the building.

'I need to get home,' she said. 'My room-mate will be wondering where I've got to and I don't want to have to explain to her.'

'Embarrassed by me?'

She paused, thinking how to respond to his question.

'If not for the fact that this club is illegal, I really shouldn't be out in the blackout. She would worry whatever I was doing, and I have a boyfriend.'

'I know,' he replied, but even still his face dropped. 'I was hoping we would have more time together, but I can see I was being selfish.'

She shook her head, but she didn't know how to tell him he wasn't being selfish, that she had had a good time and would have liked to stay longer. With him.

'Thank you for tonight,' she said. After a beat she stood on her tiptoes and kissed him on the cheek. 'I needed to see another side of German society I don't normally get to see.'

'You're very welcome.' The grin on his face was genuine and he touched a hand to his cheek. 'You're not like anyone else I've ever met. You truly understand what it's like to live in Germany now. We're kindred spirits, Charlotte.'

A taxi was coming along the road and he hailed it, then handed her some notes. 'On me,' he said.

She turned to leave. It was long past the time she was due home.

'Charlotte.' His voice was almost a whisper. She didn't turn back, in case she didn't want to leave. 'You'll come again?'

'Yes,' was all she said as she opened the door and stepped into the taxi.

Chapter Twenty-Eight

Saturday, 28 June 1941

'Where they hell have you been?' As Kurt paced the kitchen he bunched and relaxed his fists. Charlotte didn't know what to say to appease him. She hadn't expected him to be there when she got home. Her plan was to slip in, not wake up Hilda, and go straight to bed, but apparently Kurt had been waiting for her all evening. Hilda gave her a look when she came in and retreated to her room.

'Please, I don't want to talk about it now. It's been a long day.'

'I've been worried sick about you. It's not the first time you've disappeared recently and ...' he hesitated '... with everything that's been going on, who knows what might have happened to you?'

What had he been about to say? Was it something his beloved party would have disliked?

'I'm fine, Kurt. I'm fine.' She stroked his arm as an apology and to get him to calm down. 'I was just playing music with some friends, but I'm here now.'

The lie rolled easily off her tongue. But it wasn't completely untrue.

'I'm sorry. I'm in a bad mood. My parents . . . you know how it is?'

'I don't, my parents aren't here anymore, remember?'

'I'm sorry. I wasn't thinking.'

'Don't worry. I know you didn't mean anything by it. And you're allowed to talk about your parents.'

He reached for her hand. Apparently he just needed to be close to her, and she could understand that. Even if all she wanted to do was to climb into bed and close her eyes.

'It's not them,' he said. 'Although they never have understood me. I know I will argue with my father again. It's the only way we ever communicate.'

'I can imagine.' She put a hand on his chest and then leant her head on his shoulder. 'Talk to me about it. They've always been kind to me, but I've seen how much they push you, how strict they can be. I don't know what it's like living under their shadow, but you're a good man and you work hard. I know that.'

She was thankful that the conversation had moved away from where she had been. She couldn't explain the evening, why she had another reason to always look back over her shoulder every time she turned a corner. As far as she knew the Gestapo didn't know about the club, but if they turned up here she would have more to worry about than telling Kurt what had happened.

She made a cup of tea to calm her nerves. She handed Kurt a cup first, feeling that he needed it even more than her. Something had happened, but he wasn't ready to talk about it. He knew she would be there to listen if and when he needed to, but it was no use pushing him. She led him to the sofa, but he shook his head.

'Not in here,' he said. 'The bedroom.'

Kurt shut the door behind him. They were alone in her room. It wasn't the first time of course, but there was something about the way he stood there that made it feel different. His body was awake with agitation and not a single part of him kept still. If she did not know him as well as she did then she would have found it intimidating.

'I've been called up by the Wehrmacht.'

'No!' Her hand shot to her mouth to stifle the sound that came out. She had always known the war would take him from her, but she had hoped she was wrong. It was one of the reasons she had refused to marry him. She had been too afraid to admit it to herself before, but she didn't want to be a war widow, it would be too much to bear. It would be enough losing him.

'I'm to report on Monday. I have no choice. It is my duty to serve the Vaterland.'

'Kurt, no.' She couldn't think of any other words. She wanted to cry out at the world to stop. To thrash against the walls of her existence and say that this wasn't fair.

'I knew the telegram would come sooner or later. My older brother Henrik is already serving. It's my duty. My parents won't accept any excuse and I can't even think of one. It's my duty.'

'You keep saying that, but don't you also have a duty to your family? What if Henrik doesn't make it home? They need you.'

'How can you think that? Henrik is an excellent soldier. He will be fine.'

'That's not the point. You are not that naive, Kurt. Your family needs you. I need you. Do you remember Peter? He died. Fighting.'

He gulped then took her arm in his hand. It was gentle. He looked into her eyes, forcing her to stare back at him. Neither of them blinked for a few seconds.

'I need you too,' he said. 'But what am I supposed to say? "No, I won't go"? That will not end well. I will be tried as a coward. Sent to the front line anyway. Or worse, they will just have me shot.'

'Kurt—'

'I am not a coward, Charlotte. It's up to all good German men to join the fight and make sure we win. So that the others, like my brother, can come home safely.'

'What about the party? Won't they help?' She knew she was clutching at straws, but she would try anything.

He scoffed. 'The party are the reason we're at war. What reason could I possibly give them for not fighting? I thought my work at the factory would be enough, but even that hasn't prevented them from posting me out to the front.'

'Do you know where you're going?'

He shook his head. She could ask the Abwehr for help. They would likely refuse. They had no reason to interfere with Wehrmacht postings, least of all low-ranking soldiers, but she could ask them for a favour. Only, a favour would mean that she was in their debt, and that was dangerous. Who knew what they would actually do if she asked, but she knew it wouldn't be as simple as allowing Kurt to stay at home. They would send him off to some guard post somewhere in the newly taken territories, which could be equally dangerous. She would have to be careful in exactly what she asked for, and prepare for what they wanted in return, but she would do it for Kurt. She knew he would do the same for her if their roles were reversed.

But she still couldn't tell him. She couldn't tell him she was working for the Abwehr. Even with his party connections she dreaded what he would think of her, and that she had lied to him about it this long. And knowing would only put him in more danger. They could use that against him. They might recruit him.

Although that might not be such a bad idea. It would keep him away from the fighting, but then their line of work wasn't exactly risk-free.

There was no good solution.

'I don't want to lose you.'

She grabbed his arms and pulled her towards him. He followed suit and wrapped them around her. After a few seconds like that, she reached up to the back of his neck and pulled his head down for a kiss. She pressed her lips against his and held them there. If she made that moment last as long as possible then maybe he would never leave.

To make sure she took it one step further. One button at a time she undid his shirt, then ran the tips of her fingers down his chest, past his navel, and then she was undoing his belt. He didn't let her go any further, pulling her blouse up and over her shoulders and nuzzling his lips in her neck as he hurried to undo the rest of her clothes. He pushed her back on to the bed, which creaked in response. As she lay there he kissed her from head to toe and back again. Her skin prickled with sweat as they joined together. It was furious, fast, and passionate, as if it was the last time they would ever lie together.

Then they were sprawled on the bed next to each other, panting. Their hands and legs were intertwined.

'I had better go,' he said eventually, letting go of her hand. 'It's night shift at the factory. My parents will be angry with me if I'm late. But you know I would rather stay here.'

He gave her a kiss on the cheek and stood from the bed. The mattress filled back in, his absence almost toppling her to the other side. She really should replace that mattress sometime. If only they had enough money.

He dressed and then leant down and kissed her on the forehead. 'See you,' he said.

She lay there as he left the apartment, wondering if others ever felt like their thoughts were obscured by thick cloud. She knew her mind was racing, but none of the images or words that whirled around inside made any sense on their own. It was almost impossible to reach for them, like chasing a leaf in the wind. It wasn't fair to say it was a blur. If anything the thoughts were moving too fast, being pushed out of the way by another before the other part of her brain could truly understand what he had been through. If only she could articulate this feeling to others, she could ask them if they ever felt the same way, but for now, as in most things, she was alone. Alone with her never-ending thoughts, the miasma of her mind.

Charlotte was smoking on the sofa when Hilda came in. Her roommate crept like a child sneaking to open Christmas presents, but upon seeing that Charlotte was alone she walked more confidently.

241

She never spent time with Charlotte when Kurt was here. Charlotte wasn't sure whether her friend was giving them space or avoiding them, and she didn't want to ask. Hilda would talk to her if she needed to. They hadn't had a chance to talk about Hilda's new job yet.

'What's wrong?' she asked. Charlotte's tears had dried, but the signs would still be there. So she explained.

'Hang on. I have just the thing.'

Hilda returned a few moments later with a bottle.

'I've had enough to drink,' Charlotte said. 'Thank you.'

But Hilda wasn't to be deterred. She poured them both a glass of peach schnapps and they drank in silence for a few minutes. The wind buffeted the building and whistled at the windows, but at least Charlotte didn't feel alone when Hilda was there. She pushed Kurt from her mind. There was nothing she could do.

Hilda poured Charlotte another glass of schnapps. It was cheap and home-made. Given the government's rationing of alcohol many had taken to making their own, but Hilda wouldn't tell Charlotte where she had got it from. Charlotte wouldn't press the issue. She was just happy for the chance to drink and switch off the thoughts in her head. There was a curious sediment in the bottom of the glass. But Charlotte supposed that it was exactly the kind of thing students should be drinking. They weren't as pretentious as everyone thought. The liquid was sweet, but as it burnt her throat it was warming.

'To your new job.' Charlotte clinked her glass against Hilda's and the other woman smiled.

'A new start,' she said. 'To my new job. It's an odd feeling to say that. I feel like I've been a student for years.'

Hilda had taken an administration job at Blohm and Voss, the largest ship builder in the city, and it was a big deal. There were times when Hilda had admitted she thought she wasn't going to graduate and the two of them had consoled each other. It was nice to finally be celebrating some success, even if Charlotte's own studies were being obstructed by her other activities.

'I'm glad I managed to find it.'

Charlotte nodded, lost in her own thoughts. She was due to graduate next year, but only if she managed to catch up with her studies. Then she would have her degree and try to find work like Hilda had. She liked the idea of teaching, but she didn't know whether she would be allowed. But she had to do something with her life before she could marry Kurt.

'It's not much but it is at least something. There are too few women in jobs, even with the war on. You'd think they'd need us more.'

Hilda was right. It might not be the kind of job a graduate would be looking for, but at least it was work that would provide an income. Their apartment wasn't cheap, but it was at least subsidised by their respective parents. Without that help and without Hilda having a job they might not have coped.

'I don't think I could manage another summer break doing manual labour for the Nazis.'

She seemed to realise what she said and covered her mouth as she turned to Charlotte.

'It's all right,' Charlotte replied. 'I was lucky not to get forced into it myself. I still can't believe they think students are just there waiting to be indentured workers for them.'

'How exactly did you manage to avoid it?' Hilda took another sip of her schnapps. Charlotte had to think fast.

'How about another toast?' Charlotte felt her face drop at the memory. 'To Greta. May we remember her forever.'

Hilda's face took on a different aspect. A frown crossed her features and she slammed her glass on the table, the clear liquid jumping into the air and coating the wood.

'No,' she said. 'Not her. Not that woman. I know you two were friends, but she betrayed everything she believed in. Her family.'

Charlotte didn't realise Hilda had known Greta more than in passing. Hilda wouldn't say any more, and Charlotte wouldn't ask. Not yet. She was learning a lot more about Greta than

243

she had realised, but even still she was no closer to finding out what had happened to her. It seemed even her friends had motive, but it couldn't have been any of them. It just couldn't. She knocked back the rest of her schnapps. It was about time she tried to sleep, but it would be a fitful sleep.

The uniformed soldier stood at the top of the stairs leading down to the platform, his kitbag by his feet. She didn't have much breath left after running from the U-Bahn to the Hauptbahnhof, but still she closed on him. She grabbed his arm and turned him to face her, thankful that it was indeed Kurt.

'I'm sorry I'm late.' She stopped at the top of the stairs to catch her breath. Below them trains were pulling in to and out of the station, the steam from the engines rising up to fill the rafters. The station was a flurry of activity, people constantly on the move, but in that moment it seemed as if time itself had slowed down.

Kurt's frown broke into a smile as he saw her and he wrapped his arms around her, pulling her into an embrace without hesitation. The wool of his greatcoat was warm as it enveloped her, but it was a welcome warmth. She didn't know when he would hold her like this again.

'I thought you had forgotten,' he whispered.

'Never.'

They hugged and held on to each other until their warmth had time to pass from one to the other. There were so many things she wanted to say to him, but she didn't know how to articulate them.

'Whatever happens, Kurt. I will never forget you. If there's one thing I want you to believe in, it's that. I could never forget you and everything we've been through together.'

'I hope that you'll have no reason to forget me. I hope that I'll be back soon. And I will do everything in my power to come back to you. I promise you that. And once you have your degree, we can get married.'

He took her head in his hands and kissed her on the lips. His freshly shaved face was warm against hers and she pressed into it, dreading how cold it would feel when he pulled away. Thankfully he didn't for a good few seconds. They stood there like that, breathing each other in, sharing the moment. It didn't last long enough. It never would. Kurt would have to leave and despite his confidence she had a sinking feeling that he was never coming back.

She pulled him closer to her. If she could hold on to him a bit longer then maybe, just maybe he wouldn't leave. She could hear his soft breathing against her ear, and his whispered soothing sounds to her. Neither of them spoke. What else could they say? Their silence was filled with all their doubts and questions. There were no answers, only the faint whistling of the breeze across the windowpanes. Time would tell.

She stood in the Hauptbahnhof for a long time, watching the trains come and go. It was amazing how many people came and went, and Kurt wasn't the only young man, young boy, in uniform heading off to war. She hoped they would all return safely to their families, but she knew that was a forlorn hope. For many of them this would be the last time they saw their home city.

She choked back a tear, feeling a burning sensation at the back of her throat. While her father had never stopped her from crying, he had always encouraged her to think instead. Crying, he said, was important, but it wouldn't save the world. Only action would. She hoped this war would end before it took Kurt from her permanently, and she would do whatever she could to hasten its end.

Kurt had been a constant in her world since she was a child. They had always worried that he might be posted to the front, but she never thought it would actually happen. His family being senior party members and his job at the factory were supposed to stop that, but the Nazis needed more young German men for their war.

She couldn't stand what the Nazis were doing to her country anymore. At some point soon she would return to Sweden, and she would stay with her mother while she found work. But before she did, she had to find out what had happened to Greta. That was the only way to protect her friends and then find a way to get out of the Abwehr's clutches.

Charlotte knew she would be all right without Kurt, but that didn't mean she didn't feel lost at his departure. There was another gaping hole in her life. First it had been her father, then her mother had left, and now Kurt. Was she destined to lose everyone she loved? Would she end up like Greta, lost and alone? No. Charlotte would never take her own life, if that was truly what happened to Greta. She didn't have the strength to do it. The only strength she had was to fight.

Chapter Twenty-Nine

Friday, 3 October 1941

Kurt had abandoned her months ago. She was sitting on her bed and couldn't move. It was so quiet. It wasn't that it was not normally quiet in the morning, but when Kurt was here it was filled with the sound of him, his breathing, his movement. She hadn't realised before now how much he filled the space, even on the occasions when he hadn't been there. This was a different kind of absence, one that she couldn't quite describe.

It was as if he had left without saying goodbye and was never coming back. She knew it was irrational, but she couldn't help but blame him for leaving her. She pulled a cushion from his side of the bed and hugged it close, laying her head on the top and closing her eyes. A tear rolled down her cheek, but she let it go. Just as she had let Kurt go. Of course they argued, but she had loved him since they were children. His smile, the way he held her. Both stuck in her memory, vivid, but only fuelling the anger at his departure.

She should have married him, but it wouldn't have made a difference. He would still be gone. The Reich needed soldiers and he was a young, fit man, ready to fight. She had wanted to run to the local party representative and plead with him, even though she was certain it would have made no difference. There was no favouritism for party members in this regard. Not even dutiful ones like Kurt. She wasn't even sure that the local party representative knew who Kurt was. Why would he?

It was too late for any of that now. He was gone, and she wasn't sure when he was coming back. What was he doing now? Was he sat on some pallet bed somewhere as she was? Was he thinking about her too? Wondering what had gone wrong? She knew he loved her, but why hadn't he fought to stay for her?

She couldn't expect him to give up everything for her, no more than she would allow him to ask her to give up everything for him, but this was not like any of that. They had both read about what had happened to young German soldiers in the last war. Even those who survived were scarred. If Kurt came back would he even be the same man who had left? Whatever he was doing now she was certain that he would be changed by whatever he was living through. It added to her sense of abandonment. The Kurt she loved had gone. Any man who came back would be someone else. She couldn't shake that feeling. It was similar to when her father had died.

She pulled the cushion tighter, using it to stifle a sob. There wasn't even any sound in the rest of the apartment. Her roommate had yet to rouse, and for that she was glad. She didn't want Hilda to pass her door and hear her upset. She couldn't explain what she was feeling and she didn't want Hilda to see her like this.

In truth she missed Kurt, but she was glad that he wasn't around to see what she had become. There was a part of her missing, a part that she thought she would never get back, even if he returned. But she had to find a new self, to embrace what she was doing with her life. With or without Kurt. At least with him away from Hamburg, wherever he was posted to, he couldn't get in the way of her transition.

She wanted him to hug her, to feel the reassurance of his presence. He had always reminded her that there were better times in the world, and she needed him now.

One day the old couple were gone. They were always in the café, but now they were gone. Charlotte asked the waitress if she had seen them, but she simply shrugged and went to serve another table.

Even though the café was busier than usual there was a sense of emptiness as she looked over at where the old couple habitually sat. It was a sign of the changing landscape of Germany. Many things were being modernised and there was a sense of constant change. In this instance it was a change that Charlotte was not at all happy with. She may never have spoken to the old couple, nor did she even know their names, but they were always there. Their presence was somehow reassuring, solid, constant.

In place of the old couple, a younger married couple were leant over the table talking. Actually it was more accurate to say that the husband was doing the talking and his wife was humming assent at the required pauses in his speech. It was as if Charlotte had gone back in time. He was dressed in a tailored suit, with a maroon tie and a swastika badge pinned to his lapel, and she wore a voluminous skirt, white blouse, and pearls.

He was pouring over a copy of the *Völkischer Beobachter*, finding something to complain about on each page. She was sure every country had similar publications, but the Nazi daily newspaper was particularly troubling. At first it was the Jews who were ruining everything, but everyone in the café was used to that argument. But next he turned his attention to dock workers and the disabled. All of them were too lazy and that was why Germany was not as prosperous as it should be. If only the disabled could be forced into work, he said, or 'moved on' then they would be less of a burden on good tax-paying Germans like him. At no point did either of them suggest a way of helping them, but no doubt it was easier to get rid of them than change anything.

Charlotte desperately wanted to move her focus away from his conversation, but he was so loud that she couldn't concentrate on anything else. No one else in the café seemed to notice, which was probably why he talked so loudly. She hummed a tune to herself, but it wasn't enough to drown him out. At this point he had moved on to students and how they were not studying what he deemed to be important subjects any more, like science. But the Jews had ruined science in the Reich.

If not for the personal attack, Charlotte had already had enough. It struck her as interesting that the couple were complaining about workers and this and that when they were sat in the middle of a day in a café. By the looks of them they had never had to do a solid day's work in their lives. So what did they know about hard work and how to get by? Relatively speaking their lives were easy. What was the point in complaining, when they could help people instead? Perhaps a university education might have provided them with some compassion. But looking at them, she didn't think they had ever been capable of such an emotion.

Charlotte realised she had become more socialist as she had got older, but not to the kind of socialism the Nazis claimed they believed in, but real actual socialism that was all about helping each other. She had never had to work for anything in her life either, but she could at least appreciate that others didn't have it as easy as she did and no amount of complaining would change that.

She opened her mouth to say something, but thought better of it. She was already in enough trouble and it was likely they were party members. They'd report her to the Gestapo before they actually listened to her. She didn't want to end up in a concentration camp for an argument in a café. She had much bigger things to do.

Two young men in Wehrmacht uniforms were sitting at the table next to where the old couple usually sat. They kept glancing in her direction and smiling. She did her best to deter them, focusing intently on her book and frowning at them whenever she accidentally made eye contact. She could imagine one of them coming over to proposition her and she hoped she could avoid that. If she was fortunate the person she was meeting would turn up soon. She had never thought she would have been glad to see him, but his presence would at least put off the soldiers.

One of the soldiers smiled at her and stood.

At that moment Hermes sat down opposite her. The smile slipped from the soldier's face as he realised that he had missed his chance, and for once Charlotte was thankful for the presence of the Abwehr agent. As usual, he placed a rolled-up newspaper on the table and ordered a coffee. He didn't seem to mind the bitter ersatz taste of the coffee they now served.

He didn't ask how she was, didn't make any idle chatter. Why would he? He simply told her she had another mission in Sweden and enjoyed his coffee.

She couldn't take much more of this. Even though he had recruited her he had absolutely no respect for her. There was a part of her that wanted to prove to him that she was far better at being a spy than he had ever imagined, but the rest of her wanted no further part of his schemes. But she still needed him, and it was about time she started getting what she wanted.

Charlotte stared out of the window as the U-Bahn rattled along. She wasn't particularly aware of what she was seeing. The red brick and stone of the buildings were a blur along with the greenery that rushed past. It was only when her train passed Moorweide Park on the way into Dammtor that her eyes focused and she took note. She knew the small triangle of grass well from her journey into the university. It was typically quite empty, but today a large group of people stood in lines upon the square. They passed out of view as her train entered Dammtor station. Without breaking a step, she left the train and exited the station, her mind's eye focused on that group of people as if she could see them through the walls. She had to cross the road to get a view of them again, but immediately she saw they were not the protestors she had initially imagined.

Approximately a thousand people stood in tight lines, clutching bundles to their chests. There were young and old people, families with babies in arms, all dressed in drab brown clothing, standing, waiting. The thing that most stood out were the yellow Stars of David sewn into their coats.

Everyone else on the street was almost pointedly looking anywhere else than at the Jews, but Charlotte couldn't help herself. She was drawn across the road to them. She had not seen anything like it before. She was used to crowds and parades, but this was different. There was an air of melancholy about the gathered group, like a cloud hanging over them. Their drab brown clothing only added to the scene. Like the passers-by most of them refused to look back at her, but one or two made eye contact with her. Each of them looked away as soon as they realised what they were doing, until one man stared at her. His eyes were grey like steel and his gaze was just as unbending. But even still, behind that façade she sensed he was willing her to come closer to reach out to him. Without thinking she raised her arm.

'What are you doing, fräulein?' a male voice barked from beside her. She turned to face him, slowly like an animal caught by its prey. As if she hoped that by slow movements she would not be caught, but in truth she was in a daze.

'Sorry, what?' she replied, not knowing quite where the words came from.

He wore the field grey of a Wehrmacht leutnant and a frown. He held one gloved hand out in front of her, as if it would prevent her from moving away.

'You should not be here, fräulein. Some of these immigrants are dangerous.' He almost spat those last words in a way that suggested they were somehow unfit for his tongue.

Rather than answering she looked back over the group of dishevelled people and wondered how any of them could be a danger to her, but she was sure he was just being overly cautious. The Jewish man had gone, blended into the crowd. She searched for him, but he was no longer there. She was certain she would still be able to see those deep grey eyes for some time yet.

'They can't hurt me when you're here, leutnant,' she said, deciding that flattery was the best way to deal with a man like that. He had an inflated sense of importance and a compliment would always appeal more than disagreement.

He smiled down at her, like some kind of reptile from a zoo. 'Watch them try,' he said.

In truth she didn't know what she had been doing. From the second she had seen the Jews from the train her legs had brought her here almost of their own volition. She had read about the deportations in the newspaper, but she had not expected to see them lined up and waiting like this. She had thought it would happen one by one as each case was assessed and processed. The bureaucracy of the Reich was more efficient than she gave it credit for.

They weren't people. Not as far as the soldier was concerned. He had been trained to see them as something else, something less. They had been lined up like cattle, but even cattle were treated better than this.

It wasn't just Wehrmacht soldiers who were guarding the square. As she stood there she noticed there were also Gestapo officers and policemen. This was quite the spectacle. She saw a leather coat, but she couldn't be sure it was him. Even if it wasn't she had decided that it was no longer safe for her to be there. How could she explain away standing so close to those Jews?

None of the other passers-by were looking in their direction. They just hurried past to carry on with their lives. Hamburg hadn't seen anything like this before and they weren't sure what to do. It had become safer to claim ignorance and look after yourself. But Charlotte had learnt that a long time ago, when her father had died.

There was nothing she could do for them, not with the soldiers watching her, but as she made her way to the university she made a decision. She would speak to Stefan and together they would fight this. Somehow. She didn't know when or where she would make a difference, but she knew now that she had no other choice. She had to save her country.

Chapter Thirty

Friday, 3 October 1941

She shut the door of Stefan's office behind her. She hadn't knocked but she didn't think that mattered now. They couldn't stand on ceremony in a world like this.

'Have you seen what's happening in the park?' she asked. 'In plain sight.'

He put down the papers he was sorting and looked at her over the top of his reading glasses. After a second he took them off and placed them on his desk.

'This is far from the first time something like this has happened, but it's the first time they've rounded Jews up in Hamburg. I wish people were more aware of it, but maybe they will be now. It seems it's opened your eyes.'

'Why don't more people know what's happening? Why don't you talk about it in class?'

'It's not that easy. The Nazis control the press; they censor everything. I have to go along with what the Nazis want in class. They could quite easily find a way to send me out to the front in a grey uniform. So for appearances' sake I do what they ask.

But I do what I can to subvert that. There are loopholes, subjects they know little about and have yet to ban.'

She thought about the Thomas Mann book in her apartment. 'I know something about that, but it's not enough.'

'Thankfully not all my books were burnt in 1933. We managed to keep quite a few in the archive here. God knows what they teach in Berlin. I'm not sure I would even want to be a fly on that wall.'

They were standing close together, and Charlotte hadn't realised how small his office was before. There was no room to take a step back, but she didn't want to. Right now she wanted to feel close to someone, to feel the touch of another human being.

'The truth is, Charlotte, we're all afraid. I'm afraid of them finding something more useful for me to do than teach. I've argued it's a protected profession, but it's only a matter of time before the recruiters turn up at my door wondering why I haven't yet joined the great German war effort. But who will teach Germany's young if all of us are sent to fight? I don't know how long my argument will hold up, but I have to keep trying, and in the meantime I will do what I can to fight the Nazis. Even if not directly.'

'What if the Gestapo find you? Whatever they do to you, it'll make being sent to the front seem like a much better option. I worry about it every day. I can't sleep at night.'

'I'm touched by your concern for me,' he said. All of a sudden she was in his arms with his soft eyes looking down at her. There was a faint grin to his lips, which suggested he was joking. 'I can't worry about that. They could be around every corner. We have to keep going, otherwise they will win. They want us to be afraid. It's how they control us. But we have to stick together.'

'What can we do? They control everything. They control us, decide our every move.'

'I'm not saying take unnecessary risks, but we can't jump at every shadow either.'

'I can't take it anymore.'

'You have to. You can't give in now. We've come so far. We have to stick together. You and me. Together.'

She was lost in those eyes. The compassion there was almost overwhelming. 'Yes' was the only word she could utter.

'I've wanted to kiss you since the day I first laid eyes on you.'

She didn't hesitate, she pushed upwards and against his lips with her own. His flesh was soft and supple against her pressure and there was the faint taste of chocolate, before he returned the kiss.

He was somehow rough and gentle at the same time. Because he was taller than her, his weight pressed down on her, but his hands were soft, probing slowly and delicately, as if he was examining an artefact from the archive. He kissed her impatiently, in a way that suggested she would soon realise what he was doing and pull away. But she didn't want to. She thought of Kurt, the betrayal. But she pushed the thought away quickly. She wanted this. She wanted Stefan.

The bristles of his stubble rubbed against her cheek, chafing. But it was a welcome pain. His hand slid down from her lower back to her backside, but it wasn't unwanted. She let her weight shift into his hand and he responded by pulling her closer. Everything about him was warm, his lips on hers, his hand on her buttocks. She wanted him to wrap himself around her, but she resisted.

'Not here.' She placed a palm against his chest so that he would slow down. 'Somewhere else.'

She didn't really want him to, but something about this place made her feel uneasy. They could barely keep their hands off each other, but within seconds they were out of the university and on the way to his apartment. She wanted him to wrap his fingers around hers, but that would arouse suspicion. She wanted much more than that, but it would have to wait until they were in the privacy of his apartment.

Chapter Thirty-One

The tortoiseshell cat rubbed itself against Charlotte's legs and weaved between them, before it looked up at her and meowed. She squashed her cigarette into an ashtray and sat up.

'What?' she asked. 'Hasn't he fed you?'

The cat meowed again and rushed away towards Stefan's kitchen. It was amazing how they always seemed to understand what you were saying, even if there was no way they could. Stefan's home was very much like his office at the university. It was as if someone had been through it looking for something but unable to find it and growing increasingly frustrated. Books were discarded in seemingly random heaps. In other places papers were piled, curled up, or folded. There was no pattern to any of it.

Charlotte searched the cupboards for some sign of food, but couldn't find anything until the cat rubbed itself against an unopened door. Inside was an opened tin of food with a battered bronze fork sticking out of it. The lid was bent as if it had been opened in a hurry. At least Charlotte wouldn't have to open it with a knife.

'Is that what you want?'

Charlotte thought she could hear a faint purr from the cat, so scooped out some of the food into a shallow bowl and placed it on the floor. The cat went right to it, lapping up the food, Charlotte forgotten.

So she went back to the living room and sat on the chair by the window waiting for Stefan to return. Her mind drifted to what they had done, how they had lain together, and something stuck in her throat. Desperation welled up in her. What had she done? She put her head in her hands and sobbed. Something had taken over her when she had seen the Jews rounded up like cattle. And Stefan had come to her rescue, as he had done before. But this time it was different. This time she had got carried away. Her mother always said she was driven to flights of fancy, and that it was her father's fault for encouraging her to believe in stories. But this time it wasn't her father's fault. There was something within Charlotte, and now she didn't know what to do.

A minute or two later she heard another meow from beside the chair. The cat looked up at her then sniffed the air. Charlotte realised her hands were crossed in her lap and as she lifted them the cat jumped up and landed on her legs. It circled for a moment, before finding the perfect place to rest against Charlotte's stomach. The cat instantly purred and fell asleep. Charlotte reached for its neck, but there was no collar or name tag. Instead, she gently stroked the cat's fur. There was something calming about the motion.

She couldn't have said how much later it was when Stefan opened the front door and stepped into the apartment. She had drifted off into an almost catatonic state and it was only the sound of the door opening that roused her.

Stefan was silhouetted by the light in the hallway. He stayed silent and stopped where he was.

'I made a new friend,' she said, to fill the silence. 'You didn't tell me you had a cat.'

'I don't,' he replied. He laughed one short laugh and shut the door behind him. She sat up straight.

'What do you mean you "don't"? Who does this cat belong to, then?'

'She's a stray.' There was still a hint of amusement in his voice. 'But she comes by every now and then for a bite and a cuddle. She reminds me of someone.'

Charlotte could feel herself frowning. Still, the cat purred on her lap, and the soft vibration helped to calm Charlotte.

'I suspect if I took her to a vet, the party would have her put down for daring not to be part of a good German family.'

He smiled, but it didn't reach the corners of his mouth. There was a sadness in his eyes that she could well empathise with. It wasn't just the thought of the poor cat, but neither she nor Stefan could be considered to be part of a good German family and sooner or later the party would catch up with them.

'You know, I could get used to coming home and seeing you sat there in the sun with a cat. There are far worse things to return to.'

He smiled at her, but Charlotte didn't feel its warmth. Why did every man want her to be 'at home'? Why couldn't she be the one who returned home from work to them? Stefan's words reminded her too much of Kurt and the thought brought a wave of sickness to her. As if sensing her discomfort the cat rose and jumped to the floor, disappearing into the other room.

'I'm not sure that would be a good idea,' she said.

His faced dropped, but he didn't respond to her comment.

'She gets bored easily,' Stefan said, gesturing to the cat. 'She'll either come back in a few minutes or I won't see her for a few days. God knows where she goes in the meantime, but someone must own her. That or she's made a home of every apartment along the street and gets fed by all of us.'

'I wouldn't be surprised. It's quite a racket, especially in times of rationing. I wonder whether I could do something similar.'

'Don't I feed you enough?' He chuckled to himself. 'Not that there is enough food to be going around.'

'Shhh. They could be listening.'

'Who? The Gestapo? Unlikely. I check my flat regularly for anything that shouldn't be here.'

She looked around sceptically and raised an eyebrow. 'In this mess?'

'Ah,' he said, a glint in his eye. 'The mess is entirely on purpose.'

She didn't relinquish her frown, so he picked up a pile of papers and waved them in her direction. 'I know exactly where everything is supposed to be. If anyone comes in here and moves anything then I will know about it.'

She thought of Kurt's home and how perfect it was. There was never so much as a piece of dust on any surface or anything left where it shouldn't be. Kurt had said he found it stifling, and now she missed him more than ever. What was she doing here? She had betrayed her love, the man who had always been there for her, and for what? A messy apartment, and an older man? She shouldn't be here. She had a plan, she was going to finish university, find work, and build a career. Then she was going to marry Kurt. That had been the plan for so long, she hadn't even thought about anything else. She almost stood up, but how could she explain it? She would have to see it through.

'And the genius of it—' he waved the papers again '—is that it will confuse them just as much. Like you they will think that this is mess and their job will be easy. They'll get sloppy. They'll think I'm an idiot. But I'll know. And they won't know that I know, and that gives me the advantage.'

His smile was infectious. She realised it was one of the things that had drawn her to him in the first place. While he had at first impression seemed like a dour academic, the kind of man she expected to deliver stuffy lectures, that had changed when he had first smiled at her. She couldn't remember what she had said, but she could remember his smile and the laugh that accompanied it. If only he smiled more then he might not have been on his own, resorting to sleeping with students. If only he had the confidence to use his sense of humour more in his lectures. She supposed that was not expected of him from the university, but then neither would her being in his bed.

'I do hope you're joking,' she said. 'If the Gestapo decide they want to listen to you then they will. You should stay wary all the same, no matter how smart you are.'

The smile dropped from his face and he tilted his head up, regarding her from the edge of his nose.

'Ahh, but if I am joking then I wouldn't tell you, would I? You're right. Trust no one.'

She nodded. Was there an irony in the words?

'You know,' he continued. 'When you first started studying at the university I thought you were a member of the party. You certainly looked the part: blonde hair, blue eyes, the perfect Aryan. But then I suppose I saw it everywhere. Your generation were the first to come through the Nazis' youth projects, to have grown up in a world where they were in charge. You are all a part of it.'

'I suppose I was, in the beginning. I remember them coming to power. I'm not that young. But my whole life I've been told that they're going to make Germany great again. That all of this . . .' She gestured vaguely to the outside, knowing he would understand exactly what she meant. 'All of this is for our benefit.'

'So what changed your mind?'

She thought for a moment. There wasn't an easy answer to that question. It was a combination of things.

'Time, mostly. I've started to see what everything they promised means. They've been in power for over seven years and what has got better? Nothing. The more I saw of what they're doing, the terrible things they do in the name of Germany, the less I could agree with them. Seeing things from the inside, I guess it opened my eyes.'

He perched on the chair next to her. She could still smell him on her, and now that he was closer it was even stronger. When she was home she would have a shower; she couldn't do that here.

Everything was happening too quickly, and she hadn't forgotten Kurt. This betrayal would hit him hardest of all. She couldn't believe what she had done, even though she could talk to Stefan and he understood her better than anyone. She didn't know how to fix it, but she couldn't tell Kurt what had happened. It would break his heart as hers was already breaking.

'It's a shame,' he said, 'that most people are too naive to even question the Nazis' motives. Time will not help them I think.'

'I wasn't naive to what the Nazis stood for before, but I did at least think that they were trying to make the country better. We all want Germany to be a better place to live, but not at the expense of people's lives. The war, the senseless deaths, people disappearing. My friends have died. It's too much.'

'I couldn't have put it better myself. We've all lost friends. If only more of your peers would have this revelation, then perhaps we might get on with stopping the Nazis. Those in the orchestra carry on as if everything is the same.'

She thought about asking Stefan about Greta, but surely by now he would have told her if he knew anything. He couldn't have been referring to her, but the other students. 'I think some of them are, but it's not easy. As you said, we've grown up with it. It's a part of us. But we shouldn't be having this conversation here. Someone could be listening. If the Gestapo hears any of this we're done for.'

His lips formed a tight line and he nodded. She didn't really need to tell him how dangerous everything was. Especially with their relationship on top of things. But they had to keep each other on edge. A moment of laxity, a lack of concentration, could cause their activities to be discovered.

There was a power dynamic in their relationship, whatever that was. He was an older man, and in reality she was a young girl. Even though she felt older she had to be realistic. She was only a student and Stefan had his doctorate, was an experienced lecturer. There was no way their relationship could be equal.

She wasn't even sure what the university would think if they found out about the two of them.

It would probably be best for them if it didn't last much longer. But then she genuinely cared for Stefan. And he seemed to care for her. What would she do when Kurt returned from the front? She had promised to marry him one day, and she definitely didn't want to marry Stefan. That wasn't the kind of relationship they had. In truth she couldn't imagine playing housewife to either of them, but if it was to be one of them it would be Kurt. They had always been together. She felt most herself when she was with him, and even though he supported the party, she knew she could trust him. When it really came down to it, he would support her. If the party won the war they would be stuck with them for a while yet, and she would need all the support she could get. She felt a little guilt for what she had done, but then, she supposed, as she left Stefan's apartment, she had felt so much guilt that there wasn't any left.

Chapter Thirty-Two

Saturday, 4 October 1941

The key rattled in the lock and eventually opened. 'Hilda? Are you in?' Charlotte called. There was no sound from inside the apartment, but that wasn't unusual. The door was thick. She hoped Hilda was in. She wanted to lock herself in her own room and pretend the world had gone away. The guilt was eating her up inside. But Hilda was different, she was like a sister, and Charlotte could do with some sisterly love.

She walked into the living room and stopped. Hilda was packing things into a box. Tears streamed from her eyes as she moved various items from a small leather suitcase. It took Charlotte back to that night of broken glass. Hilda hadn't noticed Charlotte come in, and jumped when she felt Charlotte's presence. The fear in Hilda's eyes reminded her of the man in the park. No matter how many times she closed her eyes she couldn't forget his face.

'What's going on?'

'I need to tell you about my friend Rudy.' Hilda closed the suitcase. 'This was his.'

'Rudy?' Charlotte asked. 'Do I know him?'

'No, but you should do. Everyone needs to remember Rudy and those like him. Especially those of you who consider yourself Aryan.'

Hilda handed her a photograph. It was an image of four young people, much like their friendship group, but it was Hilda with another girl and two boys. They were all looking towards the camera and smiling. Hilda pointed at one of the boys, with thick, curly hair and a smile that transcended the still image.

'Rudy committed suicide. His name was amongst the list to assemble in Moorweide Park, but he couldn't take it. We all know where they're taking them and he took his own life rather than to suffer that. Do you understand? He would rather die than be sent to the concentration camps. Can you imagine how afraid he was to take his own life?'

The tears flowed again.

Charlotte didn't know what to say. She had been a part of this and she felt responsible for Rudy's death. While her work for the Abwehr had not involved the Jews, as far as she knew, she had helped the Nazis and that was enough to weigh on her conscience. Her own actions were putting Hilda, her friend, at risk. Not that the Abwehr would come to her house, but the more they controlled Charlotte's life the closer to Hilda they would get. And if the Gestapo were also keeping a track of her activities then it was just becoming even more dangerous. Yet, she had to let Hilda maintain the lie. Even still, it didn't quite make sense.

'You're German. A Hamburg Jew. Those Jews in the park were immigrants. They're being sent to Poland to find work.'

'Rudy was a Hamburg Jew, yet his name was on their list. And do you really think they're being sent to Poland to find work?'

'You sound crazy. Why would they lie about that?'

'They lie about everything, Charlotte. But we're too used to it to tell the difference. They may be heading to Poland, but they're not sent there to work; they're sent there for the concentration camps. Even if they work in the camps they won't be recompensed for it. They won't have a life, or families. They're prisoners, worthless. Just like me.'

Charlotte wanted to pull her into a hug, but she knew it would only be patronising. A hug was the last thing Hilda wanted now. She wanted to feel safe. Charlotte could at least empathise with that.

'Their possessions are being redistributed amongst those who've suffered bomb damage. That means they're confiscating property from Germans.'

Charlotte could still see the face of the Jewish man in the park, those quietly imploring eyes, the pockmarks on his grubby cheeks on what would otherwise have been an elegant, slender face.

'Exactly. But Jews are no longer German citizens. They all think the Jews are wealthy, that because of a few money lenders we own everything and keep it from everyone else, but I tell you, it's not true.'

'I know, but those hoarding wealth have set a bad example.'

'I've worked for everything I had. My parents had nothing. Most of those Jews you saw on that square had nothing, even less now. Everything in Hamburg, from the factories to the department stores were set up by Jews. They wanted to help people, build the city, but Hitler was jealous of them. Why do you think I had to change my identity?'

'I'm sorry—'

'No, no. Let me finish. You've been taught your whole life that Jews are the problem. That everything is our fault, that if it wasn't for us, Germany would be a better place and everyone would live happily ever after. I don't blame you for that. What else are you supposed to think? Sometimes I even start to believe it myself. When times are tough I wonder if they're right, that maybe I'm not good enough. That I don't belong in this world.'

'That's not true. You're important to me.'

The look Hilda shot Charlotte was one of deep pity, her lips pulled into a tight line.

'I know that you believe that, but now you know what you know, it will change. It always does. But I will ask you one thing. Now that most of my kind are gone, their money and their livelihoods taken, is Germany a better place?'

Charlotte hesitated, but she knew the answer without having to even think about it.

'No,' she said, closing her eyes as the words truly hit home. She had been trying to convince herself of the lie.

'It's not just about me,' Hilda continued. 'My life is worthless. I have already accepted that I may not live to see another new year. But there is more at stake than the life of a single Jew. You turn me in and nothing really changes. They send me to a concentration camp and you all carry on with your lives as if nothing happened.'

'I wouldn't do that. I have no desire to see you in a camp. They're for criminals and people we need protecting from. You're not one of them.'

'How can you be so naive, Charlotte? Truly. You're an intelligent woman, but you have been taken in so deeply by their lies. If the concentration camps were just prisons, why do they send anyone who disagrees with them there? You could end up there simply for being my friend!'

Charlotte dropped onto the couch. She couldn't take much more of this. She was tired, her brain was full of fog, and she couldn't make sense of what was happening, but she had to listen to her friend. She couldn't abandon her now. Hilda didn't have anyone else.

'Charlotte, I had a daughter. A daughter!'

Charlotte looked up at Hilda. Her eyes were more red than before, and her cheeks matched the colour. Charlotte knew Hilda wasn't angry with her, but she couldn't help but feel crushed under the weight of it all.

'I sent her away just before I moved into this apartment with you. For her own safety they took her to Britain. I had to get away and start a new life. It was the only way I could let her go.'

Charlotte gave in. She stood again and put her arms around Hilda. She didn't know how else to react. It was the only way she could show her friend that she was listening. Hilda was like a rock in her arms; she didn't relax, but carried on with her lecture. It was as if a dam had finally broken and she was desperate to get the words out.

'The Nazis made this country so unsafe I had to send her away. Can you imagine what it is like to send your child away on a boat, not knowing whether you will see them again? I've hardly slept since, because all I can see when I close my eyes is her face.'

'I can't imagine what that's like.' The face of the man in the park returned to her mind's eye, but that was different. She didn't know him. Charlotte realised that Hilda had had no one else to talk to for years. Her early anger that Hilda hadn't been able to confide in her had seeped away, replaced with her own anger for what Hilda had been through. She let go of Hilda and offered to get her a glass of water.

Hilda nodded. It was the only movement she had made in minutes.

'I'm sorry,' she said. 'But you need to hear this and I need to say it. I don't care anymore. If not for your precious Nazis, then I would never have had to abandon my daughter. How can a child, even if they are a Jew, be so terrifying to these men? What do they truly fear? They want to control you, blame all your problems on anyone else but them. That is what we represent. A solution to a problem. But once they are done with us, once they have exterminated us all, then they will only find someone else to blame. What if they just chose to blame women? What if you do not produce enough babies for the glorious Reich? What then?'

Charlotte returned from the kitchenette with a glass of water and handed it to Hilda. There was no use in telling her to keep her voice down. If anyone was listening to them, then it was far too late. Even still, the entire time she had been talking, she had been tapping her finger on the table or her foot on the floor to confuse any microphones. It was a trick she had learnt from the Abwehr, and she was sure they never expected it to be used against them.

'Charlotte, we're not even considered human in the eyes of the party. We're vermin. That's what they called us. Stealing jobs from honest, hardworking Germans. How dare we try and earn a living when we were nothing but *untermensch*?'

'You know I don't think that way, Hilda. It's just these are difficult times. Unprecedented times.'

'That is what every party member has said since they first took over, but when will it end? When will we be allowed to live again? This isn't going to be over until the Nazis are gone, until their ideas are gone. The only way I will ever get to live a life again is if I keep my head down and survive until someone saves us. Can you imagine what it's like to give up your own child? No, of course not, you don't have any children.'

'I don't. And I don't want any children. I don't want to bring babies into this world of war and destruction. What kind of life is that? It's not fair.'

Hilda nodded. It felt like the first thing Charlotte had said that was right and that the other woman could empathise with. After shouting at each other, had they finally found a common ground? Charlotte didn't dare to hope. She knew she had been complicit in her friend's suffering, and she wasn't sure there was anything she could do to make amends for it. But it had helped her in a decision that had been forming in her mind over the past few months. She was done with the Nazis and she would do what she could to bring about their downfall.

'What am I supposed to do?' she asked. 'All I've ever known is the Nazis and their promises. Why would I ever question them? I'm not naive, but I'm just one person. How can I stand against them?'

She didn't dare tell Hilda that she worked for the Abwehr. Especially after being angry with Hilda for not confiding in her. Her friend would never trust her again. But Charlotte would have to find a way out of that sooner or later. Only, the Abwehr had threatened her friends with the Gestapo. It wouldn't be that easy.

Hilda reached out for Charlotte, and they clasped their hands for a few seconds. In other times it would have been a small gesture, but in this moment it was significant. A merging of ideals, of comfort.

'I have no idea,' Hilda said. Her voice was a lot calmer than it had been. 'In the Reich women's lives only have worth as wives and mothers.'

'We should have left before the war.'

'And gone where? It's easy for you, you can go to Sweden and live free. But where would I have gone? I'm not wanted here, but that doesn't mean I'm wanted anywhere else.'

'We would have found somewhere to exist. Together.'

'It's not that easy, Charlotte.'

'No, perhaps not. But you're missing the key word there, Hilda. *Together.* Things are never easy, but if we stick together it becomes easier.'

'I know, I know, but I'm scared. Do you understand how much it has taken of me to trust you so far? I've learnt to distrust everyone. Ever since they took my baby away, since this all started when I was a child, I have not been able to trust anyone. Some Germans have come to know a better world, but I'm not one of them, and it's difficult to find hope.'

Charlotte opened the suitcase and started putting things from the box back into it. There were journals, photographs, all sorts of personal belongings. Hilda didn't comment on what Charlotte was doing.

'Why did you stay?' she asked. 'I never understood why you didn't go with your mum back home to Stockholm. Why stay here when you have a choice? With all this going on?'

'Stockholm isn't my home.'

'That doesn't matter. It could have been your home. It's safer than living under the Nazis.'

'Why did you stay? Why didn't you go with your daughter?'

'That's not the same thing. I would have gone with her if I could. They weren't taking parents, only the children. I couldn't have got out of Germany if I wanted to. I wanted to—'

'Stay here and try and make a difference.'

Hilda's mouth stayed open after Charlotte interrupted her.

'You know?' she asked. 'I didn't think anyone understood.'

'Of course I understand. It's the same reason I'm still standing here. I couldn't abandon my friends. I can't abandon my country to these gangsters. I have to do something, and the only way I can do that is by being here, a part of it.'

'We have to survive them. Tell outsiders about everything they've done.'

'Somehow we will. Together.'

'There's that word again.' Hilda flashed a faint smile.

'I don't want to be remembered as someone who just did what they were told. Someone who took the easy path. That has never been who I am, and I will not fall into that trap now.'

'I knew I could trust in you, Charlotte. There's just something about you.'

Charlotte wouldn't let her friend down. Never again.

Before they could talk anymore an air-raid siren whirred into life. The alarm echoed around their city, and Charlotte had got so used to hearing it in her nightmares that she took a moment to check it was real. Hilda glanced down at the suitcase.

'Under the couch.' Charlotte helped her hide it under the chair before they made for the door. Charlotte would escort her friend to the bomb shelter. It was the least she could do. She would have to sit there all night as the bombs fell above them, turning the city to dust. Charlotte shuddered and locked the door behind her.

Chapter Thirty-Three

Wednesday, 8 April 1942

It had been a long night, and once again Charlotte had gone without sleep. There has been many nights of bombing since October, and she had not yet learnt how to sleep in the shelter. Others in the shelter had managed to nod off, but Charlotte was awakened by every rumble, as the dust dropped down to cover her hair. The first thing she wanted to do when she got into her apartment was to have a wash.

It had sounded as if there were over a hundred bombers overhead, and as they ascended into the city once the all-clear had been given there were signs of damage everywhere. One building no longer had a wall, another was missing its roof. The firefighters were still putting out flames even in the dawn. With each bombing raid there were more flames than firefighters.

Charlotte and Hilda got to the top of their stairs and in their corridor, they bumped into Andreas. He was short of breath and almost doubled over when he stopped in front of Charlotte.

'There you are,' he said, in between breaths. 'I've been looking for you all morning.'

Charlotte wasn't sure how that was possible, as they had only just been allowed out of the shelter, but she didn't press him. He was clearly distressed and in a hurry to tell her something.

'Haven't you heard? Part of the Winmer factory was caught in the bombing. There are a number of casualties.'

'I'd better get over there. What if Kurt's family—'

'Go!'

Charlotte couldn't help but be glad that Kurt was not in the city. He could have been in the factory during the bombing. He could have been one of the casualties. She ran back down the stairs, fighting off the urge to sleep and forgetting all about her wish to clean her hair.

Charlotte felt completely out of place in the Winmers's house even though they often treated her like family.

'It's Friedrich.' She didn't recognise who the voice belonged to, but she had a number of questions, such as what was Friedrich doing in the factory at night, but now wasn't the time. She was here to support Kurt's family, her one-day parents-in-law. As Kurt wasn't here he would want her to be, to offer what aid she could.

Maybe she should have become a nurse rather than studying at the university. She could have avoided the Abwehr, but she wasn't sure she could have coped with the things she would have seen. She wasn't squeamish, but it took an iron stomach to be a nurse in wartime.

They wheeled the gurney in. All of a sudden the room reminded her of a hospital. The plush sofas were pushed out of the way, the walls became starker, somehow more sterile. People rushed about, many of whom she didn't know. Had she seen them before somewhere? Were they factory workers invited in to help with Friedrich, or were they doctors and nurses? Charlotte couldn't tell. They were dressed in everyday clothes, and she was the only one covered in dust from last night's bombing. The room was awash with people, and she had been pushed to the back, a silent observer.

The shape on the gurney was still from what she could see. A white sheet had been draped over his body up to his shoulders and every so often as someone moved she caught sight of red-brown stains on the sheet.

It also reminded her of something else, but she didn't want to go there. She had pushed that memory far from her mind and had not allowed it to surface. The thoughts overwhelmed her, so she threw herself into the moment.

'How can I help?' she asked of Simone. 'What can I do?'

Simone didn't speak. She was as white as the sheet that covered Friedrich. Charlotte thought she could hear a faint groaning sound coming out of Simone's mouth, but it was hard to hear over the cacophony of people. It couldn't help Friedrich to have so many people in the room.

'Perhaps I should go,' Charlotte said to no one in particular. As she made to go a hand gripped her arm, squeezing so tightly that she thought it might leave a bruise. Simone stared at her but still said nothing.

'All right, I'll stay,' she said. Simone didn't relinquish her arm, but she turned back to the scene of her dying child. They both stood there as the others worked, using towels and cloth to clean Friedrich's wounds. They came in with fresh bowls of water, taking away the stained ones. It was like witnessing a birth, only this was a life leaving the world rather than entering it.

Charlotte couldn't see how he would recover from such wounds, but they were giving it their everything. She felt completely lost and out of control. Given what had happened recently she was an imposter here. She had betrayed Kurt and by abstraction his family. If they had known what she had done then she would not be welcome here, and yet now was not the time to tell them. She remained silent, forcing away the sick feeling in her stomach. She hadn't even had time to have breakfast yet.

Charlotte had never liked Friedrich, but she didn't want to see him suffer, nor his family for that matter. Another life lost in this war was nothing to celebrate. It didn't matter to Charlotte whose side they were on, no one deserved to lose their life. Not even her enemies. She had seen some terrible things, but she was no killer.

Simone still held Charlotte's arm, and she was starting to feel pins and needles. One of the men extracted himself from the group and made his way over to Simone. Her grip on Charlotte's arm tightened and she wanted to break free, but knew she couldn't. The man didn't say anything but shook his head, appearing to confirm Simone's fears.

At first nothing happened, then the tears came as if in a flood. A wailing sound erupted from her mouth and she turned and buried herself in Charlotte's arms. All Charlotte could do was to hold the woman and let her grieve. She had lost one of her sons, the other two were off fighting and her husband was nowhere to be seen. Charlotte was all she had, and regardless of the circumstances, she would have provided this basic human courtesy for anyone. She wondered whether she had made the same sound when her father had died, but she couldn't remember. It was a different life.

She laid the pen down. What could she possibly say to Kurt? He knew very well that she had not been fond of his brother. He was not overly fond of Friedrich himself, but that was in a brotherly way. It was almost expected of them, but Charlotte had always felt as if she should have made more of an effort to get to know Friedrich. Maybe there had been a softer boy underneath that Hitler Youth façade.

Perhaps it was up to Kurt's parents to inform him of Friedrich's death, but Charlotte had already offered to write to him. It felt right. She wanted to reach out to him, to feel close to him somehow. The only problem was she didn't know what to say. In the past she would have asked Kurt himself to help her draft the letter, and it drove home how much she missed him.

There were so many things she wanted to say to him, but none of them she could put in a letter. She owed it to him to admit all her faults in person, face to face.

She wanted to get it into the post before it left. It was a wonder that despite the war the postal service still worked. Say what you like about the Nazis, but they did bureaucracy well. Only, she couldn't think what to say about Friedrich. The only thing to do was to get straight to the point. She then spent the rest of the letter telling him how much she missed him and how they could talk about their future when he got back. She was surprised how much she meant it. At first she had wanted to give him some solace, wherever he was, but the more she wrote the more she realised she genuinely wanted to think about a future with him in it. Only, life wasn't that simple.

She folded the letter into an envelope and got to the door just as the postwoman was about to step up to it.

'Aha,' Charlotte said. 'Would you mind taking this for me? It's for my boyfriend at the front.'

She wouldn't normally put it like that, but she knew exactly what she was doing. The postwoman pushed the bundle of letters towards her before taking her letter to Kurt and beating a hasty retreat. Had there been a knowing look on her face? Charlotte wasn't sure, but she sensed the postwoman knew more than she had let on.

Now that she was no longer being watched, she flicked through the letters looking for anything that might suggest it had come from Kurt. Most of the letters were subscriptions she had been meaning to cancel, or advertisements, but there was one in a brown-paper envelope that looked more like a formal letter than the others. What did the postwoman know about this letter? She must see thousands every day, must be able to tell them all apart and have an idea where each of them came from. The postmark was Hamburg so it must have been sent from within the city, but that didn't mean anything. There were offices within the city that dealt with all manner of things. It was naive to think that any war correspondence would come from Berlin only.

She didn't dare open it. What if it was from Kurt? She couldn't bear it. If anything had happened to him . . . She needed to speak to him, to hear his voice. It was the only way she could absolve her guilt of what had happened between her and Stefan. Everything would come out sooner or later; the best thing to do would be to tell him everything. She couldn't write to him – that wouldn't be fair. He had to hear it from her directly.

Any letter could also be intercepted by the Gestapo or a censor and then who knew what would happen. She couldn't tell him that way, not least because she would have to leave out details. No, it had to be in person, but she knew she would be too scared to say anything in the end.

It was no good, she would have to open the letter. She couldn't distract herself any longer with idle thoughts. She ripped back the brown paper but turned the letter slowly, hoping that the mere action would prevent there from being any words on the other side. She just knew the sending address would be a Wehrmacht office in Hamburg. She knew it would contain Kurt's name, as well as their apologies, but that he died in service of the German Reich. She knew all this and more would be written there, so why even turn it around? Why read it? She had been dreading this day since Kurt had first been posted with his unit. She would never see him again, of that she was sure. It was time. It had to be his death notice.

She held her breath and turned it over.

It wasn't that at all. Of course, they would send Kurt's death notice to his parents rather than her. It was something almost as bad, but at least Kurt was unharmed. It was a letter from the Abwehr. Since when did they send her letters? She was sceptical, but it had the correct address on the letterhead. The letter contained information she had requested about Greta, her links to the Abwehr and to Hermes, but they were asking why she needed it. She couldn't believe it had taken Hermes this long to fulfil her request. She had kept asking him and he had replied tersely that he was working on it. But that was Nazi bureaucracy for you. Slow. Now she needed to explain her actions. She was running out of time and couldn't deflect them anymore. She crumpled the letter into her pocket. It would be safe there until she could read it more carefully. No one could see it yet. She had risked too much.

Chapter Thirty-Four

Monday, 29 June 1942

Charlotte wasn't sure why they were protesting outside the university, and she didn't know what they hoped to achieve. The square was full of students, but that wasn't unusual. This wasn't a place where their message was likely to be heard. It was the local government buildings, the Reich's offices where they needed to go. Only there would they find the people who could make a change. As they had seen, the university had no power. All they could do was work together, to learn and understand. But that alone would not change the world.

The university was full of echoes, reflecting similar ideas back and forth. They could all sit around and make the same noises, agree with each other, but what good would it do? They weren't far from where the Jews had been assembled, but if that was not enough to make everyone see what was happening then what difference would this make? It was dangerous, and yet Charlotte couldn't drag her eyes away.

A young male student was stood on a small wooden box, shouting to the assembled crowd. It reminded Charlotte of the videos of Hitler addressing thousands of enraptured Nazis, but with less of the pageantry.

'We cannot go on strike,' he shouted. 'They banned strikes. We have no unions. The only way we have to fight back against what they are doing is to protest and fight.'

He paused for a second to let them take it in.

'If we don't, many more will die.'

The crowd cheered their agreement with him.

'They brought in rationing, indentured workers. The war takes everything we have, but it was supposed to give us more! We can barely afford to live and many of us come from a wealthy background. Imagine what people with less than us have to do.'

They waved their placards and signs. Charlotte would never have expected such a response. She assumed her fellow students were as convinced by the propaganda as she had once been, but apparently they too had had enough. Sadly, it wasn't each other they had to convince. They were young, they had no power and were easily dismissed by those in charge.

'The newspapers and the party will say they should work harder, get another job. But how? How, when they are already working all hours of the day to put food on their family's table?'

A shape appeared at her shoulder and she took a step away. Except it was Stefan.

'Come away from here, Charlotte.' He grabbed for her but she ducked away from his hand. 'It's not safe.'

She had to see what was going on. Stefan may have been right, but it wasn't the first time in her life she had been in an unsafe situation. She could handle this more than him and she didn't need him to look after her.

'I'll be fine. You go,' she replied over her shoulder as she marched towards the university. She was pulled back as Stefan finally made purchase on her arm. He spun her around to face him.

'You don't understand. It's not that the protestors are going to hurt you, but being seen here will seriously harm your prospects. Yours and mine. Do you think the party will take kindly to anyone involved in these protests?'

'No, of course not, but we're not involved in them. Merely watching.'

'They won't see it like that. If the Gestapo see us here then we'll be sent to a concentration camp with the rest of them.'

She struggled to relinquish his grip, but his hand was firmly locked around her arm.

'Be sensible,' he said. 'We can't win the fight like this. It's too open, too dangerous.'

'Go if you want, Stefan. I'm no coward.'

He closed his eyes and let go of a breath. She didn't know what he was thinking but when he opened his eyes again she could see the concern deep within them. She stopped struggling as the shouting from the crowd intensified.

'What's going on?' she asked, hoping Stefan had a better vantage.

'It doesn't look good. There are brownshirts. Seriously, Charlotte, we shouldn't be here.'

At that moment a gunshot rang out. The protestors ducked, but didn't move. No one appeared certain about what they'd heard. Then there was another bang, this time closer and louder. Everyone scattered, making for the trees.

'All right, all right. I don't want to run into the brownshirts any more than you do. Where shall we go?'

'Back to my apartment. It's closest. We can't go to the university now. I'll have to call them later to find out what's happening, but for now let's keep out of the way in my home.'

Once in the safety of Stefan's apartment, he reached for her, but she pulled away and went to the window to look out. It was similar to the day she had confided in him about being followed, but things seemed far more serious than they did even then. She sat on the couch and put her head in her hands. She could still see the rows of Jews lined up for deportation, but now they were intermingled with the student protestors.

'My father took me to see a protest once.' She was mainly talking to herself, reliving the memory. But she stared at him

282

as if she could make him see her father, make him understand her entire life. 'He said it was an important thing to see, but he didn't say any more than that. But I'm starting to realise that he wanted me to see how important they are. That they're the only way some people have a voice. That is of course until the Nazis banned anyone from protesting.'

'I knew your father. He was a good man.' Stefan looked out of the window as if he was recalling a memory. She was growing weary of his revelations, but more so of his secrets. This was not exactly the place for this discussion, but as usual he had her intrigued.

He sat next to her and she sat up. The scent of him was strong and she took a moment to breathe it in. She placed a hand on his chest in part to push him away, but to also feel his heartbeat.

'How did you know him?' she asked.

'Who didn't around here? He was a very popular man. I liked him a lot, so did many others.'

'You know that's not what I mean.' She tutted. 'Details. I thought you were a man of detail.'

He laughed. It was deep and reverberated through his chest. She longed to hear it again, to feel it through the pads of her fingers. But she didn't know how to make him laugh. He was a dour man, but not like Kurt. He was always concerned; Stefan was aloof. The thought of Kurt made her stomach drop and she took her hand off Stefan's chest. He took it for impatience and leant in closer. His shallow breaths were warm on her face and smelt faintly of mint. He smiled at her, showing his perfect teeth.

'Your father helped me get work at the university,' he said. Something in his tone suggested it should have been obvious, but Charlotte knew of no link between her father and the university. He had always encouraged her to get a university education, but he had always encouraged her no matter what. There was no specific reason for him to want her to go to university, but maybe there had been and she hadn't known it.

'When the Nazis were starting to make noise the Jews worried about their positions. Your father heard that the university were reluctant to hire more Jews to professorships, so he put me forward. He knew I was a good academic, that I had my doctorate and hadn't managed to find work since.'

'He was a good man,' she said. 'I remember he was always helping someone or other. There were always people coming by our house. Some of them I got to know, but many I didn't. They all moved on eventually and I assumed that he helped as many of them as he could.'

Stefan sighed. 'What the party did to him was deplorable.'

'The party?' She shook her head. 'I don't understand. What do you mean?'

The thought of her father, what had happened to him, always sent a wave through her. She couldn't sit still and pretend that she wasn't affected. It was something in her that she was unable to control.

'You don't know?' He looked as surprised as she felt. 'They're the ones who had him attacked. They thought he was a communist, a danger to the party. So they had him removed. I'm sorry, I thought you knew all about it.'

She let out the breath she had been holding. 'No. I had no idea. I . . . I thought it was just a fight. That he was in the wrong place at the wrong time.'

'As with most things, it's far more complex than that. You really didn't know?' he said again, which only made it worse. It was as if he was talking down to her, relishing in the fact he knew something that she didn't.

'My father was a very private man.' It wasn't strictly true, but it was something that she had over Stefan. She knew whether it was true or not and he would have to find out in his own way.

'You're right. He was in many ways.'

Damn him! Did this man know everything about her life and everything she didn't? She supposed it was the air of an academic,

284

but it was so infuriating feeling like she was a step behind the whole time.

'But he was also everyone's friend, Charlotte. If there was someone in need Max would do what he could to help them.'

'I know that. Don't you think I know that? My father was a good man and I miss him every second of every day.'

'Of course you do. I wasn't trying to suggest . . . I'm sorry. I honestly thought you would have known everything about him. It wasn't supposed to be some kind of competition or me showing off. I didn't mean that at all. I can see I've upset you.'

'I'm not upset. It's just you have a way, I don't know, a way of making yourself sound superior. That you always know more than anyone else. As if you're always the smartest in the room. I know you're a lecturer and I'm a student, but it can make others feel, well, inferior. I feel like I'm just a child when you talk and I don't like it.'

He played his thumb and forefinger along his bottom lip as he did when he was thinking. She knew she had gone too far, but it was too late now.

'I'm sorry,' he said eventually. 'I . . . I'm not sure what to say. I fear anything else I say will only make things worse.'

He pursed his lips and shook his head.

'I suppose that I'm just used to explaining everything. It has nothing to do with being superior, but well, it's my job. I have to show everyone that I know what I'm talking about, that I know what I'm doing. I don't mean any disrespect, but can you imagine how difficult that is?'

'You have no idea,' she replied, picking up her coat from the back of the sofa.

Meanwhile he stroked his bottom lip again. He didn't reach for her as Kurt would have done and in a way she was disappointed.

'That's exactly why I talk to you, Charlotte. Why I confide in you. Not to show you how much better I am than you. You don't just agree with what I say. You don't just take it as the absolute truth; you question me, make me think. I know that I can always have a challenging conversation with you and I know that you are at the very least my equal. So I'm sorry if I've ever made you feel like you're not. That was never my intention, but I can see how it felt that way and I tell you this now so you know. Whatever you decide to do. If you walk out that door then know that I respect you.'

'Thank you,' she said, but kept hold of her coat. She hadn't yet decided whether she was staying, but she had questions. She wanted to know what Stefan knew about her father. It was about time she heard what kind of man he was. 'How well did you know my father?'

'That's a difficult question to answer.'

'Try.'

He pulled the nearest chair back and sat down. Then he gestured to the other chair. Despite his words of reassurance he still acted every bit the lecturer.

'If you would like,' he said alongside his gesture, 'I will tell you everything I know about your father. The times I met him, the times he helped others. Everything I can think of. Then you may decide how well I knew him.'

She took the proffered seat, laying her coat across her lap. She wanted to demonstrate some kind of barrier between them. She hadn't completely forgiven him yet.

'Your father was a good man. But you knew that already.' He fell into a manner of telling a story, or perhaps giving a lecture. His eyes glanced to the ceiling as if seeing a different place or time, recalling a distant memory. She could remember why she had been so drawn to him in the first place. The easy tone of voice that drew you into the tale. In another world she could see him earning money from public speaking tours, like a German Charles Dickens. That or a salesman. She suspected, given his way with words, he could sell anything. He was just like the Führer in that, only quieter, more restrained.

'Your father wasn't exactly a communist, nor was he a union man. He was somewhere in between. If he was anything he was a social democrat, which I think is how he met your mother, but you would have to ask her about that.'

'My father always said that joining a political party was too much commitment, that he didn't agree with any of them. He even refused the party when they asked him, though he knew it was dangerous to say no.'

'Your father was a shrewd man. If he was a member of anything other than the National Socialists he would have been locked up. But that didn't mean he wasn't involved with the parties. He just didn't want a paper trail.' He took a sip from a glass of water on the table. Then spat it out again.

'Cat hair,' he said, laughing.

But Charlotte didn't join in. She had no humour left.

'Where was I?'

'My father's involvement with the parties.'

'Oh yes, of course. He got involved with the senate, which at the time was a coalition between the SDP, the social democrats, and the KPD. When the Nazis came to prominence and the Jews started to get worried he appealed to the senate to do more for them, but they refused.'

He leant forward in the seat and interlaced the fingers of his hand on his lap, as if he was teaching her. In a way he was. She thought she had known her father, but his life had been kept secret from her.

'He was friend to any man, but no matter how much he tried to broker peace, to support the unions, the Jews, even the communists, he just got more and more in trouble with the Nazis. Until one day they'd had enough of him.'

She gasped, despite herself. 'You're right. I had no idea.'

Except, she had always suspected that her father had got on the wrong side of powerful people, but she had been living in denial. In her mind it had been an accident, a fight gone wrong.

287

'I suppose he thought he was protecting you.'

'He shouldn't have. He should have told me. Then things might have been different. I could have helped him.'

Tears were wetting her cheeks and she wiped them away with her sleeve.

'No. There was nothing you could have done.' He reached out to clean away her tears, but she brushed him off. 'If the Nazis wanted your father gone then they were going to get rid of him whatever happened. You should be glad that he saved you from that. If he didn't then you wouldn't be here either.'

He leant in. She thought he was going to kiss her, but he didn't. Even though she wanted him to take her, help her forget everything that had happened, the horrors of the world in a moment of ecstasy, he simply brushed a strand of hair back behind her ear and put his arms around her. He felt like a father figure, rocking her back and forth. But she didn't want a father. She'd had one of the best fathers possible. The Nazis had taken him away, and nothing would bring him back.

Monday, 10 February 1936

The waiting room at the hospital was as sterile and dull as the rest of the building. It did nothing to quell Charlotte's fears. Each way she turned there was a white wall.

'It's your father, Cha-cha. I think you'd better sit down.'

'Don't call me that, Kurt.' Her fingernails were cutting grooves in her palm. Damn his politeness. How dare he use the nickname her father had given her. 'Out with it. What's happened to Pappa?'

'I'm sorry, my love. He never recovered. The first attack caused lasting damage, and this latest attack only made things worse. The doctors said there was nothing they could do.'

Why did men always talk in euphemisms when they were too scared to say what they had to say? She paced the room as a band closed around her chest, constricting and constricting. She couldn't speak even if she had anything to say. It would have been a garbled mess, just as her stomach was now.

She had always known this day would come, just not like this – when her father was older, not when he was in his prime. She hadn't even had a chance to say goodbye and she would never forgive her father for that. After the fight that had left him battered and bruised she had always known it could happen again. She hoped that it wouldn't, but it was too late for hope now.

'Say it, Kurt. I need to hear the words.'

His eyes widened but he did what he was told.

'He's dead, Charlotte. Your father passed away an hour ago.'

Unbidden her hand shot to her mouth and her jaw trembled. Her body told her to sit down more than she had ever felt the need in her life, but she couldn't. Sitting down felt like giving in. And she knew that even if she did sit, she would be back up again in a heartbeat. She was full of energy, the thoughts in her mind giving her body motion. She couldn't keep still for a second. She moved to quieten the trembling in her jaw, to numb her mind.

Kurt reached out to her, but she took a step away. He looked every bit the young man in that moment, his eyes downcast, his feet shuffling. Even his uniform did nothing to save him. She understood that he wanted to help, to comfort her, but that was not what she needed in that moment. She needed her pappa; she needed to punish whoever had done this to him.

'I'm sorry, Kurt.'

'You're sorry?' he asked, understanding failing him. He was a smart man, but in this moment he was at a loss. She felt for him. If only he could reach inside her head and hear her thoughts, understand how she was feeling. Then he might know. But she had no way of communicating it. Words failed her. There weren't words to communicate her feelings. Was it anger? There was plenty of that, but there was also something else. Something she couldn't name. Perhaps this was what grief felt like, but she had thought she had felt grief before.

'Where is he?' She moved towards the door, but Kurt stepped in her way.

'Not now,' he said. 'They won't let you see him yet. And you need time.'

She placed a palm in his chest and pushed, but he stood firm.

'There's never enough time,' she replied. 'I need to see him.'

'No. Wait a while.' Kurt matched her steely stare. She couldn't remember, but she thought it was the first time he had ever stood up to her. She pushed again, but he wouldn't shift.

'Please, Kurt. I must.'

'No,' he repeated.

She used both arms to try and wrestle him out of the way, but he gently gripped her arms and held them away from him. As a wave of tears hit her, she gave in. It was as if her body collapsed beneath her, all motivation gone. She fell into Kurt's waiting arms. He took her in, wrapping his arms around her and taking her weight.

She sobbed as he made soothing sounds. It was the last thing she wanted to do, to admit defeat, but if she was going to do it in front of anyone she was glad that it had been Kurt.

Pappa looked so peaceful, even though his face was marked with bruises. She wanted to reach out and touch the lines of his face, commit them to memory, but she couldn't move her hands. Her arms were pinned by her sides. This was precisely the situation for which she needed him. She needed him to tell her what to do, to speak those words of wisdom he always had for her. Without him she was completely lost. She no longer had a guiding light.

Kurt tucked his left arm around her right and took her fingers in his. For the first time that day she let him comfort her. She turned her head so that she could see him out of the corner of her eye. Perhaps Kurt could be that guiding light she needed now.

Chapter Thirty-Five

Sunday, 26 July 1942

The knocking on the door was becoming more insistent. It reminded Charlotte of when Kurt had come round and thought she couldn't hear him. But it couldn't possibly be him. He was serving with the Wehrmacht somewhere at the front. Charlotte came out of her bedroom and stared at the wooden barrier as if it would turn transparent and reveal who was outside.

Hilda's head also poked out of the crack in her bedroom door. Her eyes were wide and she glanced from Charlotte to the door.

'Go back inside,' Charlotte said to her. 'I'll see to it. Don't worry.'

Those words were useless. How could Hilda not worry? And how could Charlotte not worry about her friend? She should have taken her to Sweden by now and saved her from this. If only she could think of a way. Every step towards the door was like a nightmare, bringing a thought about who it could be. But she had no choice but to open it as the knocking continued.

'Inspector Richter?' She stumbled across the words like a drunk. 'What are you doing here?'

He didn't seem to notice her hesitation, and pushed his way into the apartment. If anything the inspector was leaner than the last time she had seen him. Had he been exercising more? She doubted it. It was far more likely that the effect of rationing was taking its toll on his body, like it was with all of them. She could see that he had once been a handsome man, but that was some time ago, before he had let the job get to him.

'I thought you'd never answer. What the hell kind of game are you playing? I'm here to see you, of course.'

He cast a look around the apartment, then his gaze settled back on her. It was the same as it had been in the police cell. He was watching her, analysing everything and judging her.

'What on earth could you want with me?'

She let the words hang.

'Don't worry, fräulein.' He gave her a grin, which felt genuine, but did nothing to reassure her. 'I'm not here to arrest you.'

The thumping in Charlotte's chest slowed ever so slightly, but it wasn't enough to repress her anxiety. She had heard false promises before and while he might not be here to arrest her now, it may have been a ruse to get her to say something incriminating so that he could arrest her later. No, she would still have to be careful around this man.

'I was hoping I wouldn't see you again.'

'Now that's mean. I was hoping quite the opposite.'

'I don't know why.' She took a step back from him, wanting to put as much distance between them as possible. He may not have been from the Gestapo, but the Kripo were almost as dangerous as them. 'What is this? Why have you come here?'

'Remember your friend Greta? I have more information, like the fact that her father has been arrested.'

Charlotte felt a jolt go through her. She glanced over at Hilda's door, which was still mercifully shut.

'We can't talk here. My room-mate—'

His gaze followed hers. 'I understand. Where should we go?'

293

She ushered him out of the door and pulled it gently closed behind her. She hoped Hilda would just assume she had gone out. There was a certain strangeness about the situation. Last time she had seen the inspector he had her locked up in a cell; now she was leading him to a bar. How far she had come.

One they'd got a seat in the bar around the corner she turned to him. 'Look, Inspector, I don't know what you want with me, but I have things to do.'

The bar was mostly empty. One old man was sat one end of the bar nursing a glass of pilsner as was no doubt the same in bars around the world, and the barmaid was rubbing at dirty glasses with an even dirtier rag. Charlotte had ordered a tea, but it didn't look like it was forthcoming.

'I haven't forgotten about you, Weber,' Richter said. 'How could I?'

A few seconds later the serving girl arrived with two coffees. Charlotte didn't think there was any point complaining.

'I didn't think you were interested in Greta's death. When last I saw you it had been dismissed and almost forgotten about. A closed case you said.'

'Oh, I didn't mean that. Not exactly. Although that has given me an excuse to find you again. I meant how could I forget you . . . personally.'

She took a sip of ersatz coffee and grimaced, but it wasn't just a result of the bitter taste. He continued despite her silence.

'You know, you look so much like what the party considers to be the perfect Aryan woman that it almost encourages one to agree with them.'

'Are you here to talk about Greta or to ask me out to dinner?'

He let his mouth hang open, but there was a faint smile at the corners of his lips and his eyes glowed with humour.

'Coffee is the next best thing.' He chuckled.

'You're not here just to have coffee. Why have you taken so long to find me? Greta's death was some time ago. I had almost forgotten her myself.'

It wasn't strictly true. The image of Greta's hanging body would stay with her forever, but she wanted to make a point. What good were the police if they took years to solve cases?

'There's been a lot going on. And it wasn't a priority.' He shrugged. 'But I knew I would track you down sooner or later. We don't have the resources we once had. A number of my men have been reassigned. Some have gone over to the Gestapo and a lot more have been sent to the front. Your friend's case is in a file in a drawer somewhere. All but forgotten. But it never sat easy with me. I didn't trust the doctor's report at the time, but there was pressure on us to move on and put the case to bed.'

Did Greta's life really mean so little to him? She had resolved several times that the responsibility had fallen to her to find out about what had happened to her friend, but then she had also been busy. Perhaps she could sympathise after all.

'What brings me to you now then? And why didn't you just use this information yourself?'

He took another sip of coffee and glanced at the old man at the end of the bar. He was still staring into his drink, so Richter continued. 'We were passed a list of handwritten names. Each of them had something to do with resistance networks. Most of it was out of date, but your friend's name was on our list. And it got me thinking. What if she was got rid of?'

'She *was* "got rid of". I tried to tell you at the time, but you wouldn't listen.'

He gave her a look that she thought was supposed to demonstrate he was sorry, but only made her angrier. It was as if he was passing the blame on to someone else.

'It wasn't my fault,' he said, almost reading her thoughts. 'The Nazis control the police, not just the Gestapo, but the Kripo and the Orpo. A girl like that is found dead, but unless her parents are party members there's no resources to investigate.'

Charlotte pushed the coffee to one side. The acorn taste was giving her a headache. 'She was murdered. I'm sure of it. She had no reason to take her own life, but the police didn't even bother to investigate it properly.'

'I never forgot about that case. None of it made sense. Why you were there, why she was bleeding but also hanging. I think they assumed, given her looks, she was a Mischling. No one thought it worth investigating at the time, but I'm a criminal inspector; my job is to solve crimes, regardless of who is committing them, or who the victim is. Her father has just been arrested in Paris for being a Jew. I recognised his name because I used to enjoy reading his books.'

It made no sense. Andreas had told her that Greta was a member of the Nazi Party. How could she be half Jewish and a member of the party? Unless Andreas had been lying? What could he possibly be covering up? But maybe Greta had joined the party to cover up her Jewish background, used the Abwehr as a way of protecting herself, but she had been betrayed. Was that why Hilda had no respect for Greta?

The detective gave Charlotte that lopsided grin and she had to stifle a shudder.

'I hadn't forgotten about you,' he said, using an informal address as if they were friends. 'I told you we would meet again. That was my way of saying I hadn't given up. And here I am.'

She made to get up from her seat, but he stalled her with a hand.

'Look, I'm sorry. All right? I'm sorry about your friend, and I'm sorry it's taken this long to talk to you about it. No one deserves to die and be forgotten. God knows there's enough young boys doing that at the front.

'You want to look into it? Be my guest. But there's no way I can help you. Even if it would mean spending more time with you. That would be worth it, for sure. But I'll lose my job and then I won't be able to save anyone.'

'How am I supposed to do that without police help?' She couldn't tell him everything she knew, but she wanted information out of him. 'I'm just one person. I have even fewer resources than you.'

'You'll have to ask questions. I'll help where I can, but unofficially. But whatever she was doing, she was doing it to save her parents. Think about it. She was a Jewess, maybe not directly, but close enough. If the Gestapo started probing her family then they would find out exactly what she was, and she wanted to stop that. She wanted to make a good impression, be useful.'

The barmaid walked past and asked if they wanted any more drinks. Charlotte pushed the half-full coffee cup towards her and shook her head, but Richter asked for another.

'It's better than the stuff at the station,' he muttered under his breath.

After the barmaid returned with a jug of coffee and a fresh but dirty cup, Charlotte pushed the conversation on.

'What if it was the Gestapo that got rid of her?' she asked. 'How am I supposed to go up against them?'

'I have no wish to get caught up with the Gestapo, but this isn't their doing. Not their style.'

'Not enough dungeons?'

'Something like that. We're all supposed to be police, but their remit is a little different from ours. I could ask them for help, but then they would just take over. And who knows what they would do with the information. Besides, I don't want to do their job for them.'

She could imagine just what it was like working with the Gestapo, and she wouldn't wish it on anyone.

'Why do you think you can trust me?'

He took a long hard look at her, his coffee raised halfway to his lips, before he placed the cup back on the table and shook his head.

'I don't trust anyone, not even my colleagues. That's the problem. You can't trust anyone in this country anymore and quite frankly I've had enough.'

He sipped some of his coffee, some of the black liquid sitting on his top lip before he licked it off.

'They're supposed to be police, but it isn't our job to round up people and torture them. We're supposed to uphold law and order, but they're a law unto themselves. When the Gestapo was created it didn't sit easy with many of us. It was as if our ability to do the job was being questioned. Then when we found out what they were really up to it only made that feeling worse. We are just traffic police and garbage collection now, and when things get really bad, scapegoats.'

Charlotte wasn't interested in a history of the German police forces, but she could understand why Richter was telling her this. He was still apologising for not investigating Greta's death.

'I understand, but I really must go,' she said. They had been sitting in the bar for too long, and she was due at the university. She couldn't put her life on hold for his idle reflections, not if she was going to find out who had killed Greta. 'If you can't help me then I think our conversation is over. Thank you for the information you have given me.'

She turned in the chair and stood up.

'Wait,' he whispered. The way he rubbed his hand on the back of his neck was as if he was warring with himself, trying to come to some decision. 'Here.'

He slid a handwritten list across the table.

'The Gestapo are short-staffed and want our help. A list of suspected resistance members. And even better, another one of the possible double agents.'

He slid a second sheet across the table.

She grabbed them before he could take it back and slid them into her handbag. Even a glance as she did so told her one thing. She recognised some of the names on the list.

She didn't thank him as she left. It was too dangerous having the lists in her possession, and too dangerous to be near the inspector. She all but ran back to her apartment. She would have to find a safe place to hide them and analyse them later, but it wasn't the only thing hidden in her apartment that could see her sent to a camp.

Chapter Thirty-Six

Tuesday, 28 July 1942

'Stefan. I'm so glad to see you.' She shut the door to his office and walked over to him.

'What's wrong? Has something happened?' He took her in his arms, and gently brushed her hair. 'You look as if you've had a run-in with the Gestapo again.'

She pulled away from him, not wanting to be coddled. In a situation like this she didn't want a father, she wanted a colleague, a comrade.

'It's something like that, and if the Gestapo knew what I knew then I wouldn't be standing here.'

Stefan turned from her and pulled the blind down to cover his window. He clearly didn't want anyone to see them. Then he lit a cigarette and sat on the edge of the desk. He offered her one, which she declined, before idly tapping his finger on the wooden top. Where had he learnt that? She wanted to ask him, but she didn't think he would tell her. She took the sheets out of her handbag.

'Don't ask me how I came to find it. I can't explain and if I try to I will put people in danger. But I have a handwritten list of possible members of the resistance, and I don't know what to do with it. And a list of suspected double agents.'

'Give them to me.' He made to snatch for it as his voiced rose and she pulled it away. She put an extra step of distance between them.

'Why? What can you do with it that I can't?'

'Excuse me. I didn't mean to make you jump. I can pass them on to the resistance. They will want to know they have been exposed. And they can get information to London, or the Americans. Ask for help. Maybe somehow it will give them a way to put pressure on the Nazis.'

She wasn't sure. His outburst had surprised her and she didn't want to let the copies out of her sight. Perhaps she shouldn't have come to him in the first place. It would have been better to keep him out of it.

'What good would that do? The British tried to put pressure on the Nazis in the beginning, but no one wanted to listen.'

'They may do now.'

'Maybe. But I can get them to the British through Sweden. I don't need you for that.'

'You're right, of course.' He smiled and shook his head. 'These situations get to us all, don't they? They want us to lose our heads. That's how they catch us and torment us. I'm sorry, Charlotte. I should know better, but it's not always easy.'

'I know exactly what you mean. I haven't been myself recently.'

'I think it's about time you met some friends of mine.' The smoke from his cigarette wafted around his head. She desperately wanted to ask him for one, despite already declining his offer, but she didn't want to deprive him and be in his debt. She'd quit sooner than owe him anything. It was the same reason she didn't accept any of his rations.

'What do you think this is, Stefan?' she asked. She knew she was being obtuse, but she wanted him to say it, to be more direct. She was tired of his euphemisms. 'I haven't introduced you to my friends. Why would I want to meet yours?'

'Oh I think you're going to want to meet these friends.' There was a spark in his eye as the faint light caught it. He looked over his shoulder as if they could be overheard here. 'They're more colleagues than friends, and not from the university.'

He scribbled an address on a piece of ripped paper. 'Meet me here at eight o'clock.'

She took the note and made for the door. Whatever she had hoped to achieve by coming here, she was sure it had had the opposite effect.

'Oh, and Charlotte.' His tone had reverted to that of a teacher to a student. 'Make sure you keep those lists safe. Who knows what will happen if anyone finds you with them.'

Charlotte looked down on the docks. This place was her home. How could she think about leaving it behind? But somehow she had to find a way to get her friends out. She thought she was on the right path now, but a number of things would have to fall into place before she could bring her plan to fruition. And that didn't mean it was easy. She and her friends could just as likely be sent to a concentration camp. But that didn't mean she shouldn't try. Her father would have encouraged her to try, despite the odds, and she wished he was here with her now.

At times the smell in the air was unpleasant, filled with salt and brine. It wasn't as clean, as peaceful as Stockholm, but it was home. She had grown up here, lived through the Weimar Republic, worked her way into the university. Despite all its faults it was home, and that had a certain pull on her.

She met Stefan at the address he had given and he led her across the road and around a warehouse before they got to where they were going. There was a young man smoking outside an iron door. When he spotted Stefan his eyes widened to take in Charlotte, then he touched the brim of his cap and rapped three times on the door. The sound reverberated and it took a few long seconds before someone opened it. They were admitted to a

301

reception area that must have been an office at one time, leaving the young man outside.

It was like the club again, but this time there was no music, only a tense silence and the menacing stares of the men guarding the warehouse. There were various pieces of fishing equipment, nets, and other pieces of maritime detritus that she couldn't identify. The guards took her handbag without asking, then took both their coats. It wasn't quite the maître d' experience, but she expected they wanted to search their belongings. She was given a rough pat-down, then Stefan and one of the guards grunted to the other, who opened a door leading into the main warehouse.

Inside a group of men had already gathered. As far as Charlotte could tell she was the only woman there. They were stood in a circle facing each other, as if making some kind of deal, or in a stand-off.

'Who is she, Stefan?' one of them asked without preamble. 'And why have you brought her here?'

He was shorter than the others, by half a head, but better dressed. He wore a deep navy suit that made him look like some kind of clerk, while the others wore rough cotton pants and tunics. She guessed they were dock workers.

'If she's just some student you're fucking, then you needn't have brought her along. That's for your own time.'

Charlotte felt her cheeks go red. Stefan placed a hand on her arm to calm her, but it only made things worse. She had been asking herself the same question. What was she doing here? Why had she come?

She knew one answer, but she couldn't tell them that. Greta had been involved with them somehow, and she needed to find out how.

'She's like us, Jurgen. She's seen what's become of Germany. She wants to help us fix things.'

In a way it was sweet the way Stefan talked about her as a fellow conspirator. It was almost naive. He had no idea the secrets

302

she kept, but if the resistance found out then they would surely kill her. She had to play their game, at least while she was here.

'She's just a woman. What can she do in this Germany, that we can't?'

'I can fight.' She was just as surprised at the words that came out of her mouth as they were.

Jurgen laughed. It was the kind of laugh that had no warmth, as if he just wanted the others to join him. The others just stared with dead, emotionless faces. This was no social gathering.

'She had this on her.' The brute from the doorway held up her pistol between two fingers as if he was wary of touching it. The other guard handed them back their coats and her handbag.

Jurgen walked over to the guard, pulled a handkerchief out of his pocket and took hold of the pistol.

'You know how to use it?' he asked Charlotte, talking directly to her for the first time.

She nodded, it felt like less of a lie that way. While she had been trained in the use of firearms at the Abwehr school, she had never fired one in anger. Her trainer had assured her that the two were entirely different. She couldn't tell them that. She couldn't tell them that she had carried it since Kristallnacht. They wouldn't believe a word she said. They had already made up their minds about her.

Jurgen flicked the pistol around in his hand and she braced for what was about to come, but he simply handed it to her then folded up his handkerchief and put it away.

'I don't trust her.' One of the others spoke for the first time, rounding on Charlotte.

'I vouch for her. I'd swear my life on her loyalty.' She didn't know why Stefan was risking so much on her. He didn't know her half as well as he thought he did, and she felt guilt at the secrets she had kept from him. But maybe in the long run they would keep him safe. If the resistance found out what she had done, who she really was, then maybe they would believe they he had no idea. They would only blame her for it. That was what she hoped. But if the last couple of years had taught her anything, it was that life wasn't that simple.

Jurgen held up a hand to stall his companion. 'What is she to you, Stefan?'

It was a question she had been asking herself. What was going on? Why was Stefan suddenly so confident in her abilities?

'You're right about something,' he said. Oh no, not that, Charlotte thought. 'She is one of my students. But one I've been preparing for this role since day one.'

Charlotte turned to him sharply. What did he mean he had been preparing her? Was this part of some plan he'd had all along?

'She can help us. I know she can. She's intelligent. She has a Swedish passport. She can go places we can't.'

Before she could open her mouth to ask what the hell was being promised, there was a thump from outside. Then another and the door through which they had entered crashed open. Everyone turned to see what was happening. It was the young man who had been smoking outside the warehouse. He was out of breath and in the gloom Charlotte could still see the sweat pouring off him.

'Raid!' he shouted to no one in particular. 'Gestapo.'

Before he even uttered the second word it was drowned out by the sound of moving feet. Boots stamped and shuffled on the stone floor as the men ran. Stefan grabbed her arm as she stared at the boy.

'What are you waiting for?' he asked, pulling her alongside him.

'I don't know where to go.' She had been frozen, she realised. Stopped dead by two simple words. In that moment she wondered why they had ever chosen her to be a spy. She had thought she was capable, but when it came down to it she had frozen. Without Stefan she would have stayed there until the Gestapo caught up with her.

He didn't hesitate. He grabbed hold of the neck of her coat and dragged her after him. A few seconds later there was the report of gunfire. She saw the man who had questioned her loyalty kneel down and point a pistol in the direction of the door. He fired one shot, and then another. From between the shelves and crates she caught a glimpse of a face she recognised. It was the boy from the library; she was sure of it. She hadn't seen him in so long, but that meant he was with the Gestapo as she had originally suspected. The ramifications rushed through her brain, but then one of the other men pitched forward. He lay still. Stefan bundled her towards another door. Before she had a chance to see what had happened they were through the door.

It led to a walkway between warehouses. Several metres below them was the cold dark water of a canal. The walkway was rusty and pitched from side to side as they ran over it. When they reached the other side, Stefan shouted over the crack of gunfire.

'Help me,' he said, then started undoing one of the bolts that held the walkway in place. Charlotte worked on the other side. She had to use her coat to get enough grip as the bolt was stuck, but after a few moments of struggling it came free. With a horrible scraping sound the walkway dropped, hitting the warehouse wall as it sank to the depths below.

'Now run as fast as you can and don't stop until you get to my apartment.' He pushed her in front of him. 'Go!'

Chapter Thirty-Seven

Charlotte didn't know whether it had been the tension of the evening, the Gestapo chase, or whether she had simply wanted to, but she had ended up in Stefan's apartment again and stayed the night.

She had left him to his shower, and the sound of running water could be heard from the bathroom.

As she tentatively tiptoed around the room barefoot, she took it all in. The wooden floor was worn in places, and curved from where water had damaged it, but it was smooth on the soles of her feet. It was also cold, and she looked for something to warm herself, but there were no blankets on any of the chairs. The place was functional, a functional mess.

The sun was coming in through the window shutter and she wanted to feel it on her face. Something about this whole experience felt like a new start. It was as if she was finally an adult, finally capable of making her own decisions and not being dragged along by events. She was here because she wanted to be here. Even if there was a wave of guilt every time she thought about what she had done. It wasn't just that Stefan was one of the lecturers at the university and in a position of power over her, it was Kurt too. He was her childhood sweetheart and she had always thought that they were meant to be together. That they were soulmates.

But she had needed something else. It was hard to explain. But what she had done with Stefan felt right. Just as much as she and Kurt had always been destined to be together, last night had been destined to happen. She didn't believe much in prede-termination. Her parents weren't particularly religious and nor was she, but sometimes there were things in the universe that just fell into place, whether you wanted them to or not. It was like there was some universal story and you just had to make decisions on the way leading you down certain paths. It was like music. You could play different notes, but at some point they all fit within a scale.

Of course, if anyone was to find out she would be in trouble. The thought made her tremble and sit down on a pile of papers on a chair by the window. If Kurt found out it would break his heart. She couldn't do that to him. She loved him too much. A tear escaped her eye and rolled down her cheek. She didn't deserve him. He was too kind, too sweet for her. Why hadn't she thought of him before? She had thought this was all meant to happen, but she had been lying to herself. She had been rebelling against his choices, against the world, and Stefan had seemed like the perfect opportunity to find herself.

She wondered where Kurt was now. If only she could speak to him, she felt it would make things better. She wondered desper-ately if he was all right, but she had no way of knowing. He could be doing anything, suffering anything and she would have no idea. Her tongue seemed to stick in her throat, her stomach clenching as if she had swallowed something too large to digest. She missed him, but it was so much more than that. There wasn't a word for the absence she felt, not in German nor in Swedish. It wasn't like a part of her was missing; that was a cliché. It was as if there was a hole in the world, a piece of a jigsaw irretrievably missing, or a story without an ending. It was just . . . wrong. That was the only way she could describe it.

She had tried to tell him once, but he had misunderstood. There was no way of communicating it. She had tried writing it down, but that wasn't much better.

She wondered whether the pile of Stefan's papers that she had sat down on were important. You would think so to look at them, one of the many discarded piles around the living room, but you never knew, especially with academics. Her bedroom was not much different, and while at first she had been glad they had not gone there, it was at least tidier than here. She had many of the same books next to her bed, discarded when she had lost concentration and been unable to read any more.

She lifted herself from the seat on one arm and pulled out the wad of papers. The top one had been crumbled by her backside, and she folded the corner back down with her hand, trying to smooth it out. She couldn't help but read the first few lines. The notes appeared to be some form of lesson plan. The page was divided up into sections and various books and philosophers were scribbled in the margins. As she flicked through, unable to stop, she noted there were names she didn't recognise. But that didn't surprise her. She was only a student and there would be any number of philosophers and critics she had yet to encounter. The strangest thing was that each of the notes appeared to be written with a different pen, often in different colours, and at some points the handwriting appeared to be from another hand.

She knew she shouldn't be reading, Stefan could come in at any moment, but at least the notes didn't appear to be private. He wouldn't just leave them around if they were. But maybe he had not expected anyone else to be in his home.

She looked over at the bathroom, but the door was still shut, so she returned to the notes, fascinated. Most of them were the same scribbled writing, with questions to himself. At one point there was a series of four digits. They were written in the same blue as the majority of notes, but for some reason that made them stand out. She couldn't remember if she had seen any other numbers at all on the page, except for maybe the divisions between sections. It could have been anything, but it drew her attention. It could have been a telephone number, but it was missing two digits and why would a telephone number be written in his notes when there were directories for numbers?

It might have been someone's birth date – there was a slightly larger gap between the pairs of digits – but that didn't make sense. He could have scribbled it when someone told him while he was taking notes, but that didn't seem to fit the pattern of writing. It was as if it was deliberately concealed within the text. A reminder to him, but something that would look innocuous to someone else. It could have been a code to a lock or something else, but that gave her as many questions as the telephone number. She knew it was nothing to do with her and yet she was intrigued. Her analytical mind ran through the various things it could be, but none made any more sense than the others. She could ask him, but then she would have to admit she was looking through his papers, and for some reason she was wary of the number. She committed the numbers to memory, thinking them over and over again like a prayer, so that she could check them later.

She collected the papers back together. Typically she would tap them on the bottom to make sure they were in line, but for some reason she didn't want Stefan to know she had flicked through them.

As she went to lay them on the windowsill a glossy card fell out of the papers and landed on her lap. The light caught it. When she realised it was a photo she let the papers fall onto the sill. The top sheets slid off, but she didn't care. She had recognised the faces in the photograph. She didn't dare pick it up. To do so would be like admitting that it was real. Charlotte sat there as if a spider was crawling across her lap, quietly recoiling as if any noise would bring its attention to her.

309

It couldn't be. Stefan looked the same as he always did, except for the smile on his lips. The curly black hair next to him was instantly recognisable. The same hair she had last seen covered in blood that fateful day she'd entered a friend's apartment. It was Greta. It couldn't be anyone else. She hadn't known the other woman well, but she had recognised her before she had recognised Stefan. Those big eyes stared into hers in still life as they had done in death. It was as if they were imploring her to help, but that was impossible. This photo has been taken at least a few months before her death. Greta's hair was shorter, less curled. Just like Stefan she had a big grin on her face.

Charlotte didn't know they had known each other, but here lying on her lap was evidence that they had. Since the photograph had fallen on her lap the temperature in the room had increased a couple of degrees. The noise in her head rose to a buzzing that pressed at her ears as if trying to get out. She could feel the pressure behind her forehead and escaping through the window became a tempting prospect, but she couldn't move. She was rooted to the chair. Bile rose in her throat and she retched, but it was dry and pulled at her throat. She had felt this way before, but only when something triggered it. She kept asking herself the same question, but the answer would not come in any way resembling sense. How had they known each other?

She daren't look closer at the photograph, but her fingers grasped the edges, crumpling it in the middle as she raised it from her lap. They had their arms around each other.

At that moment a door clicked open. Quickly she pushed the photograph back between the pages, not caring whether it was the correct place, and looked up to see Stefan's smiling face in another form.

'*Morgen*,' he said, beaming at her as he came into the room. He picked some papers up from the floor and placed them on the table, apparently making an effort to tidy up. 'Forgive the mess. I've been working on a paper, but I can't seem to get it right. Perhaps I need a fresh set of eyes on it.'

When she didn't respond, he came closer. The look on his face did not drop for an instant. She smiled back, hoping to avoid saying anything. She would talk to him eventually, but right now she wanted to be anywhere else but here.

'You've found my reading seat,' he said. 'I'm not surprised. It's my favourite place in the room. The way the sunshine comes in without being too much, is perfect. Although I hope you haven't been reading my notes. They're not quite ready yet.'

His smile broadened as he indicated the pile of papers on the windowsill.

'Oh, those?' she replied, a little too quickly. 'I just moved them there so I could sit down.'

She could feel a bead of sweat rolling down her temple, but it wasn't the first time she had been in a situation like this. Although on those occasions it hadn't been trying to deceive someone she knew, someone she cared about.

'I really need to do something about this place.' He leant down and kissed her on the cheek. His bristle rubbed against her skin and it took all of her strength not to recoil. She didn't want him to notice her discomfort. There would be time for that later. First she needed to process it all in her own mind, then she would investigate what was really going on here. She didn't want to have to ask him difficult questions before she could make sure that she was in charge of them.

'Next time you stay it will be tidier. I promise. I'm not used to having women stay.'

Only a few months ago she would have thought that his behaviour was sweet, endearing, but now she could cast an altogether more critical and mature eye upon the situation. He was positioning himself in a place of power over here, abusing his role of academic. It was easier for him to say there would be a next time. There was no doubt in his mind because that was what he wanted, but she wouldn't let him control her.

Part of her thought that she should trust him. She had become too cynical, and he had always been good to her. But wasn't that exactly what he was counting on? She wouldn't make any rash decisions; that was always dangerous.

'My turn,' she said, heading for the bathroom. He reached out to embrace her, but she rushed past with a forced giggle. In the bathroom she turned on the tap and let the water flow.

His words rushed around inside her head, like a stuck record. He had known Greta. That much wasn't surprising. The university wasn't large and they could have seen each other in the corridors. But there was more to it than that. He had *known* her. His words implied so much more. Charlotte had become used to listening to what wasn't said, not trusting any word she heard at face value. Perhaps she had been overthinking it, but that felt like a part of her brain that was denying the facts.

Had Stefan been sleeping with Greta too? Charlotte couldn't believe it. He didn't seem the type, but then how many women before her had thought that they were the special one? Perhaps he thought he was doing it for a reason, as if sleeping with her and other women was a means to an end.

She splashed water on her face, but it wasn't enough to get rid of the sensation. She wanted to rub her skin clean, until it was red raw and free of any trace of him. Free of the marks of betrayal. She rubbed one palm along the other arm. Had it always been so rough and pockmarked? Had the corruption of this world already affected her skin? Even water wouldn't change that.

She turned off the tap and stood back. Closing her eyes only made the voices in her mind louder, but at least it helped her to focus on them. She would need to think carefully before she chose her next steps. Did she trust Stefan? She was no longer sure. Anything she said to him now would have to be even more guarded than it had been before. She would listen to everything he said, write it down, read it back to herself, and analyse it. If he changed what he had said then she would know. Then she could decide what to do with that information.

There was a faint knock on the door. 'Charlotte? Is everything all right?'

How could she reply to that? Nothing was all right. Nothing had been all right since she was a child. Since her father had died. Since she had joined the university.

'Just a minute.' Her voice sounded weak, child-like. She cleared her throat and tried again. 'I'll be out in a minute.'

She smoothed down her clothes and retied her hair, before looking into the mirror and forcing an expression of confidence onto her face. She only hesitated for a second, taking a deep breath, before wrenching open the door.

'I have to go,' she said, wanting to speak as little as possible.

'So soon?' He pursed his lips and scratched his head. 'I thought we might spend the day together.'

'If only I had the life of an academic,' she said, but the joke felt as forced as the smile on her face. 'I'm sorry.'

He waved it away. 'I'm fortunate. Very fortunate. Others in our country are not so, but that's a discussion for another day. I won't keep you, although I desperately want to.'

It only took her a few seconds to leave the apartment building, past the concierge who flashed her a confused look. Outside she crossed the road, putting distance between her and Stefan. She could barely think of his name.

Charlotte staggered over to the kerb, doubled over, and vomited into the storm drain. She wasn't prone to sickness, but there was a bile she needed to get out of herself. It burnt her throat on the way up then swirled around the drain as the rain caught it. She heaved again, with nothing more to give, and then spat in the drain to clear the taste away.

She couldn't shake the feeling of Greta looking over her shoulder. Charlotte could feel her close, as if Greta's breath was on the back of her neck. What if her friend had slept in that same bed? She could picture Stefan putting his arms around Greta and Charlotte retched again. She had to get away from here; she couldn't think straight while she was still so close to Stefan's home.

She looked back. Was there a shadow in the window, a flick of the curtains? She couldn't be sure, not with the gloom and the rain. Her mind was playing tricks on her; she was seeing shadows, being followed everywhere. The stress of her situation, of her life, was finally causing her to lose her mind. It was a wonder it had taken this long.

She stumbled away from the house like a drunk. A man in a long raincoat frowned at her, then gave her a wide berth, muttering something under his breath, but Charlotte no longer cared what anyone thought. They couldn't hurt her anymore.

Chapter Thirty-Eight

Monday, 9 November 1942

Going to the resistance meeting had been a disaster. Charlotte had kept her head down and stayed out of the way since then. She had wanted to talk to them more, to get to know them and see who was on the list that Richter had given her. That way she could trace them back to Greta. But the Gestapo had got in the way. It seemed they had a habit of that, and once again she wondered if they had been tracking her. It didn't matter so much now; she knew what she had to do. She had a plan, but she needed to talk to her friends first.

She opened Andreas's door because she was in a hurry. He had walked into her flat so many times without knocking that she only thought it fair.

'Andreas?' she called as the door swung open.

He was inside with his back to her. She stopped in her tracks, because as he turned to face her she realised he was not dressed as he usually was.

'Charlotte, no!' He raised his voice and rushed to shut the door. 'No one is supposed to see me like this, not even my friends.'

He was naked from the waist up except a band of cloth that

was tied tightly round his chest. The skin was purple either side of the cloth as if too much pressure had been applied to it. She should have looked, but the underpants he was wearing betrayed his secret. His hair had grown out into little blond ringlets.

'I'm sorry, Andreas. I had no idea.' She didn't know why she was blushing, but the whole scene felt intimate. She was seeing into something she shouldn't be seeing, and with that came a certain privilege. If what Charlotte suspected was true then like her Andreas had a secret to hide. An even bigger one.

Then there was the danger. This was a secret she didn't think was hers to keep. She knew she should tell the Gestapo, but how could she? Andreas was her friend, no matter what, or who she was. Charlotte could not betray her, no more than she could betray her own family.

'It's all right, Charlotte. Now you know.' He grabbed a dressing gown from the back of a chair and wrapped it round himself. It made him look more like the man Charlotte had come to know. 'I doubt I could have kept it a secret from you forever.'

'You're posing as a man?' she asked, knowing she had no right to pry.

'Not exactly posing. I'm just Andreas, the same person I've been since you've known me.' He poured a glass of water and handed it to her. Then leant on the kitchenette worktop with the other hand on his hip. 'Have you ever heard of a Doctor Hirschfeld?'

She took a sip of the water – it was cool and refreshing – then shook her head.

'I didn't think so. The Nazis destroyed his work, beat him up, and ran him out of the country. Here, here, come and sit down. Please. We need to talk.'

He led her over to the sofa and perched on the arm. His flat was much like her own, but she hadn't noticed until now, her attention was too distracted.

'He ran the sexual research institute I told you about.'

'I remember,' she replied. 'You made it your life's work to carry on his studies, but they wanted to stop you.'

'You see, it's about more than that. It affects me too. I'm not a woman. Despite what my parents may have thought. Despite what you may see when you look at me now. That's not who I am. I don't know how else to describe it. I have never been what they wanted me to be. It never fit what was inside myself. What I saw when I looked in a mirror was someone else. It was like looking through a train window at a platform and seeing someone who looked like someone you recognised, but realising it wasn't really them.'

'I'm glad I finally know, and that you feel you can talk to me about it.'

After what had happened with Hilda, Charlotte had expected a shouting match. She still felt guilty about the things she had said to her friend, that Charlotte had called her crazy and believed the lies that she had been told about the Jews. She worried that Hilda felt she couldn't confide in her. She wanted to be there for her friends and she wanted to understand everything.

'I'm sorry for asking, but I'm trying to understand. It must be so difficult for you. This is . . . delicate. How do you cover up your time of the month? If there's anything I can do.'

'That's simple, Charlotte.' His voice had returned to the tone she knew so well, as if he was giving her a lecture, but it was kind and she was hooked. 'I don't menstruate. I never have.'

'Never?'

He shook his head. 'Never. I . . . I have female genitalia, but no womb, no ovaries. I can't menstruate even if I wanted to, and I'm increasingly sure I don't. I'm sorry if this is confusing for you.'

'No. Please, go on. I feel now that I'm finally starting to get to know you. The real Andreas, not just the face you put on for everyone else.'

'My parents spent a fortune trying to understand what was "wrong" with me. But there was nothing wrong with me. I'm exactly

317

who I'm supposed to be. If my parents were not old Prussians then I would not have had the money to live the way I do. And I don't just mean in relative luxury. My papers are false. If you must know Andreas isn't even really my name. At least, not the name my parents gave me.'

'What is the name your parents gave you?'

'Julia.'

Charlotte couldn't think of anything to say to this friend she'd had for years. Nothing she could think of stood up to the truth that Andreas had revealed. Charlotte was quickly learning that she didn't know the first thing about anything. Was everything a lie? Could she trust anyone at all?

But then she was a hypocrite. Her own life was a lie. None of her friends knew that she had been keeping her own secrets from them. As far as they were concerned she was just a university student who made ends meet by playing her violin. She was just like them, and yet she wasn't. They all had their secrets to keep, secrets that they wouldn't need if they lived in a different country. She couldn't possibly articulate this to Andreas who still stared at Charlotte as if waiting for a response. What could she possibly say? That she understood? She didn't understand, but she wanted to.

'Say something, Charlotte. Your silence is worst of all. I can't stand it.'

'I'm sorry. I don't know what to say. I'm just thinking and thinking, trying to make sense of what you've just told me. I just know you as Andreas and that's how I'll always know you.'

Charlotte tried to look at her friend, but her eyes kept dropping to the floor. She found it easier to think when she wasn't trying to maintain eye contact.

'That's exactly how I want you to know me, Charlotte. Andreas is who I am. I am Andreas.'

'I know. But this is a lot to take in.'

He leant forward on the chair again, and she could see the warmth in those familiar eyes.

'Let me tell you the rest of the story. The Nazis destroyed the entire Institut für Sexualwissenschaft back in 1933 when they seized power. They set back research into sexuality and gender by hundreds of years by destroying everything they could find. They wanted to make sure that from then on all people would know about is binary gender, but biology is not so simple.'

'How do you know all this?'

'I have friends, researchers, people in hiding just like myself. I am not an anomaly, a freak. There are many more like me, and there are many not like me who wish to help those like me. We talk when we can, but of course . . . it's dangerous. Anyone could turn us in to the Gestapo at a moment's notice.'

Charlotte swallowed, but bile caught in her throat. Had she been responsible for any of Andreas's friends being caught by the Gestapo? She hoped not, but she would never know.

'The party just wants us to be happy little families, man and woman, fucking and making as many little happy Nazis as we possibly can. Women like you mean nothing more to them than as baby-making machines. And I know that's the last thing you want to be. I've seen you grow, Charlotte, learn, become somebody. Don't let them take that all away from you. Don't let them take a future away from us. We deserve more.'

'Don't worry, I have a plan.'

'Be careful. Do you swear you will tell no one? They'll do far worse to me than throw me in a camp. They wouldn't understand who I am, what I am. What did you even come to see me about?'

'It doesn't matter now, but I wanted to ask you about Greta. How you knew her.'

'Her? I don't know why you're obsessed with her. But if you must know, that horrible woman thought she knew something about me, but there's no way. She tried to blackmail me, and I refused.'

* * *

319

Charlotte was writing down some notes when there was a knock on the front door. The fist only rapped twice, as if it expected to be heard and knew how well the sound travelled around the apartment. She put the pen down on her desk and shuffled her notes into a folder. If she waited then maybe Hilda would answer the door or whoever it was would go away. She didn't want to be disturbed and thankfully the light from her room was not visible from the front of the apartment. Whoever was knocking wouldn't know that she was in. She didn't know who it could be. Stefan wouldn't take the risk of knocking on her door. He had never stepped foot in her apartment building.

The knocking came again, louder. Had the Gestapo finally tracked her down? Or had Richter come back? He promised he wouldn't. The Abwehr wouldn't come here either. It had to be someone looking for Hilda, but then Charlotte didn't trust who that could be either. Not with what she knew about Hilda. Her friend was far more vulnerable than even she was.

Kurt beamed as she opened the door. She almost collapsed. 'You came back?' she whispered.

'I did.' The grin didn't leave her face.

He wore his uniform and it was cleanly pressed. Unlike everyone else she had seen recently he didn't look gaunt and faded. It was as if army life had done him good, but there was a look in his eyes that was different. It was as if he was looking through her.

He took hold of her hand and spun her around before pulling her into a hug. She let him wrap his arms around her and breathed in the scent of him. She had forgotten what he smelt like. She had become far too used to another smell. Another man. She closed her eyes.

'I applied for leave and they granted it,' he said. 'I'm as surprised as you are.'

'But I thought you would want to spend your leave with your family. Why aren't you with them?'

He still held her. She was in shock and barely hugged him back. Her arms were loosely wrapped around his back. His body felt different, leaner. She wasn't sure how that was even possible, but they must have not been feeding them well at the front.

'I don't know why, but I could tell something was wrong. I had to see you as soon as possible. To make sure you are all right. I know you don't need me to look after you, but even with that in mind, something didn't feel right.'

'Even out at the front you were more worried about me?'

She could already feel the tears pricking at the corners of her eyes and she wiped them away with a finger. She should tell him what had happened between her and Stefan, but now didn't feel like the right time. She was too much of a coward. He had come back for her and her betrayal would break his heart. Just as the look that he would have in his eyes would break hers. She couldn't handle that. She couldn't handle any of it. She was a liar and a cheat, everything that she despised in other people.

'Of course. I always worry about you. Me? I'm a lost cause, but you? You're important, you mean something to the world. I'll always put your needs above my own. I had to come and find you and make sure that you were still you.'

Kurt looked at his shoes. He never knew what to do in these situations, but somehow he always knew what to say. Even when they argued he said the right things. It was usually she who got it wrong, but that didn't stop her getting angry with him.

But this time, she simply pulled him closer to her, wrapping her arms around his waist and resting her head on his chest. It only took him a second to hug her tighter. He let out a sigh.

'There,' she said. 'Just hold me for a while and everything will be all right.'

The embrace was a return to the before time, before the war, before she had become embroiled in the affairs of the Abwehr. She wanted to keep her eyes closed so she could pretend nothing had changed, that they were both safe, warm and well fed. As soon

321

as she opened her eyes she would see his uniform, be aware of everything it represented, see the state of the city, feel the cold, the emptiness of her stomach.

It was too bad her mind had already wandered away from her. She couldn't keep those thoughts away, no matter how hard she tried. She had changed. It had happened even before he had left and had continued since. She was a different woman to who she had been, and in many ways she was glad. She just hoped that Kurt could still see the good in her, because without that she might as well give up now. If he didn't believe in her then she was not sure she could either, and she would need that belief to get through what was coming next.

Chapter Thirty-Nine

Charlotte had never felt tiredness quite like this. Sure, she had experienced times of exhaustion from her studies, or from the work she did in the League of German Girls to make sure she got into university. But this went beyond exhaustion. The constant pressure of looking over her shoulder had worn out her mind. Anyone in Germany could be watching her, assessing her movements, ready to turn her in at any moment. It wasn't just the Gestapo. Even a regular citizen was a threat. Even in Sweden she wasn't safe. They claimed to be neutral, but that wasn't enough of a protection. If the Nazis wanted something from them, then they would give it to them. Even if that was her.

She couldn't remember the last time she had had a full night's sleep, let alone a restful, complete sleep. Especially not since Kurt had returned on leave. He had stayed with her for a few days, holding her in his arms, clearly reluctant to let go, before he had to return to the army. Now, she couldn't even remember what sleep was like. It wasn't even a dream. She longed for this war to end, so that she could finally sleep, finally be safe. It almost led her to do whatever she could to help the Nazis, but that was no longer who she was. The party had broken every promise they had ever made. They had lied, and they had destroyed Germany. It would never be the same again. The Abwehr had her running errands across Hamburg, delivering letters from one administrator to another, but she was determined not to just be a messenger. She had to get information. She wouldn't sleep until this was done.

She lifted the cup to her mouth and took a sip, letting the liquid play around her mouth as she closed her eyes and let the taste linger. It was real coffee, nothing like the stuff they had back in Hamburg. She had almost forgotten what it tasted like. The rich bitterness, offset with creamy milk. The milk in Sweden was different too, almost more pure. She closed her eyes and savoured the taste. She would have to see if she could take some home. The letter in her purse suggested she could do what she wanted when it came to the border, but she didn't want to push things.

She opened her eyes again and looked at her mother across the dining table. 'Why didn't you tell me?' she asked.

'What, dear?' Her mother was also lost in the cup of coffee. All they were missing was her home-made cinnamon buns, but Charlotte didn't think she could eat anything.

'About Pappa. What happened to him. How could you have kept it secret? We never keep secrets. But you lied to me. His whole life was a lie and now I don't know who he was. He was everything to me.'

'I didn't want you to worry. It wasn't your responsibility.'

'I should have known.'

'No, Charlotte. You shouldn't. I know what you're like. You're like him. You take everything into your own hands and you would have run off to avenge him or something equally stupid.' Despite the anger in her mother's voice there were tears in her eyes. 'Can you imagine what it was like for me? In a foreign country and my husband had just been beaten up by his own government. Taken away from me, forever.'

She placed a hand on Charlotte's cheek.

'I could not stand to lose you too. So I had to protect you. It was the only way, and I'm sorry I had to lie to you, but sometimes you lie to protect those you love more than anything, and you are the only thing left to me in this world that I love. I hope you understand that.'

'Of course, Mamma. Of course I do.'

She moved her chair and pulled her mother closer. She was still angry about the lies, but she could at least empathise with what her mother had done. Charlotte had also had to lie to protect those she loved, and it had been necessary. She wanted to tell her mother about everything, but knew that it would only harm her.

No one could know what she had been up to: that she was working for the Abwehr and the resistance. It was safer that way. It wasn't that she didn't care about Stefan, but he already knew. He had been the one to bring her into all this and then the Gestapo had got wind of what they were up to. In a way it was his fault. She could have carried on working for the Abwehr, doing bits and pieces, but ultimately slowing them down rather than being useful, but thanks to Stefan she had to live a double life. Except it was more complicated than that. No one else knew about Stefan and her, and she wanted to keep it that way.

She realised then that she had been lying to them all in some way. None of them could trust her. She was a complete fraud. How many times had she considered giving up before? When Kurt was obsessed with marrying her. When she had started her studies. When all this stuff with the Abwehr had started. And now the Gestapo would not be far behind. She had led them to the resistance and they would track her down again somehow. She had wanted to end it all, somehow retreat from the world and just be at peace. But life wasn't that simple. It never had been, and likely never would be. But sometimes that wasn't the problem.

Every time she had wanted to quit as a child her father had picked her up again and smiled at her in that way of his. "If we give up, then we'll never have the chance to achieve the things we want," he would say, while giving her a big hug. "The only thing that holds us back is ourselves."

The significance of those words had meant nothing to a child who desperately wanted to avoid school and anything to do with it, but she had gone along for her father's sake. Because he believed in her, and that was the most powerful motivation in the world. It was only later, as an adult, that the words had really stuck with her. If only he was here now then she was sure he would give her that hug and say those same words.

But he was with her in a way. She could still hear those words in his voice and she reached for the charm hanging around her neck. It was something he had always worn and now she wore it every day as well. She clasped it, encasing it in her fingers and closed her eyes. She often looked to the sky in these situations, even though she didn't consider herself religious, imploring whatever existed out there beyond their realm of understanding. Imploring them to help her, support her, and keep her strong. Sometimes she thought they listened; other times she wasn't so sure. Now was one of those times.

Her mother went to get ready for church. Charlotte had no desire to go, but she had agreed for her mother's sake. She didn't know when she would see her mother next, or if she even would. She was almost at the end now, and finding out who had killed Greta might result in her own demise. She had come to Stockholm to further her plan, but she couldn't leave without seeing her mother.

Charlotte was utterly alone in this world. But she had ever felt that way and it had been even worse after her father had died. After he had been killed, she reminded herself.

'I miss Kurt,' she said aloud to no one in particular. 'He would know what to do.'

She looked around to see whether anyone had been listening, but she was alone. Talking to herself now? That was a development for the worst. Kurt may not be perfect, but she was never in any doubt that he cared for her. He had written her letters, but they were not the same as having him here.

It was crazy. She had come to realise they had different perspectives of the world. Kurt supported the party, and she had begun to see them for what they were. Kurt had been lied to by them just as much as she had, and perhaps that was why she thought there was still hope for him. If she could start to see what the Nazis were truly like, the evil they were committing in Germany, then maybe Kurt could too.

Her mother passed her coat to Charlotte and it reminded her of being a child.

'Thank you, Mamma,' she said.

She was in Stockholm at the behest of the Abwehr, but it would be harder for them to know what she was doing in the city.

Even still, she wore a wide-brimmed hat and long coat despite the unseasonal heat, and she ducked her head as she entered the British Embassy. With confidence she walked straight up to the reception desk and said, '*Hallå.*' The receptionist stared at her, with a polite smile plastered across her face.

She would try in English, but she hadn't spoken English in a number of years.

'I need your help,' she said, knowing that she would have to explain further but hoping not to have to do it in a public area.

'Many people ask for our help. What makes you think we can help you?'

She didn't have a response. She had expected questions, but not that one. She opened her mouth a couple of times, trying to find the words, but the other woman continued.

'You're Swedish, yes?' Presumably she could tell from her accent, but Charlotte decided to try her hand.

'German, actually.'

The receptionist put down her book and sat up straight,

finally giving Charlotte due attention. Her words had the exact effect she was looking for. Why would a German be here asking for help?

'I see,' the receptionist said. 'Let me pass this up the chain and see what can be done.'

'Good.' Charlotte wanted to say so much more, but not to this woman. Let her realise she was in charge here and she would only speak to someone who mattered.

She waited for several minutes. Something about the experience felt familiar, but she couldn't put her finger on what it was. After an age the receptionist returned and led her along the corridor to a pair of wooden doors. Before she let Charlotte enter she took her hat, coat, and handbag.

The doors led to an office, which was decorated with wooden panelling, a chandelier hanging from the ceiling. It resembled the dining room from one of the fancy hotels along The Strand, but much smaller.

A man in what she assumed was a Savile Row suit sat on the other side of the desk and gestured for her to take a seat.

'What did you say your name was again, fräulein?'

'I didn't. Or rather, you didn't ask.'

'Even still, I'll have to tell *them* what you're called. I'm the British ambassador, you may speak to me.'

'Tell them . . . Tell them I'm called Hilda.'

She had no reason to lie, and yet this man irked her. She would come clean to someone superior if they treated her with respect and seemed willing to help her.

'Right you are, Miss Hilda. Now, why don't you tell me why you're here and why you think I am in a position to help you.' He steepled his fingers in front of him and stared at her over them. Now it had finally come down to it, she wasn't sure what to say, so she started with the basics.

'I'm a messenger of information, on behalf of the German military.'

'I see. You understand I can't tell you anything about our operations. In fact, I know very little myself.'

'I'm not asking you to tell me what you are doing in my country. I'm only asking you for help.'

'I understand, of course. But there are so many other German citizens asking for help and they have been for almost a decade now. We cannot possibly help everyone.'

It was typical of the British to be both welcoming and unfriendly at the same time. They were so wrapped up in etiquette and tradition that they often struggled to see the detail.

'I'm not just anyone, I'm a German spy working for the Abwehr. I have links to the resistance too, and I want to help the British end this war. Can't you see that I'm useful to you?'

'And how am I to trust that you are who you say you are?'

All her items had been taken from her before she had been brought into the room, including her violin case, but her handbag contained a number of choice items that might encourage him to believe her.

'If one of your people looks through my handbag, which I suspect they already have, then they will find some letters. They won't mean anything to you at first, but if you analyse them you will be able to work out where they are from.'

He steepled his fingers in front of his face and regarded her with a cool look.

'I don't think any of my people would stoop so low as to rifle through a lady's handbag.'

'Please, I'm not naive. Why else did you take it from me if not to see what it contained? They will also find a pistol, but that belongs to me and I would very much like it back.'

His eyes widened at her suggestion. Perhaps he was not expecting that she would come armed, but she hoped that it would be testament to the veracity of her claim. He would be a fool not to believe her, but given his attitude so far she would not be surprised. After a few seconds of silence he unsteepled his fingers and reached for the Bakelite telephone on his desk.

He didn't dial, nor did he give a greeting when the receiver answered the call. 'Yes,' he said simply, without taking his eyes from her. 'Indeed. Very well.'

With those cryptic words he replaced the receiver on its cradle. He nodded at her and shuffled some papers on his desk. It was the first time he had broken eye contact with her since she had sat down in his office. An awkward minute or so later the office door opened and an aide walked in. He handed the ambassador a few envelopes and a notepad, both of which Charlotte recognised. She didn't say anything. They would either know what they were or they wouldn't. Whatever happened she was determined not to leave the embassy without help.

'We will be in contact, Miss Weber. I think it would be best if you didn't come here again unless we ask you to. Who knows who could be keeping an eye on your whereabouts.'

She didn't want to think about it. He had raised her fears from earlier. Fears she had put out of her mind to be replaced by the fear of them not believing her. She was not entirely convinced they did believe her, but the ambassador's demeanour had changed. The look of pity had fallen from his face to be replaced by something she would have described as grudging respect. At first he had dismissed her as a meaningless woman, now he suspected there was much more to her than that and she was going to prove to him that she could help.

Her bag and violin case were returned to her, then she was escorted to a back door of the building, which was shut and locked behind her. The meeting had only lasted a few minutes and now she was back on the streets of Stockholm. But those streets had changed for her. Now they seemed to close in on her, watching her every move. She would have to be even more careful than before. She had thrown her lot in with not one, but two enemies, the Abwehr and the British.

Chapter Forty

Tuesday, 2 February 1943

'I need to get on that ship.'

The chill Copenhagen wind buffeted Charlotte, but she stood firm. She reached out but the crewman blocked her path. He tutted and apologised, but wouldn't move. Over her shoulder there was no sign of her pursuers, but she knew they wouldn't be far behind. Coming to occupied Denmark had been a mistake, but it was the only way to get home from Stockholm by ship. She should have stayed on board.

'Please. I'm German.'

'Your accent is good, but I don't care. We're not taking on passengers. Captain's orders. It's too risky.'

'Even going into Germany?'

'Even that. Now go away. We've got to get underway.'

He pushed her back down the gangway and she almost stumbled. She didn't stop to shout her anger at him. The people chasing her could arrive at any minute. She thought of trying another boat, but they would turn her away just as quickly. The members of the resistance, or that's what she assumed they were, had waited for her outside a coffee house. She had spotted them and managed to get away, but she had missed her scheduled journey to Hamburg.

She ran. She didn't know where she was going, but she had to get away. They were following her; she was certain of it. They had come into her lodgings and searched through her things. What they were looking for she had no idea, but that was the only logical explanation. And now, wherever she went she could feel the shadow of someone following her, the presence of someone on her trail. They could simply be watching her, but instinct told her otherwise. They were getting too close to her and she was vulnerable. Once she was back in the Reich she would be safer, but she had to get there first.

Her shoes pounded over the cobbled streets, splashing in a puddle that sent oily mud up her legs. She had put on trousers for the boat trip, and for that she was thankful. Running in a skirt would only have made things worse, not to mention the rain and mud. She turned a corner. The road led away from the docks, but she had to put some distance between her and her pursuer. Somehow she had to throw them off her trail. As she ran she glanced side-ways for an alley or passage she could cut through, but the wall was continuous, impenetrable. If only she knew the city better.

Copenhagen was a warren and yet that shadow was still behind her. She thought about stopping to look over her shoulder, but knew that would allow them to catch up. But when would she know they were gone? Only when that feeling vanished and she finally felt alone. She turned down an alley and then past another building on a path that she thought led back to the harbour.

'Wait. Please!'

Charlotte knew she should have kept running, but the pleading in his voice stalled her. How could she run away from someone in need? Even if that need turned out to be a ruse. What else could she do? She turned to face the voice.

'I thought you would never stop.' The man spoke in heavily accented English, not knowing that thanks to her Swedish she could understand a little Danish.

He was dressed like a dock worker, with a brown cotton waist-coat over beige undershirt and brown trousers. His ruffled blond hair the only shock of colour that stood out from the otherwise dull ensemble. He was maybe of a similar age to Charlotte, the softness of his face suggesting he was in his early twenties. Despite his thin build he was out of breath from following her.

'What do you want? I don't have time for this.' She gestured vaguely in the direction of the docks, hoping that he would get the idea without her needing to be explicit. She still had no plan to get out of the city, but stopping to talk to this man certainly wasn't helping.

'I overheard you in the coffee house.'

Charlotte forced herself to shrug, but her heart rate increased. What could he have possibly heard? She had been talking to the barmaid, confided in her in a way she shouldn't have, but Charlotte was tired. Instead of claiming ignorance, she went on the attack.

'That was a private conversation. How dare you?'

'I'm sorry. I couldn't help it. At first I was daydreaming and then I couldn't help but listen to your conversation. You were sat so close to me. Even if I hadn't wanted to.'

He drifted off, apparently noticing Charlotte's frown. So it had been him that had been chasing her all this time. Not the resistance.

'I still don't think it's fair to listen to other people's conversations. You should have gone somewhere else.' She turned to leave.

'I'm sorry,' he said again. 'But please wait. I need to talk to you.'

'I can't think what you could possibly want to talk to me about. I don't even know you.'

'No, but you know people like me. You're German, aren't you?'

'What has that got to do with anything? Do you seek to blame me for what's going on here? It's nothing to do with me. None of my business. You're better off going to the German governor.'

She was scared and her words didn't match her feelings. She had had enough of people telling her she was wrong without truly knowing her.

'You're a traitor!' The words hit her just as hard as any bullet.

'I don't know what you're talking about. Leave me alone.'

She pushed him away to carry on back to the harbour. She didn't have time for idle chatter and accusations. But he stood in front of her. He was slight and she could have overpowered him, but something about his manner lent her patience.

'Whose side are you on? Truly?'

The answer to that question was far more complicated than she could articulate and so only one word formed in her mind for her to speak.

'Mine,' she said.

His eyes widened and what she thought she caught there was a sort of admiration, which was quickly replaced by a frown.

'If we weren't in this mess, then I would think that very selfish.'

'What else am I supposed to do? Sometimes it's important just to survive. That's all I ever wanted.'

'At what cost? Who will you sacrifice for your own survival?'

'Not my friends. Never my friends. They're the reason I do this. The reason I'm here.'

'Then I wish to be your friend. I need your help.'

'My help? Why me? After the things you've called me.'

'It was a test. I don't know. I wanted to be sure you were who I thought you were.'

'What do you want?'

'You! Halt!' Two German soldiers from the dock had caught up with Charlotte, but it wasn't her they were pointing at. The Dane looked one way and then another, like a trapped animal, his teeth bared as if they would defend him.

'Halt! Come here.'

Charlotte hesitated at the contradiction. But there was nowhere to go. The soldiers had them trapped in an alley.

'You brought them here.' The Dane shot a glance at Charlotte, almost spitting the words. 'Damn you.'

Charlotte noticed then that they were trapped. The alley was a dead end and neither she nor the Dane had any way past the German soldiers. They stepped closer, but slowed. Their chase was up and there was no need to expend any more energy on their prey.

The first soldier landed a punch on the Dane's jaw. He spun around and almost bounced off the wall. He clawed into the masonry in apparent effort to keep him up. But it was no use as the other soldier kicked his left leg from beneath him and he fell to the ground with a thump. He raised his arms over his head, but it wasn't enough to stop them. A rifle butt cracked against his elbow and he let out a whimper.

'Please,' he said between gritted teeth. 'Please.'

Charlotte was frozen to the spot. She wanted to help the Dane. She wanted to run as far away as possible. She could do neither. Her body decided that she must witness what was happening, for better or for worse. She had no idea whether the soldiers would turn on her next, but even that was not enough to make her flee.

'There.' The first soldier spoke in German and held out a hand to her. The kind of gesture one might make if he was trying to help her from a boat onto the shore. 'We saved you, fräulein. There's no reason to be scared of this scoundrel any more. You're safe.'

She wasn't sure that was true. How could she ever be safe with men who would not only partake in such violence, but would also seemingly enjoy it? She took the hand. What choice did she have? Spurning her saviours would not go down well and she did not want to anger these men. They could easily turn their anger on her, even though they seemed to know she was German. Even though she wanted to be nowhere near them, they could help her find passage home, to the city that no longer felt like her home: Hamburg.

Chapter Forty-One

It was the same bench on which she met Hermes, but if it was safe then it was safe now. The British agent had taken an incredible risk in coming to Hamburg and she wasn't about to let him get caught. But the tide of the war was changing and the Nazis' attention was in the east. It was darker than it had been; the city council had erected a canvas across the lake to disorientate the British bombers, and it was like sitting under a massive tent. The lake had lost its previous sheen.

He sat down heavily and let out a noise that sounded in part like a deflating balloon. He wore a cream jacket and stood out more than she had expected. His rotund belly suggested he liked food and that he had no intention of running should it come to it. She liked him already.

'Hilda?' he asked. She had almost forgotten the false name she had given the British. It had been dangerous to use her friend's name, but it felt right in the moment.

She nodded and said the name she had been given: Hans.

'You're not the type of German I'm used to meeting. You look like something out of a fairy tale, but more Christian Andersen than Grimm.'

She knew it was a compliment, but it was clumsy, especially in German. 'We're not all schnitzel-eating, lederhosen-wearing mountaineers, you know?' She meant it as a joke, but it came out more forcefully than she had intended.

'Yes, quite. I travelled around the country a fair bit before this blasted war. It's why I was chosen for this job. But you don't want to hear my backstory, nor do you want to hear my humour, apparently. I'll keep it to myself and get to the point.'

'I really wish you would. We don't have a lot of time.'

He barked a laugh. 'What I have always loved about you Germans is that you are so direct. I'm English, dear. I go around the houses; I speak in euphemisms and terrible similes. You ask too much of an Englishman if you expect him to speak his mind. My ancestors would faint at the very thought, indeed.'

His words actually brought a smile to her face. He may have been a buffoon, but there was something endearingly disarming about him. He had the manner of a lecturer mixed with that of a stage performer. But she suspected it was all an act. His travel around Germany, his command of the language, weren't the only reasons he had been selected and dropped into the country to work with agents. His manner had a way of drawing you out of yourself, and she could see herself giving him information she didn't want to, if she did not watch out.

'It's a wonder you managed to forge an empire.'

Her words stopped him, and he turned to regard her with a look that was entirely different from the jovial charm of before. He appraised her as if she was a prize horse, but not in the way that most men did. He wasn't looking at her as if he wanted her; he was somehow looking through her, as if he could see into her mind and beyond.

'Yes,' he said. 'Yes, you'll do. You'll do very well.'

He looked ahead again, his appraisal finished and she had apparently passed whatever test he had been conducting.

'What do you mean by that?'

'You're obviously very astute, dear. They picked you well. You saw through me from the very beginning and you're not naive enough to believe we're on exactly the same side.'

'We're not. We never will be. But we can work together.'

'Indeed. And that means that you won't just do what you're told. Some of my colleagues like people they can push around, but not I. I want someone I can work *with*, someone who is capable of making their own decisions. In our game one needs to be able to react to changing circumstances. Having your own mind will certainly help you in that. It's clearly served you well so far.'

'I haven't let the Nazis cloud my mind and judgement, if that's what you mean.'

'I'm not sure that it's quite as simple as that, my dear.' If he was not an Englishman then she would find his tone condescending. However, it was just the way they talked. My dear this, sweetheart that. It was almost as if they were trying to copy the French, but lacking all of the charm. In German it just sounded silly and almost made her laugh, but to do so would concede control of the situation.

'If we don't stop this war soon, then your lot won't leave much left to save.'

'Your air force have been bombing us, not our own.'

'That's true, you're right. But what choice do we have?' He paused, the frown on his face indicating he was trying to think of a word. 'It's tit for tat.'

Again, she suppressed a smile. His code-switching was almost from some bad comedy movie, and the fact that he switched naturally between accents only worsened the effect.

'That's why we need to end the war. Too many of our boys are flying over here and never coming back. The same for yours. They don't deserve to die for a few men in suits.'

'That's very glib. I didn't take you for a political philosopher. You struck me more as the pragmatic type. For King and Country and all that.'

'No, you're right. Time was I would have loved a good scrap, get stuck into the enemy. Show them what for. I used to box, you know? No, that's not important now. I fought at the tail end of the old war. No, I know I don't look old enough.' There was a twinkle in his eye, which Charlotte couldn't quite decipher. Was he more self-aware than he appeared, or was it part of his arrogant British charm? 'But I saw what those trenches did to the boys. I vowed I'd never let it happen again, yet here we are.'

'I feel like you'd fit in very well with some of the society figures in Berlin. If not for the war they would love your decorum and manners. Here in Hamburg, things are a little different. There's more dockers than Nazis, not that they have any of the power, you understand? But they're the ones who make the city move. If they're not being sent off to die for the Reich.'

Charlotte wanted to stand, to stretch her legs, and there was a part of her that wanted to run as far away from this conversation as possible. She was supposed to be a student. A musician. The same old doubts rushed through her mind, while the man was speaking. An occasional word dropped into her consciousness, but she was too busy asking her the same old questions. How had she found herself in this position? What was going to happen next?

Of course she had wanted to help her countryfolk, but she had thought she was. As always, things were becoming more and more complicated.

'Are you listening, dear?' he asked.

She looked at him suddenly and nodded. By now she should have learnt that it was dangerous to potentially miss important information, but something about the British agent suggested that she didn't want to show him that she had been daydreaming. He had probably been rambling anyway.

'It's just you looked like you were in a world of your own there.' There was almost a look of concern on his face, which reminded her of her father when he had been worried about her. 'In truth I often find these meetings quite boring. However, you seem more interesting than most. Perhaps we should just get to the point, yes?'

'So, what do we do next?' She was eager to get started. Her plan couldn't wait any longer, and this was only one of many steps. 'What do you want of me?'

There was that question again. The same question she'd asked of Hermes all those months ago in the Hotel Vier Jahreszeiten. She expected the answer would be the same.

'For now? Just to know that you're on board. Sadly things don't work very quickly on our end. I was asked to set up an initial meeting, assess your willingness to cooperate, and then report back.'

'And that's it? I just wait to hear from you, meanwhile I am still working for the Nazis?'

'I'm afraid so, my dear.'

'If they find out I've met you, they'll kill me. Or worse.'

'I'm afraid that's the game.' He seemed afraid of everything, but she thought better of saying so. 'You're going to have to play them for a while longer yet. It's the only way we'll get any useful information.'

'I will bring every piece of information I have on the Abwehr and the German forces in Hamburg to the British Embassy in Stockholm. It's the least I can do.'

'That would be very good of you, but be careful. We've been at this too long. If I'm gone much longer they will start to worry and send a search party.' He grinned at her. 'The king will miss me dearly if I'm lost behind enemy lines. Who knows to what lengths he will go to bring me back. I dare to think what would happen to this fair city in that case.'

He hauled himself from the bench and went to leave, but she stalled him. 'I need you to do something for me,' she said. When she explained he nodded and said he would see it done. Charlotte didn't expect she would ever see him again, but if he did this task for her then she would be forever grateful.

* * *

As usual, when she arrived in Stockholm a few days later, Åke was sitting in her mother's kitchen, his hand around a mug of coffee. She didn't expect there was any coffee left in the cup, but he still held it as if it was comforting to him. He stared into the middle distance until he noticed her and his mouth broke into a broad grin. She had found herself in Sweden again, but this time she was not here for the Abwehr; she was here for herself. She had delivered a package to the British Embassy. It wasn't much, but it was something to prove her willingness to cooperate.

'Charlotte,' Åke said, rolling the r in that way of his.

He was like a piece of furniture in the house, a permanent fixture, but on this occasion she was glad he was there. She had come looking for him, not her mother. She didn't bother to flatter him with pleasantries. He was a direct man, and it was one of the things she liked about him.

'I need your help to get some friends out of Germany,' she said.

He put his coffee cup down and regarded her with those bear-like eyes. 'Friends? Why? What have they done?'

'Their crime? Existing in a Nazi world. One of them is a Jew. The others, well, they just need your help. And mine.'

He took a deep breath.

'Do you understand what you're asking me to do?' Åke placed his big hands on the table and stared directly at her. The frown above his eyes showed exactly what he was thinking.

'Yes. Completely,' she replied, matching his gaze. 'I've thought about it a long time. A very long time. I wouldn't have come to you if I didn't fully understand the consequences. I wouldn't want to put you in danger if it wasn't entirely necessary.'

He scoffed and she almost backed away from him. Gone was the lovable bear she had known for years. In front of her now stood an altogether more serious man. The playful light had dropped from his eyes and had been replaced with something more calculating. She wondered whether she had adopted that same expression when she had first been dragged into all this.

'It never really made sense,' he said, shaking his head. The curls of his hair waved as he did so. It was endearing.

'What didn't?'

'That you were able to come and go as you please, as if there was no war. It never made sense, but I understand now.'

'Believe me, it isn't that easy. I've had my fair share of scrapes getting across the border. I could tell you a story or two.'

He let go of the table, and she didn't realise how white his knuckles had become. The frown was still a feature on his forehead, but he turned to face away from her.

'This is some kind of trap. I don't know why, but you're either playing a trick on me or trying to trap me in something.' He turned back to her. This time his eyes were narrowed. 'I think I should go.'

He moved to walk past her and she grabbed his upper arm. Her hand only wrapped around half of his bicep and she could feel the tension there.

'Please, wait,' she said. He looked down at her hand and blinked. If only she could hear the thoughts going through his head, but all she got was his frown.

'I've got a lot to tell you about. It's not easy, and a lot of it still may not make sense, but I will try to explain. I've been working with the Abwehr, German Military Intelligence.'

He walked past her again, heading to the door. He shook his head all the way, but she carried on.

'And the British. I'm no Nazi.'

He stopped again.

'I trust you implicitly. It's why I asked you. I haven't told anyone else about this, not asked for anyone else's help. Please. Just listen to what I have to say. It was the Gestapo who first sent me here, but I never agreed with what they wanted me to do. I was using them.'

It was a half-lie, but she hoped it would hold water. It was the only way she was going to get Åke to listen to her and to understand.

He had to believe that she had been playing the Gestapo and not him the entire time. So she told him the rest of the story. How they had approached her, how she had fallen in with the resistance and then the British. She told Åke what the Nazis were really doing to Germany and how she hoped to defeat them somehow, but first she had to get her friends out.

For the first time that afternoon Åke listened intently without interrupting once. She told him all about Greta, how she had been caught up in her murder. The case of mistaken identity with the Abwehr, and everything else. He listened in silence and was quiet for a long time once she had finished telling him her story. Then he opened his mouth a few times to speak, but for the first time since she had known him appeared to have difficulty finding words.

'I'm sorry, Charlotte,' he said eventually, when she thought he would never speak again. 'I've always loved you, like a little sister, but you must know that I'm not doing this for you. Those people need my help and if helping you helps them, then I will do it. Anything to stop the Nazis.'

It was a revelation to her, but she didn't show her surprise. She had always thought of Åke as a big brother too. He had always been jovial and carefree, far from the kind of person who she would describe as a freedom fighter. She had thought his only concern was getting through life unharmed, and she thought he might help her as family, but if he was willing to help her friends anyway then she would have to reassess her opinion of him.

'Well, thank you.'

She appreciated how much it had taken for him to agree to what she was asking and to tell her how he felt.

'So what do we do? You're the expert at this. I am just a humble sailor.' There was a flicker of humour in his eyes and he smirked. Charlotte was glad to see some semblance of the old Åke back.

'Don't sell yourself short. You're far more than that.'

He waved a hand, dismissing her words.

'Ach. What did you have in mind?'

'We need to get a boat up the Elbe. Find somewhere to moor without arousing the attention of the harbour guards and get aboard.'

He whistled. 'That's not going to be easy.'

'No one said it would be easy.'

He held up his hands again. 'All right, relax. I know this is serious. But it will take a lot to get a ship anywhere near Hamburg. Can't we go to Copenhagen, or somewhere else in Denmark? It may be occupied, but the dock masters turn a blind eye to the odd boat.'

'No. It has to be Hamburg. It will be too difficult to get my friends out of the city by train or even road. There are border checks, guards everywhere. They'll need papers.'

He nodded along to each of her words, his hand clasped around his chin. Every few seconds he looked as if he was about to say something then decided better of it.

'It has to be the harbour. We can get them on board, and then we're away and out to sea. They won't be able to follow us and even if they want to they won't spare the resources needed to chase us.'

'I don't know,' he replied after a few seconds. 'It isn't just a case of sailing up the Elbe and into the harbour. We will need a reason to be there, have to register it with the authorities.'

'I think I may be able to help there.'

Chapter Forty-Two

Thursday, 22 July 1943

Charlotte was exhausted from her trips back and forth between Sweden and Hamburg, and from the constant pressure she seemed to be under. Everything in Germany was getting worse, but she had a plan. She just wasn't sure how it was going to work. That was why she had invited her friends to her apartment. They were all part of the plan. She would have included Kurt, but he had already returned to the front. Her heart felt sick for him and she wished he was here, but there was nothing she could do. She had written him a long letter, and she hoped that she could find a way to get him out of Germany one day too. She thought of Peter whom they had lost to the war, and stopped. It would only make her worry about Kurt more. Andreas and Hilda were the only two left.

They were arguing as they always did and it reminded her of that fateful night when Britain had declared war on Germany. She couldn't help but smile at their words. How long would it be before the British and the Americans were marching through the Reich? Andreas asked. They had poked a sleeping dragon and it had woken up with fury. What would happen to all of them then?

If the reparations from the previous war had caused Germany to suffer before the Nazis came along, how bad would it be now? They couldn't make the same mistakes again.

How different their lives would have been had they not declared war? The other difference from that night was that she was not an observer in the conversation. She was leading it.

'We pushed each other apart,' she said. 'Feared everyone. Forgot how to love, to live, to be people. All in the name of National Socialism. What does that even mean? It's a contradiction in terms.'

Andreas agreed with a nod. He had let his hair grow longer and his head was now covered in little blond curls, but he still dressed as smartly as he had ever done.

'We need to help each other, not fight,' Charlotte continued. 'We work together.'

'Admirable, but the world doesn't work like that. Men will always fight amongst themselves.'

'It's not just men though, is it?' Hilda asked. 'There are women complicit in what the Nazis have done too.'

'And they will get what they deserve when the British and Americans come,' Andreas said. 'I just hope we don't get caught up in it all. It's going to get a lot worse before it gets any better.'

'That's why I have a plan.' Charlotte grinned. She had been waiting for this moment. 'I'm going to get us all out of Germany.'

The other two stopped talking, their mouths almost hanging open. Hilda shook her head, more in defiance than disagreement, but it was Andreas who was first to recover.

'How?' he asked. 'How are you going to get us out?'

'I've arranged for a little trip. We're going to Denmark to play a concert.'

'What? I don't understand. Denmark is even more dangerous than Hamburg. It's part of the Reich now, but they're suspicious of everyone there.'

'But don't you see? That's exactly why we need to go there.'

'No. I don't. This is crazy and you're going to get caught.'

'It's the only way I could get permission. Denmark is part of the Reich. Therefore the foreign office will allow us to go and play a concert for Nazi officers there. Then we can get on a boat and go. We don't even have to go to Denmark. We can sail anywhere.'

'She's right, Andreas.' It was the first Hilda had spoken, but Charlotte was thankful for the support. She hadn't thought they would just go along with her plan easily. She was mad, but she was determined to do what she could to save them from the Nazis.

'You make it all sound so easy. But how did you manage this? And how are you just going to sail away?'

'It's not easy. But all three of us have secrets, reasons we can't stay here any longer.'

The other two stared at her, then at each other. Charlotte didn't know if they each knew what the other was hiding, but that didn't matter now.

'I had to call in some favours. Make a few requests. You're the only people who know the whole plan. And the answer to your last question is something I'm going to have to keep to myself for now. If it works out.'

'What? What do you mean if it works out? You're mad, Charlotte.'

'You know? I think I probably am. I think this country has turned me mad. We're all part of a collective madness, and unless we do something we're going to get dragged down with the Nazis. They were never going to fix this country. They were only ever fixing it for themselves. And so many of us fell for the lies and enticing promises. I've seen the worst of them and I want no part of it anymore.'

Andreas flopped back into the chair and put his head in his hands. But Hilda stood and came over to Charlotte and took her hand.

'I'm with you,' she said. 'I'll follow you to hell and back, because I've already seen hell, Kristallnacht, what they've been doing to my people, and I know that with my friends at my side, wherever we end up, it will be better than this.'

All Charlotte needed now was Andreas. He still had his head in his hands, and she waited for any kind of response, willing him to agree. Her plan wouldn't work without him.

'All right,' he said eventually, through the palms of his hands. Then he sat up again. 'I presume you need us all to do something. So, what is it?'

'Do you still have access to the biological labs at the university?'

He swallowed and then nodded. She knew what she was about to ask him would not sit easy and that he already suspected what she was going to ask, but they had no choice now.

'Then you know what I need?'

'I think so. It's not going to be easy to find a perfect match, but I think I'll be able to find something close enough.'

'I can give you measurements.'

'There's no need. I know enough already; I can do it by eye.'

'Here.' She picked up a cloth bag and handed it to him. She wouldn't need it any more. If they managed to leave the country then she wouldn't be able to take her belongings with her.

He undid the clasp, glanced inside, and nodded again. 'I see,' he said, refastening the clasp.

It was an ambitious plan and this perhaps the most ambitious part, but she trusted Andreas to get it right. Not just because she knew his secret, but because he was a good friend and he was relying on their plan every bit as much as she was.

Charlotte spent the rest of the morning telling them the plan. She only left out details that would confuse things, and the details about the last task she had to complete before leaving Germany: to find out who had killed Greta.

After they had left to go to their respective workplaces, Charlotte opened a notepad and pen. It was the same pad she had used to write the letter to Kurt, fine quality paper she had managed to keep from before the war. She had thought long and hard about what she was going to do. It would only take the slightest error for her plan to go awry and land her in more danger, but she had to do enough to entice the person she was writing to.

She wrote a number of identical letters. The letter would only make sense to one person, but it was only one person she wanted to act upon it. To the others it would seem like something innocuous, a friendly note from a friend, some further details about their escape that would only make sense in the context of certain conversations she'd had. But to one person it was so much more than that. She hoped it was not too subtle. But her problem was, she didn't yet know who that person was. Tomorrow she would find out, of that she was sure. Then what? She had no idea.

Chapter Forty-Three

The warehouse was cold and smelled of salt. It belonged to the Winmers, but they seldom used it, which made it perfect for her needs. It was right by the water, but close enough to the city to be easily accessible.

She was making a round of the perimeter wall when a thumping noise made her stop. She hadn't asked for anyone's permission to be here, and footsteps told her someone was coming. She hadn't expected anyone to come, not yet. They were early. She wasn't ready.

The person entered through a door on the city side. They were silhouetted in the darkness, but she recognised their outline and her heart jumped a beat. It couldn't be. It couldn't be Kurt. Not him.

'Charlotte,' he called. 'I know you're in here somewhere. Come out. It's all right. It's me.'

She let him walk towards her, unwilling to believe it was truly him. But then he was only a couple of metres away. She couldn't hide any longer.

'Kurt?' she asked, extracting herself from behind a container and into the light. 'It is you.'

'I told you I would show you that I love you.' He pulled her into him and planted a kiss on her lips. 'I've been waiting to do that for so long.'

'Kurt,' she whispered, relishing his name on her lips. 'You know you hypnotise me. Always. But what are you doing here? You're not supposed to be here.'

'I had to come back for you, of course.' He kissed her again, apparently making up for lost time. 'I went to your apartment, but you weren't there. Hilda told me where to find you.'

It was stupid of Charlotte not to give Hilda explicit orders to tell no one where she was, but in a way she was glad. If she had then Kurt may never have found her. Now he could go with them.

'I'm not going back to the front again. I'm not going to let them send me out to Russia. I'm not dying for the Reich and I'm not dying for those bastards.'

'But the party?'

'The party? I never believed in their shit anyway! I just did what I had to do to survive. To save you.'

'What? What are you talking about? You are a member of the party, you believed in it all. I saw it with my own eyes.'

He scoffed and turned in a circle, agitated. His hands were waving in front of him as if he wanted something to grasp.

'Make Germany great again and all that rubbish? You really thought I believed all that? Blaming the Jews for all our problems. I've known plenty of Jews, and other "undesirables" and not one of them has ever caused me any harm. It's always been the Nazis we should have worried about.' He took a step closer. 'But they were dangerous. The people who didn't take them seriously enough were the ones who suffered. I never wanted anything to do with them, but my parents did. And my brothers. But you know I'm not like them. I never have been. It was all an act.'

'Why didn't you tell me?'

'Because I had to keep you safe. The less you knew the better, the less danger you were in. If I openly opposed the party then

351

they would kill me, and then they would come for you. It wasn't safe. It still isn't safe. I shouldn't be telling you now, but their days are numbered and I had to do something.'

'We could have worked together. If only you'd let me in on your secret.'

It was about time she told him her secret, but she couldn't do it. Not yet.

'I knew all along that you didn't trust them either,' he continued. 'It's why you wouldn't marry me, why you wouldn't join the party. But I couldn't say anything. I had to keep you safe. Not knowing what I was up to meant you couldn't be dragged into it.'

'I know a little of what you mean. I understand the secrecy, but I wish it hadn't been necessary.'

'I should have known. I should have known you well enough to realise that it was all an act.' He smiled. 'I was good at playing the role, eh? Maybe when this is all over I should try my hand at acting!'

She put her arms around him and breathed in his scent, and then stood back, still holding his arms. She couldn't believe they were having this conversation in a smelly old warehouse. She had so much to tell him. The guilt had been eating her up. But she couldn't tell him everything. Not about Stefan. Now wasn't the time. She'd only just got Kurt back.

'I've got my own secrets to tell you,' she said. 'Now might not be the time for all of them, but you have to know I've not just been working for my degree here in Hamburg. I've been busy myself.'

'I know, the orchestra. You have a life too. I've always supported it. Truly.'

'I'm a spy.'

His face dropped and he pulled back from her. So, she told him everything, and how much she had wanted to tell him. He frowned through her story and she knew she was saying the wrong things. She didn't have the words to explain; that was why she had written the letter.

'If we hadn't had that argument that day, I would never have got to know Greta, and we probably wouldn't be here now. Who knows what would have happened?'

After a long pause he spoke. 'It seems we were meant to be. We've both been leading a secret life. Pretending to be something we're not. I had my reasons for not telling you and I'm sure you did too.'

'I don't know about that. There are all sorts of philosophers who say we have free will, but perhaps there is a reason we keep coming back together. We're better together than on our own.'

'We can fight them together.'

'But it's not just us. There are others we need to help.'

'Of course, of course. For too long in this country we've been selfish. Just like my family. What's the point of living if we're alone and only thinking about ourselves?'

'Why didn't you speak like this before?'

He stared at his shoes, reminding Charlotte of the Kurt she had known as a child.

'I was scared. No terrified. I had no idea where your loyalties lay. Although I knew you couldn't really be a Nazi, not the woman I love. But I was scared of everything. The Nazis controlled everything. I may have had the protection of my family, but how long would that last if they thought I was working against them?'

'Of course I didn't believe any of it.'

She had never seen Kurt so angry. It was as if he had been bottling it up for years. He paced, balling his hands into fists, but he kept his distance. This anger was not directed at her; that much was clear. It was directed at the world around him. And she could empathise.

'The things my parents did to their workers. And you liked them.' He turned on her, fixing her with a bloodshot gaze. 'You went along with them. They thought you were one of their own.'

He stared at her for a few seconds, his shoulders rising with his breaths. Then he looked at the floor and let out a sigh.

'You didn't know. Couldn't really know what they were like. I'm sorry. They put on a front for you, a performance.'

'It was convincing. But I never completely trusted them. I didn't trust you either because of them. But now I know I should have known better.'

'I couldn't see any other way than to go along with it, with them. Not when they were my family. At first I tried to encourage them to help the Jews, find them work, make false papers, use our money for good. But they thought I was weak and sentimental. I knew then that nothing I could say to them would make any difference.'

He needed to get this all off his chest, and it didn't matter that she was running out of time. She owed this to Kurt. 'We're descended from the Portuguese Jews who settled in Hamburg and stayed through all the religious laws and persecution. But we don't talk about that. They changed their names after years and thanks to my parents' influence nobody knows about it. We were lucky where so many others were not. If not for the factory, we might have ended up in the ghetto or the concentration camps ourselves. But my parents wouldn't listen. They weren't scared. They had money, a good name, reputation, and they were members of the party. They couldn't possibly be Jews and they would hear no talk of it. Why should they help those who had been foolish enough to keep practising that religion in Germany where they weren't wanted?'

'So you had to do what little you could.'

'I had to do what I could. If not for you and your father taking me under your wing when I was younger, I may well have turned out like them. There were times when I helped the workers at my parents' factory sabotage the equipment. We slowed down production as much as we could, until it became too obvious.'

'I would have helped you with that.'

'There was no way to get you in; it would have been too risky. My parents liked you and I didn't want to jeopardise that

354

or your safety. Of course, we couldn't do too much, otherwise someone would work out we were damaging the equipment. I think that's why I was sent to the front. Someone knew. Then the bombing did the work for us.'

'I wish I'd have known at the time. In a way it would have made things so much easier.'

'I wish I had known that you were being used by the Abwehr. I could have helped you.'

'You couldn't— We're having the same argument again. We were keeping each other safe.'

He held up a hand and then pulled her into an embrace.

'I don't care what happened. I've known you since I was a boy. You're the best of us and I love you. You did what you had to in a difficult situation, and now we have to do the same . . . to survive. It's the only way.'

'And to help as many people as possible along the way.'

'Of course.'

She sat on an upturned wooden crate. 'When will it all be over?' she asked him, not really expecting an answer.

'I have no idea, but I think we have reached a point where our little acts of resistance might actually make a difference. The army are failing in Russia. The allies are bombing us relentlessly. The Nazis have nothing left. Surely they have to give up this stupidity soon?'

'We always knew it would end up like the last war. That's what Andreas said. So, what do we do now?' For once it was her asking him.

'I have absolutely no idea. But quick, we need to go before someone discovers us. It's not safe here.'

'Where is safe? Nowhere in Germany!' Her voice echoed in the empty warehouse and she lowered it again. 'Listen, I have a plan, but I will have to explain as we go.'

An air-raid siren whirred into life. Even though it took a second for it to emit its piercing wail there was a change in the air that signalled its start. It was as if Charlotte had learnt to predict them. It was an extra sense she hoped would keep her safe.

Kurt turned like a frightened animal. 'We have to go. Now. The bombers are coming.'

'I hear them. I hear them in my dreams. Every night, without fail. There they are. Then I wake up and the city is still there but everything is a little bit worse.'

It reminded her of the time she and Kurt had first sat watching the British bombers coming in over the city. Then it had seemed almost exhilarating. When they thought it was a threat and before they had seen the damage that could be wrought on the city. Now, it was just terrifying.

They ran from the warehouse, knowing that it was one of the most dangerous places to be in the city. Charlotte explained her plan as they ran; Kurt clasped her hand like they had done as children. The dark was all encompassing, and if they weren't careful they could trip on the rough floor and detritus. But Charlotte had got used to running, and what was one flight of stairs from another?

Chapter Forty-Four

Sunday, 25 July 1943

She had left Kurt to deal with the final parts of the plan at the warehouse once the raid was over. She hadn't told him what she was going to do next. He didn't need to know, and she didn't want him to see this side of her. Not because she was ashamed, but because she couldn't break his innocent belief in her like that.

Greta's flat hadn't changed much. Thanks to her death and the bomb damage the building had received it was still abandoned. Not even the city's many homeless wanted to call this home now. But it was the final piece of the puzzle. Why had Greta been killed, and why had she been killed here? She didn't know who it had been yet, but she had her suspicions.

There was a sound from the hallway and she looked up. Her expected guest had arrived. While she paused there was no further sound. Perhaps it had been something else, the wind. The violin case stood on the table next to her, and she thought about using it as a weapon, but there was no point. That was not how this was going to go. There was still a patch of wooden flooring stained a dark reddish-brown, reminding her of what had transpired here.

There was another sound. This time it was the creaking of a

stair. Charlotte was thankful for their warning sound. Someone was definitely coming up the stairs. The person she had invited. A shadowed figure appeared. Her heartbeat thumped in her ears.

'It was you. You killed her.' It wasn't a question. The figure appeared to push themselves further into the shadows as she spoke as if in guilt. 'It was you all along. I should have known.'

There was confusion as the shadowy figured looked to go back down the stairs, but it was too late, Charlotte had seen them, and they both had to see this through.

'What was it?' she asked. 'Did she reject your advances? Was I going to be next? Was that part of your plan?'

'I had to.' The voice was muffled, but clearly recognisable to her. 'You wouldn't understand. Her death was necessary.'

Stefan stepped into the apartment. He was wearing a long coat and a wide-brimmed hat, but it was unmistakably him. She let her anger drive her words. The betrayal.

'How can you say that? How can any death be necessary?'

Her heart raged inside her. How could he kill her friend like that? She was a girl. She had her whole life in front of her and he killed her for what? It would never make sense to Charlotte.

'You lured me here?' He gave her a grin she didn't recognise. It reminded her of Hermes. The look of a killer. 'I always knew you were clever, but perhaps too clever for your own good.'

She ignored his threat. She wanted answers to her questions.

'The code was for Greta's violin case, wasn't it?'

He took a step closer. 'How did you find that?'

She stepped back. 'I saw it written on the papers in your apartment. I thought I recognised it at the time, but I was too confused.'

'The violin case wasn't important. I just had to get back what she was hiding. What linked her to me. She had to die because she was no longer useful. She refused to do what was needed of her. Her death fulfilled more purpose than she ever did in life. Her family's background would only have made things difficult for her. They were all she cared about.'

His face took on a sour expression as he said those last few words.

'Haven't we seen enough death? How can you say that now after all this?'

'If she had not died then you would not have been brought in to take her place. You should be thankful for that at least. She was a traitor. I had thought she was good like you, that she would work hard to bring the Abwehr and the Nazis down, but all she wanted to do was to make a name for herself. She wanted to climb the Nazi ladder and I couldn't allow her to do that. You were so much better than her. You hate the Nazis just as much as I do.'

A part of the puzzle fell into place. 'You arranged for me to take her place, didn't you? You wanted me to meet the Abwehr agent.'

'She was supposed to meet him, but she was working for the Reich to protect herself. But it was never going to end well for her. She would have ended up in one of the detention centres sooner or later.'

Here was a man who had known her father. Had that all been lies too? She had trusted him even when she knew she should have trusted no one. Everything in her life had been turned upside down. Throughout her life she'd had to re-evaluate things, and this time was no different, but in many ways it cut deeper than the others. It was a betrayal, a feeling that sunk to her bones and shook her like a steam train. She would not double over and vomit, no matter how much she wanted to. She would not give him the satisfaction.

'You took longer to train, but you were always going to be better than her. You could see through the Nazis' lies.'

'I saw your name on that list. At first I thought it was because you were a member of the resistance and I thought about destroying it. But then I realised what it meant. Then there was the photo and the code in your apartment.'

'It was stupid of me to leave those lying around, but I couldn't

359

bring myself to get rid of them. She did mean something to me, you know? You both did.'

'Don't say that. You make me sick.'

His face contorted into a snarl. 'Can't you see? I did it for you. Because I care about us. For us. For Germany. There was no other way.'

Sweat was dripping from his brow, and she suspected it wasn't just because of the heat in the apartment.

'That's not true. You worked your way into the Abwehr before I did; you betrayed everything you said you believed in. You were controlling me all along. For what purpose? What did you want in the end?'

Everything was falling into place. She was just ashamed it had taken this long. His relationship with Greta. It had never meant anything to him; it was only a means to an end.

'It wasn't like that. I had to do something. You've seen what the Nazis are doing to this country. They would never have trusted me fully. I had to see what information you could get for me. Greta wouldn't play ball – you don't know what it was like.'

'I don't care what it was like. You killed her, a young woman you took into your apartment. You probably told her you loved her too. Let her trust you, and you killed her. For what?'

'For you.'

'Stop. Stop lying to me. To yourself. You did nothing for me.'

It was about time she stood up to him. It had taken her long enough, and she should have made a stand long ago, but he had got into her head. He had done the same with Greta, used her and used her up. If she was not careful, he would do the same to her.

She felt the weight of the pistol in her handbag, where it always was. She had never told him it was there. But she couldn't reach for it now. He was too close and he would get the jump on her before she could bring it to bear.

He ran his finger along his lips, but now it was more frantic than it had ever been before. His other hand was in his coat pocket.

'You don't understand,' he whispered. 'You never understand. I knew you could do it. I just had to make sure that they knew you could do it.'

'Of course I understand,' she almost spat at him. 'You manipulated the Abwehr to make sure they chose me as their agent. You had worked out that they were going to use Greta and when you realised it would be her, you got rid of her. You couldn't manipulate her like me.'

'No, no, no.' His face was bright red, the words loud and harsh. Anyone could overhear them, but he didn't seem to notice. 'I never manipulated you. Don't you see? It had to be you. You were the only one they wouldn't get to. Your father—'

'Don't you dare mention him. For all I know you killed him as well. Was that part of your game?'

'No. Those party thugs killed him for helping a Jew. I had no hand in that. I wouldn't. I loved your father.'

'Not as much as I did. He would hate to see what you have become now. He would hate what I've had to do to make sure I wasn't done away with too. To get along with the party. The things I did for them.'

She spat on the floor, her throat suddenly filling with bile. He reached for her. Black-gloved hands flashed past her face as she turned and ducked him. With all the training she had received, she was more prepared for this moment than ever. She twisted again as he grabbed at her, trying to wrestle her to the floor. She ducked and he kicked out, tripping her. She rolled and landed with her back against the wall. In one swift motion she had pulled the gun from her handbag and levelled it at him. The gun she had never fired in anger.

Some emotion crossed his features that she couldn't understand. It was somewhere between panic and fury.

The gun thumped back in her grip. The sound echoed around the room. Stefan crumpled to the floor clutching his chest. It all happened slowly, like a silent film, but then Stefan was on the floor, blood pooling around him. She had never fired the weapon before, but now she had killed. Someone might be alerted by the noise, but they would be too late to do anything. She scrambled to her feet and looked down at the man who had manipulated and cheated her, the man who had pretended to be something he wasn't, and felt nothing. He had killed Greta and risked her life instead to play his games, and for what? It had done no good. And now he was dead too. Nothing they could do would stop the Nazis. Only time would see the end of the thousand-year Reich. Charlotte and the others were too small to make a difference, no matter how much they tried.

That wouldn't stop her from trying, but her first responsibility was to her friends. She had to save them.

Chapter Forty-Five

Sunday, 25 July 1943

SS-Obersturmführer Schulz stood by the cab of the Opel truck as his troops piled out. He was determined not to be defeated this time. On those previous occasions he had been too hasty, gone in with guns blazing, but in doing so he had underestimated the intelligence of the woman. But never again would she escape him. He had her in his grasp.

The air-raid sirens whirred in the distance, but he was not perturbed. They had to do this now, or they would lose the chance. They could not be afraid of the British bombers. He had come too close to be put off, and any of his men who were too cowardly to do what they were told under the bombing would be sent to the camps.

Of course, he had come close before, but this time he had the warehouse surrounded. Before he had been too fixated on rounding up all of the resistance fighters. This time he had told his troops to focus on her, and her alone. If anyone else got in the way then they were expendable. He had to catch the traitor. It didn't matter how much it cost.

He pulled his leather jacket close and walked around the back

363

of the truck now that it was empty and his men had taken their positions. This time he had decided not to rely on the Orpo; the uniformed police officers were poor and he couldn't help but blame them for his previous failures to bring in the woman. The Kripo offered better men, but even they couldn't be relied on. No, this was a job for the SS and only the SS. He didn't even have to give them orders as they filed into position silently. They knew what was being asked of them. In the gloom they looked like spectres hunting their prey. He was pleased with the romanticism. That was exactly what they were.

His intelligence had been right, he noted, as he spotted the van they had been trailing. Untersturmführer Leitz was young, but he was good. His apparent age had allowed him to infiltrate the university from an early stage and ever since he had been tracking the woman. Schulz wasn't much older himself, but he had more experience and seniority. He had been angry when Leitz had lost track of the woman for months on end, but it was the young officer's intelligence that had led them here.

Schulz had checked and the warehouse had been empty for some time, even before the British bombing. They hadn't been able to find out any more information at risk of being too late. It didn't matter who the building belonged to; they could be rounded up later. What mattered was who was inside now, and he had them surrounded. Except for the gangway that led to a vessel moored up on the dock. He hadn't expected that, but no matter. They wouldn't get far.

The city was on fire. It was a hellscape, worse than any religious text had ever described. The bombings had been severe before, but it was as if the combined might of the British and American air forces were descending on Hamburg. Aircraft filled the sky, and Charlotte had no idea how they kept from crashing into each other. That would be the least of their worries when the bombs started falling. She had no idea whether the shelters would be enough to defend people, but she had no intention of being in any of them. It was as if the city was hotter, the pressure itself rising. It was palpable.

There was so much fire. The drone of aircraft engines was ceaseless, and the staccato explosions of the bombs kept up a regular rhythm. If there was ever a time to get out of the city it was now.

They only had one chance to get this right. If they were caught then that would be the end for them. She would find herself in a Gestapo cell, at the mercy of every torture technique she could think of, and her friends would end up in the camps. Who knew what would happen to them then. They had only one chance, and there were too many factors that had to fall exactly into place for her to pull it off.

Charlotte heard the trucks approach. She had known they would come and for once she was calm. Everything was in place now and there was nothing else she could do. The trap had been laid.

If he managed to catch the turncoat spy he would be in line for a promotion. He was already one of the youngest Obersturmführers in the area, and to be promoted was no easy task. He may even get to meet the Führer himself and that was worth every effort in catching the woman. He didn't care what her name was; she didn't deserve a name. She was the worst of all traitors.

He crouched down by the wall, and gave the signal for his men to close in. They stormed the warehouse in single file, making as much noise as possible to distract the enemy. She was sure to have accomplices with her, and if he could round up the local terrorists too then he would definitely garner favour. Schulz waited for the inevitable gunfire, but there was nothing, only the sound of the bombers encroaching.

One of his men appeared back through the doorway. 'There's no one here,' he shouted over the noise.

Schulz ran towards him. 'What? What do you mean? You followed this van. How could you let them escape?'

The man shrugged. He actually shrugged. Schulz could have cuffed him around the head, but what would be the point?

'Find them!' he barked instead.

They ran up the gangway together. First Hilda and Andreas, then Charlotte and Kurt. Her friends had been given the time and place to meet, but she wasn't sure that they would follow her instructions to the letter. Thankfully Kurt had managed to round Andreas and Hilda up in a truck while Charlotte drove the decoy into the warehouse and snuck out the back as she had done months before. The rest of their cargo was already in place.

Åke wouldn't wait long. He had been given clearance to moor in the docks and pick up cargo, but with the air raid and the coming bombers he would want to set sail. He had already done too much for her, and he wouldn't risk his life. She couldn't blame him for that.

Kurt held her hand as they ran, and she vowed she would never push him away again. She expected the bombs to begin falling at any moment.

There was a crack. At first she thought it was the creak of the boat, then she realised it was the report of a rifle. Other bullets started to ping off the hull of the ship as the Gestapo found her. They'd finally caught up with her. It was now or never.

'Damn it,' Schulz shouted over the din. She had been clever, but not clever enough. The empty warehouse had been a ruse. The van that had driven in was empty and the driver had run off into the night. But it had been Schulz who had spotted the boat moored at the next dock.

Then he had spotted her. He'd actually laid his eyes on her for the first time in months, her blonde hair waving behind her as she ran up the gangplank. The boat was almost underway, as it began to turn away from the mooring. With a shout he ordered

366

his men to open fire. He couldn't let her get away. Who knew what secrets she would take with her? It was too late to take her in now, he'd have to settle for her death.

'Kurt, no!' she screamed, but it was lost against the backdrop of the ship engine and the bombs. He pushed her away with one hand, but kept a hold of her hand in his other.

'I can't go with you,' he said, shouting to be heard over the din. Bullets pinged around them, but they kept their heads low. 'You know I can't.'

'I can't leave you here. Please, Kurt. Don't do this.'

'It's the only way. You won't get away unless there is someone here to finish off the plan.'

'You don't need to. I need you—'

'You don't need me, Charlotte. You never have. I have always loved you and I know you love me too. You may push me away, but you've only ever done it to protect yourself. I understand. But you will be fine without me. I'm a German soldier; I won't be safe even in Stockholm.'

She was at a loss for words. Anything she attempted to say got caught in her throat. He pulled away from her, but neither of them would let go of the other's hand.

'I will keep you safe,' she said, eventually.

'No,' he replied. 'I have to do this for you. It was always for you.'

She wouldn't let go, she couldn't. She gripped his hand, but it was slipping from her grasp.

'Now,' she shouted to the crew. 'Do it, now!'

She felt a pain in her side and she went down. His hand slipped from hers, but with one final lurch of strength she pushed him away, towards the safety of the boat. He fell back with a pained expression on his face, but he was finally safe. 'No!' he shouted as he looked at her. She mouthed *I love you* and dropped.

* * *

367

A heavy shape fell from the boat. It seemed to hover, then go, lost from sight, before splashing into the cold, salty water of the dock.

'Cease!' Schulz shouted over the din of gunfire. 'Cease fire!'

He ran to the railing and looked down. It was impossible to tell for certain, but down below floating in the dark waters was the body of a woman. In the occasional flash of an explosion he could see the blonde hair and the clothes tattered by bullet wounds.

'It's over,' he said to himself. 'She's dead. The Reich is safe from traitors again.'

Aftermath

Saturday, 31 July 1943

He stumbled along the road, struggling to stay upright. His skin burnt, but then the very world around him tasted of ash. The air was thick with smoke and the aftermath of the bombing. Walking was a struggle and not just because of his weakened and battered limbs. He had nowhere else to go. His home, as so many others, had become a raging inferno, engulfed by the explosives that had been dropped on them. The nights and nights of bombing had seemed endless. At first they had come out into the dawn hoping their city was still standing and seeing the damage wrought before them. As it had continued for two, four, and now over a week of flame and noise, they had all become numb. A firestorm.

Family by family they had lost their homes. It had taken him until this last night of bombing, but eventually the bombs had come for him too. He had lost his family a few days prior. His last glimpse of them shrouded in smoke and the orange miasma. Searching through the rubble, cutting his hands upon broken bricks, had brought no relief. They had simply gone. Vanished. Exterminated from existence.

Now he stumbled along the road, only taking minor note of the other families that had lost their homes, their loved ones. He barely noticed the burnt corpses lying against the walls, looking as if they were simply asleep. He had become too used to it. Far too used to death.

Moth-bitten gloves handed over a bowl of thin brown soup. The look in those eyes said: *You need this more than me.*

The young man was a Jew, or at least a Mischling. The Jew was a good few years younger than him, only just old enough to fight in the army, but that was one thing that the Jews could be thankful for. They had been forbidden from enlisting. A small mercy.

Here he was, an Aryan, standing in line at a soup kitchen with Jews, Mischling, queers, and gypsies. It didn't matter, they were all hungry, had all suffered the effects of Allied bombing.

He had been persecuting Jews for years, but now he was amongst them. The Führer's great plan had failed. How could they ever maintain the thousand-year Reich if the British and Americans were bombing German cities to hell? How many Germans had to die for this?

He was only ashamed it had taken him this long to see through the lies. That it had taken the horror of war coming to their doorstep, losing his own family, to find empathy. If that was what it took, then he was not worthy of redemption. He deserved death.

At the front of the queue an elderly woman passed him a wooden bowl. He had no idea what was in it, but it didn't matter now. It was food, and he was grateful. His stomach rumbled and it was painful, like a dagger in his gut. Next to him a young man had just finished his bowl and was asking for more. He wasn't impolite, simply asking if there was any left at the end.

He looked down at his own bowl and felt remorse. Why did he deserve all of this when others were in need? He turned the wooden spoon around in the bowl so that it was facing the younger man.

'Share?' he asked, moving the bowl a little closer to his companion.

The smile that accompanied a nod of acknowledgement almost made up for his guilt, but he knew he would never shake that. Not in a thousand years. He was called Hermes and he would take his story, the story of what the Nazis had done, to anyone who would listen.

The SS Arvika slid past the white cliffs as it headed for its mooring in Dover. The wind was bracing, but not in the same way as Hamburg. The smell of salt was thick in the air and caught in the back of the throats of those on board. For this mission, there was only a skeleton crew. It would have been too much of a risk for any other crew member than those needed to operate the vessel. The ship was now escorted to its docking point by a British warship painted in a dull grey. They could just about make out the naval ratings in their uniforms. The reception seemed overly grandiose given the passengers on the ship, but given their nature it was more through caution than ceremony. Its huge cannons were pointed at the Arvika's hull, but whether it was on purpose or not was not clear. Navy personnel had boarded the Swedish boat before it had been allowed to enter British waters in the Channel. They couldn't go to Denmark, or to Sweden. There were too many Nazis there. They had thought they could simply make the short journey across the sea from Hamburg to Hull, but it seemed the British wanted to keep an eye on them and had escorted them to Dover.

When they docked, a blonde woman walked purposefully down the gangplank, followed by a mismatched group of people. None of them were sailors, but the water and the salt air were familiar to them. All they hoped for was some hot water and a meal. Any other comfort was something they only expected in their wildest dreams. They were friends who had been through thick and thin and who were now embarking on the next step of their journey.

The woman had thought about dyeing her hair, but there was no way to do it on board, so she had remained herself. Besides, those who were after her back in Germany thought her dead.

There would be no way to identify the body they had thrown overboard. For all intents and purposes it was the body of Charlotte Weber. Andreas had made sure it would appear that way, and she would make sure that the Nazis never found out the truth.

What awaited the friends in Britain was not something they could guess, but it had to be better than what they had left behind in Germany. They were all fugitives, but they would return someday – that was for sure – and the woman probably sooner than that, but none of them knew when. For now the Nazis held sway across the Reich, but their days were numbered. The friends would only be safe when the Nazis were gone, and the woman was going to do everything she could to make sure that happened.

Author's Note

The Violinist's Secret is a work of fiction, but as with all of my books I try to portray a sense of what happened during this time as accurately as possible. Many of the stories contained within are true. I have tried where possible to research and make sure events are as accurate as possible, and if they are of my own invention that they are grounded in plausibility.

Spies by their very nature are secretive. I found no evidence of a German spy working in Sweden, but I'm sure that it could have happened. Because trying to force Sweden into the war, did happen, although the letters in *The Violinist's Secret* are a fabrication. The Nazis wanted an easy route to their conquered territories in Norway, and the easiest way was going through Sweden. But the Swedish government was proudly neutral, not wishing to be drawn into the war. Over time the pressure the Nazis put on the Swedish government meant they were forced to allow German troops to travel through their country, or risk invasion.

Hamburg was heavily bombed throughout the war. Its role as a port made it a prime target for allied bombing. And this increased until Operation Gomorrah in 1943, which created a firestorm across the city for eight days and seven nights and killed 37,000 people. A lot of the dates used in the book are dates that bombs were dropped on Hamburg, even if the action itself may not include a bombing raid.

University education suffered heavily under the Nazis. Science subjects were emphasised at the expense of art and humanities, in order to support Nazi Germany's expansion and military efforts, despite the fact they were pushing out the very academics researching these areas and lost many great minds to the United States because of their non-Aryan, often Jewish, background. The arts and humanities were heavily controlled and censored, with only subjects and texts that were considered German being taught. As a result critical thinking and examination studied.

One of only two faculties to speak out against the removal of Jews from German universities was the faculty of Philosophy in Hamburg. In 1933 philosophy staff asked the Dean of the university to write a letter of protest. And the later student protests between 1942 and 1943 actually happened. Although I could find no evidence of this in Hamburg, I suspect that there was dissent amongst students in the city, being so far from Berlin. Many of these students were arrested by the Gestapo, with some being tried, with no defence, and then executed by guillotine.

The Nazi book burnings of 1933 are famous, but the story of Magnus Hirschfeld is less well-known. His Sexual Institute in Berlin existed and was at the forefront of gender and sexual research in Europe at the time. The Nazis did burn all of their research and forced Hirschfeld, a Jew, out of the country. There were many people like Andreas across Germany before the Nazis took over and forced them into hiding.

There are many more instances of the terrible atrocities the Nazis committed shown in this book and I hope that through Charlotte and her friends you have seen what oppressive governments can be capable of and hope that it never happens again.

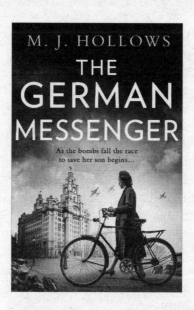

M. J. HOLLOWS

THE GERMAN MESSENGER

As the bombs fall the race to save her son begins...

Liverpool, 1940. "Where's George?" Ruth didn't realise that she had grabbed hold of the other woman's arms. "Where's my *son*?"

Journalist Ruth Holt is struggling in the terror of the Blitz when her young son is suddenly snatched away in broad daylight. Soon after, the kidnappers' demands arrive. They are working with the Nazis, and she has no choice but to co-operate, or the authorities will learn that she is harbouring secrets of her own.

Ruth's job gives her access to critical information, and if she does not share it with Britain's enemies, her child will face the consequences. Desperate, she falsifies information, lying to everyone: her employers, her family and her lover. But as the demands increase, the knife edge she walks on grows increasingly thin. If she falls, she will never save her son.

Dear Reader,

We hope you enjoyed reading this book. If you did, we'd be so appreciative if you left a review. It really helps us and the author to bring more books like this to you.

Here at HQ Digital we are dedicated to publishing fiction that will keep you turning the pages into the early hours. Don't want to miss a thing? To find out more about our books, promotions, discover exclusive content and enter competitions you can keep in touch in the following ways:

JOIN OUR COMMUNITY:
Sign up to our new email newsletter: http://smarturl.it/SignUpHQ
Read our new blog www.hqstories.co.uk

https://twitter.com/HQStories
www.facebook.com/HQStories

BUDDING WRITER?
We're also looking for authors to join the HQ Digital family!
Find out more here:

https://www.hqstories.co.uk/want-to-write-for-us/

Thanks for reading, from the HQ Digital team